ST. LEGIER

THE JESSICA KELLER CHRONICLES: VOLUME 7

BLAZE WARD

KNOTTED ROAD PRESS

St. Legier
The Jessica Keller Chronicles: Volume 7
Blaze Ward
Copyright © 2018 Blaze Ward
All rights reserved
Published by Knotted Road Press
www.KnottedRoadPress.com

ISBN: 978-1-943663-87-3

Cover art:

© Innovari | DepositPhotos.com - Spaceship battle cruiser assault

Cover and interior design copyright © 2018 Knotted Road Press

Never miss a release!
If you'd like to be notified of new releases, sign up for my newsletter.

I only send out newsletters once a quarter, will never spam you, or use your email for nefarious purposes. You can also unsubscribe at any time.

http://www.blazeward.com/newsletter/

ALSO BY BLAZE WARD

The Jessica Keller Chronicles

Auberon

Queen of the Pirates

Last of the Immortals

Goddess of War

Flight of the Blackbird

The Red Admiral

St. Legier

Additional Alexandria Station Stories

The Story Road

Siren

The Science Officer Series

The Science Officer

The Mind Field

The Gilded Cage

The Pleasure Dome

The Doomsday Vault

The Last Flagship

The Hammerfield Gambit

The Hammerfield Payoff

Doyle Iwakuma Stories

The Librarian

Demigod

Greater Than The Gods Intended

Other Science Fiction Stories

Myrmidons

Moonshot

Menelaus

Earthquake Gun

Moscow Gold

Fairchild

White Crane

***The Collective* Universe**

The Shipwrecked Mermaid

Imposters

PART 1
OVERTURES

OVERTURE: JESSICA

The door chime brought Jessica Keller up from the day's paperwork. The never-ending battle. She shouldn't have any more meetings tonight. That was the whole point of staying up late and diving in now, when it might have waited for tomorrow.

Get more done now. Then go to bed. And then start the whole mess over again tomorrow with a little bit of a head start.

She still wasn't sure if it was economical to repair the horrendous damage that *Steadfast at Dawn* had done to *Auberon* on that last jousting pass. Any lesser vessel that had survived such a mauling would have been de-commissioned and scrapped at this point. The flight back had taken twice as long as normal, just to limp home to base.

And Jessica was finally willing to admit how badly she had underestimated her foe. Not *Steadfast at Dawn*, but the being known as *The Eldest*, according to Yuur Ul.

That had been the hardest part: Admitting she was so wrong about this entire campaign that they should all be dead now, but for luck and timing. Good on her part, bad for many others.

Jessica considered the door. Her office was the usual mess when she was working uninterrupted. Piles of notes on paper to enter into the system, or just memorize and then burn. Her favorite sippy cup mug with less than two centimeters of cooling coffee left in the bottom.

She flipped a coin in her head. Someone had walked up to Willow

Dolen, guarding the outer chamber, or pinged Jessica's assistant Marcelle, and asked for a meeting right now, instead of scheduling it. And whatever it was had caught their attention enough that they decided to bother her with it, instead of putting it on her calendar for later.

Both women were trained and cognizant of the needs of their boss.

Jessica pushed the button on her desk that opened the hatch. A shadow entered.

Marcelle.

Just from the look on her face, the wry smile, Jessica knew it would be good news, or at least a most interesting change from the current piles of crap.

"*Pint-Sized*," she announced in her quiet, alto drawl, bringing a smile to Jessica's face.

Normally, Centurion Moirrey *zu* Kermode was introduced as simply Moirrey. As far as Jessica knew, only she and Moirrey's best friend from school, Dina, ever called the petite engineer by her junior high nickname.

And Marcelle wouldn't, unless the Evil Engineering Gnome was up to the best kind of absolutely no good.

"Will I need more coffee?" Jessica asked, assuming that this might take a while.

Marcelle considered things.

"Yes," she said. "Decaf?"

"Please," Jessica replied.

Probably going to take a while.

Marcelle stood to one side and Moirrey entered, a stack of non-regulation notebooks tucked under one arm. At least she was in uniform, the black and green that marked them all, or had, when Jessica was younger.

Before she became The Fleet Centurion, in white. Or an Imperial admiral, in red.

"Sit," Jessica said.

Moirrey grinned and plopped down into one of the two chairs, putting three notebooks on Jessica's desk. None of them were the same size, or color, being black, red, and teal. Marcelle departed with Jessica's mug to get out the good coffee.

Jessica noted that Moirrey was practically fidgeting tonight. So, they were back nearly a decade, then. Before this young woman had grown into herself and become the serious scholar who had shaken empires.

Before Moirrey had grown *still*.

Tonight did not promise seriousness.

"Am I going to become an accomplice, just by listening to you?" Jessica opened the conversation.

Moirrey screwed her face sideways as she thought about it.

"Mebbe," she replied slowly, grinning so wide her hazel/blue eyes nearly disappeared.

"And it's not in any computer system, is it?" Jessica continued, pointing at the notebooks.

"Nope," Moirrey nodded. "Dinna think worth commitin' tha'folly. Least not yets. Mebbe, ifn's you ken."

Jessica powered off the slab she had been typing into and considered this woman. This *Advanced Research Weapons Technician.* This Evil Engineering Gnome. This woman looking so innocent right now that butter wouldn't melt in her mouth.

"Out with it," Jessica said.

"So's," Moirrey began with a long drawl. "Bin readin' reports from the *Trusski*-guy. The Khan. Ex-khan. Whatevers. Lookin' fer idears."

"Okay," Jessica prodded, when Moirrey ran out of words.

"M'I'llowed ta gets filthy, stinkin' rich, if'n's I invents something totally awesomes whiles in service?" the tiny woman asked. "Somethin' fer civil folks?"

"Depends," Jessica replied. "Military things are part of your job, so probably not. Yan's a civilian now, and designing starships being built by three governments, so far. He gets licensing fees. What are you up to?"

Something was off about the woman. Not bad, just not right. Fidgety.

"Buts they never dealt with planetary invasions'n'stuff," Moirrey continued her thought with an almost scholarly tone. "*Buran*-folk. An' Vo's gonna hafta go do something like that. Gots ta thinkin'. An' maybe me'n'Yan'n'Willow mighta been a little drunk. Designed some crazy stuff. Vo took it with him."

"I remember," Jessica said. "I read your notes. He did specify exotic."

"Yups," Moirrey agreed. "Then I hads'n even betters idea."

Jessica held her breath as the woman leaned forward and flipped open the top notebook to page one. She spun it around for Jessica to see.

The image Moirrey had drawn in colored pencil was an angel. Well, no. Angels don't carry a pistol in one hand and a sword that looked nearly two meters long in the other. But the creature, the woman, had wings. Stubby ones, barely half again as wide as the person's arms. Maybe three meters across total. Two rows of feathers.

The figure, the woman, was also wearing some kind of suit. It didn't look like a simple skinsuit, but it also wasn't heavy armor. Maybe a modification of an armored lifesuit. Close enough, anyway. The helmet was strange, looking like an ancient gas mask or something similar, but it also swooped way up in back, like the skull came to a point nearly a foot above a normal, human one. Feathers trailed off the top of the helmet's crest, like something an even-more-ancient Hellenic warrior might have appreciated.

Jessica glanced up. Moirrey nodded and flipped to the next page. It was the same person, now seen from the back. The wings looked metallic in this image. Two stubby tubes rode on either side of the spine, from collar to kidneys. Two more, much smaller, were visible on the wingtips. Jessica could see fins on the woman's calves.

"Interesting," Jessica offered, unsure where Moirrey was taking her.

"So I hads this crazy idea in th'shower," the engineer said. "Does my best thinkin' there. Ya takes a repulsor pod off'n a zip-bike, and tunes it down *significantly*. Hafta customize each lifter every time ya wears it, just to keeps it in synch with mass'n'weather conditions. Power pack'll need work, but I figger Yan's good at that sorta thing. But you could fly."

"I've seen similar things in civilian use," Jessica said. "Personal lifters that could loft someone and give them gliding capabilities."

"Yup," Moirrey agreed. "Totally unsafe fer anythin' but bridge inspectors and emergency parachutes, unless yer complete crazies. Howevers. I wanna mix in a thruster pack from the zip-bike, too. Add mosta the electronics from a space pilot's flight helmet. Puts you in a body suit with some armor so's yer not street pizza first times you fly. Adds you to a planetary invasion. After *Fourth Saxon*, somebody's gonna be lookin' for weird. Ain't nobodies gonna sees this comin'."

Jessica pulled the notebook closer and flipped a few pages. More schematics, getting progressively more technical and detailed as the woman's thoughts had come together. Variants with heavier weapons, different shaped skulls, bizarre logos painted onto oversized foreheads.

"Why?" Jessica finally asked.

"We come up with a giant, robot-looking tank fer Vo," Moirrey chirped. "Man-shaped, but eight meters tall. Weird looking and intimidating as hell, but not something we'd ever build. *Buran* might, though. We needs ta know hows to kill it."

"With you so far," Jessica replied.

"So's the tactics book always reminds ya on page one that the enemy ain't no three meters tall, but ain't no one meter tall, neither," Moirrey continued. "We got no idea what *Buran* might have fer land army. But they ain't got no ideas on us, same same. So maybes we can be three meters tall and scary alien angel of doom. They won't know better."

"Purpose?" Jessica felt herself dropping into strategic and tactical thinking now.

"Scoutin'," Moirrey replied. "Ya gotta be total loon to strap that thin' on and fly into combat. Them folks fit. Plus ya get major mobility on the surface, so's they can hit from s'prise flanks and corners, 'specially ifs ya put them on zip-bike that're smart 'nuff to coast to a safe stop when the crazy pilot jumps fer sky. Scary-ass critters comin' fer yer liver, lady."

"This one's a female," Jessica observed dryly. "*Fribourg* won't let women into combat like that. Not in our lifetimes, anyway."

"Yup," Moirrey agreed. "Easy 'nuff to make a male version. Bigger torso half-plate that don't need to cushion boobs. But I figgers crazy folks like the rednecks from *Saxon* might wanna play. You 'magine a whole legion of these loons coming over a ridge at you?"

"I can," Jessica said dryly. "So where's the getting crazy rich part?"

"I start building these things, an' every bored kid in the Republic's gonna wanna have one," Moirrey said. "Any maybe a few of them nice ladies from *Fribourg*. Wanna nail down all the copyrights and trademarks'n'stuff first. Then license 'em and start rolling in the Levs."

"Sounds good," Jessica decided, imagining the craziness such a trend might entail. And where. "Mark it all highest security clearance for now, and then tell someone in the Legal Services department you have my approval for them to handle that side of things, at least until my brother can get involved and advise you."

"Woo-hoo!" Moirrey swept up everything and vanished as the door opened and Marcelle entered, swerving to barely avoid being run over.

"Looks like I missed the party," Marcelle observed, placing the two mugs of coffee she had made on the desk. A moment later, she shrugged and started drinking the one she had made for Moirrey.

"*Pint-Sized* might have outdone herself, this time," Jessica agreed, reaching for the fresh mug. "Hopefully, it won't actually come down to brass tacks and we'll never have to find out if it would work."

"Amen to that," Marcelle said.

OVERTURE: EMMERICH

Emmerich Wachturm, Grand Admiral of *Fribourg, Commander of the Fleet,* Hereditary Duke of *Eklionstic,* etc., sat and waited with something approaching dignity as the door to the conference room opened.

He had chosen to take this meeting close to the place where the Inner Staff met: Joh and the cousins of the Imperial blood. It would rank close to that in overall importance, even if his spies and aides had warned him that the situation was likely to be far less serious than one would normally expect.

Em rose from his seat on this side of the heavy, oaken conference table as the signal turned green. Formal affair. Handle it as such, for at least as long as he thought necessary.

Four guards were visible in the hallway outside when the hatch opened, to go with six more inside. Heavily armed men prepared to unleash the very hounds of hell at the drop of a hat.

Em suspected they would be even more confused by the coming performance than he would have been, but for the private letter of introduction Jessica had sent along with the visitors.

Republic Senior Security Centurion Amala Bhattacharya came first, dressed in elegant civilian robes done up in a soft color somewhere less than teal, but more than aqua. A product of one First-Rate-Spacer Vibol Harmaajärvi, *Scholar of Fashion,* according to Jessica.

Whatever that meant.

The woman was average for height, so shorter than most Imperial Ladies. Darker as well, with skin tending towards a golden brown of the ancient, South Asian Diaspora, rather than the red-brown Hispanic that was more frequent in *Fribourg*. Black hair longer than appropriate for a security marine who needed to put it under a sealed helmet, plus dark eyes alive with barely-suppressed laughter. If there was anything that stood out about the woman's face, Em probably would have said the nose, oversized with a mild hook, but even that just lent her face character.

Bhattacharya bowed and smiled at him.

"Amala Bhattacharya," she said distinctly. "Scholar. Ambassador to the *Khan of Trusski*. Personal Representative of Queen Jessica of *Petron*."

Em nodded back. No mention of her military duties, currently on hold as she escorted the man behind her.

Telling, that.

"Ambassador Ul Banop Cheani Yuur," Amala said, stepping to one side as the man followed her into the room.

Clan name: Ul. Crèche name: Banop. Family group: Cheani. Personal name: Yuur. The presumably-former Khan of *Trusski*.

Em found him short, barely taller than Bhattacharya, with the same darkness of skin, perhaps even more golden and less brown, with piercing blue eyes, a bald skull, and a similar nose. The man wore pants and a tunic in a sand color today. Formal, but neutral.

According to Jessica's notes, while he might still be technically a Khan, and probably a Minister of the Eighth Rank, the man was probably also a fugitive with a *Buran* bounty on his head.

He certainly acted the part of an Ambassador well enough, coming to a serene rest and smiling lightly at Em before bowing formally.

"Grand Admiral, it is a pleasure to finally make your acquaintance," Ul said in a soft, high-pitched tenor.

Em bowed back and gestured to the table as the marine by the hatch sealed them in silently. He sat and watched the two of them settle down.

A moment of companionable silence passed.

"I'm given to understand that dealing with the two of you occasionally appears, to the uninformed outsider, as some sort of improvisational comedy act," Em broke the silence.

Jessica HAD warned him in no uncertain terms not to underestimate the two of them, but not to read too much into that performance, either.

Em appreciated the way Bhattacharya blushed, ever so slightly, while the Khan grinned like a Cheshire Cat, all eyes and cheeks.

"And that all requests to *Buran* for official diplomatic relations have, ere now, been met with firm negation," Em continued.

"Ah, but those were delivered with a gun, Grand Admiral," Ul replied quietly. "Ill-mannered barbarians raiding civilized villages. Red Admiral Keller chose a different approach. A more subtle one, if you will."

Em felt the sarcasm infect his face. Let it. Let them see it. Was rewarded with more grins.

Seriously? This was not how diplomacy was supposed to be conducted.

"Acknowledged," Em said. "And now you have now appointed yourself Ambassador to the Barbarians, Minister Ul?"

"We live in ignorance of one another, Grand Admiral Wachturm who was once the much-feared *Red Admiral*," the man noted. "Only the Warriors communicated, leaving the Scholars unfulfilled. My mission is to find more Scholars disguised as Warriors and help them to learn the folly of warfare. To that end, I have requested security clearance to read more of your books."

"More?" Em asked.

"I found *Jessica Keller, Volume One* most enlightening, sir, if a touch self-aggrandizing," the Khan replied.

Em bristled just the slightest bit, but thought he managed to suppress it. Apparently not, from the knowing grin on the stranger's face.

"And I feel I would learn more about you if I were to read your books in publication order, following the development of your tactical and strategic genius up to the point it ran into the irresistible force that is Keller," Ul continued. "Already, I have learned a tremendous amount about your culture from the audio works of Centurion *zu* Wiegand. Specifically, her symphonies."

Casey?

"How so?" Em asked, aware that he had already lost control of the meeting, but willing to follow the twists and turns of this man's mind. Nobody had ever gotten inside *Buran*'s head.

"As *Princess Kasimira*, she wrote music that spoke to the soul of *Fribourg* itself," the Khan said, his eyes staring into the distance. "By opening myself to that, I was able to understand more of your nature. You are a proud, martial folk beset by a slight cultural inferiority complex, but upheld by bedrock principles. Generally happy, but sadly limited."

All that from music?

Em made a note to buy Casey's entire catalog and listen to it with a more critical ear. Before this, it had been merely background music that had become amazingly popular with the populace even before the woman became the Savior of the Empire.

Em felt his hand come up to interrupt the stranger, but Ul nodded graciously.

"And I am aware that my observations on the topic would not be generally welcomed here, beyond a very circumscribed circle of Scholars, such as yourself and Amala," the Khan nodded. "I wished to make my position clear as a Scholar, and not a Warrior or a Spy, Grand Admiral. One suspects that I would find my return to *Winterhome* something less than welcome, at present."

"I see," Em said. Maybe he did, at that. "What, then, is your purpose, if we cannot guarantee you safe passage home?"

"I wish to write a book, Grand Admiral," Ul replied, his high voice suddenly taking on great gravity. "I wish to tell my story, and that of my people, the children of *The Holding*, that you might understand us, as I have come to understand you. To speak to the Scholars and Artisans, and not just the Technicians and Warriors."

"A book?" Em forced the skepticism out of his voice before he spoke.

"Yes," Yuur Ul pronounced. "It will be entitled *Lord of Winter*."

OVERTURE: DENIS

Denis Jež gave up trying to suppress the grin on his face and sighed happily at the sight. Through the wide portal, a brand new ship was docked in an interior bay. She looked average-sized until you saw the Imperial light cruiser in the next slot over, looking like a new-borne puppy cuddled up against his mother for warmth. Only then did the immensity of the warship become obvious.

"I take she meets your approval?" the man on his left asked in a droll, knowing voice.

Denis turned to Emmerich Wachturm and smiled.

"Even Yan Bedrov didn't believe that the old designs for a warship were so vulnerable, Grand Admiral," Denis opined. "A couple of degrees to the left and the flag bridge of *Auberon* might have been annihilated. Along with Jessica, Casey, and everyone else. We need something better."

"I've seen her reports," Wachturm said. "And Bedrov's. And yours. That Star Controller has no business on the front lines. And carriers are an even worse idea, although Bedrov tells me he might have a solution to that. My grain of salt awaits his genius."

Denis nodded, sober but still grinning.

"You'll get her home safe?" he asked. "And not steal all her secrets?"

"Jež, my spies are exceptional," the Grand Admiral smiled back. "I had the complete as-built plans for *Auberon* even before you went off to *Corynthe*. Nothing you did there under Whughy altered that significantly.

I'll have a skeleton crew under Iskra Vlahovic get your battered, old vessel and her flight wing home safely. I need you back out there with Jessica too much to do anything else."

"And this, sir?" Denis continued, pulling on the sleeve of his new white jacket. "What will the First Lord and the Senate say?"

It felt weird, being in someone else's uniform, even if it had been tailored for him. Baggy, blue slacks. White, button-up shirt with a folding collar. White, double-breasted jacket with gold trim and a single, thick ring around both wrists.

"Jež, you are the Command Centurion of the flagship of *First Expeditionary Fleet*," Wachturm turned deadly serious. "In *Fribourg* service, that's an admiral's slot, not a captain's. I appreciate that you want to be a warrior like Aeliaes or d'Maine, so you'd rather remain a command centurion, instead of becoming a Fleet Centurion. But I want my people treating you like you deserve. If Naoumov has a problem with that, she's welcome to come to *St. Legier* and argue with me and the Emperor. I have his backing on this."

Denis nodded, still shocked, but letting it flow through him.

Denis Jež, Imperial Admiral of the White.

They both turned to the ship waiting out there.

"And *Auberon* was a flagship, Jež," Wachturm continued, pointing at the ship before them. "I need you and Jessica in another flagship, and safe, so you can continue the war."

If *RAN VI Ferrata*, Bedrov's Expeditionary Cruiser design, was a long sword, this monster was a greatsword. She had the same general lines, but was nearly a third bigger in all dimensions.

IFV Vanguard. The first of another revolution in naval warfare.

Imperial Fighting Vessel. But so much more.

Something so new, so big, that Yan Bedrov had run out of adjectives to describe the design. Not that he had given it much thought. Most of his effort had been on the three Expeditionary Star Controller designs he had finalized for Jessica and the *Aquitaine* Senate. But all of them had been carriers. None would likely ever be built, not after *First Trusski*.

Only by luck and the Grace of God had *da Vinci* and her wing come back with as minimal casualties as they had at that battle. They should have been simply obliterated, stomped like ants.

And everyone here knew that. Even the pilots weren't bitching too much about going home, those who had survived.

So now, instead of a Star Controller, the Grand Admiral was sending him out in a pure warship. Four administrative shuttles and two fast couriers comprised her total flight bay. Tucked inside a lot of engines, generators, and guns.

What Bedrov had called a Heavy Dreadnaught in his design notes.

DH-001. Vanguard.

Denis knew that her first sister ship was about a third completed now, almost halfway around the planet at a dedicated shipyard. *IFV Valiant.*

But *Vanguard* would be his. Denis Jež and Nina Vanek would get to go on the big raids with *VI Ferrata* and *VI Victrix* now, instead of hiding safely behind Tomas Kigali's skirts, even as dangerous as *CA-264* had proven herself to be.

Denis had originally earned his stripes on a Strike Carrier, but done it in direct combat. It would be good to get back to that.

He absorbed Wachturm's words about Jessica needing to be there in a flagship to command, and him needing to be her commander, just like they had done with Auberon.

"We'll do you proud, sir," he said.

"I'm counting on that, Denis," the big man said. "Very soon, I plan to take the war to *Buran.*"

OVERTURE: VO

The field was huge. Perfectly level and grassed over, such that you could have had at least a dozen separate rugby matches going on simultaneously, with space left over for fans on all the sidelines. It promised to be a warm day, but only later. The morning sun was just now burning off the low clouds.

General Vo *zu* Arlo watched on a monitor from the cooler confines of his command transport as the last of the troops filed into place. For now, over six hundred vehicles were lined up for review in several rows across. The tanks and self-propelled artillery loomed heavy at the rear, with a variety of skiffs: both assault and scout versions; closer in. Just over five thousand men as well, grouped nervously into teams and crews, forwarded from other units whose commanders felt that those men met the strenuous requirements Vo had set forth.

His own command transport was parked behind a small stage in front of those men, built high enough so that most of the men out there could see him when he climbed the stairs and started today's events.

The factory had taken a basic assault skiff and turned it into an armored box capable of holding Vo, his communications team, and the support group he kept close at hand. Old timers, for the most part, men who had been with him at *St. Legier*, and before that, *Thuringwell*.

Killers like Hans Danville and Iakov Street. For those times he needed that.

But today would be an entirely different process. Five thousand men hoping to make the cut. To prove that they belonged.

"Sir, it's time," Danville said quietly, standing and checking his weapons: the pistol, plus the various knives and other implements he carried everywhere he went. Around him, the rest of the team followed their own similar rituals.

Vo nodded and stood. One of the modifications that he had required for his transport was ceilings high enough he could stand without bashing his head, unlike most models. He figured that being in charge allowed him that small perk, adding forty centimeters of space to the original design.

"Field team, go ahead," Vo ordered, just as quietly. "I'll follow in a minute. Comm team will handle everything from here."

Vo watched as half the men filed out, his bodyguards, leaving him with the remaining six. Nobody was going to attempt an assassination in the next two minutes. Not here.

One more heavy breath drawn deep. Shortly, the entire world would change for a number of people.

Normally, Vo would have been in the green and tan splattered field uniform he preferred for maneuvers, but this was official business. So instead, he was in sage, the Class Two uniform he would wear while inside the building at headquarters, or calling on government officials and higher-ranking officers.

He stepped to the hooks beside the aft hatch and grabbed his leather belt. Matte black, 12mm revolver in a holster on the right. Scabbarded long sword on the left hip. Six kilograms of metal, plus all the cartridges across the back, like an ancient cowboy from a vid.

Vo turned to the man on the other side of the hatchway as he strapped it all on. *Command Decanus* Reese Borel. No longer a Master Sergeant, but the senior non-comm in what would become this new unit.

His new unit.

Borel was the man who was becoming his left hand, even as Danville and Street were his right. Communications. Organization. Details. A military unit like this required soldiers and drivers, but it also needed mechanics, cooks, and personnel managers like Borel.

"Audio pickups are live, General," Borel said simply. "Talk in a normal voice once you emerge on the stage and we'll make sure the men hear."

Vo nodded, unwilling to trust his voice right now. He was too far into the zone.

There had been a speech he wrote for this. Well, rewrote half a dozen times before he realized that reading something to these men was the wrong way to approach them. He could have sent it in the mail if that was what they needed.

This had to be from his heart. His soul.

Vo stepped out into the mid-morning sun and assaulted the wooden steps up to the platform. There was an awning over it to provide some shade, but it was a nice day yet.

Below, thousands of men came slowly to silence, faces intent on the stranger, this famous foreigner who might yet become their commanding officer.

Vo looked at the small group down front, immediately below the stage. They were turned at an angle to the rest, so they could look out over the field, and be seen by those men. But they could also look up and see Vo standing close at hand.

They had earned their place here.

Master Sergeant Edgar Horst. Color Sergeant for the 189th Division. Now Color Decurion for the 189th Legion. Nearly thirty years in uniform, and currently the longest-serving active-duty man in the unit. In one hand, the pole with the unit's proud flag, dating back to before the original conquest of *Thuringwell,* an event memorialized by Karl IV with an Eternal Guard. A group of men that had come painfully close to being annihilated by Fourth Saxon and Ninth Pohang during the invasion, but for Horst.

And one Centurion Vo Arlo, Grand Army of the Republic.

Vo paused and stared out at the men. Let the moment build. He had written words, but they failed him. They were just words. He needed something bigger today.

"*Our* story begins on Imperial Date April 30, 174," he began in a low voice that nevertheless boomed across the field as Borel was as good as his word. "At a place called Yonin, on the little-known planet of *Thuringwell.*"

Vo glanced down and picked out the four men who had stood that day, and all the rest who had stood with them. With him.

"The *Republic of Aquitaine* launched a full planetary invasion on that day," Vo continued. "At Yonin, the men of the 189th Division stood firm. They would have gladly died at their post, because they were doing their duty. Sometimes, that is what is called for."

Many of those men glanced up and smiled.

"But it was not their day to die, even as they had resigned themselves to doing their duty with honor. Those fifty-seven men survived. Some have retired and others will join them soon, once this last task is done. Many of the others will return to *Thuringwell*, where Fourth Saxon is currently holding the Eternal Guard for us, so that they could all be here. Because they wanted to stand here today. Eventually, all of you who remain will serve a hitch on *Thuringwell*, guarding an Imperial monument on a Republic world, so you can understand what that dedication to duty looks like."

Vo took a deep breath and looked up at the field, sage with uniforms and vehicles.

"Later, twenty-four of those men were selected to come here, to *St. Legier*, to honor the man who had kept them from being slaughtered. When the Emperor made me a *Ritter*, and Honorary Colonel, Third Regiment, 189th division. Those men have earned their place on this field. The rest of you have not."

A sound went through the crowd. Perhaps a low moan. Maybe a touch of a growl as well.

"If you look at those twenty-four men, you will see they only wear two tags on their dress uniform," Vo challenged the men now with his tone. "My first standing order on taking command was that no other tag was necessary, if they wore one of those two. The first is the *Defense of Thuringwell* medal, given to the fifty-seven men who stood that day, and forged by Michele Ali al-Inverness, the Armourer of Fourth Saxon herself. The woman who also made all the swords the Honor Guard bears to this day. That badge comes from the same bronze that was used to make the plaque placed at the front of the older memorial, ordered by the *Aquitaine Senate* to honor the peace, when war was the option."

Vo found himself pacing now, walking in slow, measured steps first to the right, and then back and across. It helped center him as he spoke.

"The other medal is for *Imperial Honors*," Vo said. "For those twenty-four men who stood with me when we found it necessary to challenge the entire Empire. To do what was right, rather than what was merely expedient. In one of her only official acts, Emperor Karl VIII commanded that the divisional flag for the 189th be modified to include these words across the bottom: *We stood.* Gentlemen, that is what the 189th Division means, to me, and to those men. *We stood.*"

Vo let the pause draw out.

"But this is no longer the 189th Division, even as we inherit the history, the honors, and the memories. The Grand Marshal has commanded me to create a new thing, a *Legion*, and to build it on the bones of that old division and her troops. Two hundred and seventy-three of you chose to volunteer for this new duty. The rest were honorably transferred to the 17th Division and we wish them well. The 17th is another training unit, as the 189th was, and those men who left us will turn out better troopers, some of whom will find their way here in future days. That unit patch on your shoulder was your invitation to join us today, but you have not earned your spot, either."

Vo turned and faced the field now, squaring his shoulders and bringing his head up as the fire took hold.

"A Legion is not comprised of regiments, but of cohorts. And cohorts are made up of soldiers. There are only five thousand of you here today because I set very high standards for those men who would be allowed to volunteer for this duty. Four years active service in a line unit. A willingness to learn a whole new way to soldier. And an expectation that earning your place here will be the hardest thing you ever do."

Vo paused. Studied them for a moment.

"The ancient Romans used the term *decimation* to describe a punishment. Every tenth man would be removed from the line and executed. I intend to punish you almost as hard if you stay, in order to winnow you down. There are seventeen percent more men here than will make that final cut. One in six of you will not measure up. Will not be tough enough, smart enough, or hungry enough to stay. The price you pay will be blood, sweat, and tears, gentlemen. The reward will be belonging to the best unit in the Imperial Land Forces, when the Grand Marshal is looking for a unit to put at the tip of the spear. Because we are going to war, you and I. Together."

Another sound. A short, sarcastic laugh, perhaps, chopped before it fully developed. The reaction of the common foot soldier to the suggestion that a flag officer was going to get his boots muddy.

"You and I," Vo repeated. "I will march every mile with you. Qualify every weapon with you. Eat from the same kitchen. Face the same danger. The cohort commanders you will inherit have already been through that fire with me at Field School, so they can testify. The rest of your officers will face the same tests, the same duty. None of them have earned their space here, either."

Vo found himself pacing again, the mad energy similar to what had taken hold of him in a small clearing behind the Imperial Palace, just before launching his historic assault on an entire empire.

"Some of you are here because you believe yourself to be warriors. Heroes," he snarled, letting the fury take hold and burn itself out. Better they find it out today, so they could slink away before their stupidity got someone more worthwhile killed. "I have no use for warriors. None. I want *soldiers*. I require men who understand that driving a truck full of food and ammunition is just as important a job as leading a tank charge against a fortified position, possibly more so. We are links in a chain, and this unit, this *Legion*, will only be as strong as the soldiers doing the dirty work, in the corners or in the scrum. A cook in a field kitchen contributes more to the war effort than a man with a rifle, because the cook makes sure that hundreds of men are fed and ready to fight when the time comes. Gentlemen, that is what it means to be here, if you are allowed to stay. We are a *Legion*. Let the rest of the Army come to fear and respect what that means. Fear and respect us."

Vo raised a meaty hand and pointed at a small unit off to his left, a small patrol of assault skiffs, holding a smaller standard than the 189th's.

"That man is Cohort Centurion Alan Katche," Vo announced to the assembled men. "In a legion, the senior line officer, the one who commands the First Cohort, is known as the *Primus Pilus*. It mean *First Spear* in the ancient tongue. The man who will be the first to engage with the enemy. You will follow him into battle, because he will be in front of you getting there. I chose him for exactly that reason."

Below, the standard of First Cohort was raised, held, and then lowered again, a silent rallying point for the men to see. Katche had been one of the stars of Field School with Vo, and happily joined this new adventure.

In the center, Horst raised the divisional colors in salute as a response.

"But I will not be far behind you," Vo continued, drawing his 12mm revolver from the holster and holding it sideways in the air for the men to see. "This is the weapon of the Fourth Saxon Legion. It is now the weapon of the 189th Legion. A firearm throwing a metal slug at supersonic velocities. You will learn to use it, qualify in it, master it. As I did."

He had them now. Vo could feel it. The energy crackling off of the men was nearly palpable as he spoke, thankful for all the classes in command and public speaking that Command Security Centurion Crncevic, *Navin the Black*, had insisted on as part of a rounded education for a dumb punk from the slums.

Vo holstered the big pistol and reached across to draw the sword now, holding it aloft to reflect the hazy sunlight.

"And this is not the cavalry saber I used at *Thuringwell* when I invaded that planet and took it away from you," he said, engendering a quiet, almost-unconscious growl from the men. "al-Inverness forged it for me, but it is not mine. This sword is yours. It belongs to the commander of the 189th Legion. It *is* the 189th Legion. It can be worn with dress, as I am now, but it will also work just fine to kill a man, if I have to."

Vo slid the sword home in its scabbard and paused to scan the entire field, left to right, front to back.

"You men are all volunteers," he said conversationally. "Are you ready for the challenge of your lives?"

"Sir. Yes, sir," came the reply.

"Really?" Vo sneered. "Is that all you have? I need bad-ass killers, not kittens. Are you ready to sweat for me? Bleed for me? Kill for me?"

"SIR! YES, SIR!"

"Better," Vo said as the immense sound receded. "One final history lesson for you men. In ancient times, a captain raised a unit, but he only got paid when he was able to march the men in front of the paymaster. When he could *muster* them and present a military unit worth the name to the king who was hiring. Those of you who remain, I will only make you wear these nice uniforms you have on twice in any year. First will be on Empire Day, and then on the anniversary of today, which will henceforth be *Muster Day.* I expect the rest of the year you will be training or fighting, and too busy to get all dressed up because you are the meanest, toughest bastards in the Army. Are you men prepared to cross that line and learn what it means to belong to the 189th Legion?"

"SIR! YES, SIR!"

Louder still. Vo smiled.

"Primus Pilus, muster the Legion."

PART 2
EMERGENCY

CHAPTER 1

"I have the watch," Captain Colson said as he took command of the sentry room.

"Standing down," Captain Siembieda replied, saluted, and left.

Arn Colson had already confirmed that the eight men on watch were sharp and prepared. The men rotated through on two-hour shifts, one departing every fifteen minutes as his replacement arrived. The never-ending watch decreed to protect the capital world from another raid.

It was no longer enough to keep fleets close at hand. *Buran* ships could jump rapidly to the edge of scanner range, center themselves, and then land their next jump, the shorter one, with deadly accuracy. Fleet Headquarters had been utterly savaged three years ago, a combination of internal sabotage and treason that allowed a Mako an unchallenged raking pass at the closest possible range.

Grand Admiral Wachturm had other plans, if *Buran* ever tried it again. Thus the watch.

"Alert," one of the men called. "Unknown signal in section fourteen."

Colson reached out a hand and flipped up the smooth, metal plate protecting the button that would trigger something approximating Armageddon: alarms on all decks, warnings sent to all ships, and the deadly minefield coming live.

That was why a full naval captain had this duty. The minefield. There were always going to be issues, firing weapons without gunners first carefully identifying targets downrange.

The Grand Admiral had complained that enough alerts weren't being identified, but he had also made it clear that the only time a captain would get in trouble was by not being paranoid enough for this duty.

The button was red. Glowing with internal light as a malevolent eye in the darkness, even as bright as the room was.

"Confirmed," another voice chimed in. "Enemy warship has jumped into near space."

Buran had returned.

Captain Colson smashed his fist into the button. Immediately, the sirens started up.

But more importantly, the station's shields activated automatically. The eight men in this room now had unlocked control of the various weapon stations around the facility, at least until gun crews could roust and take control themselves.

Those after-action reports had suggested a difference of more than forty seconds doing it this way, which might be life and death in this situation.

The first Type-4 beam fired into the darkness, clear at the edge of effective range, against a ship that would jump again in a matter of seconds. But it was a statement of purpose.

This time, *Fribourg* was prepared for war.

CHAPTER II

IMPERIAL FOUNDING: 179/11/10. IFV FIREHAWK,
ABOVE ST. LEGIER

"**B**ring the squadron to full alert," Admiral Tom Provst growled as soon as he entered the flag bridge of *IFV Firehawk*.

One look at the screen in his office had told him this wasn't a drill.

"Already done, sir," Commander d'Noir replied, secured at his station and running things well enough. "All escorts are cleared and we are ready for maneuvers."

"Bridge, Provst here," Tom said as he got to his station.

Captain Al Kistler's face appeared on a screen immediately. Tom still found him to be a lean skeleton of a man with droopy eyes, but they made a great team. Tom was looking forward to taking command of *IFV Valiant* in a few months when she was completed. *IFV Firehawk* was a proud vessel, but she was old by the standards of warfare Yan Bedrov had unleashed on the galaxy. Him and Lady Moirrey Kermode.

"Here," Kistler said simply, glancing at the camera occasionally while focusing his attention elsewhere.

"Al, I can't imagine they came all this way to attack the station," Tom said. "Get us deep, clear down to the edge of the atmosphere, and then keep all the escorts high, so we and the cruisers have a clear field of fire across and up for the primaries."

"Another bombing raid, Tom?" the man asked in a quiet tone that was sharper than the eyes ever looked.

29

"Bad feeling," Tom admitted, listening to the ominous rumble deep in his gut. It had always served him well. "And keep us close enough that we can fire upwards in support of the station with the heavy stuff and not hit friendlies."

"On it," the captain said, cutting the circuit so he could get to work.

"d'Noir," Tom turned to his Flag Commander. "What are we facing?"

"The single biggest fleet of *Buran* vessels I have ever seen, Admiral," the man replied. "And I've been to *Samara*."

Tom cursed under his breath. *Samara* was where Imperial fleets went to get their asses kicked. If *Buran* had come here instead, this was going to get ugly.

He pressed a button and a projection took shape over the standing table between them. *St. Legier* at the center as a grapefruit. Fleet Headquarters in orbit as a grape. A mind-numbing collection of dots in red, dancing around dots in white and green, friendly warships and civilian traffic in orbit.

"Four capital ships, Admiral," d'Noir continued. "Including a JumpCarrier, what the system calls a Megalodon, and two Carcharias. At least ten cruisers of various configurations we're still trying to identify, plus a dozen Hammerheads floating around, mostly as escorts, but also moving like wolf packs on any solitary vessels they can catch."

"Confirming a Roughshark," a new voice called. One of the men around the outside of the room watching monitors and data feeds from all directions. "I have bombs in the air. Repeat, bombs in the air."

"Send a signal to ground forces, just in case they missed it," Tom ordered. "Missiles will never catch them. Order any vessel with decent parallax on beams to try to shoot down bombs. Let's avoid firing Primaries into the ground, though. We'll let a missile hit the planetary shields rather than knocking them down ourselves and opening the way."

Assents from all sides. Monitors turning sideways as *Firehawk* pitched down and rolled to get closer to the atmosphere. Hopefully, other squadrons would recognize what he was doing and do the same. Plus, getting his ships low made it harder for *Buran* to maneuver, since jumping down on them from a much higher elevation took tighter control. Not that they wouldn't, but it made them come out at a flat angle, rather than diving. Easier for gunners to line them up in the thirty seconds you had to shoot.

Tom didn't figure anyone was crazy enough to take him on directly. He was in the shadow of the station, where those big beams could fire in support if someone tried. Plus, his battleship had three cruisers and eight escorts close at hand, a mix of old frigates and the new corvette designs coming on line as fast as the yards could roll them into space.

Hopefully, it would be sufficient. Al Kistler had a particular young man on his bridge, a Lieutenant Wiegand earning his rank and learning the craft of being a sailor from some of the best men Tom knew. A man with places to go.

"Contact," a voice called from the comm. Kistler, forward on his bridge. Tom felt his shoulders come up and forced them back down. "Enemy squadron incoming. Stand by to take fire. All weapons engage the enemy flagship as you bear."

Tom stared hard at the second screen, showing the close-in trouble that had just dropped on top of them. One of the Great Whites was coming, with a small pack of Makos trailing in his wake.

Someone wanted to play. And this was going to get messy.

Firehawk's Primaries and Type-3 beams poured into the Carcharias about to pounce. Around them, the Imperial squadron did the same.

The bow of the beast even looked like a great white shark, from this angle. Three tines coming out of a triangular mouth that served to focus the three Mag-Shear emitters.

Firehawk wasn't one of Bedrov's new designs, armored and insulated to take on a squadron like this. She was of the generation that was meant to destroy *Aquitaine*, back when that had been the goal.

The first shark belched fire and all Tom's screens turned to hash.

CHAPTER III

Emmerich Wachturm looked at the screen in his office and decided that this might be the day he died in battle. But at least he was in orbit where he could command things more easily, rather than being stuck on the ground, helpless to do anything but watch.

Buran had sent an entire sector fleet, somehow snuck them across the tremendous distance from the border, and the even vaster one from beyond *Ninagirsu*. Had done so after Em's scouts had begun to locate and dismantle the highways of secret transmitters that *Buran* had hidden in the darkness between stars, where neither *Fribourg* nor *Aquitaine* ever looked.

Somewhere, there was an *entire region* of *Buran* space left undefended. If Em could have, he would have telepathically linked with Jessica and told her, just so she could go out there and do something about it.

He had never imagined that *Buran* would ever return to *St. Legier*. And never with an Armada this vast.

A signal chimed. Em pushed a button and the hatch opened.

Lt. Commander Gunter Tifft entered. He had grown into himself, from the self-conscious Quartermaster aboard *Firehawk* into a steady, capable aide, good enough at his job that Em could afford to leave Hendrik Baumgärtner, his long-time aide who was now an Admiral of the White himself, at home more, rather than chasing all over space with the

Grand Admiral on surprise inspections. Or send Hendrik to do them for him, like now.

"Orders, sir?" Tifft asked simply. He was good at that. Everything Em needed from the man and nothing more.

"I have good admirals in charge tactically, Gunter," Em said. "We'll let them fight until they ask for help. Anything I do at this point is likely to muddle things at the moment they will need diamond clarity. We have another problem."

"Sir?"

"That fleet out there is not normal, Tifft," Em fumed, tapping on the monitor to emphasize his point. "They have never, as far as I know, assembled that many warships into a single formation. Certainly not outside of their homelands. Not even defending the places we've attacked."

"Smash and grab, Admiral?" Tifft asked. "That's enough force to destroy this station if they wanted to."

"Not without suffering horrendous casualties in the process, Gunter," Em replied. "We've upgraded the guns and I have enough firepower in close orbit to do that job. *Buran* has never been that careless about lives. They fight when attacked, but almost never provoke."

"Would this be an attack on the planet again?" Tifft asked. "One Roughshark was able to drop a dozen bombs. The damage was minimal, but they were only trying to be seen, not to do significant damage."

Em watched a blue dot appear on his screen.

"Good call, Tifft," Em said. "The first bomb has launched, a scramjet pointed straight down. Order all vessels to engage any Roughshark they can locate."

"On it, sir," Tifft said.

"Hold," Emmerich said. "Let's move to the flag bridge now. If they come, I'm feeling too close to the outer hull for comfort."

Em rose and grabbed a briefcase with key papers. Everything else was electronic, and he would feel better, buried deep in the insulated bowels of the station, where the Mauler hopefully couldn't get to him.

They exited the hatch just the lights and grav-plates flickered.

Somewhere, someone had just mauled the station.

And it was likely to get worse before it got better.

CHAPTER IV

"That's one," Tom Provst yelled triumphantly as the bomb exploded mid-flight.

A ragged cheer went up from the men around him on *Firehawk*'s flag bridge. The ship was hurting, but the Carcharias, one of the so-called Great Whites, had hopefully been hammered at least as badly on her pass.

The Makos accompanying on the first pass had escaped relatively unscathed, but that was the result of better tactical doctrine from *Fribourg* these days. All the new corvettes kept their pair of Type-3 beams tuned for short-range, close-in work when on patrol in the home system. At least until they had a reason to adjust them. At that range, they hit like Primaries, a dull sledgehammer wielded by an ogre. If the older escorts couldn't pour as much firepower into someone swooping by, Tom still had several cruisers handy. All of them had fired on the lone capital ship as it passed and ignored all the cruisers with it.

In past days, the cruisers would have gone after the escorts, each trying to overload the power absorbers so that they could score a kill. Jessica Keller had taught them better, finally.

Kill the biggest beast by hitting it from every direction at the same time. It can't shift power around or fill the batteries fast enough, and then it becomes vulnerable.

Tom was just mad he didn't have the Heavy Dreadnaught *Valiant* or some of the new Expeditionary Cruisers. Type-4 beams or Bubble Guns would have been a lovely tactical addition right now. And the better range would have let him hit some of those scramjet missiles that were getting through the gaps in coverage.

Already, two had gotten low enough to explode, with massive, orange mushroom-shaped clouds that had hopefully been deflected by the planetary shields below. Communications with the ground had gone to hell as a result. Contact with the other squadrons defending low orbit wasn't much better.

Tom looked at the tactical plot projected between him and d'Noir.

"How many bombers are we dealing with?" he yelled over the din of raised voices.

"At least four, sir," someone volleyed back. "They've turned off all IFF signals so we're having to track vessels by engine signatures alone. Makes it messy."

"Affirmative," Tom called. It made sense, damn them. "Someone let the Grand Admiral know. He's up on the station instead of the ground, so maybe he can do something. Meanwhile, shift the squadron farther away from the station. We need to be able to shoot better at those missiles. Change targeting priority to go after any Roughshark we can get first, and then the big boys later. Alert the other squadrons as well."

"Roger that, Admiral."

Provst took a deep breath and leaned back. Already, the rank smell of adrenaline and sweat had made the flag bridge's air go sour. Bad locker-room smell. Shitty day getting worse.

Red dots appeared and vanished. White dots ran like hell for deep space and jumped as soon as they could, just to get away from the chaos below and the risk of an overshot blowing starlight through them.

That left more green dots than red, but the green were all bunched up in a few places, rather than smoothly spread out. It helped them protect one another, but left too many gaps where bombers were able to appear, fire three missiles downward, and then vanish.

None of this made any sense, but Tom wasn't about to stop fighting for a reason as silly as that.

Those bastards had come all this distance for some reason. He just had to figure it out and stop them.

CHAPTER V

Em entered the station's bridge and signaled to Admiral of the Blue Frankenheimer that the man should continue what he had been doing, even as the station commander rose and started to say something.

"Keep at it, Ralf," Em called, finding an unoccupied station to one side. "I wanted a better view than I could get in my office. Have you launched all the flight wings?"

"We have, Em," Frankenheimer replied. The man was tall and getting paunchy, but his voice was as firm as his eyes. "Only a few had missiles, but everyone with a gun is out there."

"Good," Em ordered, sitting. "You stay tactical. I'm going Big Picture."

Rather than reply, Frankenheimer went back to issuing orders and updates. Em powered up the monitor and began typing furiously.

"What are we looking for, sir?" Tifft said from the next station.

Em paused and thought about it for a moment.

"A mining marker playing music to eternity," Em replied cryptically. "Something that doesn't fit the pattern."

Tifft's eyes got a far-away look in them, and then he got to work as well.

What did *Buran* hope to gain from a raid of this scale?

Tom Provst had possibly crippled one of the capital ships on their first pass, having learned how to face a charging shark from Bedrov & Keller. They would learn eventually not to fly right through the middle of a squadron of escorts. Hopefully not too soon.

Em made a note to himself to ask Bedrov what it would do to tactics when *Buran* swapped the Mag-Shear device for some Type-4 beams instead. Jump to a corner, fire the heavy guns, and jump away, rather than risk stepping on a rattlesnake.

Another, damned arms race, but at least he was winning this round, as near as he could tell. With fire discipline, the fleet was inflicting better than it got, and *Buran* still had to make it home.

But what the hell were they up to?

CHAPTER VI

"**C**onfirm that?" Vo asked as he took two steps up into the back of the command skiff. Decanus Borel and his team were at their stations, dinner already forgotten in the moment when the first alert sirens sounded.

"Raiding fleet overhead, General," one of the man called. "*Buran* vessels. Bunch of them. Nuclear-tipped, scramjet missiles already in flight, dropping on various places all over the planet. None coming this way at present."

"Get all the air defense teams in a ready stance," Vo ordered. "Unlock all batteries that have beam weapons and get someone on the scanners, identifying everything above our horizon. Nobody should be overflying this base, but warn anybody who is that this is a live-fire exercise starting now."

Decanus Borel gulped and nodded.

"Rules of engagement, General?" he asked in a steady voice, if a little loud.

Vo nodded. Reese was a damned good non-comm, but he had never been at the sharp end of something like this. Never had *incoming orbital fire* demanding the right of way. Very few men and women had.

"If they're flying horizontal, take a second look before engaging," Vo ordered. "Anything moving in a dive is to be killed by any and all guns with bearing immediately. On my authority. We don't have planetary shields overhead, but I'd rather answer to the Grand Marshal about how I shot down a civilian than to lose the legion today."

"And the rest of the command?" Borel asked.

"Get everybody mounted up and secured," Vo said. "I want armor around people if something happens. Everyone else move into secured shelters until the all clear sounds."

"Sir, we have some rough-enough terrain just south of the laager," one of the men in the far corner called. Curator Stolz. A man who often looked like he wasn't sure which end of the gun the bang came out of, until he started talking. "Tanks could park on the slopes and provide adequate secondary fire support for the air batteries. The hills will make up for the low elevation on the guns."

"Send the orders to Bleushan, Stolz," Vo nodded gratefully.

He didn't have to do it all. Just surround himself with competent men and let them find answers.

It was almost like being home with Fourth Saxon, except he missed that big, stupid, brute of a horse, *Shevi*. Maybe he would name the command skiff after his first mount. A few of the men here would appreciate the joke, and share it with everyone else.

"What else do we know?" Vo asked the room.

Heads were down on monitors. Headphones were on as the men listened to feeds from all directions.

Reese looked up.

"It's a firestorm up there, General," he said grimly. "Fleet unlocked the minefields and launched everything they had. Four capital ships. Over a dozen cruisers. Another dozen Hammerheads. Bloodbath on all sides."

"Makes no sense," Vo agreed. "Doesn't have to. Our job is to hold our airspace. If this is a strike putting commando forces on the surface, we have to be able to intercept or engage. Otherwise, help the good guys any way we can. What's on the command net?"

"Mostly static," Borel called. "First bombs went off just above the shields, but didn't crack anything. EMPs are rippling out like waves on a pond right now, but the bombs look clean enough."

"Order everyone to prepare for fallout, just the same," Vo ordered. "And put that up on the civilian emergency network as well. All people shelter in place indoors as much as possible."

"On it, sir."

Vo decided to keep his belt on for now. He wasn't wearing the big sword, having stowed it in an overhead bin, but he still had the pistol. Hopefully, he wouldn't need it any time soon.

What was *Buran*'s game this time?

CHAPTER VII

"Order all but one of your escorts to continue the battle while you retire to the rendezvous point and begin repairs with the other," Director Ul Turin Dyana Vor tasked the other man from the bridge of the *Angustidens*-class vessel *Glory in Duty*. The Nightmaster. "We are within range of the outcomes predicted by *The Eldest* at this point. Yours was the bad luck to draw a competent foe."

"I obey," Director Au nodded, cutting the circuit from *Defend the Homeland*.

Director Ul looked at his own bridge with a smug feeling. *Glory in Duty* was as yet undamaged, even though he had led the first charge, raking *Fribourg's* orbital command station at a very high speed, escaping on the Capriole drive before the barbarians could respond effectively. Two of the Makos accompanying him, however, *Called to Battle* and *Hope in Morning* had trailed on the run and caught the full fury of the defender's guns. Both were out of the fight now, with *Called to Battle* effectively crippled and already withdrawing.

Director Au's Carcharias, *Defend the Homeland*, had simply encountered a competent force commander when they attacked. All of that squadron's ships had fired on the biggest enemy, rather than engaging the closest, as had always been *Fribourg's* preference. Au looked like someone had graffiti-ed his vessel with black paint and a sledgehammer, from all the damage lacing his hull.

If *Fribourg's* new vessels were as capable as they appeared, it would be necessary to inform *The Eldest*. Changes would be necessary, as it appeared that the barbarians were finally learning how to fight a civilized foe.

Still, the overall battle was proceeding according to plans as transmitted by the Four Mandarins. Damage was inevitable when titanic forces engaged on a scale such as this, something only commanders who had served at *Samara* had previously experienced.

"War Advocate Ko," Director Ul called. "Begin drawing the defenders away from our target area. Proceed with Phase Five of the plan."

"Phase Five initiated, Director," the man replied, barely looking up. "Maneuver Advocate, inform the fleet."

"I obey," the other man said, already pressing keys to route the signals to all vessels, in addition to the four cruisers *Glory in Duty* normally carried.

Glory in Duty was the flagship of the entire squadron today.

Director Ul studied his next target. It was a manufacturing facility located just over the horizon from the main enemy base, forward as the planet orbited. Far enough away that vessels would have to shift their coverage to keep his hungry sharks from pounding it to orbital scrap.

Not that he would be staying long enough to actually do that, but it was necessary to redirect the barbarians away from the target zone.

And it would be nice to inflict some surprise on *Fribourg* today, in recompense. The extensive minefields had proven to be a most unwelcome development, and he could not decide which version he hated more. One apparently contained what the Imperials called a Type-2 beam as well as a generator, allowing it to fire repeatedly at any available target close enough, while the other was simply one of their Primary beams that would fire once, and then be done.

A constant surge of damage that must be absorbed and controlled, or an icepick that might lance right through and damage the hull before the crew noticed?

At least they were developing a detailed map of the minefields. That would be critical when it came time for Phase Nine.

CHAPTER VIII

"**S**till not making sense, Admiral," Em heard his assistant grouse under his breath.

Em had to agree.

First *Buran* had attacked the station. The last time, that had worked because traitors had disabled the defensive systems on the platform, allowing one Mako free reign to make a slow pass with their mauler. The results had been horrendous.

At least the station had better armor and insulation now, thanks to Bedrov.

And two of the Makos on that first pass had gotten their snouts kicked in when the Type-4s came on line in time.

Then suddenly, they backed off and went after the defending squadrons around the planet, damning the minefield to go full steam ahead.

But *Firehawk* had proven the new tactics sound, even in an old *Amsel*-class battleship, hammering on one of the two attacking Great Whites and blowing holes in the vessel before it could escape. *Firehawk* was hurting, but she was an old design, not even one of the *Paladin*-class vessels that were supposed to be able to engage *Buran* vessels more evenly, to say nothing of monsters like *Valiant*, where Tom would be raising his flag in a few months.

One Great White knocked out of the battle. One battleship seriously afflicted. A frightening number of vessels damaged on both sides, but *Fribourg* had the advantage in tonnage and home pitch. There wasn't much Em could do about the missiles detonating in mid-atmosphere, except make sure that all the defending squadrons paid attention and tried sniping when they could.

Tom Provst had even managed to kill one. Someone else had gotten another. But with four or five Roughsharks out there, that was at least seventy bombs that could be dropped on the planet. Possibly ninety.

Even with planetary shields in place around important facilities, the damage would likely be nightmarish.

"New signals, Admiral," Tifft broke in on Em's concentration. "Several sharks are making a run at the Petrograd Heights Station."

One of the Empire's key orbital manufacturing facilities. And a playground for the rich and powerful. It had shields and some guns, but not enough to hold off a concerted rush.

"Ralf," Em called Admiral Frankenheimer. "Who do we have that could shift around to protect Petrograd?"

The man checked his boards with a fierce scowl.

"Tom Provst and his team have been sitting on our flank," Frankenheimer yelled. "They're in the best position right now."

"Move them," Em ordered. "Hopefully, *Buran* will see that as an opening to attack us here again."

"I would enjoy that, Em," Ralf beamed. "Not everyone got a chance to fire last time. Next time, we could crush a few of them."

Em nodded and went back to his boards.

Something was still missing. Granted, he was dancing to someone else's tune, something Jessica had forced him to do time and again, but this was more mechanical. It was like *Buran* was working their way down a checklist that involved damaging a wide range of targets, but not staying anywhere long enough to destroy anything.

And the costs they were incurring in the process could not bear the outcomes.

Somewhere, somebody was up to something.

CHAPTER IX

"Anything?" Vo asked his men.

More than an hour had passed. None of the dropping missiles had come close enough to be engaged from the ground, but Vo's legion was literally in the middle of nowhere, a huge training base several hours flight south of Werder, designed to let large ground formations practice war without neighbors even noticing.

"Negative, sir," Stolz replied, keeping a wary eye on his boards. "Still several vessels engaging in a game of tag around Petrograd, but the only missiles even remotely in our region have all been fired at Werder proper. Those shields have held, but some of the outlying areas have gotten splashed."

"Make sure all the medical teams are packed up," Vo ordered. "As soon as all this is done, we're likely going to need to move close to Werder to support. Hospitals and medics will be a priority, followed by transport."

"Acknowledged, General," Decanus Borel chimed in.

Vo closed his mouth at that point. There was no reason for the men to see his frustration. They felt the same.

It went back to conversations with the Fleet Centurion first, and the Grand Admiral and the Grand Marshal later. You could invade the surface of a planet, but everything important would happen in orbit. And from orbital space, there wasn't much a fleet couldn't do to someone on the ground, up to and including dropping large rocks at high velocity until you nailed him, like the galaxy's most patient sniper chasing a fly.

Hitting the edges of the shield instead of the center made a crude sort of sense. Even thermonuclear-tipped scramjets moving at several thousand kilometers per hour weren't getting through those shields, but they could scorch the distant suburbs.

Vo could almost taste the waves of anger that would come bubbling up from the natives of this planet, to be orbitally bombarded a second time.

"Confirm that we have a good link to the planetary emergency network, Borel," Vo finally commanded. "We'll need to move quickly when we get the orders from Werder."

"Yes sir, General."

Vo lapsed into silence.

Nothing so maddening as to simply sit down here and wait to see when it might be his turn to do something.

CHAPTER X

Director Ul Turin Dyana Vor had always felt a moderate level of derision towards the barbarians known as *Fribourg*. Primitive. Rigid. Wild animals unfit for human interaction.

Today, that had grown to anger.

Vor had discounted the lurid tales from the campaigns around *Trusski*. *Steadfast at Dawn* had made poor tactical and strategic decisions, and the Red Admiral Keller had exploited them.

But this, here, lent credence to those tales.

Fribourg, that never-to-be-sufficiently-damned realm of barbarians intent on conquering the galaxy under their aboriginal ways, they had learned. Changed.

Vor had served at *Samara,* facing idiot assaults derived of linear thinking. *Fribourg* had not changed their tactics, nor even their tactical doctrine, in a century.

Until now.

It did not bode well for the campaign to pacify humanity, that *Fribourg* had finally awakened to the threat. Nor that they had learned how to fight the current generation of *Sentient* warships. Vor had a list of notes for the Scholars of Naval Design as to future needs.

Still, they might not be necessary. Not after today.

Ul Turin Dyana Vor could see a future where all of *Fribourg* lay broken at his feet. Supine and vulnerable.

Ready to accept the lessons of *The Eldest* and transform themselves into willing participants in the great mission. And as they only understood strength, *The Eldest* had found it necessary to impose his will upon them in the most spectacular manner possible.

The barbarians would finally come to understand just how hopeless their resistance was.

And he would be accorded the glory to hold the blade itself.

"War Advocate, are all squadrons in place?" Vor called out over his bridge. Calm. Firm. None of the fury underneath that had made this a necessity.

Fools.

"They are, Director," the man responded instantly.

Vor could taste the rage in the man's voice. Another jousting pass with the battleship known as *Firehawk* had gone badly, but at least the *Fribourg* vessel had been savaged this time, and forced to withdraw some.

"Maneuver Advocate, are the maps complete?" Vor continued.

"We believe so, Director Ul," the man said. "Three Hammerheads have been crippled or destroyed in the process of scouting them, but all of the heavy mines appear to have been triggered and the lighter ones will not have sufficient power to alter the outcome at this point."

"And the approach has been identified?" Vor continued. He could taste victory at this point. The greatest defeat of a foe in centuries.

"It has," the Maneuver Advocate replied.

"Confirm that *Sukhoy Nos* is in position and then communicate Phase Nine to all vessels," the Director of *Glory in Duty* commanded. "One last surge to push the barbarians off balance, and then all vessels scatter and form up at their rendezvous points. Transmit 'Well done' to all commanders."

"I obey, Director."

CHAPTER XI

"What the hell is that thing?" Em heard a voice say.

It might even have been his.

A new signal had appeared, high and well away from everyone else, as if it had been hiding out in the darkness before now. Pointed inward, like Damocles' sword hanging over the heavens. Moving swiftly, but pointed down, rather than along an orbital insertion path.

It made no sense to maneuver any vessel like that. They would just have to flatten out from that much deeper in the gravity well, or jump from so low that even *Buran*'s best navigators would be hard pressed.

"Admiral, all *Buran* vessels have just jumped at the same time," Tifft noted out loud. "They haven't done that once today."

Em turned a quizzical eye on the man.

"Not once?"

"No, sir," Tifft said.

"Ralf," Em yelled loud enough to drown every conversation. "Bums rush."

Admiral Frankenheimer paused, cursed under his breath, and began yelling orders rapid-fire.

"Bums rush, sir?" Tifft asked, painfully confused.

"They are about to launch a full, frontal assault on us, while that whatever-it-is does whatever it came to do," Em said before turning to yell at Ralf again. "Where's Provst?"

"*Firehawk* has withdrawn with serious damage, Em, but most of his squadron is still guarding Petrograd."

"Get them after that new thing," Em ordered. "This feels like the end of the battle, right now."

"On it," Ralf yelled.

Em sucked a deep breath into his lungs. It only felt like the room was choking him with smoke, when everything was clear as spring.

The new signal blinked off of the scanners. Em counted to eight, and it appeared again, at least at the very edge of Type-4 range, if not safely beyond. Ralf's gun batteries opened up anyway, but that would be like tickling a whale to death at this range.

"What's he doing?" Ralf yelled over the orders going back and forth.

"Unsure, Admiral," a man's voice responded. "Target is not maneuvering as expected, and most vessels are now engaged with the other *Buran* ships that have come out of jump."

Not maneuvering? Why would a ship that big not maneuver?

Em felt his stomach go cold. His whole soul.

"Ralf, that's a bomb," he yelled. "Get everyone on it now!"

Em watched his old friend's face turn white as the implications hit. The Roughsharks had delivered missiles as big as Starfighters. This thing was the size of a battleship.

"Tifft, order planetary forces to engage that thing as well," Em turned to his assistant. "Anyone and everyone who can. Drop everything else to stop that."

Tifft had gone pale as well. He turned and began barking orders into a microphone, but the planetary network was a mess from all the previous explosions. Nuclear bombs had scrambled all radio below the ionosphere, and it would take hours for the energy released to dissipate.

The bomb was right around three thousand kilometers above the surface right now, but it was moving at a tremendous velocity and accelerating away from the various ships and stations taking shots at it. It would hit some terminal velocity imposed by the thickening atmosphere, the ship's spear-shaped design, and the materials that comprised the outer hull, but it was still just minutes from reaching the ground, if it was a bomb.

The Imperial Capital of Werder was directly beneath the beast.

CHAPTER XII

His Sovereign Imperial Majesty Karl Johannes Arend Wiegand, Hereditary King of *St. Legier*, Emperor Karl VII by Grace of God, looked over at the stunningly-beautiful woman seated next to him on the couch. At fifty-eight standard years, her hair had finally faded from the gorgeous blond of younger decades to a pure silver. She was still tall and willowy, as befit most Imperial women of her station and heritage, and those green eyes had lost nothing.

Kasimira Ekaterina, of the House of Alkaev.

The Empress Kati.

Her eyes were troubled now, but she remained silent. All four hands were tangled up in each other on laps as they watched the battle unfold overhead on a monitor.

Joh knew what that thing was as soon as it appeared at the edge of the atmosphere. Knew there was nothing Em or anyone else could do at this point to stop it.

But he also knew that Ekke and Casey would escape the Beast's wrath. And that the Empire was more resilient now that it ever had been in his lifetime.

The Emperor leaned over and kissed the most beautiful woman in the galaxy one last time.

"I love you," he whispered.

CHAPTER XIII

"Nothing?" Vo demanded angrily. "Fire all batteries anyway. We must do something."

"Firing now, General," Borel announced. "But we're too far south. It won't overfly us until it flattens out."

"It's not going to, Reese," Vo growled. "That's a bomb, not an aircraft."

It made sense now, the targeting they had done earlier. Finding the exact edges of the planetary shields protecting the capital. And perhaps their strength. Vo could see the next step with astounding clarity.

And there wasn't a damned thing he could do.

Or perhaps there was.

"Reese, override all emergency signals that you can reach," Vo ordered in a calm, quiet voice. His emotions had come close to getting out of hand a few times today. He was at the precipice now. That wasn't what the men needed. What everyone needed.

"Sir?" Borel turned, ashen-faced. He could do the math as well.

"Order all aircraft, civilian or military, to ground immediately," Vo commanded. "Repulsor craft are to land on skids and deploy ground anchors. Tell the tanks to get to level ground immediately. All personnel are to seal themselves tight. Vehicles closed and on internal air. Bases go to emergency lock-down procedures. *Now.*"

Vo put word to deed and flipped down a jumpseat, strapping himself down tight. He turned to the men of his bodyguard and his admin command.

"All of you, buckle up," Vo continued, letting calm wash over him and the mad energy of the last two hours recede like a tide. "That's an order."

He took an immense breath and watched the dot that was the *Buran* ship plummet towards the surface of *St. Legier*.

"Put that warning on loop, Borel," he said. "All hands, brace for impact."

"Impact, General?" Stolz asked in surprise. "Where?"

Vo turned a sad face on the young man. He had no words to describe the horror he could see coming. The impending doom. It was there in his mind, perhaps the greatest fear he could imagine.

Greater than even the sort of personal nightmare of a battle that got all his men killed and left him untouched. Even that did not measure to this scope of failure.

Outside, the sky suddenly flashed whiter than the sun.

And then darkness fell.

CHAPTER XIV

To the end of his days, Em would never be able to move past his guilt. To admit that the first thought that had crossed his mind, watching the sun fall to earth over Werder, was that Freya was home on *Eklionstic*, and not at their palace in the capital, not far from her favorite park.

That he hadn't just lost her.

The room had fallen to utter silence, perhaps punctuated by quiet sobs. Em could only hear the pounding of his heart in his ears, as he watched a white-hot plasma cloud engulf his city. From this elevation, he could see the shockwave as the atmosphere raced away from the explosion's epicenter, trailed by the earth itself moving like waves in a pond as the massive bomb exploded and brushed aside the planetary shields protecting the Palace like curtains.

This was what failure tasted like.

This was what it meant to lose everything. Almost everything. Freya hadn't been there. And that tiny, greedy thought would haunt him forever.

Joh had been down there. Kati. Cousins. Loved ones. Comrades.

Gone.

Em slammed a fist into the monitor hard enough to possibly break the bones in his hand, but the screen was made of tougher stuff and continued to show him his failure to protect the people who had counted on him.

Tifft was silently crying, a spectacle echoed by many of the men around him. Those with any expression at all. Many had simply vanished inside themselves.

The silence was astounding.

The pain never-ending.

Em unbuckled his harness and rose.

Ralf Frankenheimer looked like a three-days-dead corpse, mouth opening and closing like a fish, even as no words came out.

Em wasn't sure there were words.

"Ralf, you did all you could," Em said, stepping closer to the man. "I'll take it from here."

Ralf responded like a marionette whose strings had been cut, collapsing to the floor before Em could catch him. Only the sobs emanating from the man's chest let Em know that Ralf hadn't simply willed himself to die.

Em could understand the feeling.

He blinked back the tears. He had spent decades fearing this moment's arrival, ever since Karl VI and Empress Ailina had died in a tragic accident twenty years before.

He had never expected to have to stand on this deck. To say these words.

He would not cry. Not today. Perhaps not ever, but he would have to face Freya at some point. His reserves of strength might not be equal to that task.

"All hands, continue engaging any *Buran* vessels," Em ordered. "No quarter given."

He didn't expect there to be many of the invaders remaining. It was obvious now what they had been up to. The tapes would just confirm what he already knew in his soul. One last push to distract everyone, so that they could drop a battleship-sized bomb on Werder.

"Someone get me eyes on the planet that aren't obscured by a fireball and mushroom cloud," Em continued, amazed that he was able to function at all, let alone give orders.

Some things were bone deep.

Tifft seemed broken, along with Ralf. Only the blinking eyes and falling tears confirmed that his aide was still living.

"MOVE IT," Em yelled at the men, all of them currently cowed into submission and lost.

Something broke free in one of them. A man suddenly pushed a button with shaky hands and began talking into his mic. Slow and labored, but functioning, however minimally. Others struggled to follow.

On the monitors around him, Em could see the red dots vanish one by one. Many had already fled, reappearing well out and moving away from the planet at high speed, but he needed to be sure. The casualties Em had been able to inflict on them today had been utterly devastating. They wouldn't have stood for it, but for the knowledge that they were here for a larger purpose.

To bomb *St. Legier* again. To destroy Werder.

Em wondered how badly damaged the planet itself might be, given the scope of that explosion. The entire hemisphere might have heard it. Within minutes, they would feel it.

"Engineering, concentrate on that blast," Em ordered the room, uncaring who responded, as long as someone did. They were all hard men, professionals. That training was still underneath, and would carry them, if he could reach it.

Or it would break them.

"Find out what that thing was," Em continued. "How big was it? What type of explosive? What are the fallout risks? What's the state of communications with the ground?"

"I am receiving no signals from Fleet Operations in Werder, Grand Admiral," one of the men replied in a mechanical voice. "Nor Imperial Land Forces Headquarters. Nor the Palace."

"Find me someone on the ground," Em countered. "Anyone."

"Sir, I have Admiral Provst aboard *Firehawk*," someone yelled. "Asking for a private channel."

"I don't have a private channel," Em snarled. "Put him through on the main board."

Tom Provst's face appeared on the screen and Em's heart fell the rest of the way.

He had known the man since Ensign Provst had first earned his transfer to the original *Blackbird*, twenty-five years ago. Had guided Tom's career along the right lines, until *Captain* Provst had commanded the *Blackbird* at the battle known universally today simply as *Third Iger*, the battle where a young, Republic destroyer squadron commander named Keller made her name, preventing Emmerich Wachturm, the dread *Red*

Admiral of older days, from mousetrapping a Republic fleet and annihilating two fleet carriers commanded by that idiot Bogdan Loncar.

"Tom?" Em asked, but he already knew. Could see it in the man's haunted eyes.

"I put him in the safest place I could find, Grand Admiral," Tom Provst's voice sounded like glass ground into shards. "The bridge of a battleship surrounded by the best squadron in the fleet."

Tom's voice broke. Perhaps his mind as well. The eyes got wild for a moment.

Em found his own center, forcing himself to be there now for this man, one of his students. One of his best. One of his few true friends.

"What happened, Tom?" Em breathed slowly, trying to hold his sanity together with both arms.

"That last pass at *Petrograd*, Em," Tom said. "They learned from what we did to them the first time. Every ship ignored my escorts and fired on the '*hawk* with everything they had, just before they ran like hell for deep space. We took a bridge hit. Bad one. Al Kistler's dead. Everyone's dead."

He gulped, and Em could see insanity take root in the man's soul.

"Crown Prince Ekkehard is dead."

The room itself groaned.

Em felt like someone had walked up and punched him in the stomach as hard as they could, driving all the breath from his body.

"I failed," Tom continued in the voice of a precocious six-year-old discovering death for the first time.

"I failed you, Tom," Em interjected, trying to get inside the man's mind while he still could. Tom was rapidly losing himself. "You did everything you could."

"It wasn't enough," Tom cried in pure anguish. "He's dead."

"I know, Tom," Em said in a quiet voice. "So is Karl VII. So are a great many people."

"Are you sure?"

Em glanced at another screen, a jittery image from a frigate that was flying as low as it could with the shockwave and smoke battering and obscuring.

"Looking at the images of the ground, Werder's been destroyed, and everything around it."

"What do we do?" Tom asked.

The madness had fled his eyes, Emptiness had taken hold instead.

"There are procedures in place for this, Tom," Em said, taking a deep breath. "We keep moving forward and hold it all together until everyone else recovers. The Emperor is dead. Long live the Emperor."

"I can't," Tom Provst whispered fiercely. "I failed the boy. I can't live with that."

"Tom. TOM," Em yelled as the man's eyes lost focus. "Look at me. Now. Good. I need you, Tom. I have to go do the single hardest thing I think I will ever have to face, and I need you here, holding things together until I get back."

"I can't do it, Em," Tom whispered. "I'm broken."

"Tom, I need you. It's as simple as that," Em countered. "I need men I can trust. What happens next will test the entire Empire. Give me a year. Promise me that, and I'll give you anything you want."

"Anything?"

"Tom, I'll even load the gun for you and walk away without a word, but I need you right now. Things will come apart while I'm gone, without men like you holding it together."

"Gone?"

Tom's swarthy skin had gone white, but there was something in his eyes finally. Some note that the insanity that had burned everything else out, hadn't completely consumed him.

"I have to go retrieve the Emperor, Tom," Em said. "Whether she likes it, or not."

CHAPTER XV

IMPERIAL FOUNDING: 179/11/10. ARMY TRAINING
DEPOT "KING OLAF," ST. LEGIER

"General, I have the Grand Admiral on channel six for you," Vo heard one of the men say quietly.

Everything was quiet. Only the life support system refused to be silent, slowly blowing cool, clean air, even as a terrible sirocco unfolded around them, hot winds outside racing outwards from a wound to the planet's soul.

"General?"

Vo shook himself like a wet dog, coming back into his body from whatever place he had gone to. He blew out all the air in his lungs like it would help and pulled fresh in.

Some men respond to shock by going cold. Hollow.

Others simply broke and never quite recovered themselves.

Vo had learned early on how to put his sanity into a safe place and hold it there, regardless of what the outside world did. It had served him well in a life of petty crime. And the inevitable stint in jail. And marine boot camp.

And all the stupid places he had gone since.

"I'm here," Vo said, marveling at how normal his voice sounded.

He wasn't an emotionless automaton. He simply could not afford to let any emotions out right now, lest they all come, like the residents of Pandora's box freed by him leaving any crack.

"Channel Six, General," the man said carefully.

Vo could feel all twelve men staring at him. Needing him to be steady. Giving them a rock upon which to stand.

He had spent a lifetime doing that.

It wasn't going to get any easier tomorrow.

Vo cleared the channel and put Wachturm on conference mode. He might have to keep secrets from the rest of the Legion, but the men around him would be necessary accessories to anything he did.

"Wachturm, you're on speaker," Vo said simply, warning the Grand Admiral.

"Acknowledged, *zu* Arlo," Emmerich replied.

Vo could hear an even-greater pain in the man's voice, but nobody had leveled the Dragon Gates with fire, back on *Anameleck Prime*. This was merely Vo's adopted family.

It was Wachturm's home. His whole life.

The Grand Admiral paused for another moment, probably composing the words to sound better, knowing that the 189th would be hearing them directly instead of filtered first.

"Werder has been destroyed, General," the Admiral said. "The primary crater measures roughly seventeen kilometers across and nearly a kilometer deep in places. They are still estimating the magnitude of the planetary shock, but the number is simply catastrophic. Somewhere above an eleven on the Richter scale. For a primitive society, this would be an extinction-level event, to quote one of my scientists."

"Yes, sir," Vo agreed. "We are still feeling it down here. What are your orders?"

"Vo, I need your competence," Wachturm said grimly. "I have to go and retrieve the emperor. The palace was destroyed. Crown Prince Ekkehard was killed in the battle. I'm not even sure how much of the Army High Command has survived, because yours is one of the few units of any size that I could reach. Admiral Tom Provst will command local naval forces while I'm gone, but I have to have somebody on the ground, organizing things."

"Sir?" Vo asked.

"Men I can trust Arlo," Wachturm's voice turned heavy. "Men *she* can trust. There are other divisional commanders, Army commanders I could reach out to, but you are the only *Ritter* in command of a military force on *St. Legier*. And the only one I know well. The planet has been nearly shattered. The population will start coming apart without someone to rally them. To give them orders. And to bury whatever bodies they can find."

"Can't the fleet do a better job organizing, Grand Admiral?" Vo responded.

"Possibly," Wachturm agreed. "But this is the exact reversal of the conversation you and Anthohn and I had, when you first took this job. We can hold orbit, but we cannot be there on the surface doing things. You have your experience with Fourth Saxon. You have the men of the 189th. You have the *zu*. And you have my faith that you will do the right thing. I don't have anybody better suited. Neither does she."

Vo would not cry. Not now.

He would hold himself together until this was all over. Stable. Rigid. Upright.

Vojciech *zu* Arlo hadn't known what kind of man he was, until he walked into that dingy hall to meet with retired Senior Judge Holman Metharom.

But he would do what was right, as *Navin the Black*, Jessica Keller, and Karl VII had taught him.

"Acknowledged, Grand Admiral," Vo rasped, still right at the edge of that precipice.

He would not fall. He would not fail.

"What are your orders?" Vo managed to repeat in an even voice.

"You will take command of all Imperial Land Forces on *St. Legier*, General *zu* Arlo, under my authority as Grand Admiral, speaking for the throne. You will coordinate rescue and relief efforts. You will exercise *Palatine* authority on the surface until the Emperor returns or I relieve you. Right now, she is the only person who outranks me, and that will remain so until the House of Dukes can conclave. And that might take more than a year, given how many of those men were likely in Werder yesterday. The fleet supports her, and me. Provst will command naval forces in the system, but only to the edge of the atmosphere. Questions?"

"Will they accept her?" Vo asked.

It was a technical as much as political question, but one that would have had a very resounding negative five years ago. Before Lady Casey became Emperor the first time. And there were still people out there cleaving to the old ways. Those fools would be a problem.

If he let them.

Which was why the Grand Admiral was asking him, and not one of the others who might have different ideas.

"The fleet backs her, General," Wachturm growled. "In *Fribourg*, that's really all that matters, but she will also have the 189th. And she is beloved of the general populace on a variety of levels. It will be enough."

"Where do you fall in the Line of Succession, sir?" Vo asked, drawn by the tangent.

Yesterday, that would have been an academic question. Today, the galaxy might hinge on it.

"Depending on who you asked?" Wachturm replied sadly. "Tenth or eleventh. Yesterday. Some of them were in Werder, so I'm not really sure. And I don't give a damn, because number three is alive and well. And counting on us. Does that help?"

Vo took a breath, held it, released. There were twelve men around him, but they were as little, white mice in the cupboard now, fearful of being noticed as Imperial Policy was made before their eyes.

"It does, sir," Vo replied, pushing his anger down until everything came out flat. "You have given us an impossible task, with an impossible deadline. We will fail at it as well as we can until you can return with whatever help you bring. But we will not fall."

Vo looked around at the faces surrounding him. Saw the calm assurance break through the sadness. The reassuring nods. Men who would march into Hell with him.

Again.

"Fail, General?" Wachturm was slightly perplexed.

"We are the 189th Legion, Grand Admiral," Vo said, giving hope to these men, and to the others who would hear this story, this legend, repeated for as long as those unit colors survived. "*We stood.*"

"Thank you, Vo."

Vo cut the channel while his emotions would still allow it. He turned to Decanus Borel and ground his teeth for a moment.

"Put the entire Legion in motion, Reese," Vo ordered, soul gone to ice. "Get all the scouts as close to Werder as they can safely travel, as fast as they can get there. Once Fourth Ala clears, send the tanks north as a unit and then have everybody else break down our base here, pack it all on every vehicle we have or can requisition, and start north. Designate roadways and have Fourth Ala keep them clear of refugees so we can move upstream as a force. Once the scouts finds us a spot, plan to build a base ten times the size we need, for all the people and supplies that we'll have to handle, with a landing base for shuttles from orbit."

"What about other units, sir?" Borel asked.

Vo paused and thought about the logistics of the thing. Invading *Thuringwell* had been an afternoon on Hogan's Alley, by comparison.

"Have them start building bases well out," Vo decided. "A ring around 400 kilometers from the center, every fifteen degrees of arc from zero. We'll send them people once we get organized, and they can feed and house them far enough away that they're not in our way. We'll handle the vicinity of Werder, both for logistics and security. Provst can send down some of his marines once we own the territory."

Vo unbuckled and rose from his seat. Perhaps split open his cocoon to emerge into summer for the first time.

"I will be back as soon as I have a chat with the kitchen," he announced. "This will be our last meal together as a team for a very long time. I won't say that we should enjoy it, but we need to remember this, too, when we get there and have to hold an Empire together."

CHAPTER XVI

IMPERIAL FOUNDING: 179/11/11. FLEET HEADQUARTERS, ABOVE ST. LEGIER

Amala did not like the waves of fury boiling off the bodies of the marine squad escorting her and the Grand Admiral through the halls of the station. Mostly they were here for the Grand Admiral. She felt like an afterthought.

As a diplomat and a foreigner, she had been locked down hard yesterday, isolated by security protocols enforced with adamantine ruthlessness. Cards no longer opened any doors, including her own suite, so she had spent the last twenty hours sealed in a space measuring twenty-three square meters, at least with an attached bathroom. Two men with guns had delivered dinner and breakfast without any words whatsoever.

Amala had known the station had been attacked. The whole platform had rattled with incoming fire, and she had been there enough times with Alber' to know the sounds of battle.

Grand Admiral stopped so suddenly she would have plowed into the man, but one of the marines behind her grabbed cloth with an angry fist and pulled her up short. Wachturm turned to face her in the empty hallway.

"Has anyone briefed you?" Wachturm asked her blankly, standing in the middle of a broad hallway, surrounded by a dozen men with guns and body armor. And rage.

"No, sir," Amala replied, trying to keep the resentment from showing in her voice.

Wachturm nodded grimly. Paused, looking for the words. Fixed her with eyes that stared death across the meter between them.

"Yesterday, *St. Legier* was subject to a major assault by *Buran* forces," he began sharply.

"Acknowledged," Amala said.

Keep it short, tight, and professional. These men are all out on some edge. Death was not far from their hands.

"Werder was destroyed by an orbital bomb, Bhattacharya," he continued.

"Destroyed?" Amala felt all the blood drain out of her body, leaving only a cold, hard knot in her belly.

"Leveled," he said. "The Palace, the Emperor, the government, and much of the military's command structure on the ground is gone. I am facing a significant crisis and have to be six places at once."

"How can I help, Grand Admiral?" Amala asked.

He paused, measuring her. Perhaps seeing her for the first time as a person, and not an object representing somebody else.

"Be understanding and flexible, Ambassador," he decided. "And not take anything personally while we work this internal matter out."

Amala nodded.

"I will be leaving the system shortly," Wachturm continued. "You and the Minister will be accompanying me in an official capacity. If I left him here, I suspect some level of malice would befall the man."

As in, someone would sneak in and kill the old *Khan* for no greater reason than the nation of his birth. The man barely left his cabin to begin with, spending all of his time reading whatever books they would deliver, and writing his *Magnum Opus*. He had certainly had nothing to do with the attack, unless his mere presence here, having escaped *Trusski* and the wrath of the Warriors in *Samara*, had somehow been a trigger.

"Understood, Grand Admiral," Amala said.

Wachturm nodded and turned again. He started walking with those long legs, forcing Amala to skitter along in his wake, but at least the guards seemed to have relaxed some. She had spent enough time on the other side of those guns to feel the difference in the sound of their boots on the metal floor.

The angry waves came back when they reached the Khan's hatch. No verbal grumbling, but it was there in the set of the shoulders, the hands, the eyes. Men with unrequited rage issues.

Amala made a note to dial everything down around these marines for a while. And to warn Yuur, if possible. This goon squad had no sense of humor anymore.

Wachturm waited politely while one of his men keyed the bell, waited a beat, and then opened the hatch with a card. The first two marines were in and stationed to either side of the door, guns up, before anyone else moved.

Yuur Ul had barely stirred. His desk was already turned sideways so he could watch entertainment videos and documentaries on the side wall. Papers were piled up by chapters on every flat surface except the cleared space on a side table where a tea service waited immaculately.

Wachturm entered. Amala followed, stepping to one side and giving Yuur a silent warning about the seriousness of the issue with the set of her face.

Yuur rose and bowed, slowly and formally.

"Grand Admiral, how may I serve?" Yuur asked, his tenor voice at once soft and resilient.

Amala watched Wachturm come to parade rest, but he still reminded her of a wild hawk.

The Grand Admiral was a giant presence. Combined, she and Yuur maybe out-massed the man, and she was half of that herself. Yuur was a short man, thinly built.

But he was also a willow tree, resilient in the face of the storm.

Wachturm was the oak.

A moment of electric silence passed.

"Yesterday, *The Eldest* launched a major raid against this system," Wachturm began, using Yuur's term for the *Sentient* computer, the undying god who ruled *Buran*.

"I suspected as much, given the sounds and the response," Yuur replied carefully. "If I may ask, how bad was it?"

"*Buran's* fleet dropped a number of nuclear bombs on the planet," Wachturm said. "The same as the prior raid, but with several Roughsharks instead of the one. And then they attacked with a larger weapon, a bomb roughly the size of a battleship. The Imperial Capital of Werder, along with every man, woman, and child in it, was destroyed."

Amala watched Yuur collapse into his chair silently. For a moment, she thought he was suffering convulsions until the sobs became audible.

But Yuur Ul was also a Scholar, a Minister of the Eighth Rank. He controlled himself after a few moments and looked up.

Amala would remember the pain in the man's eyes on her dying day.

"*Sukhoy Nos,*" the Khan whispered angrily. "Damn them."

His shoulders slumped even further, but then he rose and faced them again. Another bow, deep and slow. Tears spilled down his face.

"Grand Admiral, if you need to execute me, I have only one request," the Scholar stated.

"That is?" Wachturm replied, apparently knocked off his train of thought by Ul's reaction.

"Do not ever make the video public, sir," Yuur said. "*The Eldest* will use it as justification for the second attack, regardless of the timing and the purpose."

Yuur surprised Amala by stepping to one side and gesturing to the papers on the desk.

"Burn this," he ordered. "Or bury it as deep in your archives as you wish. It is of no value now, save to Scholars of History. And spies."

"Minister?" Amala spoke up before she could stop herself.

Yuur turned to her, all the pain evident.

"No value whatsoever," he repeated, livid.

"Why?" the Grand Admiral's anger was evident in his voice.

"The purpose of *The Holding* is to provide an example of a just and intelligent society, Duke of *Eklionstic,*" Yuur explained. "To show a better option for all mankind, an aspiration for greatness. It is now a worthless gesture."

"Worthless?" Wachturm asked, centering in.

"Through Amala Bhattacharya, I have come to know *Aquitaine,*" Yuur said, gesturing with one hand. "Through you, and more helpfully Centurion *zu* Wiegand, I have come to know *Fribourg.* I had hoped to bridge the gap of communication, to allow the Scholars to know one another, that there could be peace, as Keller hoped. That will never happen now."

"Never?" Amala had to ask.

Yuur turned to her, focusing his terrible *intent.*

"*The Eldest* has just committed the most grievous sin, the most unimaginable crime *known* under the laws of *Fribourg, Aquitaine,* and any of a dozen other nations, Scholar Bhattacharya," Yuur pronounced with a voice of angry doom. "*The Eldest* has proscribed the ancient penalty on *St. Legier.* He has tried to destroy an inhabited world without any provocation. *Fribourg* will never forgive that. Period. *The Holding* could overwhelm and conquer the Empire tomorrow, and children a thousand years hence would still be secretly taught about that crime. *Aquitaine* has exactly one exception, in their entire legal structure, regarding *Sentient* systems, so they will gladly join in the holy crusade to destroy *The Eldest*. Every free nation in the galaxy will as well, frightened that they will be the next to suffer."

Yuur took a deep breath, turned back to the Grand Admiral, and bowed again.

"I will no longer serve *The Holding*, Grand Admiral," he announced. "You may execute me as a free citizen, instead. Both our consciences will thus be clean."

Amala held her breath. Wachturm studied the man, fought some entire war in his head, and then nodded. Not much, just enough to establish a tone of communication.

"Free citizen?" he asked slowly.

"*The Eldest* has chosen to bombard an inhabited world," Yuur replied. "To kill countless millions of innocents. Keller had the same opportunity, and chose to drop a javelin into my garden and deliver an Ambassador to my Court. *I will no longer serve such evil.*"

"Yuur?" Amala asked.

"No," he snapped harshly. "I will no longer accept that name. Henceforth, I renounce my birth. No longer will I be Ul Banop Cheani Yuur."

"What shall we call you, then?" the Grand Admiral asked in a surprisingly-agreeable tone.

Amala watched the former-Khan's eyes lose focus for several moments. They came back with a new fire inside. Angry and implacable. A mirror for what Amala had seen in Wachturm's, out in the hallway.

"I do not believe your histories cover the man sufficiently," he said. "But his name is taught in *The Holding* as an example of the old prophets, the old dreamers. As is his legacy. He failed, but we all fail, given enough time. The lucky ones die as heroes rather than living long enough to become villains. I will see *The Eldest* fall for the evil he has committed."

"Sri?" Amala asked.

She was a security marine. Or had been. Keller had ordered her to remain as an Ambassador, and allowed her to remain a personal representative of the Crown of *Corynthe*.

But there were only so many books, so much knowledge, she could pack away in her spare time. Even as impressive as the list she had consumed already had grown.

"Rama Treadwell, Scholar Bhattacharya," Yuur said. "His preaching and his words formed much of the intellectual underpinnings of an ancient star-spanning effort known as the *Union of Worlds*. It was itself destroyed in one of the imperialist convulsions of the *Pocket Empires Era*, paving the way for the later rise of the *Concord*. But his teachings live on fifty-nine centuries later."

"Fifty-nine centuries, Sri?" Wachturm asked, incredulous.

"Why not, Grand Admiral? There are those who follow the Prophet of Allah to this day. Or The Christ. The Great Buddha has conquered entire sectors of modern space since his death fourteen thousand years ago. But Treadwell taught that all humans are united and must seek the greatest ethical interactions with one another. Yes. I am not sufficiently advanced to call myself a Shepherd of the Word, but I will be known as *Seeker*. Personally, I am not even certain that the Shepherds survived the Great Darkness, but many of them wrote of their dreams in the long, pleasant afternoon before. I discounted it all as worthless drivel when I read it before, but that was when I believed that *The Eldest* had the greatest utility for mankind in his plans. The last year has unfortunately been an education."

The man now known as Seeker bowed again, first to the Grand Admiral, and then deeper to Amala. She presumed he honored Keller, who had shown the Scholar that not all barbarians are uncivilized, and that the so-called civilized could be monsters in their own way.

"What is to be my fate, Grand Admiral?" Seeker asked simply.

Amala could sense no fear in the man whatsoever. No trepidation. None of the hesitation to simply walk off a cliff. Wachturm was within his rights to execute the diminutive Scholar, as *Buran* had refused all other diplomatic overtures.

But his action grounded her. And she had never felt ungrounded before.

A door opened in her mind suddenly, warming her with unexpected light.

Wachturm cleared his throat and assessed the man.

"I would appreciate you completing your first document, Seeker," he said. "For the historical context, if nothing else. After that, perhaps a new ethical standard would be welcome. *Fribourg* and *Aquitaine* have been at war almost since the Empire was founded, in one way or another. Keller upset the ancient balance and *Buran* has destroyed the scales upon which such things were measured. A new kind of Emperor will take power, and her reign will hopefully be the dawning of a new age, as well as an expansion of a war to heights previously unseen. We need to remember who we are. Is that sufficient?"

"It is, Grand Admiral," Seeker replied, taking a deep breath and turning to face her with a serious face. "Scholar Bhattacharya, I embark upon another new adventure. It would please me greatly to have you accompany me."

Amala nodded and bowed.

"I look forward to following, *Seeker*."

CHAPTER XVII

It should have been a celebratory moment, launching this silver beast, this brand new cruiser, from her dock into free space.

Yan Bedrov had even let Ainsley talk him into getting a new suit made, of a very fashionable bent according to Imperial standards. Back when they planned today to be a party.

The first *Escort Cruiser, Expeditionary* in *Fribourg's* fleet.

IFV Indianapolis, CEE.

Being aboard her for the final bits of *Builder's Trials* before *Acceptance* had been why Yan and Ainsley hadn't been down there on the surface, at the office of Bedrov & Keller, three days ago.

To die by fire, like so many of his contemporaries had done over the decades. Only Faisul and Mori had been there in the office, two promising, young pirates that each had the touch to maybe design some pretty decent ships, given a few more years and some guidance they would never receive now.

Yan supposed some might classify his as a charmed life. Being the only survivor, so many times, probably had that look to it.

At least to an outsider.

Ainsley must have been reading his mind. She leaned against his side and squeezed his hand as they watched the flag bridge's main screen, showing an image from a camera secured over on the dry-dock wall. A fierce, tiny tugboat pushing the big cruiser out of her sandbox.

Because *Indy* was designed to be a flagship for a squadron of *Expeditionary-class* vessels, the flag bridge was extra-spacious. Because Yan had designed it, everyone was seated, either in facing pairs, or with a singular, clear view inward, to where they could look up over their monitor screen and see the flag officer gesticulate madly in battle, as they were frequently likely to do.

It was the way Yan did things. The *Corynthe* way, because space was always at a premium. *Aquitaine* had liked it. Grand Admiral hadn't thrown that big of a hissy fit once he stopped and thought about all his years of staring at the backs of heads, and how much human communication was non-verbal.

Not that Yan would have listened to the man. Emmerich Wachturm might place the orders, but Karl VII officially *Accepted* the ships into service.

Had.

Would have, too, with *Indy*. Would have come up here with them and stood on this deck, next to where the Grand Admiral was sitting now, the surviving man's face frozen in a rictus somewhere between a scowl and tears. Yan and Ainsley were off to one side, civilians with the best ticket in town.

And nowhere else to be right now, with the *Fribourg Empire* suddenly going through what *Corynthe* had when Jessica took over.

The Revolutionary Future.

Technically, all of Yan's contracts had been with the government of Karl VII, when there had been such a thing. At the direction of his true sovereign lord, Queen Jessica.

He wasn't sure what the future was about to bring, but Yan was a man all about brass tacks when it got down to contract language. Not that he would ever call this a vacation, never even more than whisper that to Ainsley in bed, with the music turned way up and the lights dimmed. Nobody but her would understand and appreciate what he meant without being offended at the words themselves.

The wonders of finding love in middle age.

Because if *Buran* thought that blowing up the damned planet was going to cause *Fribourg* to suddenly roll over and play dead, those people were as dumb as a mud fence post. You were probably safer, and smarter, kicking a rabid porcupine.

Yan squeezed Ainsley's hand in return. Her eyes twinkled with all the jokes they'd shared during the project that were entirely inappropriate to mutter aloud, surrounded by these serious men. Ainsley had only been half-joking when she thought that Wachturm needed a hug.

It would be like comforting a tree. A Russian olive, at that. All thorns.

"*Indianapolis*, you are clear of the dock and we are withdrawing to a safe distance," the voice came over the loudspeaker. The captain of the tugboat sounded just as fierce as his ship. "Smooth sailing."

"Acknowledged, *Foss-Six*," Captain Kingston's voice replied. "Stand by for powered flight."

On the screen, the tugboat had bounced backwards like a hand accidentally touching a hot stovetop. Yan grinned. There was almost nothing he could do to improve that little ship's design, except maybe let Moirrey loose on the exterior with some paint. Not that Imperials would appreciate speed lines, but it would look good on the screen.

"Grand Admiral," Captain Kingston continued in a mechanical tone. "Your orders, sir?"

Yan watched Wachturm rouse himself from whatever funk had overtaken the big man.

"Come to Zero-Three-Zero, ahead full," the Grand Admiral ordered, his voice finally sounding like him again. "Transition to JumpSpace and I will send you the current set of coordinates for Forward Base Delta."

Current. Yan grinned over at Ainsley, who grinned back at him.

A freaking mobile base. JumpSails on a monitor-class killer runt, parked out in the middle of the *M'Hanii Gulf* somewhere, threatening all lines of communication between the original area of *Buran*, what they called *The Holding*, and the new colonies around *Samara* that were such a threat to *Fribourg*.

Jessica being her usual, evil self.

Yan was looking forward to seeing what she and Jež had done with the Heavy Dreadnaught supporting Kigali, Aeliaes, and d'Maine. While he missed carrier operations, and had worked with his new partner-in-crime to create a jump-capable strike fighter, Jessica's war would be big guns.

And whatever other swords his Queen needed him to build.

CHAPTER XVIII

Vo studied the airy news studio around him. Off-white walls. Soft-textured, hanging ceiling. Ugly tile floors with scrapes of something gouged into them randomly. Two dead cameras, like drunks leaning on chairs, or maybe tombstones in the middle of an empty space.

He flashed back to a day this last spring, addressing the men who desired to become the 189th Legion. That had been a clear field, orderly lines, a pleasant day. What stretched out before him now in all directions was hell brought to Earth.

His scouts had located a spot in Mejico, a satellite suburb of Werder that had been close enough to be largely protected by the planetary shields, and far enough away that the explosion that knocked those same shields down had more or less leapt over the shallow valley, leveling the heights on both sides, but leaving the core of the city, down below on a small river, mostly intact. At least physically.

Psychologically, the place had been crushed. War did that to civilians. Soldiers, too, but they were trained to overcome that. These people had just watched their world be annihilated around them.

But enough of the town survived. And the downrange hilltop had been more parks than houses, so the 189th had put down markers and started building a base amidst the fallen trees.

Survivors were slowly trickling in. Some were whole, at least

"

physically, and Vo's men put as many of them to work as wanted. The rest got evacuated to further-out bases as fast as places could be identified and tents deployed.

There were far too many.

Vo was surprised how many people had managed to survive: the initial blast and fireball; the shockwave like a tsunami of super-heated air; the ground itself moving like gelatin; buildings falling in or catching fire.

But humans were resilient creatures. Vo knew that. Hard to kill. Easy to make angry. He had seen the first embers burning in the eyes of some of the people who had passed through. Most were still numb. But not all of them.

As the non-comm in charge of the HQ detachment, Reese Borel hadn't gone for a big, outdoor stage today. Instead, they had simply imposed martial law and evicted most of the local video news staff, extra bodies who would need to be fed at a time when he needed to work.

There would be no evening sportscast or traffic report for the foreseeable future.

Vo was standing today, resting his hands on a lectern he had dragged into the room. Reese had wanted to seat him behind a desk, but Vo had vetoed that. He worked and thought better standing up. Even if it was designed with a much smaller person than him in mind.

Today was already going to be the worst day of his life.

He wore sage. That damned Class Two uniform, when he had wanted to do this in his field gear. Battle dress. But he had to project the right image. And he understood the value of that image, especially today.

Grand Admiral had transitioned to JumpSpace eighteen hours ago. The admiral in charge, Tom Provst, was in orbit, supervising things like a hungry, angry eagle.

Vo had the whole damned planet to take care of, at least until the Emperor returned.

So he wore sage. And the bigger, gaudier awards pulled out of storage, the better to impress people. Civilians would react well enough to the uniform itself, especially as he had added the maroon cloak that marked him as *Ritter of the Imperial Household*. The military men would study his chest and draw their own conclusions.

Enough of the officers would appreciate that Vo *zu* Arlo had to be a dangerous man, to survive winning some of those.

The kind of man who had been willing to shoot pretty girls and would-be emperors.

The maroon cloak was flipped back over both shoulders. Not that he needed to get at either the sword or the pistol, but people needed to know he wore them.

That he was not playing around.

As he had in the spring, he'd written and rejected a dozen speeches. There was no model to guide this thing. None.

And Creator-willing, nobody would ever need his work as their own precedent.

Well, maybe *Winterhome*, the capital world of *Buran*.

Vo would happily stand off in orbit and bombard that planet past the point of human viability.

He was not alone in that desire.

Reese appeared in Vo's line of sight and held up a hand to get his attention. Brought him back to the present.

"Ten seconds to live, General," Borel stated calmly.

Vo needed calm. It was one of the reasons Reese Borel had this job. Street and Danville and their team did other things, but Vo needed Borel's help to stay grounded.

Vo drew an immense breath, held it, released. He flexed both hands to loosen them. Pulled his shoulders back and relaxed. Leaned forward and rested his hands on the lectern with the Imperial flag on the front.

A red light came on next to the camera.

"People of *St. Legier*, I am General Vo *zu* Arlo," he rumbled, letting the emotion, the anger, push his voice deeper. Down where maybe whales might answer. "As of this moment, all of the planet is declared under martial law. Grand Admiral Emmerich Wachturm, speaking for the throne, has placed me in supreme command of all Imperial forces inside the atmosphere."

He paused, letting that sink in. All around the world, every screen and radio had been overridden by the Emergency Broadcasting Authority. And then the Imperial anthem had played, ominously, as it did. People were going to be listening, watching.

Hoping.

Right now, he was likely looking out at the entire population of *St. Legier*, some nine billion people, minus all those who had died at Werder and in the aftermath.

Another moment, for people to study him. To prepare themselves for the news. Nothing had been official until now, as everyone had held out the slimmest thread of hope.

After four days, the Imperial Palace had been declared a recovery zone, on the off chance that the bodies of Karl VII and Empress Kati could ever be found. The earth itself had been compressed, like a boulder dropped on loose dirt. The palace grounds were somewhere around two hundred meters closer to sea level than they had been a week ago.

"The Imperial capital city, Werder, has been destroyed," Vo continued. "Emperor Karl VII is presumed to have been killed. Crown Prince Ekkehard was slain aboard *IFV Firehawk* during the fighting."

Vo took a breath, partly to steady himself, but partly so he could scowl at the camera.

"Emperor Karl VIII will resume the Imperial mantle," Vo commanded the people listening. His tone left no doubt. As he intended. "I will enforce the Grand Admiral's will until she returns, and then hers until she sees fit to remove me. People of *St. Legier*, hear my words, and hear them well. There will be no second chances. Under Martial Law, many crimes are punishable by the simple expedient of a quick firing squad. Looting, theft, robbery. Those looking to make a quick florin cheating the military or their fellow citizens, will face a rough and unforgiving nemesis. Me."

Vo let the raw anger spill out now. Trying to hold it in would damage him in ways nobody would understand. Except perhaps Moirrey, but she would have her own demons to contend with.

"I am a foreigner welcomed into your lands," he growled. "But I swore an oath. The same oath the many men around me did. To uphold the crown again all threats. *All threats*. And they have killed my Emperor. Our Emperor. But they also killed a great many of your friends, your relatives, your countrymen. There was a young woman, Annette Fuchs, who was like a daughter to me, after her father, Walter, helped me save the Empire the first time. She was sixteen years old and filled with joy and love. I will never dance at her wedding. And for that, I will visit unto *Buran* a most terrible wrath."

Vo let the tears run down his face now. Stopping them, denying them, would hurt more than letting these people know his loss. He felt like one of the ancient gods of destruction, come to earth and given an avenging incarnation. And he was.

"But that is a task for tomorrow," Vo continued, breathing slowly enough that his voice didn't crack and fail. "Today, I need your love. All of it. Scientists estimate that more than twenty million people were killed in the initial attack. Another two hundred million are at risk now, because their entire lives, their entire world, has been shattered. In many cases, they have literally nothing but the clothes on their backs. They have watched death claim their families, their friends, and total strangers in the aftermath."

More breathing. More tears as well, but that wasn't stopping anytime soon.

"I need you," Vo implored. "I need your love. I need you to open your churches, your schools, and your homes to total strangers who have nothing at all left except life. The devastation around Werder will be generations healing, and I need to save as many people as I can. But I cannot coordinate something so large. Nobody can. I need you to come together, in your kirks, your fraternal organizations, your towns, and figure out how you can help. How many of the lost you can feed, can shelter, can rebuild, while I try to simply find them all and get them to you, to safety. There will be retribution. I will bear the sword that destroys *Buran*, if it is the last thing I do. I cannot make good your loss, but I will never allow it to occur again. That much I promise."

Vo stopped there. He had nothing left. Nothing at all.

Reese saw that. Understood.

The little red light went out and the lights in the studio came up to daylight.

Vo's hands hurt.

He looked down and realized that he had unconsciously gripped the metal of the lectern hard enough to torque fingermarks into the thin steel.

And he was crying.

But Reese was crying as well. So were all the other men visible.

Tears were necessary. To mourn a good man. And the millions of innocents lost.

Before the 189th would be allowed to come for *Buran*'s soul.

PART 3
EMPERESS

CHAPTER XIX

Jessica smiled at the man, perhaps taking a bit too much advantage at his discomfort. She liked the way he kept tugging at those perfectly-tailored, white sleeves, as though the fit was wrong. But then, she didn't suppose Torsten Wald had ever spent the florins necessary to have a uniform like that. Nor had someone like Vibol Harmaajärvi do the work.

Jessica might have sent Amala Bhattacharya to *St. Legier* with the Khan, but she had kept *The Tailor*, once she had come to understand the man's genius for draping cloth.

She supposed that Torsten just wasn't prepared to live his life in white. As an Imperial Captain, the man had worn a blue jacket for a decade.

But Em had insisted.

If Forward Base Delta was going to officially remain part of the *Imperial* war effort, it needed an Imperial officer in command, even if only technically. On paper, as it were, while Arott Whughy did the work. He would act as Chairman of the Board, while Whughy continued as Chief Executive.

And so, Torsten Wald, Imperial Admiral of the White.

They were alone in his cabin, preparing to join the others for dinner. She leaned close enough to kiss him. Because she could. And because she liked the idea of kissing him. Torsten treated every kiss like it might be the last.

Jessica had never been *cherished*.

She grinned as she leaned back, matching his smile. He shifted just enough to present an elbow, always the Imperial gentleman.

"Shall we, *Fleet Centurion?*" he asked with a humorous lilt, referring to her own white tunic.

"Certainly, *Admiral*," she fired back across his bow, watching the impact the words had on him, even now. The way his eyes grew both serious and proud at the same time.

Jessica supposed she and Torsten looked as bad as Yan and *da Vinci* some days, but she wouldn't trade.

No, not *da Vinci*. Ainsley. The woman had made good her threat to retire at the Brevet Command Centurion rank, plus an honorarium awarded by the Senate, and gone into business with Jessica's second-favorite pirate/design genius.

One of these days, Jessica had to introduce *Pops* Nakamura to Imperial society. Make good the threat of an open design competition for naval architecture. Set a budget and revel in the outcome. Suck in all the talent in the near galaxy, perhaps as far as the Spinward Reaches, for new design aesthetic.

Tomorrow.

Tonight, a celebration.

She took Torsten's arm and pressed it against her side as they walked.

The wardroom had been cleared and cleaned. Dinner by invitation only. There would be a larger party tomorrow on the actual date, but tonight, something smaller and special: a birthday dinner for Denis Jež.

Birthdays weren't a thing that was generally marked in *Aquitaine* with a celebration. Certainly not very formally. They had welcomed him to forty a year ago with a *petit* occasion, but they had been in route to *Trusski* and a final battle at the time.

This year, Casey had insisted. *Fribourg* put more weight on birthday events, and Denis had turned into something like her second favorite uncle, after Emmerich Wachturm. She had declared that there would be an *Occasion*.

Robbie Aeliaes was already there supervising things when she and Torsten arrived. Alber' d'Maine was apparently in the middle of a hilarious story with Tamara Strnad and Arott Whughy, based on the gales of laughter. Kigali and Nina Vanek were talking off to one side, heads leaned in like conspirators planning an assassination, while Vilis Ozolinsh and Navin the Black were already seated and enjoying themselves immensely, each with a glass of wine, sharing a cheese plate.

People who had been with her for a long time, since she first took command of the Strike Carrier *Auberon*. But more importantly, people who had generally known Denis longer. Everyone was here except Tamara.

Torsten grabbed two glasses of wine from a roving steward and handed her one with a grin. She breathed in the calm, festive air of her senior commanders and smiled. Her Merry Men, as Nils Kasum had christened the group privately, back when he was still First Lord of the Fleet.

The force had taken a small break from the high operational tempo of the last several months. Trading the badly-damaged Star Controller for a brand new Heavy Dreadnaught had let Jessica make devastating attack runs on less well-defended systems: blowing up empty stations, looming suddenly overhead, chasing off badly-outclassed patrol forces, all across *Buran*'s invasion front.

It would be even more interesting in another few months, when Yan Bedrov's new fast strike bomber design would finish testing and enter service. Turning *Il Augusta* into a true Strike Carrier would let Jessica plan even more audacious campaigns.

So tonight, they could relax.

The main hatch opened and Casey escorted Denis into the room. She might be on his arm, like Jessica was Torsten's, but he was obviously just along for the ride. Casey practically glowed with excitement.

"My friends, the guest of honor," Casey announced, beaming.

Denis accepted their congratulations and ribbing with equal aplomb. Like Torsten, he wore white tonight, marking this as an Imperial thing.

It was odd to Jessica, watching the two cultures, blood enemies for so long, slowly transform into a genial, if fractious, family. She hoped that Yuur Ul might be able to work some of his own merry magic on the Imperials, opening a path for relations that didn't involve guns. War was unnecessary, but while *Fribourg* had learned that there were other options, the deathless *Sentience* in control of *The Holding* still carried on with his implacable mission measured in centuries.

Jessica banished those thoughts as stewards got everyone seated around the single table in the center of the room. Wine and anti-pasti, and good conversation, were the order of the day. Soon enough, they would ramp things back up.

Torsten was on her right. Kigali had ended up on her left.

"How soon until we make a pass at *Samara*?" he open the conversation innocently.

You had to know the man to see the fire in his eyes. Alber' was on the end next to Kigali, facing Casey down the length of the table. He *always* had that fire.

Jessica wasn't fooled. Neither were any of the others. They heaped good-natured scorn on the idea.

"You could just starve them out, Tom," Arott teased. "Without the *Pochtovyi Trakt*, the postal road of beacons that we've been steadily blowing up, they might get lost."

Kigali snorted with derision.

"You can't starve a planet, Arott," Robbie joined in. "At least not for food. Parts, maybe, since they don't have a big drydock yard close, and would have to run a gauntlet, but this *Buran*. There's nothing they do better than that."

"How soon until they start to abandon some of their newer colonies?" Nina spoke up.

She was still a tiny woman, an almost-ethereal redhead just over the minimum height and weight requirements to remain in the fleet. But there was nothing small about the woman's mind or personality. She was Denis's First Officer because she wanted to be *here*, on the front line, rather than off commanding her own cruiser on a quieter frontier, or teaching tactics somewhere.

All of them were like that. Serving in First Expeditionary Fleet because it was where the action was. They wouldn't have come if they weren't all warriors.

Even Arott had learned to relax, given enough time.

"Understand that they work on decadal or generational scales, Nina," Jessica began.

The woman nodded, but her question hadn't been born of ignorance. Rather, insatiable curiosity. What she needed to prepare for over the next year.

In battle, Nina commanded *Vanguard*. And could give Kigali or Alber' a run for ferocity.

She was still one of the best Tactical Officers Jessica knew.

"We've been at this barely a year, and before that, *Buran* had been slowly, inexorably, pushing *Fribourg* back for perhaps as long as fifty years," Jessica continued. "By now, we have their attention, and we're starting to force *The Eldest* to dance to our tune. But he has been in command over there for millennia. They won't give up any ground easily. That's in their nature. Push into any opening, and then hold against all pressure."

"So we need a bigger lever?" Arott asked. "Who's mind do we have to change?"

He and Nina were the two that went strategic, when the others were generally experts on the tactical.

"According to Yuur Ul, our renegade Minister of the Eighth Rank, the decision comes from the very top," Jessica said. "But it must be interpreted and enacted at the layers below that."

"The Mandarins?" Vilis inquired.

Oz represented the bluest of blue-blood in *Aquitaine*. Direct descent from several of the Fifty Families, the group that had helped Henri Baudin *found* the Republic, four centuries ago. But for a love of engineering and tinkering, he would have never stayed long in the fleet.

His accent was the crispest of elite, the wealthiest of the very rich. Even if he was still a practical joker on a scale with Moirrey, some days.

"Those four, and the Ministers of the First Rank," Jessica agreed.

The Holding was a function of Scholars, not Warriors, as Ul had told them. *The Eldest* spoke, having access to vast databanks of historical and current information input from all directions. Four Mandarins interpreted and directed: The Minister of the Left Interior, The Minister of the Right Interior, The Minister of the Left Facet, the Minister of the Right Facet.

Below them, a few hundred Ministers of the First Rank listened and commanded. A few thousand Ministers of the Second Rank executed, the scale growing decimally, all the way down to Ministers of the Eighth Rank, as Yuur Ul had been, as *Khan* of *Trusski*.

A conservative society, conditioned by a lifetime of service to the deathless god in charge. Stubborn. Ruthless. But also efficient.

Jessica knew she would only beat them by destroying that efficiency, that harmony that the ancients called *Wa*. Introducing chaos into their careful plans.

Look what she had achieved on *Trusski*.

Not all planets would react as well, but Jessica understood that.

"*Trusski*," Casey said aloud, as if reading her mind. "And all the raids along this frontier. It's *Cahllepp*, all over again, but I'm missing something."

"You can drive a rat crazy faster with a random selection of punishments and rewards than you can a diet of steady punishment," Denis, of all people, spoke up. "As Jessica reminds us. Not every station gets destroyed. We even decided to steal that one. And sometimes, we just drop small radio satellites into orbit that play music at them. At least until someone destroys them after we leave."

"What will the Red Admiral, that crazy bitch, do next?" Robbie grinned as he spoke.

The rest laughed. It felt good to laugh with these people. And drink wine. And belong.

Torsten squeezed her hand and everything was good with the universe.

Not all of Moirrey's Mischief involved blowing things up, although she had never slacked on that frontier. Music station satellites. Orbital fireworks that made pretty designs in somebody's night sky, especially if fired inward from the edge of a solar system on the tip of an invisible, ballistic missile, to arrive silently, weeks later.

And, on two occasions, javelins dropped into somebody's back yard, as a reminder that Keller Marie Jessica was a Warrior, and would be coming for them, eventually.

Never forget that part.

Keller was coming for you, one of these days.

With Torsten by her side, she could do anything.

CHAPTER XX

"Sir, we're being challenged," a voice broke into Em's reverie. "*RAN VI Ferrata* and escorts."

"Put them on the main screen," he ordered, glancing around at the faces he could see on the ship's flag bridge.

Bedrov had been right. Being able to look these men in the eyes had made it much easier to work. Em silently cursed all the conservative ideas he had clung to for much of his naval career, unwilling to adapt to things until forced. In that, Bedrov & Keller had done him an immense favor.

Em glanced over at Bedrov and Barret, seated off to one side as… He supposed *Witnesses* was as good a term as any. There would need to be many.

Today, he would repay the rest of the men around him for the duty they had embraced so willingly, so unquestioningly on the flight here, dropping into the middle of empty space at nothing more than a set of coordinates when they had wanted to be home at *St. Legier*, helping. He could have retreated to an office to talk to Robbie Aeliaes, but these men deserved to know the whole truth. It had only been rumors up until now.

Operational Security at the highest level possible.

A face filled the main screen. It wasn't the man Em had been expecting.

Then his brain registered that *Indianapolis* would look like a threat, arriving off-schedule and without prior clearance. Even an Imperial warship. Command Centurion Aeliaes would have put his Tactical Officer in charge. Guns armed and sailors ready to kill.

Senior Centurion Harden Glenraven. *Hardie.* She was close enough to her commander in looks that many people had expected them to be siblings. Em had made that mistake, the first time.

"This is a secured zone, *Indianapolis*," she announced in a flat, challenging voice.

She reminded Em of Alber' d'Maine that way. Cold, ruthless, unforgiving. Another of the warriors drawn into Jessica's gravity well. The toughest, meanest force in the galaxy, as far as he could tell. Certainly, the best.

First Expeditionary Fleet.

"I'm aware of that, Glenraven," Em answered simply. "I need you to round up the key players and get them aboard the station as soon as feasible. I have news that I am unwilling to transmit, even encrypted."

A moment of silence after the signal arrived over there five seconds later. Further yet to the bigger dots of light representing *Vanguard* and the station itself.

Em watched her eyes grow shrewd. She glanced off to one side with a flicker, returned her attention to him like a mongoose hunting.

"Acknowledged, Grand Admiral," she replied after a beat.

The screen went dark. Em took a breath.

"Captain Kingston," Em spoke in a loud, commanding voice. "Prepare a shuttle with yourself, your senior officers, and an escort detail with your color guard to accompany me. We'll be raising the Imperial Standard on my return."

There was no cheering. Normally, men would applaud to be aboard a vessel transporting the Emperor. Today, they just sat a little straighter, shoulders back and heads up.

There was honor in duty, but every one of these men would have gladly not had to be here, Em included.

Tomorrow would be worse.

CHAPTER XXI

In the four hours it had taken to arrange everything, Jessica had snuck off and had a quick nap, a shower, and a snack. It wasn't her station being subject to a surprise inspection from the Grand Admiral, nor one of her ships. And Denis and Arott would be happier not having her underfoot.

Because it was Em, and because he had arrived without any warning or fanfare, she had dug out the red, Imperial day uniform, rather than the white and black she normally wore in semi-formal circumstances.

And Em's private message to her, once he got closer, had been specific. Certain names to be present. Nobody else, not even Marcelle or Willow. And no ceremony when the shuttle docked, other than Arott welcoming Em and about a score of sailors and marines, and escorting them down to whatever conference room where she waited.

Jessica. Torsten. Arott. Denis. Casey.

Robbie. Alber'. Kigali. Tamara. Enej.

Moirrey had been the one name that stood out. That assured Jessica this was official business. What that might be, she had no clue, Em having outrun all news getting here, but it could not be good.

Briefly, Jessica wondered if Karl VII had decided to act early and had found Casey a husband. Perhaps he had sent Em to finally rein the Princess in and bring her home. Jessica would argue almost as loudly as Casey did, but if this was official business, she would be overruled.

Both of the women answered to Emmerich Wachturm, and he only answered to the throne.

Moirrey and Casey both wore their best dress uniforms today, but more importantly, the maroon cloaks and swords that marked them special.

The only two living, female, *Ritters of the Household.*

Everyone else was also formal. Red, white, or black and green. Plus the maroon.

The hatch opened and Arott entered, walking around the table to where Jessica sat and coming to attention. Something in his face as he walked had Jessica already halfway out of her chair, so Whughy's next words did not catch her off guard.

"All rise," Whughy ordered in a sharp tone as Em appeared at the hatch. "His Excellency Emmerich Wachturm, Hereditary Duke of *Eklionstic*, Grand Admiral of *Fribourg*, *Commander of the Fleet.*"

The rest rose quickly, chairs slamming back almost as fast as if an alert had sounded. A mixed group of other men had accompanied Em, including a Captain and several Commanders. They entered far enough to spread out along both walls, just inside the door.

Em stopped at the far end of the table from Jessica and scanned the room with a face that might have been carved from a granite cliff face. He finally came to rest on Jessica, his eyes inscrutable.

"*Wildgraf* Keller," Em acknowledged, gesturing her closer, to stand at Casey's side, off to his right. "Queen Jessica of *Corynthe* and Lady Moirrey of *Ramsey*, would you please join me?"

The words were ritual. Rote. There was no emotion underneath them. But at the same time, none of the men accompanying Em were keyed up, or angry. Nervously calm, if anything.

Jessica complied, taking up a station just behind Casey, where Marcelle frequently stood for her.

Em cast his terrible visage across the room one last time, before it came to rest on the Princess. The *Ritter*. The Centurion drawn up almost defiantly before her uncle.

Em drew a breath, swallowed.

"Princess Kasimira, I come bearing news," he continued in that hard voice. "Emperor Karl VII is dead. Crown Prince Ekkehard was killed in battle. Long live Emperor Karl VIII."

Jessica understood then why Em had asked her and Moirrey to stand close. Casey would have collapsed to the floor, had she not had the two of them there to catch her. Casey weighed almost nothing, but it felt like all the burden of Heaven rested on Jessica's shoulders as Casey fell into her arms. Moirrey was there a moment later.

Emmerich Wachturm stepped back and went to one knee. The rest of the Imperial officers did the same, followed a moment later by all of Jessica's people. Only the six marines along the outer wall remained standing, besides the three women.

"All hail the Emperor," Em called, voice heavy with dread.

"Hail," came a ragged volley of voices.

Jessica was bewildered, unprepared for this moment even in her worst nightmares.

But she had also stood over Ian Zhao's body, having wrested a crown from him in the process.

She held Casey as the woman's flesh went cold and clammy. Felt the taller woman's tears spill on her hair and neck. Moirrey wrapped arms and cloak around them both.

Jessica could feel the silent shudders inside the woman, suppressed, but more importantly, hidden by the maroon cloth covering them.

The room had dropped five degrees in as many seconds, or perhaps all the blood had poured out of Jessica. Emmerich Wachturm had been there that day as well. Ian Zhao had been part of his plan, thwarted by Jessica.

Before.

Their eyes met now. Kneeling, Em was only slightly shorter than Jessica standing.

She could see all the way to the bottom of the man's soul in that moment. He had helped bury Karl VI. And now Karl VII. And was perhaps young enough to envision outliving yet another Emperor, one he had held as a newborn.

The tears she could see in there would not be shed. Perhaps ever. But they were there. She could see them. Jessica could cry them for him. Something else Em had taught her along the way.

How had the universe come to this point?

Casey drew a breath to the tips of her toes and released it as Jessica held her. Jessica could feel the new Emperor force something to bay, almost physically.

Casey rose back to her immense height, pausing for a moment to kiss Jessica on the cheek and whisper a *thank you* in her ear.

Emperor Karl VIII turned to the room, rotating once on her heels to take them all in before she spoke.

"I accept your charge," she said in a quiet voice that was still hard enough to grind down mountains. "From this day forth, I will reign as Karl VIII, *Emperor of Fribourg*. Emmerich Wachturm, you will kneel."

Em looked up in confusion for a moment, before his face went white.

"Your Majesty, no," he pled.

But the Emperor would not be brooked.

"Kneel," she commanded.

Em sighed in defeat. He shifted his weight so that he was on both knees now. Casey drew her sword, studied it for a second, and then stepped close to her uncle.

Lightly, she tapped his shoulders. Right. Left. Right.

She stepped back, but still held the blade in one hand.

"I proclaim you Emmerich Wachturm, *Ritter of the Imperial Household*," Casey called in a heavy voice. "Arise, Lord Em, and be presented to this Court. You will speak with my name."

Em rose like a man walking to the gallows. Jessica suppressed the wildly-inappropriate grin that wanted to escape her soul. Em had resisted Joh wanting to do the same thing for the last twenty years, preferring to concentrate on his naval duties and avoid the politics that the other job brought with it.

Lacking a cloak for her uncle, Casey scabbarded her sword, untied the knot at her neck with her free hand, and placed the cloth around his shoulders with her own hands.

For a moment, Casey turned to Jessica with an enigmatic scowl, but she just nodded to herself and foreswore whatever thought had danced across her mind. Instead, she pointed to the *Aquitaine* marine closest to the main hatch.

"Out in the corridor, go to the right, and enter the first chamber on your right," she ordered. "Return with enough spare chairs for the officers that accompanied you."

She ignored the man as he moved, turning to face the rest of the room.

"Be seated," she ordered in a more gracious tone. "Em here. Moirrey next to Em. Jessica across from Em and Denis next to her. Admiral Wald, you will sit at the far end from me. The rest of you find space."

Casey sat. Collapsed mostly, into the chair at the head of the table and leaned forward, palms flat on the surface. She could have been cast in white bronze.

The others found spaces or waited while more chairs arrived.

Silence engulfed the room.

Finally Casey spoke. With the voice of Emperor Karl VIII.

"How bad?" she asked Em simply.

"There was a major battle at *St. Legier*. Werder was destroyed by orbital bombardment," the Grand Admiral responded quietly. The men and women in the room gasped. "Your brother was killed aboard *IFV Firehawk* in the fighting that preceded it. General *zu* Arlo is in charge of the planet until we get back."

"Vo?" Casey asked, shocked. "Will they follow him?"

"Do you know any man that the people of *St. Legier* are more likely to listen to, if I'm not there, Your Majesty? He will hold until you return. Against all the hordes of Hell, if necessary."

Jessica felt like someone had punched her in the gut. Casey looked like it.

Jessica reached out a hand and felt the Emperor take it. Only Jessica could feel the strain, the agony unseen under the remarkably calm demeanor.

She could imagine Casey suddenly watching her entire future plans evaporate before her eyes, to fall into the worst possible outcome the young woman could have ever imagined. But for the accident that claimed her grandfather, Karl VI might still be alive, the family being naturally long-lived.

They had spoken in private, she and Casey. Covered the next half decade with campaigns and plans before Casey expected to be brought to heel and forced into a political marriage of some sort. Ekke had been expected to get wed in a few years at most. Start a family. Relieve her of her duties as third in line by adding a passel of children who would inherit precedence.

All that, gone.

Karl VIII. Emperor of Fribourg.

Casey turned to her. A split second had passed, but Casey had aged a decade.

It wasn't like watching her grow up in the coup. No, this was watching Moirrey transform into the woman that the Evil Engineering Gnome was born to become.

Casey let go a breath.

"I know that you have claimed the moral high ground in your war with *Buran*, Jessica," the young Emperor said. "I will not demand that you sacrifice that. I will not demand retribution be cast down on

Winterhome from the heavens until the planet is itself uninhabitable. But I will order Grand Admiral *zu* Wachturm to put all available forces under your command for the duration. *Buran* must be punished. If that task requires that I ask *Aquitaine* for more help, or *Salonnia, Lincolnshire,* or *Corynthe,* then so be it. If *The Eldest* has returned to the old ways, then that creature must be destroyed, root and branch. This will be a war for the future of the entire human race."

Jessica nodded but kept her peace. *Buran* would be expecting reprisals for this. Even a deathless, megalomaniac computer could not be so stupid as to expect that an attack like this one would cause *Fribourg* to surrender. He would have prepared.

She expected that the Starbase at *Samara,* the thing known as *Ural,* was utterly impregnable right now. Probably reinforced by whatever force had attacked *St. Legier.*

"It will be done, Your Majesty," Jessica promised.

They both turned to Em, who nodded in turn. Jessica could see him grinding his teeth by the way his jaw muscles bunched.

"You say Werder was destroyed, Grand Admiral?" Casey asked in a cold, hard voice, steeling herself for the news.

"Indeed, Your Majesty," he replied slowly. "They engaged Grand Fleet all across our orbital defenses, and then dropped a bomb roughly the size of a battleship onto the shields, cracking them like an egg. The devastation is simply unfathomable. The city itself was flattened, as if by a giant heel driving it into the mud. The surrounding area was subject to shockwave, firestorm, and then groundquake."

"Casualties?" The Emperor requested.

"We only remained in orbit for a few days," Em said. "Best estimate at the time of our departure was twenty million killed in the first twenty-four to forty-eight hours. With perhaps two hundred million more at risk over the next twelve months."

The entire room gasped again, including the officers that had accompanied Em here.

"The House of Dukes is in Werder," Casey observed. "Was."

"Was," Em agreed. "The explosion was centered on the palace, but the House of Dukes was close enough, as was the Army's headquarters, to be flattened. I declared martial law across the entire system in your name. Admiral Tom Provst is commanding all naval forces in my name. *zu* Arlo is in command of the planet itself, until we can figure out how to handle things. There are rules and historical precedent for nearly everything, including this. At least Fleet Headquarters came out relatively unscathed. You can rule from there while we figure things out."

"No."

"Your Majesty?" Em was clearly surprised.

"I said no," Casey repeated. "I will be on the ground, with the people of *St. Legier*. I would rather reign from a squalid tent in the mud than watch from the safety of the heavens."

Jessica watched the wheels turn in Casey's head as she transitioned from naval planning to Imperial law. Her eyes came to rest at the far end of the table.

"Admiral Wald, I must demand a terrible thing of you," Casey's voice grew implacable.

"Your Majesty has but to ask," Torsten replied in a tight, angry voice.

Jessica could practically taste the rage emanating off her dear love, at *Buran's* assault on his capital. The eyes had hardened down to a rage Jessica knew lived within, but had never seen come to the surface.

She was reminded of Old Man Winter on the Eastern Front, in one of the great land wars of the early industrial age. An ancient foe slow to rouse, and utterly unforgiving when it finally was.

"Torsten, if Werder has been destroyed, my father's government has been eliminated with it," Casey began. "In addition, the House of Dukes will need to be reconstituted, possibly from scratch, a task that will take years. In the interim, I need a civilian government in place, handling day-to-day decisions. The Fleet might be the backbone of the government, but it cannot be its eyes nor its hands."

Jessica watched the man she loved take a deep breath, gulp once as the enormity of Casey's plans became clear.

"I will serve in whatever capacity you require, my Emperor," he said in a quiet, firm voice.

"You will retire in white, Admiral Wald," Casey commanded. "And take up the role of Chief of Deputies of my government *in extremis*, until the House of Dukes and the House of the People can be reconstituted on *St. Legier*. Until I can release you from this duty."

Torsten nodded. Casey turned to Jessica and started to say something, but stopped when Jessica squeezed her hand and nodded.

Sacrifice. Jessica's would be tiny compared to Casey's, and they both knew it. She might not see him again for years. But this was not the place to deal with that grief.

Later, alone in her cabin. Perhaps with Moirrey. And several bottles of wine.

Casey smiled wanly and mouthed *Thank you.*

The new Emperor turned to Arott.

"Fleet Centurion Whughy," she began. "I must remove your Imperial commander and the legality that allowed you to serve here. Will you take up arms for the *Empire of Fribourg* in his stead?"

"Your Majesty, I will," Arott replied firmly.

Casey nodded. She rose abruptly, causing the others to do the same. Quickly, everyone was standing.

"My friends, I will never be able to repay you for the love and support you have shown me, both today, and in all the time leading up to this moment," Casey intoned. "Now, I must ask the impossible of you, even as I go to face the impossible myself. *Buran* has chosen to impose what it thinks will be a telling, perhaps mortal blow on our will. It will not stand. It must not stand. I will ask for assistance from all of our old allies and enemies: *Aquitaine, Lincolnshire, Salonnia, Corynthe,* and others. We can no longer attempt to live in peace and harmony with *The Eldest,* but must cast him down from his throne. Jessica, Em, you will be my sword, to destroy him, utterly and irrevocably."

Jessica nodded grimly. Em looked fit to strangle the beast with his bare hands.

She glanced down at Torsten. He had gone white, but she could already see the new man that would emerge from all this, starting to peek out from the corners. He would be made of steel, with all the love and tenderness held deep inside, where perhaps only she would ever see it again. But she would be there to remind him.

Always.

"Ladies and Gentlemen," Casey commanded. "The Empire."

"The Empire!"

CHAPTER XXII

Torsten clenched his teeth and fought to remain outwardly calm as he waited for the hatch to his suite to open. Jessica stood at his side, so he constrained the fidgeting that wanted to erupt.

He had an hour until the shuttle for *Indianapolis* would be departing, possibly separating them forever. More than enough time to pack up what few things he would need to transport.

Nowhere near enough time to deal with the outstanding emotional issues.

And no time to handle the issue with the delicacy it demanded.

They had made promises with kisses and fingertips, but rarely words. Partly, he knew himself to be a reticent man, casting silences into gaps rather than speaking up. Jessica was the same, content to watch things unfold, gaming away thousands of responses before she ever moved, and only then, decisively.

The hatch cleared as though a glacier, deliberate and implacable. Torsten tossed propriety to the wind, grasping Jessica by the hand and tugging her into his cabin.

Even their private lives had remained largely separate. He would not impose himself on the woman and she faced monumental challenges far beyond his. If they had spent the barest handful of nights together in the last year, those had been precious gems to savor, not something to presume.

In an hour, he would depart. Torsten Wald had no doubts that the chances of him ever walking these decks again were rapidly approaching zero. If Arlo was holding *St. Legier* together by force of will, a task few other men could accomplish, Casey's Chief of Deputies would have to weave back together the frayed ends of the Empire itself with his bare hands.

There would be very little time for personal issues. Less so when he loved the woman who was about to take command of the entire war.

Inside his suite, the hatch closed with a snap.

Torsten took Jessica's hands in his and faced her from close enough to kiss.

She waited for him to speak. She always had. Jessica Keller was like that. Torsten Wald would have to cross the chasm. He had created it in the first place.

"Circumstances have conspired against my carefully laid plans," he said quietly.

She watched him with a twinkle in her eyes. It was an inside joke between them that he always spoke as if addressing an academic conference. Inside the Palace, most audiences were, to some extent.

But the grin was there. The support. The rapport. The love.

"Given the impossibilities of my task, this is the only way left for me to ask," he continued.

Having a left leg that ended mid-femur with a titanium implant that in turn connected to a hinged knee joint meant that Torsten could walk without a hitch, and stand without the shifting balance issues he had faced when he wore a sleeve over his stump.

It made kneeling, however, a carefully choreographed event.

Pitch the hips to clear the artificial foot's friction on the carpet. Draw the leg back so he could lower himself with his good leg onto the artificial ball of a knee that zu Kermode had designed for him. Settle his weight on the implant and push his good leg forward.

Never once lose his hold on her hands.

Torsten looked up from the floor to see that Jessica had gone white. She had done a masterful job of containing her emotions earlier, when Casey, when the Empire, had needed her the most. But they were alone now.

Torsten had still managed to surprise her. It was good that he could do that, especially with this woman.

"*Wildgraf* Keller of Corynthe," he began in a ritual tone he had practiced dozens of times in his head. "Will you do me the honor of joining your life with mine? Of becoming my wife, and I your husband, to the end of our days?"

The little gasp told him all he needed to know. The tears clouding her eyes. The smile.

"I will," she managed, dropping to her own knees and wrapping her arms around him.

Torsten could taste the tears as he kissed her, unsure if they were hers or his. It didn't really matter.

After a time, they settled.

"So," she began lightly, grinning. "You had not expected this timing. Does that mean you do not have a promise ring for me to wear, to warn other men off?"

Torsten shared her smile.

"I have not, milady," he answered with whatever grand dignity he could manage, given their place on the floor of his cabin. "And I could not, because the number of conspirators required would be too great."

"Conspirators?" Jessica asked.

"I have it in my head that the person I should ask to make our rings would be Michelle Ali al-Inverness," he offered.

"Fourth Saxon's Armorer?" Jessica laughed.

She had a lovely laugh.

"But for Fourth Saxon, and Vo Arlo, we would not be here, Jessica."

She sobered at that.

"We would not," she observed before grinning again. "Will the new Emperor give her blessing to this union?"

"If she will not, then I will petition *Aquitaine*'s Senate personally, as a matter of state."

"Oh, Torsten," she sighed and leaned into him. "You have no idea how much you delight me. I look forward to dragging you off to *Corynthe* one of these days and forcing you to teach economics to a group of semi-reformed space pirates."

He smiled and kissed her, forcing himself upright on his good leg and drawing her up as well so they could simply embrace.

He faced an impossible task. With her love, he could prevail.

CHAPTER XXIII

Yan held his peace as the others loaded onto the shuttle across the landing bay. It was a dignified effort, if a bit weird to watch. When was the last time an Emperor carried her own duffel bag, snarling at the poor marine who had expected to carry it for her?

Wachturm emerged, once they got Casey and Moirrey aboard, and walked over to where he and Ainsley had stationed themselves, well off to one side by the airlock hatch. Best ticket in town.

"You're sure you wish to remain here, Bedrov?" the Grand Admiral asked, coming to rest like an avalanche at the bottom of the hill. "There will be few new ships for the war effort at this point, while I work out what *St. Legier* needs and how we address things."

"I can always hitch a lift with the *Mailman*, Grand Admiral," Yan replied. "With my office and staff annihilated, there is no place other than Penmerth that would be a better place to work. Plus, I need to drop another revolution on that bastard."

"Pardon?" Wachturm asked.

"*Buran*," Yan clarified. "He's starting to react to Jessica and you. Eventually, he would figure out how to counter all the current changes, if I let him. I need to make the music faster and faster, until he trips and breaks a leg. This is as good a place as any to work. I'll send requisitions in if I need things more than Whughy already has stashed here."

"Good enough, Bedrov, Barret," Wachturm said. "I'll have *Il Augusta* back with her new flight wing, soon enough."

Yan watched the giant turn on his heel with the grace of a much smaller man and stride off towards the shuttle. Yan didn't envy the task they faced. And there was little he could do to help, other than to be another mouth to feed, or another expert with an unwanted opinion.

Instead, he turned to Ainsley. The woman who had defined herself for so long as *da Vinci*, pilot extraordinaire, before becoming his partner in crime.

"Planning to keep you kinda isolated from *Merman* and his crew of lunatics," Yan said, referring to the Senior Flight Centurion in charge of *Il Augusta*'s Wing. All but two of the man's pilots had volunteered for the new flight craziness Yan was about to unleash. With folks stepping up from *Auberon*, *Merman* had managed to fill the thirty-six crew slots for his twelve fast bombers.

She answered him by way of a single, arched eyebrow, but the amount of sarcasm she could contain was simply unmatchable by any other woman he had ever met.

"We need to go completely crazy," Yan continued. "Back of the notebook weirdness like nothing we've ever come up with before."

She grinned.

"Us?" she even managed to sound blameless, rather than his unindicted co-conspirator. "Innocent as the driven snow here, bubbles. Don't know what you're talking about."

"Three steps ahead of where that bastard thinks we're going to be tomorrow," Yan replied as the shuttle lifted in a whine and backed carefully through the lock seal into deep space. "Three steps."

CHAPTER XXIV

Arott waited patiently for Oz to finish reviewing the executive summary at the front and some of the wiring diagrams at the back of the report. He had learned the lesson of paper originally from Jessica, and it had been reinforced by Admiral Wald and *Fribourg's* fascination with the printed word. And it added a weird smell to his office to have stacks of paper, both printed and just waiting blank, stored here.

Oz had been greedily consuming the document for nearly fifteen minutes while Arott watched, sipping at his lemonade and trying to project the sort of personal professionalism that had always been his hallmark.

Arott was way outside his comfort zone today.

Finally, Oz arranged the pages into perfect alignment and placed them on the desk between the two men. He had a wry, knowing smile that Arott found extremely disquieting.

"Will it work, Oz?" Arott blurted.

Command Engineering Centurion Vilis Ozolinsh, universally known at Oz these days, affected a dry, withering look. He did that well, related to three of the wealthiest, most elite families in the *Republic*. Oz had been born with a platinum spoon in his mouth. And fallen in love with engineering, to the chagrin and dismay of his family. And turned into a goofball, somewhere along the way.

"You could ask her yourself, Arott," Oz observed with a grin Arott could only classify as evil. "She won't bite."

Arott harrumphed sourly.

"I have a reputation to maintain, I'll have you know," Arott replied. He and Oz had never been close, but they had run in many of the same circles twenty-five years ago, before the Navy claimed both of their souls. "Dry, stodgy, and academic."

"And yet," Oz's grin grew even wider. "You could have been a pretty good engineer if you hadn't had your heart set on ultimate command. What's wrong with Moirrey knowing you designed this system, Arott?"

"Flights of fancy, Oz," Arott countered. "Not my signature at all. And I wasn't even sure it would work. That's why I need someone like Moirrey to investigate."

"Oh, it will work just fine, Fleet Centurion," Oz replied. His smile had not lost a lumen of power. "I'm not sure I understand the tactical implications, but this sort of thing is purely an engineering problem, and you've done a very credible job of laying out your needs and your proposed solution. Someone on her team could take it to the next step, and then she or maybe Yan Bedrov could design and build a test system for you. You still haven't answered my question."

Arott paused to find the right words. He was pretty sure he could ask Oz to take credit for the design and not let the truth out. He just had to convince the man that it was a task worth doing.

"Arott Whughy is a by-the-numbers, stick-up-his-ass perfectionist, Oz," Arott finally offered.

"Who has managed to build the strangest, most-unnaval vessel I have ever encountered, and run it effectively," Oz fired back. "With no blueprints, no backstop, and only the vaguest suggestions of direction from Jessica. I'm familiar with the concept, Arott. Something like this will seal your fate with the Engineering Corps when you finally take over for Petia, one of these days."

And it would. They both knew it, but that wasn't the point of this conversation.

Arott sighed. He would have to tell Oz the truth. Bastard.

"Oz, if this comes from me, they'll think I miss line command and want to get back into the saddle again," Arott admitted, to himself as well as to the engineer. "My little secret? I'm past command, mentally. Running a base is an order of magnitude more complicated than a warship, even *Auberon*, and I've never been happier in my life."

He paused as he reflected on those words. They were God's honest truth, and he had never even whispered them aloud.

"Robbie, Alber', and the rest of the fire-breathers can have the glory of close combat," he continued. "I'm preparing to take over Fleet Headquarters at *Ladaux*, for my next command, if Petia will let me. And then her job as First Lord of the Fleet in five or eight years."

"Oh, shit, you're serious!" Oz was finally, genuinely surprised.

It felt good to surprise the man. Nothing Arott Whughy ever did was supposed to surprise people.

"Deadly serious, Oz," Arott said. "And we need to win this war, and do it fast, because *Buran* is bigger than *Aquitaine* and *Fribourg* combined. Given enough time, they'll grind us down and win."

"Okay," Oz shifted in his seat and flipped the document back open to the executive summary's design diagram. "So what does this type of weapon gain us?"

"A Type-2 beam is good for engaging fighters, and escorts if you get close enough for a crazed, jousting run, like Jessica's people are known for," Arott explained. "With the new Type-1-Pulse, it has fallen out of favor. Similarly, with the redesign of the Type-3 into a tunable model, you can either have point-blank firepower or extreme range."

"And sequencing a Type-2 rapidly?" Oz asked. "Why not a single, hard pulse of a beam, like the others?"

"Those Power Absorbers they use leak, Oz," Arott said. "I've spent a lot of time studying scan logs and video. And they aren't monolithic. It isn't a hemisphere they cover, although it looks like it. Each is a separate channel, covering a very specific zone of the ship. It's there in the notes of Appendix F. If I'm right, we can spike a single panel hard with the modified Type-2. While the target panel and its neighbors will catch it, a little bit of the energy should bleed through and hit the hull, instead of splashing up to be captured by the neighboring panels like our other beams do. Icepick him, instead of a shiv. Not much difference, but maybe enough."

"Kigali?" Oz asked, leaping beyond what they needed, and landing on who should test it.

"Honestly?" Arott countered.

Oz nodded.

"Kosnett on *CS-405* or Glenn on *CP-406*. Kigali won't give up his guns, even for a little while. Plus, the other two will approach this like artists, instead of berserkers."

"Point taken," Oz said. "But if this works out and upends warfare again, you're getting all the blame."

He smiled. Arott returned the smile. He could live with being associated with it, at that point. By then, it would be too late to move him back to line command, even to a Heavy Dreadnaught. He could settle into station command. And eventually, First Lord of the Fleet.

It was obvious, at least to Arott, that Jessica Keller was never returning to the *RAN*.

CHAPTER XXV

Maybe it was that year of living and training and fighting with Fourth Saxon, Vo decided as the blizzard outside his window seemed to step up another screaming notch. Very little in this world bothered him anymore, at least when it came to weather.

The *Death Zone*, what they had taken to calling the area that had been the capital region of *St. Legier* centered on Werder and the Imperial Palace, had decided to have an unseasonably cold and wet winter. With the amount of damage done to the planet, Vo wasn't surprised.

Back home, tectonically-active planets occasionally got tremblers all the way up to Nine on the ancient Richter scale, a logarithmic method of measuring energy release that dated back to the lost homeworld.

Logarithm. Vo wasn't a scientist or a mathematician, but he had dated both in his time. He had learned enough to know that a Nine was ten times was powerful as an Eight. A hundred times more powerful than a Seven, which were the ones that significantly damaged badly-engineered cities.

The ground effect of that bomb, according to a planetologist they had located, was somewhere around Eleven and a half, maybe, centralized. The shields had held just long enough to absorb some of it. Plus it was directed down, instead of up. A massive shaped charge impacting the planet.

It had still annihilated the city and the surrounding region.

Had it been an asteroid striking ground, the heat alone would have killed everyone over a much larger area, perhaps a thousand kilometers. And then kicked up enough dust and molten rock to darken the skies and block the sun for years.

Weather patterns all over the planet were reacting in bad ways. But it also wasn't even the earliest storm to drop nearly a meter of snow in the area in the last generation.

It still complicated his work to find survivors, get them to safety, and keep food and supplies flowing in.

It was an Extinction-level event for a bronze-age civilization, and it might still overwhelm them here.

How do you explain to someone that two hundred million people might starve, on the capital world of an interstellar empire?

"Reese," Vo called over his shoulder, bringing himself back to the place where he was supposed to be, in charge of the men leading the effort. "What's the latest from orbit?"

There was a pause. Vo wondered if he still occasionally startled his men. He would sit silently, meditating on his sins for long stretches, before speaking. They might think he had turned into a rock.

"According to Admiral Provst, we should be getting two big freighters of foodstuffs in the next eighteen hours, at drop points six and fourteen, plus he managed to swap out another squadron of ships, so he's scraped us up another six hundred or so marines as a labor force soon."

Vo called up the map in his head and studied it. After the coup, he had taken the time to memorize maps of *St. Legier* in much greater detail. Most of them were no longer relevant, describing streets and neighborhoods that were only memories now, but the regional terrain was still more or less intact in many places.

"Drop them on the southwest side," he decided. "Put them down on the lake shore itself with orders to build up docks and wharfing facilities. The Emperor might decide to put her new capital down there, given that it mostly survived, and we can use the water to transport heavier cargoes from a longer distance without roads. Add a note to have someone locate me the furthest distance we can easily move a barge and figure out where to build or expand a starport to service it."

"Roger that, sir," the man replied.

Vo went back to the snow. It was probably a metaphor, blanketing everything in cold, malevolent death, but he'd be damned if it would stop him. He'd be damned if anything would defeat him.

"Sir, you need to see this," another voice, a grim one, chimed in.

Curator Stolz. Reese Borel's right hand, as Reese was his. The tone guaranteed Vo's attention even faster than the words. The whole point of the team he had assembled was that they could handle most tasks, needing him only to approve decisions and step in when things got delicate.

Or messy.

Vo turned from the window and located Stolz across the command room they had assembled. It was warmer in here, but all the assault skiffs were parked right outside the door where Vo's pistol belt hung if he needed to be in the field quickly.

The room had fallen almost to silence around them, with only the sound of the furnace blowing hot air in a corner.

Stolz tapped the screen in front of him as his general approached. Vo followed the finger and read the note without emotion. It was a message from Admiral Provst's staff about someone suddenly requisitioning a vast number of civilian airliners and heavy lift aircraft.

Vo was working very hard at not feeling emotions these days. Any sentiment would lead him to either mindless rage or despair. Neither of those were constructive most of the time.

He reconsidered his choices as he re-read the words.

There was one other place he could go, emotionally, and still possibly even make it back to sanity safely afterwards.

If he cared to.

Wrath.

"I don't know Field Marshal Rohm," Vo observed airily. "Or the Seventh Guards Army. Who can fill me in?"

Iakov Street, of all people, spoke up. Decanus Street had been reigning darts champion at the Maltese Cross after the last tournament. And had helped Vo kill an Emperor before that. But he rarely spoke up in public, at least not without a very good reason.

"Political general, *zu* Arlo," Street called from the corner.

zu Arlo. Only the old timers called him that. It was the province of the twenty-four who had been there with him. The rest hadn't yet earned the right in the eyes of their comrades.

"Go on," Vo prompted the man.

"Seventh is a good Army, sir," Street continued. "Only one infantry division in the mix, with five mechanized and three tank, including 19th

Heavy Armored. They hold the whole southern continent from outside Santiago."

"What about Rohm?" Vo asked. "You said political."

Street glanced around the room. Not nervously, but keyed up.

"Everyone on mute," Vo ordered. "Now."

Hands flashed to buttons without hesitation. Street nodded.

"Betting in the NCO mess several years ago was that he was angling to marry Princess Steffi when she came of age," Street said in a low voice. "Have kids with the Imperial family. Wouldn't be surprised if he kept the idea and changed targets. Never been married, so no divorce scandals along the way. And he's what we would call a social general, rather than a street fighter."

Vo nodded sharply.

"In the *Republic of Aquitaine Navy*, we used to call them Noble Lords, as opposed to Fighting Lords," Vo replied with just enough of a sniff to convey his opinion of the former and his preference for the latter.

He turned to Reese. "Get me Field Marshal Rohm on the comm. I'd like to ask him why he's moving so many of his troops north without orders."

The visages around the room grew dark and a little terrible as Vo glanced about. He took a deep breath and walked to the middle of the room.

"And put it on the big screen," Vo continued in a tone that a stranger might mistake as light, possibly even friendly. "I'd like us to see each other as we talk."

A few minutes passed, but only a few. Vo suspected that the Field Marshal was awaiting the call. The room projected behind the man didn't look like the inside of an assault skiff. Perhaps a lady's boudoir, if Vo was inclined to be charitable.

If.

The Field Marshal himself appeared tall and lean in a slickly-tailored uniform. He had a black widow's peak and slicked-back hair on an aquiline face that somehow missed being august and settled for vaguely smarmy. At least the piercing, hazel-brown eyes showed intelligence, if a low kind of cunning.

They studied each other for a moment in silence. Vo guessed that the man expected to score points by making Vo speak first. He had the look of those sorts of playground games.

Vo wasn't playing.

"Field Marshal Rohm," Vo pronounced the name slowly. "I'll presume that you have read the same orders from Grand Admiral Wachturm that were transmitted to all divisional and higher headquarters. The one placing me in command of all military forces inside the atmosphere. So I have a simple question: Why are you disobeying a direct order to hold your units in barracks while civilian forces operate?"

If the men around Vo had slightly more of a reaction than Rohm did, everybody twitched at the tone and the words. Including the man on the screen.

"You are merely a General, Arlo," Rohm replied with something of a sneer. It might have been a pleasant, tenor voice. On another man. "And a foreigner, to boot. You do not give me orders."

Vo nodded. The preliminaries of scuffing dirt on each other's shoes was out of the way. Now they could play rough.

Vo found himself looking forward to playing rough.

"I see, Field Marshal," Vo commented. "So you do not feel that the Grand Admiral has the authority to issue orders to an Army officer?"

Another surge in the man's pupils. Even a hair of a dilation looked huge, when the man's projected eyes were the size of grapefruits on this screen. And he had probably never tried poker with people who were cutthroat players.

"I am the senior Army officer on this planet, with Grand Marshal Jenker killed in Werder," Rohm's voice got testy. "I will take command now and show you how to run things correctly. You've obviously made a mess of it, bringing in so many peon marines and civilians, and not recalling all the men I have under arms."

Vo smiled. It felt like the blizzard outside, cold and deadly. From the corner of his eye, he could see Street smile back, so it probably looked like death as well.

Street's did.

"Field Marshal Rohm, you are hereby ordered to return to barracks," Vo said, slowly and formally. "Your entire force is ordered to return to barracks as well."

"You do not give me orders, boy," Rohm snarled in a mighty voice. "I suggest you take your pissant group of fools, your so-called legion, and remove yourself from my operating theater before I lose my temper."

Yes, *Wrath.*

It had been a month of utter anguish for all the people he could not save. All the corpses they had dug out of rubble. Atop that, a year of living as a foreigner among the constant sniping from the majority of Army officers who were of noble birth.

And a decade of assholes like this one.

Vo might wear the black sword rank tab of a general, but in his soul he was still a yeoman on the lower decks, dealing with snotty spacers fresh out of training and full of themselves.

He rolled forward, ever so slightly. Up onto the balls of his feet as his shoulders hunched forward. Again, not much. Just that last warning a feral animal gives you.

"I am also *zu* Arlo, Field Marshal," Vo snarled back at the man. "*Ritter of the Imperial Household.* That means, among other things, that I speak for the throne. For the Emperor herself, until she decides to remove that privilege. That means I do give you orders. *Imperial Orders.* And I have given you an order. In ten seconds, you will be guilty of active mutiny against a superior officer during combat operations, under the Imperial Military Code. Do I have your attention, Field Marshal?"

"You think you can make me, *General?*" Rohm roared. "With one division of troops?"

"No," Vo admitted.

"Then you stand down," Rohm ordered. "You can't stop me!"

"I don't have to, Rohm," Vo replied with a tight, angry smile. Street's smile mirrored his, two men contemplating the fastest way to decapitate a chicken for dinner. "I will simply order Admiral Provst's battleships to bombard your formations from orbit until you surrender. To shoot down your aircraft and crash them into whatever land or ocean happens to be below. And then, according to the ancient codes, I will order your surviving enlisted men to be decimated by their mates, with all of the officers executed by the remaining enlisted men. You can stand next to me when I play this conversation for the Emperor, or I can carry your head into the throne room by your hair. Which will it be?"

Vo was not pleased with the way his own men recoiled at his words, even if Rohm seemed to suddenly discover the precipice yawning open at his feet. Troopers of the 189th Legion should be harder than that. He would have to add something to the training regime, after this, to toughen them up to the necessary level of deadly.

The Army might have gone stale, as Wachturm had said. It had apparently gotten soft as well. Too much time in garrison would do that. He would need to take these men and invade a hostile planet, that much was obvious.

Transform them from mere killers into something more impressive. Something Alber' d'Maine might have recognized.

The internal of that must have played out on Vo's face as Rohm watched. Probably the look of disinterested death. Rohm's face had gone white.

"You're serious," Rohm whispered in shocked, appalled disbelief.

"No, I'm done," Vo replied quietly. "Stand down, or start digging in."

Pause.

Wrath.

"We'll return to barracks immediately," Rohm's voice had a hint of whimper to it now. "Sir."

Not much. About what Vo would expect from kicking a puppy.

He felt like that, too, right now. Like he was kicking a puppy, but these men could never know that. None of them. The whole Empire needed to fear that Vo *zu* Arlo was hard enough, mean enough, deadly enough to carry through with a threat like that.

Because he was.

And right now, he was looking forward to it too much for his sanity to bear.

Vo took a quick breath and stepped back from ordering the Navy to open fire on ground targets. He forced his fists to open, as painful as that was, and blinked slowly.

"Turn over your command to a subordinate, Field Marshal Rohm," Vo said. "And report here under guard. You can help me and my men dig bodies out of the rubble with your bare hands, so you can begin to understand what the last month has been like for them. It will change your outlook on many things."

Rohm gulped, nodded, and the screen went dark.

Vo blew out a breath and let his weight settle back on his heels.

"I have Admiral Provst on channel fourteen for you, General," Reese said quietly into the emotional void that had opened in the room.

"Main screen," Vo commanded.

Tom Provst usually looked like a reanimated corpse, especially today. Vo understood why. Understood the guilt that had wracked the man. It was hard enough losing one of your own and having to write a letter to his parents. Vo had done too many of those.

Tom Provst still held himself personally responsible for the death of the crown prince.

Vo had wondered in that first fortnight if he would get a message from one of the other admirals that Provst had finally cracked and taken his life. Wachturm had warned him, as well.

"Your ships can stand down as well, Admiral," Vo voiced the words quietly, as if speaking at a funeral.

Provst studied Vo's face for a few moments before he nodded.

"I wondered, on Day One," the Navy man said with the angry drawl that seemed to be his default these days. "Wondered whether Wachturm was crazy for putting you in charge down there. Like he was crazy for leaving things to me up here. But it gave me a place to hang onto. A reason to get up and move forward. What would you have done if Rohm had called your bluff?"

"I wasn't bluffing, Tom," Vo responded.

"Yeah, I can see that now," Provst nodded again. Calm with the emotional flatness that you only got standing in the face of death. "I knew the civilians would listen to you, especially after that speech. And the fleet and ground pounders will now, too. What will *she* say?"

Spoken that way, there was only one woman Provst would refer to. Vo had to step past the Fleet Centurion in his mind and give thought to the young woman Wachturm had gone to retrieve.

"That's tomorrow's problem," Vo replied, signaling Reese to cut the channel before the ugly emotions got out of hand and he said too much.

He had no idea what she would say when she watched the video and read the reports everyone would file. And he didn't care. He wasn't here to win a popularity contest.

He was here to do a job.

A few more corpses along the way wouldn't make his nightmares any worse than the twenty million people that were already there.

CHAPTER XXVI

DATE OF THE REPUBLIC DEC 28, 401 FORWARD
BASE DELTA

Jessica entered the main conference room confident, but still on the vaguest of pins and needles. The final battle at *Trusski* had shown her how badly she had underestimated *The Eldest* and the sorts of people he formed in his crèches. The type of socialization and commitment that could turn his people into warriors. What someone might do when convinced that they had been shown *The Truth*.

In the year since, she had taken those lessons and applied them, pirate-style, across the entire sector of space on this side of the *M'Hanii Gulf* raiding almost every system *Buran* held, save *Samara*.

She had only threatened that over-secured system. Forced them to reinforce *Samara* again and again, lest Imperial fleets suddenly descend upon it if he dared move ships to defend the rest of the frontier. The other places she appeared without warning.

But that was yesterday. Jessica had something new in mind today.

She didn't need to convince the men and women in this room. She already had them. They had been with her long enough, each in their own way, to have married their paths with hers.

It had taken them to glory. It might yet take them to their deaths. But nobody had ever promised them that they would die in bed.

The main conference room on the station was huge. Suited to hold fifty comfortably, rather than the double handful here today, but it had the best AV suite, a full holoprojector like both *Auberons*, and a monster version that could hold an image eight meters across.

Jessica found it amusing that everyone looked at her as she entered, but nobody moved to stand. In the old days, the Noble Lords had generally insisted on an unwritten protocol that all lower-ranking officers stood when a superior officer entered.

The Fighting Lords had been too occupied with more important things.

Her inner team awaited her. Nils Kasum had once called the foursome of Denis, Robbie, Alber', and Kigali her *Merry Men*. There was some element of truth to the historical designation.

Today, she had added Enej, Arott, and Tamara, *II Augusta* having just arrived yesterday with a newly designed and built flight wing. Kanda would represent the survey cruiser *Ballard* as her eyes. Yan was here as well, ready for all the crazy engineering tasks that awaited, with Moirrey off helping Casey.

And it was going to get crazy.

Jessica had one moment of sorrow that Casey wouldn't be here. Jessica had looked forward to the young woman taking command of the first Imperial corvette of Yan's new design that would join this force. Without her, Jessica had asked Em to hold them back until *St. Legier* was adequately protected, and then send out a full fleet, the one that *IFV Indianapolis* would anchor as a pocket flagship.

In six months, she would have doubled her available weight on this strike force's border, but she didn't want *Buran* to have that long to prepare.

Jessica took the seat at the end and nodded to everyone, setting her mug of fresh coffee in front of her and placing both hands on the tabletop to ground herself. She picked out Arott, seated next to Denis, across from her.

It wasn't that Denis always sat in the chair furthest from her, although it had taken her time to process that. Denis was sitting so he could watch her back at all times, a movement as automatic for him as breathing.

Just one more thing that made them such an effective team. She could trust him with anything.

She smiled at Denis, and then Arott.

"We need to up the crazy," she announced simply.

Most of the commanders frowned. It was enlightening that Kigali, Yan, and Arott just grinned. They had anticipated her.

Arott nodded.

"Which vector?" he asked with a grin, as if it was a foregone conclusion, what she was asking.

"Downstream," Jessica answered. "And south."

Arott nodded. The rest were confused. It was good.

Denis turned his whole upper torso to study the man next to him, before returning his attention to her.

"Is there some sort of telepathic sense that develops, once you become a Fleet Centurion?" he asked with the slightest sarcastic tone.

It was Jessica's turn to smile.

"He and I had this conversation already," she said. "We will beat *Buran* by being unpredictable. At some point, the beast will figure out that we must have a base in the gulf itself, and come looking. So we're going to move to a different place. Logic suggests a place from which we can launch raids directly into the *Altai* sector, on the other side, so I'm sure that *Ninagirsu* is as well defended as *Samara*."

"*Ninagirsu* is spinward, Jessica," Denis noted. "We're going the other way?"

"Yes," she replied, pressing a button on the table in front of her and bringing the projector live.

It took a moment to find the right file, and then the entire projection was filled with the Imperial side of the Gulf in blue, and *Buran*'s side in gold. At this scale, stars ten light years apart appeared as close neighbors, with the vast channel of darkness running down the middle.

"If we were on a planet," Jessica began, "*M'Hanii* would be a river that served as a natural border between nations. For the longest time, it was that in space, as well. Until *Buran* decided to expand. There have been so many worlds terraformed in the distant past that nobody noticed *The Eldest* dropping quiet colonies into *Fribourg*'s gaps."

She pressed another button and the projection rotated and began to zoom.

"But even *Buran* doesn't have enough people and ships to take them all," Jessica continued. "As near as we have been able to tell, with intelligence provided by the former Khan, there are gaps and pockets over there, based purely on stellar geography and rates of birth."

A star lit up now, well downstream from their current location, and very close to the bottom. From the side, the Milky Way galaxy was a fried egg, thick in the core and then a relatively smooth flatness as one headed out to the edges. And it rotated around the core, giving spinward and anti-spinward, or upstream and downstream, meaning. On average the galaxy ran about one thousand light years thick.

"This is *Stanovoy*," Jessica said as the image grew closer and closer. "If we were on a planet, this would be something of a peninsula in a river, protecting a secured anchorage bay behind it. There is a gap that largely separates it from all the neighbors, but it is something of an industrial center, as there are a variety of fairly-rare mineral deposits that are easily accessible. According to the man now known as Seeker, the bay was caused by a massive supernova exploding in the distant past, clearing the local space and seeding all the proto-systems around it."

"What do we have planned for them?" Denis spoke up now.

She could see the look of rage underneath his face. Denis had always been the quiet, competent one, but he had also turned into another beloved uncle to the young woman suddenly thrust into the one role she wanted least in life.

Whatever Jessica asked, whatever Casey needed, Denis would make it happen, no matter the cost. It was why Em had promoted him to white.

"A month ago, we would have snuck in and frightened them, like we've done over here," she responded.

"And now?" Denis pressed.

She could see the rest wanted to ask that question, as well.

How far are we willing to go to pay back those bastards for what they've done? What they've become?

"I don't plan on dropping any bombs on the planetary surface," Jessica said in a low, dark voice. "Up until now, this has been a quiet sector for them, so I'm not expecting significant military forces at hand. And Seeker has said that they don't believe in the sorts of mass fighter formations we use to defend systems, instead relying on just beams and missiles. If we get lucky, we'll drop in and be facing nothing capable of even challenging our right of passage. Like *Thuringwell* was when we got there. That's when things will get ugly."

"Ugly," Kigali observed in a voice with no emotional loading whatsoever. "Define *ugly*, please?"

"I want you and your team to assist Alber', Robbie, and Denis in damaging or destroying every military outpost or civilian craft we can lay guns on while we're in system, Kigali," Jessica challenged the man. "Tamara's folks will pursue the ones that think they can blink away from us. Then we'll go after any civilian stations and factories in orbit, giving them just enough time to do a full evacuation, like Admiral Wachturm did at *Ballard.* I want to permanently, materially damage the economic underpinnings of this system, and this sector, before we move on to the next one and repeat it. Eventually, I want to destroy the economy of the sector itself."

"Scorched earth?" Robbie asked.

He had known her longer than anyone, at this point, having served under her back in the days when she commanded *Brightoak.*

"If it moves, it dies, Robbie," Jessica said. "Up until now, this has been a military endeavor on our parts, trying to make them stop at a border and behave. I'm past that. We're all past that. As soon as I can get a message home, I'm asking David Rodriguez to send whatever help he can. I'm asking the Senate to reinforce First Expeditionary Fleet with new squadrons, before that bastard comes any farther. *The Eldest* wouldn't listen to reason, so I'm going to resort to the kind of violence that would have made *my* name an epithet for evil and destruction, before he destroyed a planet. Any questions?"

Yan surprised her by raising a hand. He almost never brought things up in public, preferring private meetings to work out details, before springing them on the rest of the group. Either he had already done so with the right people, or felt comfortable enough with them to start cold.

"Yan?"

"I have grown intimately familiar with the contents of *Project Mischief,*" he spoke in that slow drawl he affected when he wanted your attention. "It was always deadly, but there was an element of goofy playfulness to many of the things. Archerfish drones, sure, but also Eye of God orbital satellites, made of burning magnesium visible in broad daylight."

Everyone smiled at that, at what Moirrey had perfected. Jessica was proud of the tiny woman, the Evil Engineering Gnome, and just sorry she couldn't be here with them.

zu Kermode of *Ramsey.* One of the new Emperor's Ladies- in-Waiting, as well as one of the house *Ritters.*

And a good part of the reason the rest of them were still alive.

"Go on," Jessica prodded.

She was always amazed at how far the man Bedrov had come from good-old-boy pirate, serving then as Ian Zhao's second in command; to the confident, deadly, naval architect bringing a whole lifetime of lethal experience to the field of battle. Jessica would miss having him in Tactical command of *Kali-ma*, her flagship, and losing him on the surface of *St. Legier* would have been a terrible blow.

But he was here now. And if his anger out-weighed Denis and the rest, that was a result of watching the mushroom cloud from orbit rather than just on a video.

Seeing friends die firsthand.

"I have a few designs that have not made it into any official files, while I worked out the specs and power requirements," he continued. "They will not be of any significant value while you are out raiding, but you'll need them before you go after a major target like *Ninagirsu* or the sector capital at *Severnaya Zemlya*. They are not nice. Won't work for shit against anybody but *Buran*, either. But you need to plan six to eight weeks in semi-drydock for the cruisers and *Vanguard*. Less if we send a request to Wachturm for extra construction engineers on the next run. Plus one or two of the frigates."

"Okay," Jessica noted as a placeholder. "How bad?"

"I have not gotten pissed enough to put numbers to a planet-cracker, Your Majesty," Yan growled, reminding everyone here that he only answered to the *Queen of Corynthe*, and nobody else. "Everything short of that is fair game. Plus, I'm gotten some new designs from Moirrey and from a friend of Oz."

Jessica stared sharply.

"That one wasn't from Oz?" she asked in a hard voice.

"Correct," Yan said. "I have my theories as the origin, as Oz has a different tactical signature to his thinking. But it is a very effective design, and I plan to implement it."

"Huh," Jessica grunted. "But the rest?"

"I'm going junkyard dog," he snarled in that slow drawl. "Rabid, ugly, and mean."

Even Jessica felt a chill at his words. She had seen Yan Bedrov angry. She had never seen him like this.

"You, Arott, and I will meet offline and go over them, Yan," she decided. "Everyone else, bring your crews up for a higher operational tempo. We'll send *Mendocino* and *Duncan* back for supplies as soon as we have a list, plus request any spare hands Em can send, so we may have a troopship docked here soon."

She paused to scan the room, noting the poised faces, the flickering anger. The rage buried just underneath the surface.

"This will be like *Cahllepp*, all over again," she said. "With one exception. We were trying to scare the Imperials then. I intend to punish *The Holding*. As Robbie said, scorched earth. Tamara, make sure your people understand that we're going to do this Alber's way."

Tamara nodded. Her crew were the newest members of the team, but she had been there at the beginning with Denis and the rest. And everyone understood what someone meant when Alber' said Goddesses of War.

Led into battle by the Queen of Destruction herself.

CHAPTER XXVII

Vo was doing paperwork in his personal office when a knock on the wooden door brought him back to the surface. Never enough food for everyone, so it must be parceled out carefully enough to *maybe* keep enough people alive for another few days. Fuel for heaters so people might not freeze to death in the cold. Transport to get as many survivors to safety and volunteers into the Death Zone as possible.

And wood and rope for gibbets. Looters were shot, but their bodies were still hung from posts in the ancient style, as a warning of what someone would face, if they thought they could get away with something.

Fortunately, the numbers of fools was dwindling. At least for now. Vo had no doubts that at some point the idiots would decide that he had stopped paying attention and they could get stupid again. The last two months hadn't ruined his opinion of humanity, but it hadn't done anything to improve it, either.

"Come," Vo called in reply, setting down his pen and rubbing the bridge of his nose.

He looked forward to the day he could retire someplace soft, like a strike commando team on a suicide mission.

Reese Borel opened the door, peeked in, and stepped to one side.

"Field Marshal Rohm to see you, sir," Reese said in a careful, neutral tone.

Vo rose. Not to cede authority to the man, but to greet him as equals, rather than threatening to have him executed.

Again.

Up close, the man had the tall solidity that ran through so much of the noble class in the Empire. Perhaps a hand shorter than Vo, and skinny, but it was a wiry strength. His hair had a layer of gray just visible underneath the bits that had been dyed black.

Rohm was dressed in his best class two uniform, the sage with many of the impressive ribbons. Not as good as Vo's would be, if he wore everything, but Vo didn't think there were any left on *St. Legier* who could, with Jenker dead. And the man was unarmed, as he should be.

Vo stuck out a hand as the officer trod carefully into the small office.

"Field Marshal," he said simply.

Rohm took the hand, once he realized that Vo wasn't about to attack him. Or shoot him.

"General *zu* Arlo," he replied, adding a ghost of a smile when he realized that Vo wasn't about to crush his hand, either, while shaking.

"Sit, please," Vo gestured to the chair. "Borel, have someone find the Field Marshal a full set of cold-weather field utilities that are a good fit. He'll be joining us on our next patrol round. He'll also need a pistol and an armorer to help him learn to use it."

"Yes, sir," Reese said, closing the door silently.

Vo studied the man for a few moments. It was the first time they had met in person, as far as he knew. Rohm had vocally been one of the conservative ones who hadn't agreed with Karl VII awarding a *Rittership* or a Colonelcy to a foreigner. Had Rohm been in the Navy, Vo had no doubt the man would have at least secretly supported the coup by Dittmar, if he hadn't declared outright. The Army hadn't mattered enough on that day to even be noticed.

There was a streak of conservatism that ran deep in *Fribourg*. It had served them well when things were stable and predictable, but Vo understood how much a female Emperor would challenge these men. Offend them.

How many would agitate for her to stand aside so an acceptable male heir could be located somewhere and enthroned? The Imperial Succession List existed for expressly the purpose of tracking every person with Imperial blood in case that bomb had wiped out the top five hundred candidates in one go. They would go into the second half, if they had to.

They didn't need to, with Lady Casey alive.

Vo was here to enforce that.

Rohm, for his part, seemed to study Vo just as closely. They had already had the pissing match where Rohm decided that he wasn't ready to play a game of throne or neck. No doubt the man would attempt to ingratiate himself with Karl VIII and cast aspersions on Vo's character in the future.

Vo really didn't give a shit what the locals thought. Or said. He had been handed an impossible task. The only thing he could do now was to fail as well as he could.

Twenty millions ghosts were going to haunt his dreams forever. The only question he had now was how far short of two hundred million more he could manage.

"Field Marshal, I ordered you to report to me here for two reasons," Vo began. Best to get this out of the way. "One, I don't trust you, simple as that. And I have to make an example of you so none of the other commanders out there decide to try me. The admirals have already been broken to the bit by Wachturm after the coup, and they like Tom Provst, so I don't have much to worry about there."

"I see," Rohm said carefully, matching Vo's neutral tone. "And two?"

"Two," Vo let his gaze find a point one thousand kilometers into an invisible distance. "I had to deal with a great deal of grief and snide commentary from pompous, well-borne gentlemen like yourself at Field School. You've never had to get your hands dirty, or not at least since you made it past lieutenant twenty-some years ago and could order other people to go get wet and muddy. You're going to live like me and my men for a bit and remember what it's like, before I send you back to Santiago. Or until the new Emperor decides what she wants to do with the two of us. As you've said, you're the senior surviving officer, in terms of rank and time in grade. I was just the man they put in charge of saving the world."

Vo appreciated the fact that Rohm shut his mouth rather than arguing. It wasn't a threat, so much as a promise, to throw them both onto the carpet in whatever Imperial throne room Centurion *zu* Wiegand ended up using when she got here. To let her first official act possibly be something drastic.

There was nothing Karl VIII could do to Vo that was worse than going to sleep each night.

Vo had carried it all on his shoulders for long enough. He wasn't Atlas, and he wasn't Heracles.

Rohm let the moment pass. He had apparently spent enough time introspective on his flight up here to understand what a noose felt like around his throat.

"What should I concentrate on, sir?" Rohm asked, deflecting the conversation onto careful, professional grounds.

Two officers, evenly ranked, unsure of seniority, set to working together. The newcomer asked for directions, possibly orders, on the assumption that the man already on scene might have a better understanding of the immediate situation. It was more like the *Aquitaine* way, the way the Army did it, especially since the *Fribourg* Fleet was exactly the opposite, with the senior officer immediately in charge, regardless of any total ignorance of the tactical situation.

"I'll attach you directly to Headquarters Ala for now," Vo said. "In a week to ten days, I have six hundred fleet marines that will be ready to be dropped on the southwest corner of the Death Zone, near Strasbourg. I've studied your record, and you have enough civil engineering background to take command of them as they work on docks and warehouses. I would like to turn that city into a regional transit center if we can dredge the waterfront deep enough for larger maritime ships and barges, with a new or expanded starport somewhere on Lake Zurich itself or up a river where we have open space to work."

Rohm paused as he absorbed the words. Obviously, not what he was expecting when he walked in the door.

Pity. Perhaps if Rohm had done as much research as Vo had, he would have been able to guess better at what was coming. And if he wanted to put his noble ass to work, he would earn a lot more credit with the 189th Legion. And their commander.

The moment passed.

"I can do that, sir," Rohm said quietly.

He paused again, unsure. Verging on words, but holding himself still. Still enough that Vo almost missed it the flinch.

"Speak, Field Marshal Rohm," Vo said, echoing a much earlier conversation with Jessica, still his model for this sort of thing. "Better to ask now and not be confused later."

Again the pause. Eyes up and distant, finding the right words. Mouth crinkled up, almost as if he had bit something sour, but not quite.

Finally, the man gave up.

"Why?" Rohm asked. "You aren't one of us. Weren't born here. Aren't technically even an Imperial citizen as many would judge it. Why are you doing all this?"

Hands gestured to encompass the room, the city, and the Death Zone. Maybe the entire *Fribourg Empire*.

Vo tapped the red sword patch on his chest with one meaty finger.

"I swore an oath, Field Marshal," he rumbled. "We all did, but I doubt that many of you considered what it really meant. That oath required me to storm the Imperial Palace and kill Sigmund Dittmar in order to rescue Karl VII. Right now it means going junkyard dog on *St. Legier* in the aftermath of a devastation so vast that the language lacks the necessary terms to describe it, except *Death*. I'm trying to teach the 189th everything that it entails. Not just the pride, but the cost."

Rohm studied him closer. Vo just stared at the man as he did.

Something changed. Vo couldn't put his finger on it, but Rohm's head came up a little. The shoulders squared and pulled back.

"I swore the same oath," Rohm replied, his voice a challenge.

"You did, Field Marshal," Vo answered. "I've studied your record. You're a good man, and a good officer. That's why we're sitting here talking, instead of you being tossed in the stockade until Karl VIII returns. You swore that oath, but you had forgotten that there are costs associated with what we do. We have to pay them now."

"You're going to take on the entire Death Zone by yourself?" Rohm asked.

His voice wasn't sneering, nor incredulous. Maybe midway between the two.

"I'm not alone, Rohm," Vo countered. "The 189th Legion stands with me. And the fleet. I have the entire civilian population of this planet to call on. I would like the help of the rest of the Army, but they have to understand that they aren't in charge here. They'll do it my way, or they can rot in their barracks."

"I see," the man said. "And if I had come here angry, and demanded satisfaction in a duel, to assuage my impugned honor, *zu Arlo?*"

His voice was very flat, very careful. Distant. Curiosity, rather than challenge.

"I've killed more men with pistols than swords, Field Marshal," Vo said. "One more wouldn't weigh that heavily on my conscience. Not after the twenty million I already failed here."

Rohm slammed his mouth shut. Blinked hard.

Understood that he probably would have lasted about as long as a puppy, if he had gone through with such a threat.

That much was obvious in his eyes.

Vo thought the man would say something brash and arrogant. He had that reputation about it, from everything Vo had read. Instead, he extended his right hand across the desk.

"What else can I do to help, sir?" Rohm asked.

Vo took the hand and shook it.

"Keep me honest, Field Marshal Rohm," Vo said. "Remind me what it means to be human when I forget."

CHAPTER XXVIII

It was the tiniest thing, the weirdest, little idiosyncrasy of naval architecture, but it focused Casey's eyes in the dimness of her cabin, stretched out on her bunk and unable to sleep. Yan Bedrov had designed both this vessel and *IFV Vanguard*. Casey found her gaze drawn to the seam in the ceiling where the plates met with a weld.

On the Imperial warships, the weld was a solid bead of metal, a tube mushed slightly flat to hold the two pieces of metal together. On SC *Auberon*, it had been inverted, to appear from below as if a pipe had been pressed in, and then the extra bits cut away, leaving a perfect smooth curve.

It made no sense that she couldn't look away, but Casey wasn't sleeping tonight, so her mind kept fixating on that point.

It was probably better than some of the other places her brain wanted to go.

She gave up after a restless time and rose from her bed. She dressed quickly. Em hadn't thought to bring any clothing for her, not that there would be anything in naval stores for a woman, let alone a woman Emperor, so she generally wore her normal uniform as an *Aquitaine* Centurion.

At least until tomorrow, when she expected them to drop out of JumpSpace at *St. Legier*.

Then she would put on an impossible corset called *Emperor of Fribourg*.

At least she would have two people in her immediate Household to rely on.

First, she had managed to impose herself on Em and shanghai Moirrey, with the explanation that she would need Ladies-in-Waiting, something nobody in the current incarnation of the Fleet was capable of fulfilling.

The current incarnation.

Second, First-Rate-Spacer Vibol Harmaajärvi. The lean, fussy, naval tailor that had accompanied Amala Bhattacharya to *Trusski* as part of a planetary invasion force that had consisted of nine people. A fifty-six-year-old sailor who had joined the *Republic of Aquitaine* Navy before Casey was even born. Who was currently hard at work designing and crafting what would become her Imperial wardrobe.

She would look impressive, of that Casey had no doubt. She had seen his work on Bhattacharya. But she had resisted putting anything on as long as possible, settling instead for giving the man one of her best uniforms to turn into patterns for whatever art and magic he was busy creating, down in the cabin Em had assigned the man.

Tomorrow, that would change. Forever.

Centurion Casey *zu* Wiegand would disappear into the fog, to be replaced by *Emperor Karl VIII*.

Casey found herself standing at her desk, unknowing how she came to be there. She sat, firing up the console and bringing up a menu screen. *IFV Indianapolis* lacked the sort of specialized software and input hardware she had left behind at her father's palace, so she called up a basic music program and began tinkering with the settings to get it as far into advanced mode as it was capable of achieving.

If she could not sleep, she would compose instead.

She started with the woodwinds. Brass would be too much, too imposing right now. The pain in her soul required a softer sound, one horn calling softly in the morning mist, joined slowly by others, as if searching for one another.

Lost.

Strings brought a counterpoint she thought of as *pain*. Only then could the percussion and brass join in, like hunting dogs and horsemen chasing a stag through the brush.

Casey had thought she was facing a funeral hymn when she placed the first note, but it was quickly clear that this would be the opening to her Third Symphony. There were too many notes, too much complexity for anything else.

It would not be a meditation on loss. That would only come another time. Perhaps a later movement in this symphony, layered atop a basic requiem. Something she would simply call *Father*.

Casey lost sight of the screen as the tears filled her eyes. The keyboard was proof against water and salt, so she let muscle memory add the next several bars until her brain told her she had reached a moment to pause. The play button brought it all out in one long, sonorous tide of music.

An hour of night had passed. Six minutes of an opening movement had taken shape. For a moment, she considered that an aria might be necessary, a voice raised up and commanding the music, but the only thing she could imagine at this moment was a scream of rage filling a darkened hall.

No. Not rage. Fear. A woman looking up at Death itself descending from the heavens before darkness fell. What it must have been like to be standing in the middle of a park in Werder as the shields failed and the world ended.

Casey hit the save key as silence fell. She closed up the screen and pulled her legs up onto the chair, wrapping her arms around her shins.

She thought about her father and her mother. The Emperor Karl VII. Empress Kati. Her brother Ekke, killed aboard *IFV Firehawk*. Steffi, killed in the earlier coup attempt.

And she cried.

CHAPTER XXIX

IMPERIAL FOUNDING: 179/12/26. THE DEATH ZONE,
ST. LEGIER

V o snarled back at the blizzard as he emerged from the warm building. He faced the screaming winds piling wet sleet against both the side of his skiff and the two men standing at the ass end of it, out in the cold, waiting for him. Rather than argue with them, he climbed up the two steps and found a jumpseat. Sure enough, the two were in a beat behind him, slamming the hatch shut and dogging the lock.

Temperature outside, nine below zero centigrade. Temperature inside felt balmy, but it was probably only three above right now. But it was dry and the heaters were going full tilt.

One good thing about all the armor around him was the thermal insulation designed to keep them invisible on IR scanners. Once you got the beast warm inside, it would stay that way for a long while. Someone must have been up before dawn running the engine to get it here, though.

Vo was just happy he could take off his gloves and the knit cap he kept under his helmet. Unbutton the over-jacket a little, but leave the gunbelt in place. Relax some.

It was a nasty bitch out there.

Danville handed Vo an insulated mug of reinforced coffee. Lots of cream, perhaps the slightest touch of rum. Fat and fluids to keep him on track as they went out into the storm.

Blizzards didn't stop the patrol rounds, designed to rescue survivors and capture looters. They just made the work more painful. More than once, Vo had considered finding one of the heavy tanks and riding along with them, but he needed his staff. Long gone were the days when it could just be him and a horse.

Vo glanced around the room and picked out Rohm, sitting in the forward port seat. The one closest to the interior heater. The eyes above the scarf gave him away, bundled up tight against the weather, even inside. Santiago was probably in the low thirties today. Shorts and loose shirts weather. Go to the beach and ogle the pretty girls.

Instead, he was here. Dressed as warm as Street could get him with a day's warning. And had spent a couple of hours learning how to handle the revolver on his hip and shooting it into a berm. Officers used beam pistols for the most part. Only Fourth Saxon and the 189th threw copper-jacketed-lead at someone.

Today.

That would change, tomorrow. One of the tomorrows. Energy shields really didn't work worth a damn at ground level, and required a huge generator to power. Soldiers wore insulated, semi-grounded armor to resist portable energy weapons.

Wouldn't do shit against a bullet.

Rohm smiled. Vo smiled back.

"We set?" Vo called out.

"You were last, sir," Danville replied with a grin.

"Go," Vo ordered.

Even after a year, he was still getting used to a team of men who constantly fought to be a step ahead of him. Up earlier. At shower and breakfast before he first stirred. Training laps or dojo time, with marksmanship practice in mid-afternoon. *Command Team, Headquarters Ala* was about a year from turning into a dangerous, lethal, strike Commando, at this pace. Invading a hostile planet, hell, even just raiding one with this force, would be a pleasure then.

Kill *them* for a while.

The skiff surged upwards on its repulsors just enough to clear the skids before retracting them flat against the hull. Vo had pounded into his pilots the importance of staying low, going so far as to award tank crews gold stars on maneuvers, every time they were able to lock even an autocannon on a silhouette at range.

As they had taught him on *Thuringwell*, every centimeter of height was another hundred yards farther away that someone could hit you.

Where this legion were going eventually, those tiny bits of elevation would matter. Not so much today, but it needed to become instinct.

"With the blizzard today, Field Marshal," Vo began, "we're going to go fairly deep into the zone and make a fast run looking to see who's moving around. Anyone we see is either in need of our help, or up to no good. Only someone desperate is out in this weather."

"I see," Rohm answered. "Is this for my benefit?"

Vo noted that only a few of the men bristled at that, though neither Street nor Danville did. Good. They understood that Rohm was a hard man, a senior officer, but he was being a professional, and not an asshole. The good non-comms could smell the difference.

"Partly," Vo said. "Some mechanized Patrol of the Legion is out doing rounds almost constantly, but the area is huge, so HQ Ala contributes as well. We haven't really broadcast the state of things very widely because civilian morale is too unstable. I don't need people angry or devastated right now. Or, at least, more so. The ones on the front lines with us are tough enough. The ones back home are working their asses off to support everyone we locate and ship to them. I've got churches and schools overflowing, but generally people have hot food and a place to sleep."

"Are there many survivors left inside the Death Zone?" Rohm asked.

"A few," Vo grimaced. "Too stubborn to leave. Or hurt and riding it out for now until someone can get to them. Every hunk of electronics within about seventy kilometers of the epicenter shattered under the pulse. Outside that, it was solid static for nearly a day. If someone broke a leg, they had no comm. That's where we come in. For once, we're the good guys. We just have to find them, which will be a pain in this weather, but when it is needed most."

Rohm grimaced back and nodded. Vo could see the man imagining the ground he had overflown ballistically at eighty thousand meters, suddenly up close.

Senior officers like Rohm normally got to spend their careers in climate-controlled bunkers, well away from the nastiness. Vo had little sympathy for the man, but would withhold judgment until Rohm got snow and mud inside his jacket and gloves.

Then they would see how far the rest of the Army needed to come.

"Cutlass Ten, this is Cutlass Six," a voice came out of the speaker by Vo's head. "I've got a heat signature of some sort. Strange."

Vo cocked his head at the tone. The men of the Cutlass team, his Command Patrol from the Headquarters Ala, were generally older. Fire-breathing kids were in First, Second, and Third Ala. The craziest were with the Scouts in Fourth. He wanted veterans close by, available as a fire team or support.

And they weren't supposed to be uncertain. Must be good, whatever it was.

"Pipe the feed here," Vo ordered.

The screen on the front wall had been showing a camera view forward, overlaid with a map based on sensor readings from the other nine skiffs, spread out like a pack of hunting dogs. They were covering ground faster than Fourth Saxon could have, but not at full speed. Just enough to keep their sensors sharp.

A red circle appeared on the map, then turned dotted.

"It was here, but it's gone now, Cutlass Ten," the man said. "Not too sure I didn't imagine it, sir."

Vo grinned. The rest of the men around him did as well, including Rohm, after a second.

The question was never *Are you paranoid?* It was always, *Are you paranoid enough?*

Better to hit on false positives occasionally than to miss the important things, like a man about to stand up from cover, holding an anti-tank missile as you flew by.

Still, it had been nearly ninety minutes of patrol. They were only another twenty from the area of Imperial Palace. Good time for a break. And some hunting.

"Cutlass Six, drop short and ground," Vo ordered. "Deploy your team as a backstop. Everyone else circle wide and establish a perimeter far enough out to hold. Cutlass Ten will drive them to Cutlass Six."

Treat it like a training exercise. Like they had found a looter here. Someone smart and agile might have been able to drop to cover fast enough to disappear if they knew what they were doing. Whoever it was probably hadn't counted on Vo snooping when they vanished, especially not with Danville and Street on his flanks.

Generals weren't supposed to do this sort of thing. And that was the difference between an *Imperial* General and an *Aquitaine* Legate. Declan

Burdge, commander of Fourth Saxon back on *Thuringwell*, had ridden the occasional patrol rounds with the force. Said it kept him young.

Old man was probably still tougher than Vo, even in retirement.

The ten skiffs circled now, a pod of killer whales spotting a wounded seal. Vo pulled his gloves and helmet back on, just as the others did. Rohm hadn't shed any of his.

Hands went to carbines next. Vo and Rohm had revolvers. So did all the men, but they also carried autocarbines. Good for close in work, since Vo didn't plan to swarm a defended trenchline in the clear.

The pilot grounded them in the lee of a swale. Street was out first, followed by Danville. Vo managed to make it out third, mostly by using his bulk to hip-check Decanus Colton Formain, his *Draconarius*, or standard bearer, out of the way.

The sleet was lighter than earlier, but still chewy. If things got a little warmer, it would turn to a very sticky rain, but this was miserable enough. And another good reason to use slug-throwers. This much weather would drastically reduce the effective killing range of a pulse rifle.

Thus the carbines.

Vo drew his revolver and kept it low to his hip. Once everyone was out, he was pleased that Rohm was doing the same. The man might not be comfortable with the noise, in spite of the hearing protectors built into his helmet, but he did understand weapons.

Lancer Terence Aday was out on the far left flank as everyone went to a knee and studied the immediate area. Aday was the baby of the group, being the only Lancer, but he was also a sniper that both Street and Edgar Horst had vouched for. He took up a covering spot with Curator Johan Hoga facing rearwards as his spotter.

In overbuilding his command skiff, Vo had also been able to have a larger squad as well, ten men in addition to himself, instead of the normal total of seven in a fire squad's skiff. There were twelve of them now, with Rohm. Generals weren't supposed to lead in places like this, so Vo let Danville and Street set the pace, each shifting outwards to cover a forward flank, like they always did, with the rest of the men moving carefully behind them.

This might have been a park at one point. Maybe the fabulously-huge back yard of a wealthy Duke or Landgraf, if the pile of wooden and marble ruins behind him represented a manor house rather than a resort. Cutlass Ten had set down in the middle of what might have been a rugby pitch, with shattered buildings like jagged teeth on three sides of them as they moved, and a brief bit of perfectly flat that began to roll into forest some over there.

Deciduous trees had already lost all their leaves in the winter, so the blast had just knocked some down. Evergreens had lost tops everywhere, leaving a mass of downed limbs, but very few trunks in the way. The snow was patchy, but Vo couldn't tell if the trails in it represented critter traffic or vagaries in the terrain itself. Maybe underground pipes for an automatic watering system or something. It hadn't gotten warm enough to melt, unless the few days of sunshine had sublimed everything.

"Cutlass Lead to all units," Vo spoke normally for the microphone in his helmet to pick up. "Cutlass Ten advancing towards Cutlass Six. Everyone stand by for action."

Action.

Ambush, runner, or nothing. You never knew. Best to treat every possible encounter like a training exercise with live weapons. Ten armed skiffs, plus more than seventy men, all heavily armed veterans.

They crossed the empty playing field and got to the edge of the rougher brush. Vo was back about twenty paces from the leaders, working on walking silent, with Rohm close by. The Field Marshal had never stalked a deer, that much was obvious.

Danville went to one knee with a hand in the air. Like Vo, the man held a revolver, with his carbine slung. His free hand went down and touched something, sifted it between fingers.

Vo had instituted his own version of Fourth Saxon's silent language for troops in the field. Learning it from him had moved these men out of their comfort zones. Danville signaled that he had a track.

One person. Small. Moving in the same direction. Fairly recently. The ground was mostly frozen, but there had been some sun to melt things, so maybe the snow was soft enough. Vo was concentrating on the horizon, not the turf. His job was strategic, not tactical.

That's why he had Danville and Street out front. Killers he knew well.

"Cutlass Six, look alive," Danville muttered. "Possible rabbit coming in your direction."

Someone had been here. Cutlass Six had indeed picked up a heat signature through the wind and nastiness before it vanished off their sensors.

Vo studied the area. If the ground behind him had been manicured, this area had been feral. A forest left natural. Probably a favorite hunting ground for the owner. Or a Hundred Acre Wood. You never knew with rich people.

Vo called up the map in his mind and studied it.

"Danville, hold here," he said, just loud enough for the other man to hear on the comm.

The killer nodded and remained down, pistol sniffing ahead.

Vo considered *Thuringwell*. Games in the brush with that rat bastard from Imperial Security. Before Moirrey got the guy. Vo didn't figure he was walking into an ambush, but maybe, just maybe they had found someone's bolthole, like that old mine had turned out to be.

Shattered buildings in all directions from the shockwave of wind and heat that had penetrated the shields overhead. Trees old enough, mature enough, to have been scorched, but not much more. Yeah, this would be where he would want to dig in, on Day Two.

He remembered a small creek on the far side of a rise, possibly fed by an artesian well. Pull supplies from root cellars and wine cellars and ruins. Danville had indicated a small person, so perhaps a teen or a young woman. A few tracks, but looking down, Vo would have missed whatever spoor Danville was on, so some level of field craft.

I would want a little elevation, but not so much that I could be seen. Just enough to keep watch safely.

"Danville, follow the terrain to your right about twenty degrees," Vo said quietly. "Up and into that heavier brush on the second rise. Everyone else, safeties on for now."

Approach this like a scared deer rather than a trapped bear. For now. They could all unleash a fusillade in an eyeblink.

Danville seemed to float across the snow like a wisp. Street shifted, but not as much, spreading himself out into an arc coming around the base of that heavy brush on the little hill. Gunderson and Burana shifted the other direction, opening the net wider on the assumption that their General could hold the space in the center. The five hole.

High praise, from these men. Even if he did have a noisy Field Marshal tromping along close by.

"That's far enough," a high voice called suddenly from the brush on the near part of the rise. "I have a weapon and I'll shoot if you come any closer."

Bingo. Found them, whoever they were.

Since there was no incoming fire, most of the men went to a knee, carbines and pistols up but not shooting, rather than flopping flat in the snow and raining down hell on someone.

Vo joined them, signaling Rohm to do the same. Less threatening that way.

Cutlass Ten itself wasn't in direct sight, but all ten skiff commanders were listening in on the radio and would know what was happening. Plus he could always call in the entire 189th, if he felt the need.

Hell might freeze over first, but he had options.

"We're the 189th Legion," Vo called back, pitching his voice at the spot his mind had flagged as a good place for a slit trench hiding hole. "Rescuing survivors and getting them to evacuation centers."

Long pause. Thinking about it.

"I don't believe you," she yelled.

She. Not a teenage boy. The faintest possibility of being even younger, but there was too much poise in that voice for a twelve year old on their own for a month. Even among the militant aristocrats of *Fribourg*.

Woman. No, girl. Sounded closer to sixteen. His two younger sisters, Zorana and Sonja, had both sounded like that, once upon a time a decade ago. Most likely alone. Probably scared, especially to encounter a bunch of armed men this deep in the Death Zone. Expecting the absolute worst, since the only law to be found around here were the men with him.

Or guns.

Vo stood up and holstered the revolver. He could always quick-draw in a pinch. Dash Mitja had taught him that. Instead, Vo tapped the red sword patch sewn on the outside of his jacket, over his heart. Even on a winter longcoat.

Hell, even on the outside of a suit of heavy EVA armor, according to the regulations.

"I am General Vo *zu* Arlo," he shouted. "*Ritter of the Imperial Household*. Commander of the 189th. I give you my word."

"Arlo?" she said. "The *Aquitaine* cowboy?"

Vo grinned.

Yeah, that might be one way to look at it. *Fribourg* really didn't have the right cultural matrix to grasp Fourth Saxon. They went in for Teutonic Knights, not crazy-ass rednecks.

"Yes, ma'am," he smiled in what he thought of as the right direction.

The sound echoed oddly from all the trees, but would come from about where he was facing.

About where he would put a grenade if she suddenly opened fire on them.

"Why are you here?" she called.

"Trying to save anyone I can," he explained, letting the weight of twenty million souls color his tones. "I would like to evacuate you, if I can. Failing that, we can always drop off some food packs, and maybe a zipbike if you want to leave later."

Frightened? Maybe. Armed? Quite possibly, and not a risk he wanted to push. Someone he would leave in place and check in on occasionally if she turned out to be too mean to save? Absolutely.

Long pause while she thought about it.

"Who are you, really?" she called, just the edge of sarcasm in her tones.

"I am the military commander of this whole damned planet, young lady," Vo snarled back, starting to lose the fine edge of friendly, to the point where he might be willing to let this girl perish here. "You can come out, or I can bloody well leave you here to die on your own. Cutlass force, this is Cutlass Lead. All teams saddle up and prepare to return to your patrol rounds. Cutlass Ten will be along shortly."

Danville was still. *On Point* like a hunting dog. Street glanced over and grinned. The others remained quiet and watched their zones for trouble.

Vo counted slowly to ten, but she didn't speak.

"Decanus Street, I'm cold," Vo announced loud enough to be heard in a duck blind nearby. "Get the men back to the skiff. Flag this area as inhabited for later teams."

Vo turned to Rohm with a frosty smile suited to the cold, nasty weather than hadn't eased up all that much. The man rose, confused, but remained silent. Around them, the men stood and began to crabwalk away from the hill.

They got about twenty meters when a voice came after them.

"Wait," the girl yelled.

Vo paused and turned back halfway. The others settled in, carbines ready and fingers on triggers. It wasn't just the cold that had them on edge.

"That's it?" she called. "You'd just leave me out here to die?"

From the tone, Vo realized he wouldn't have been the first to do so. To abandon her.

"Do you want help?" he called back loudly.

He'd gone through that stage, the angsty despair, with both of his sisters. Fortunately, he'd been on active duty at the time, so he only had to deal with it via letters from home.

"You're the Army," she said. "You're supposed to help people."

"And I can't make you accept my help, ma'am," Vo countered. "I'll have a team swing by every few days and check on you. You can decide when you're ready for rescue."

Vo swung back around and started to walk. There were limits to his patience, and he was at one of them. There was a box of meal packs in the skiff he could toss out the back hatch when they left.

"I'm coming with you," she decided.

Vo counted to three and took a deep breath, controlling his face before he turned. She didn't need his demons. Nobody did.

Vo spotted movement as a petite figure in splotched white and green emerged from the thick brush. She had a pulse rifle with a good scope slung across her back, with her hood pulled up and a scarf around most of her face. Bulky, warm clothing covered her, but the girl was still tiny. Perhaps lithe in the way that Nina Vanek, back on *Auberon*, had been.

At least three men had weapons pointed at her as she moved forward with open hands. Vo waited. Rohm shifted a few steps further away, but that was his training. The man handled himself professionally.

"You would have left me?" she asked in a small, hard voice as she got to within a few meters.

"I have the rest of this planet to try to secure," Vo bit the words off. "I don't have time to deal with a hard case and can always drop supplies until you change your mind."

"I said I'm coming with you," the small woman fired back angrily.

Vo would have guessed her to be more Nada Zupan's physique, although not quite so tall. Still probably slim and lanky, though.

And tough enough, resourceful enough to have survived in the Death Zone for six weeks in the worst weather in a generation.

She studied his face closely. Unlike many of the others, Vo wasn't wearing a scarf. He was rethinking that as his nose got cold.

"You really are Arlo," she observed. "But you're no Prince Charming."

"So I've been told," he replied. "Who are you?"

"Victoria Ames," she said, chin coming up in challenge.

Vo studied the petite woman. Girl. Sixteen looked about right. A hard sixteen, too. The winter gear she was wearing was comparable to his team's, though. And fit her well.

"You didn't acquire that gear recently, did you, Miss Ames?" Vo hazarded a guess.

The clues were there, if you wanted to interpret them that way. He had seen too many survivors who had emerged with nothing but the clothes on their back, or what they had been able to scrounge up from ruined stores and shattered houses. Vo had lost count of the number of cases of frostbite he had seen treated in the last six weeks.

The parts of the girl's face he could see went white for a second, and then flushed red. Not a blush, though. The eyes were too hard. This was anger, but not directed at him.

At the world, perhaps.

The chin stayed up, and not just because she had to tilt her head so far back to stare him in the face. The girl probably had a hand on the Fleet Centurion for height, and still weighed a stone less. There was dirt on her face, and hard, blue eyes.

"No. And?" she demanded.

Vo shook his head and stared walking. They were out of the rough brush and on the edge of the clearing where Cutlass Ten waited, the turret aimed in this direction but not tracking hard on the girl. Not currently, anyway.

"Street, mount up," Vo ordered, glancing at Ames and indicating she should fall in with the rest.

It wasn't the least bit accidental that three of his men shifted their attention inward towards the girl as they moved, but nobody was acting aggressive. They had all rescued enough crazed, scarred, or broken people. Angry ones were the easiest to handle.

At the skiff, Vo turned to her again.

"Is your weapon safetied, Ames?" he asked, like he would a rookie trooper on her first patrol.

"Yes," she snapped back, mildly offended. "Clean, locked, and two pair power packs in my belt, too, General."

Several men grinned. You could see it above the scarves when the eyes crinkled.

"Good," Vo said. "Rack your weapon to starboard inside and grab a jumpseat."

Vo preceded her into the belly of the beast and located the mug of coffee locked into that cupholder and waiting patiently for him to return. He needed warm.

After a moment he chalked up to shock, Victoria Ames climbed up the steps and entered his command skiff, pulling her rifle off her back under a number of very watchful eyes and putting it next to several other weapons. She looked around, and took a seat diagonal from Vo. Close to the hatch, but across the hatch from him. There weren't a lot of seats back here, but enough that she could have space on both sides as everyone else sat down.

"Cutlass Ten, this is Arlo," he said to the ceiling. "We're mounted up. All units back to patrol."

He studied the young woman for a moment. Poised. Angry. Frightened. Twitchy.

"Danville," Vo said. "Grab Trooper Ames some coffee. Cream? Sugar?"

Had he tossed a live squid into the middle of the floor, the looks he got from everyone, from Ames to Rohm, wouldn't have been more shocked.

"Trooper, General?" Rohm sputtered. "Are you mad?"

"Grand Army of the Republic is about half female, Field Marshal Rohm," Vo smirked back. "The meaner, tougher, smarter half, based on my experience."

Danville had shrugged after a moment and handed the woman a fresh mug, pointing to the supplies nearby to adulterate it.

Ames watched with hooded eyes as she sipped the black heat. Vo largely ignored her, concentrating on his own mug, at least until she decided to speak. Around them, the men did the same, wary, but relaxing a notch.

Vo pointed at three of the men as he looked at her.

"Field Marshal Rohm," Vo commented. "Decanus Iakov Street, team commander. Curator Hans Danville, team scout. We'll debrief you later in more detail, but I have one more question first. How long have you been living in that hole?"

Again the scowl. Visible this time because she had thrown the hood back and lowered the scarf. She could be pretty, but she was tense as the skiff lifted and began to move. However, she had also buckled herself in and didn't jump too hard. Gunderson or Ozawa would have probably tackled her if she made a suspicious move right now.

"Fourteen months," she challenged, waiting for the obvious next question. That other shoe to drop.

Vo nodded and went back to his coffee. Ames would talk, when she was ready. He had gone through this with Zorana and Sonja, in their time.

Silence descended, broken only by the hums and bangs of the skiff and the heaters.

"That's it?" Ames continued.

"That's it," Vo agreed. "We're headed into the area that used to be the Imperial Palace, and then will return to our laager in about five hours. You can eat with us until then. We'll drop you off at a processing center for survivors so they can get you shelter and a chance to start a new life."

It was a speech he had repeated too often for one lifetime.

"There's no place for me," Ames said. "I have no family, nowhere to go."

Vo couldn't tell if she was speaking to him or herself. Zorana, after she had divorced the grifter Karol, before she found Andrej, the dentist, had sounded like that.

"What do you want from this world?" Vo challenged, sounding like he had then.

Somehow, Vo wasn't surprised when she reached a hand back and caresses the armored wall of the skiff, as if to reassure her.

"This," she admitted in a tight, carefully-controlled voice. "I want to be a soldier."

The eyes held a challenge when they came back up to look at him. The men stirred, but held their peace.

"A girl?" Rohm interjected with disbelief. "Serving in the Army?"

"Why not?" Ames turned her fury on the Field Marshal as she pointed at Vo. "He says they serve in *Aquitaine*. The tougher, meaner half of *that* army. His words."

Vo grinned. So did Danville and Street. Probably remembering Lady Moirrey killing the general from Imperial Security during the coup, by firing a shot right past the Emperor's ear.

"Women do not serve," Rohm pronounced, heartily offended.

"Why not?" Vo asked.

Again, tossing a live squid into the room would have left things calmer.

"Are you serious, *zu* Arlo?" Rohm challenged. It was the voice of aristocracy, talking about *those* people from beyond the Dragon Gates. People like Vo. "Are you deranged?"

"No, worse," Vo smiled serenely at the man. "I'm in charge."

CHAPTER XXX

Em had considered saying something. Arguing with her, at least privately. Putting his foot down about propriety and image.

In the end, he remained silent, understanding that it was more important that she stand here with him on the flag bridge as they dropped out of JumpSpace. Because these men would take that image, and build upon it in their memories. Make it her legend.

Every King and Emperor of *Fribourg* for five centuries had commanded naval forces in battle at some point in their career. Lady Casey was no different, even if she had served under Jessica in the *RAN*. These men surrounding them had never imagined that a woman would lead them. Command them.

Only Tom Provst could legitimately make that claim, before now. It was one of the reasons that Em had put him in charge over more senior admirals. That, and to give the man a reason to continue living.

Casey certainly looked the part today, standing silent and quietly proud next to him. The man who was her new personal tailor had done her up a pair of soft, black, leather boots, knee-high in back and with a semi-rigid knee-guard in front that came up to mid-thigh as a shield when kneeling or in close combat. The heel was no more than his dress shoes, and the finish was matte, instead of polished. They looked like the sort of thing he would expect on a combat marine, under the plates of field armor.

Martial, rather than political. Both her and the tailor were making a statement of Lady Casey, the Emperor Karl VIII, as a warrior, and not a princess.

Casey wore a bodysuit in an off-white that verged on the lightest gray, with a darker-gray hexagonal pattern about three centimeters on the flat sides. The front crossed over, double-breasted, with a seam up the right side of her chest, so that the red sword over her heart was not obstructed or broken. Raglan sleeves in black mirrored her boots. Her sword belt, done in a glossy, black leather, clasped onto a large, steel ring, set on her left hip-bone instead of the center, and split three ways, one across, and then over and under the point of her left hip, anchoring the sword she had chosen to wear today.

Over that, the new Emperor wore a black and gray jacket with epaulettes and fringe, plus lacing on the short, standing collar and the cuffs. It did not denote a rank or an emblem, but still contributed to the overall military feel. The front could be closed with fourteen silver buttons and it came down to a diamond front, flat across the back at normal length for a jacket and then plunging to a point just above her knees.

Her only color today was the maroon cloak of a *Ritter of the Imperial Household*, tied at her throat and with the Imperial Eagle on the front. Her face was washed out, but even Em could see the careful effort she and Moirrey had put in, to color her into something normal. The pain was still there, new lines etched into a face too-young for that sort of hurt, but images of her taken today would show her strength and resolve, drawn from both sides of the family.

Em looked over at the countdown clock on a nearby screen. He drew a breath as it approached zero and prepared to begin giving orders, but Casey silenced him with a hard look.

He held his peace. Casey was one of the few people left who could give him orders, if she felt the need. Apparently, she had.

"*Indianapolis*, this is Centurion *zu* Wiegand. I have the flag," she said into the monstrous silence that had fallen. "All hands to battle stations."

Many of the men looked up in surprise at her voice, but shocked mouths emitted no sound. A siren whooped quietly, but everyone was already prepared. Poised.

Living in an unknown future.

Emergence.

"Captain Kingston," Casey ordered in a distant, firm voice. "You will raise the Imperial Standard."

"Aye, sir," the man replied from speakers after a beat.

Like the rest of them, Reif Kingston was adjusting as he went. It helped that Casey acted and sounded like Joh would have, had he been standing on this deck. That same, solid conviction. A leader that had seen first-line combat. A warrior who had even outdone her father and been wounded in action, however slight the injury had been at *Trusski*. It was still one ribbon Joh had never earned.

One many sailors never earned. But it had already endeared her all the more to these men.

Em watched Casey expand herself to fill the room. He had no other way to describe it as she breathed out and turned to study every man in sight.

"The flag has been raised, Your Majesty," Kingston came back a second later.

Em approved of the way Casey nodded. More legend. Her chin came up and she drew and released a heavy, loud breath, as if she could feel the entire weight of an empire on her shoulders.

She did.

"All ahead full," she ordered.

They had spoken in private, but Em had no doubts that this woman would prevail. He had seen it aboard *Auberon*, when he had first arrived to find Lady Casey wearing the uniform of the woman who had formerly been his greatest foe. Seen it again and again on the flight home, where she spent half of every day with Em's naval staff, and half with Wald, planning for how to create an entire new government after the last one had died.

Fribourg was a culture of paper. Physical objects that could be retained and preserved for centuries. Destroyed in fire. Oh, certainly there were copies stored in secured facilities, frequently the kind bored into old mountains, but paper.

More important than the papers were the bureaucrats who moved that paper around. Who gave form and purpose to need, communicating the wishes of the Crown and the House of Dukes, and to a lesser extent the House of the People, and forming those commands into policies and interpretations.

All that was gone. If twenty million people had died, more than two million of them had served the government in some direct way. That loss would be the most grievous. Epochs of experience lost in an afternoon.

Casey and Wald would have to rebuild it from nothing except her will and his experience. Em did not envy them the task, but he also couldn't think of two people better suited to pull it off. Especially with the help of the military, in the form of himself, Tom Provst, and *zu* Arlo.

And Jessica, out there holding the wall against all comers, as Nils Kasum had once said.

A moment of heavy silence had passed.

"Contact *IFV Firehawk*, Captain Kingston," Casey ordered. "I will go aboard her with the Grand Admiral for an update. After that, I will return here and then descend to the surface with my Household and *Indianapolis*'s color guard."

"Yes, Your Majesty," he replied.

She turned and Em could see the pain in her eyes. Nobody else was close enough to see the muscles in her jaw bunch as she clenched her teeth and tried not to grind them.

Em smiled softly at her and nodded. They both understood that this was all for show. For her legend, and how it would be communicated to the entire *Fribourg Empire* tomorrow.

There would be a coronation ceremony, one of these days, but that would be a formal event, filled with pomp and ceremony. They would probably require at least a year, if not three, just to figure out how to do it, given all the history destroyed below them.

But the woman he thought of as his niece would take command of the Empire today.

CHAPTER XXXI

Vo walked towards the mess hall with a sour grimace that was more than just the fresh, morning piles of snow everywhere.

In his hand, he held a slab with a message from Borel appraising him of a *Surprise Inspection* that would take place in about two hours, the shuttle already having begun the descent from orbit. It was a stupid way to code a message. Anyone with half a brain would know that there were only two people who could give him orders on this planet.

One of them had gone off to get the other.

So she was home. And coming here. Shortly.

Around him, the quad was alive with men moving rapidly every direction. Getting ready. The landing pad was all of ten minutes away by skiff, so Reese had apparently let him sleep to his normal time rather than waking him up.

Vo stomped through the last of the snow to the door, kicked his boots a few times to get the sticky white off, and pulled the heavy wooden panel open.

It had been a restaurant specializing in Hispanic food in the time before. A family-owned joint that had been working a regular day at the moment when their home across town was destroyed and they were fated to survive. The family had moved in here.

And volunteered to serve the 189th food when Vo arrived.

Borel had assigned a team to help, but Melina still ran her restaurant with an iron fist. The only change for her had been to expand operations to run twenty-four hours, the Army never sleeping at this point. She had six new assistant managers now, Army food and catering experts, but Melina was absolutely in charge.

She greeted him with a warm smile as he walked in. A table was always reserved for Vo and his staff in the corner closest to the kitchen. The rest of the main room was tapering off from a mad rush, so presumably the inspection warning had come in hours ago and the men still here were going to be off, as soon as they shoveled home the excellent breakfast burritos that Melina's husband Thurman specialized in.

Vo waded through the close-packed tables as Melina filled a mug with coffee and sat it on his table. Cohort Centurion Alan Katche, the Primus Pilus of the 189th, was already there, reading something on his own slab. He was a wiry man, with curly dark hair and eyes that seemed black at times. He was average height that always seemed taller until Vo got close enough that he was suddenly looking downwards at the man. Seated, he still looked physically bigger than he was.

Vo rested his slab on the side of the table and pulled out the chair.

"You heard?" Vo asked as he sat.

"Two hours ago," Katche replied with a grin. "Got everyone in motion. Figured you would be up all night with them, so you needed your beauty sleep."

It had turned into a running joke between them. Katche always explained the reaction of women around Vo as strength and ruggedness. Which sounded way better than tough and ugly. At least on paper.

Beauty sleep was obviously critically important.

"Anything I need to sign off on?" Vo queried.

"Only my execution papers," Katche laughed.

Vo joined him. In an emergency, all rules went out the window. The men were forced to make their best guesses as to what would be judged right, at least in the view of the lawyers who would come along later and second-guess everything in the calm leisure of hindsight.

Vo had long-since lost count of the number of things he had done or ordered in the last month that the new Emperor might find questionable. Still, she wasn't squeamish. He knew that much from the little time he had spent around her aboard *Auberon*.

But this was a much bigger arena. And Vo really hadn't spent that much time around the woman before.

"Hell, you were just following orders, Alan," Vo countered. "I'll demand that they execute me first, so that you have to take over."

"I should probably put in my retirement papers, then," the Primus Pilus chuckled. "Fishing sounds good about now."

"Take me with you?" Vo asked.

"I'm pretty sure that would make me an accomplice, Vo," Katche said.

Vo started to say something, but Nicola, Melina and Thurman's middle daughter, arrived at that moment with a plate. Thirty centimeter tortillas, homemade, stuffed with eggs, cheese, peppers, and meat. Vo would never go hungry with this place intact.

"Thank you," Vo said as the girl smiled with a blush and fled.

For the briefest moment, he wondered how hard it would be to configure a set of mobile kitchen vehicles to Melina's standards, so he could hire her to accompany the 189th into the field.

"Details I need?" Vo asked as he grabbed the burrito and took a bite.

"You've got time to eat, shower, and dress," Katche said. "Grand Admiral specified field uniforms, rather than pretty. We have the new palace in Strasbourg being prepared for her, but the note says she's going to stay with us here in Mejico for a bit."

Vo let a raised eyebrow suffice as he chewed. Katche shrugged.

"Maybe we've screwed up enough that we're about to be relieved," Alan said. "Dunno. If she's mad enough, they've got Rohm right here to take over."

Vo shrugged in turn. Too many unknowns. This hadn't been rolling logs in a river. It had been running across the backs of angry alligators in a swamp. This was the first time he and Alan Katche had actually been in the same room in more than a week, with every Ala assigned a different slice of the Death Zone to supervise and too little beauty sleep for any of them.

In two hours, he would know his fate. The Grand Admiral was coming. Lady Casey as Emperor Karl VIII would be with him.

What was the worst she could do to him at this point?

The room falling utterly quiet nearly caused Vo to reach for his pistol, even in the middle of his own base. Alan Katche's eye grew huge, staring over Vo's shoulder, before coming back to meet Vo's gaze, but it was surprise, and not aggression.

Vo glanced back and saw the cause of the commotion. He nearly laughed, but that would be inappropriate. This wasn't *Aquitaine*.

Dash still should have been here to see it.

Iakov Street was walking closer. In his wake, Trooper Ames followed. She was a skinny girl, as he had guessed, and tall, like Nada Zupan, but she still had hips and a chest. Someone had found a uniform for her, but it just emphasized her shape by being too tight across the torso and hips, in order to fit her shoulders and waist.

The men of the Headquarters Ala dropped into shocked silence as they registered the intruder, and processed that she was wearing the same uniform that they were. Vo just grinned at Katche and swallowed the bite in his mouth.

Dead silence.

Street was milking it for all he could, walking like a ghost to stand next to the table and fall into parade rest next to Katche. Ames did the same, probably about as well as most of the veterans in the room.

The Primus Pilus looked both directions, but remained silent. He did cock his head, while looking at Vo expectantly.

Vo looked up.

"Decanus," Vo said solemnly.

He sipped some coffee and reveled in the situation. Little had brought him joy in the last two months. He probably shouldn't be enjoying this as much as he was.

"*zu* Arlo," Street said in a voice louder than necessary, considering the distance between them, and all the listening ears in the room. "Considering the mission today, what special orders do you have for my team?"

Vo swore that he could see men leaning closer, all around the room, afraid that they might miss something. Not every face was turned this way, but enough ears were cocked to follow.

Casey is going to do it to Wachturm. I can do it to you men. Welcome to the future.

Vo fixed Ames with a sharp stare. She returned it in spades, challenging him as hard as any bantam ever had. A pin might have fallen, several tables over.

"None, Decanus," Vo said simply. "Cutlass Force will turn out for inspection by the Grand Admiral when he arrives."

"I see," Street replied after a moment. "Very good, sir."

Vo caught the faintest hint of a grin on his face as Street turned to Ames.

"You heard the general, Trooper Ames," he said, again louder than necessary, but not harsh. "Fall in."

Street walked past her and began to wend his way through the seated mob, Ames in his wake and all heads following, like the Pied Piper.

Alan Katche watched them exit, and then turned back to Vo as a roar of voices erupted.

"You planning to put her in First Ala?" the Primus Pilus said over the din.

Vo shook his head, letting the grin out, just a little.

"Then I don't really care, sir," Katche said.

He rose and departed, mug in hand, leaving Vo alone with half a burrito and a few sips of coffee.

Already, Vo was in better humor. He wondered what the Emperor would say, because Cutlass Ten would be the team closest to her when she stepped off that shuttle.

And what was the worst she could do to him?

CHAPTER XXXII

Casey had steeled herself with the sort of stubbornness that had served to ward off a coup. Both the Wiegand and Alkaev families were known for that. Still, she nearly lost control.

From the air, the only things recognizable on the screen of the shuttle were the contours of the land they were flying over. Lake Zurich. Strasbourg. Rivers and mountain ranges that had been too tenacious to fail.

Cities closer in were gone. Not damaged like a groundquake had struck.

Gone.

Knocked to kindling by the blast, and then covered over with nearly a meter of snow in places.

No. Her home was gone. Erased.

The pilot had added a navigational overlay to the screen, mapping what was with what had been.

That only made it worse, as she realized that they were about to fly over the place that been the Imperial Palace. A lake appeared to be forming now, as the ground itself had been compressed into a shallow bowl by the bomb.

Casey sucked a hard breath and fought to keep the tears at bay.

Moirrey noticed, from her spot across the aisle. Everyone else was a safe distance away from them, including Em, talking to the pilot on a headset.

Moirrey reached a hand out. Casey took it and squeezed, aware that the tiny woman would offer all the strength she had. Whatever Casey needed. It would keep her going.

There was a world to rebuild, and nothing in the history books about how to go about doing something like this. But none of those books covered a woman seated on that throne, either. And she wasn't about to give up that.

Karl VIII. She had faced down a coup and a revolution. Fought off an assassin in the shape of a *Sentient* warship. Become a warrior.

She could do this.

Em removed his headset and fixed her with his gaze for a moment, framing the words in his mind before he spoke.

"We'll be on the ground in sixty seconds," he finally announced simply. "Arlo and parts of the 189th will be meeting us. Are you positive that you don't want to move to Strasbourg and set up your Household there?"

"Em, the entire Household, if you want to call it that, consists of me, Moirrey, and Vibol," she retorted. "Plus whatever guards you or Vo add. How much harder will it be for them to recruit all the civilian people some folks will expect me to maintain? How much safer would I be in the middle of a Legion, as opposed to a town overflowing with refugees and citizens who might be terminally offended that a woman has the audacity to wear a crown?"

"I had to ask, Your Majesty," he said. "*zu* Arlo has been running things for six weeks in my absence. The usual troublemakers have filed the expected complaints about his behaviors and decisions, which I am largely ignoring for now. But things we'll have to deal with eventually. Once you get settled."

"I'll be settled by being with those men," Casey said as she pointed at the invisible ground. She could feel the edges of fire start to burn inside her. Up until this moment, the last two days had left her numb. Flying over what her mind was already calling Lake Werder had broken something loose inside her. "Living with them. Being protected by them. I've watched the transmission that Vo broadcast planet-wide after you'd left, and I can only imagine the impact it had on the populace. I need to be here now, next to him. Vo *zu* Arlo is the foundation of my crown, my standing with the people of *St. Legier*, just as you and Provst will anchor the fleet for me. Do you understand?"

Casey was concerned by the way Em's face clouded for a second. Then she realized.

Emmerich *zu* Wachturm, Grand Admiral and Duke, was thinking about this from a military standpoint. As he should. That was his job.

But this was a larger problem. It had a military aspect, she recognized, but it was also a civilian thing. And a human issue.

Werder had died. *St. Legier* had suffered a grievous blow. *The Eldest* was perhaps expecting it to be a mortal one.

Perhaps that was the creature's intent. She could not, would not let it succeed.

Over my dead body.

"I think so, Your Majesty," Em finally admitted after a long beat.

Maybe he understood. Maybe not. That didn't matter. Em would support her, if she could convince him that she knew what she was doing.

It was on her shoulders. And Vo's. Two accidental heroes.

She would live down in the mud and ugliness of the place that the locals were calling *The Death Zone*, because she needed these people to support her. Uphold her. Not just today, but a year from now. A decade from now. A generation from now.

Retain the Empire itself when someone came along and demanded that a woman stand aside. That they return to a past that had already failed, rather than move forward into a future where the Peace with *Aquitaine* could hold, while she fought the war with *Buran*.

Centurion Kasimira *zu* Wiegand. Emperor Karl VIII of *Fribourg, by Grace of God.*

Casey was willing to live within the corset of responsibility that came with that mantle because it came with power. But she could dream of a better world, if she could just hold the locals together for a decade. If she could bring her father's dream to fruition. Win the Peace. Save the galaxy.

All that in a flash of insight. Casey hadn't been able to articulate it, even to herself, until now. She needed Arlo. Needed his strength. Em didn't understand the power of Vo's words, the spell Casey was sure had been woven around the people fighting to save the world around them. As it had her.

On the screen, they were coming in to land. She had lost track of it consciously, but tracked it in the back of her mind.

The 189th had cleared a chunk of the landing field of starships, and filled the space with tanks and ground craft instead. Casey could see a lone bulk freighter, the kind that hauled grain between worlds, unloading into a line of trucks, over in another corner of the starport.

The shuttle came to earth with a soft lurch. Casey was used to hard landing decks on ships, or concrete runways, so the ground underneath the ship compacting under the shuttle's weight threw her mentally off balance just a little. Reminded her that she was on the surface of a planet again, for the first time in over a year.

She was an alien in this place. Princess Kasimira had gone off on her adventure to *Aquitaine* two years ago. A stranger had returned wearing her flesh.

Around her, the shuttle began its shutdown sequence, engines falling silent, unneeded. It had served its purpose, a steed bringing her to the field of a new battle.

Casey unbuckled her harness and rose, stretching shoulders and back that had gone rigid with the tension of the last few hours. Moirrey joined her a moment later, as did Em and the several men that had accompanied the flight. Torsten Wald had remained so silent on the flight, wrapped up in his reports and notes in a corner behind her, that him standing and smiling grimly at her was a surprise, like a ghost had just materialized on the deck.

Casey drew a breath and brought herself back from squirreling in on herself. That hadn't been acceptable before. It had even less place in her life now.

"Em, Moirrey, Torsten. Thank you," she said.

There were so many other things to say. She needed to remember to say them.

On the viewscreen, a swarm of vehicles moved closer. Skiffs and tanks coming in to protect her.

Men placing themselves between her and any danger. She would never again be alone, for good or ill. Casey pulled her cloak a little tighter around her shoulders and turned to the hatch.

Em was there already, along with Moirrey and several marines from *Indianapolis*. Casey moved to join them on silent feet.

She had put her foot down against a big, formal production here. These men needed to be doing their jobs, not spending a week welcoming her home with bands and banquets.

Em watched a small screen by the airlock for a few seconds, grunted to himself, and then triggered the switch. Both doors opened and a small ramp extended.

Grand Admiral *zu* Wachturm went down first, his black day uniform and matching overcoat a stark contrast to the snow everywhere.

Moirrey *zu* Kermode followed, her maroon cloak billowing out as her feet churned. She looked like blood had pooled, when she came to rest next to Em, turned sideways for Casey to walk past.

Torsten completed the set in a blue and gray civilian suit, three less likely cohorts she could barely imagine, but they stood in front of a line of troops drawn up in cold weather gear.

Casey sniffed once. The cold, bitter air had almost no smell, but it was home. Her home. The place she had come from. The world she was returning to.

She stepped into the small vestibule of the airlock and then out onto the ramp. The men drawn up on both sides were at attention. Not many, as she had demanded. Just enough that they could see her and report back to their friends. Not so many that work wasn't getting done.

Arlo was there. General Vojciech *zu* Arlo, Commander, 189th Legion, Expeditionary.

Standing 181cm tall, Casey was used to being as tall as most men who weren't immediate blood relatives. Em was taller, her father's size at 186cm, but Arlo was a giant. Two meters even. And he massed easily twice what she did, even with the muscles she had developed from acrobatics and dancing with sabers.

She stopped at the bottom of the ramp and turned to face him and the men he had arrayed behind him. Faces she recognized from the Color Guard of the old 189th Division. The men who had helped Vo save the Empire the first time.

His face might have been carved into the stone of a mountain by an ancient team of artisans. He was not a pretty man. Not even ruggedly, compellingly handsome, in the way her father had been and her uncle remained. He wasn't a troll, either, though, as much as he might call himself one, but perhaps a mountain man, come down to the valley in the spring for supplies and to have his beard shaved off, before returning to the wilderness for another year.

Cast in bronze. But she knew that. A force of utter nature that would not be brooked nor denied. Nothing less stubborn than him would have managed as much as the reports she had spent a day reading suggested. And he was a poet underneath, which she had never even guessed about the man. His written words gave him away, so she had gone back and listened to the welcoming speech he had given to the 189th when those men volunteered to serve with him nearly a year ago.

Truly, a leader.

He had brown hair, cropped shorter than would be comfortable in this weather. Brown eyes almost light enough to be called hazel. Lines that might have been etched by those same stone masons as could have immortalized him into a mountain.

"*zu* Arlo," she said with a welcoming nod, speaking louder than necessary over the soft wind, and enough that the men behind him would hear.

"Your Majesty," he rumbled back at her.

Casey looked at the others here to welcome her. Blinked in mild shock when she realized that one of those men was wearing the rank tabs of an Army Field Marshal. Then she recognized Arald Rohm's grim face, and wondered how that particular man had come to be *here*. Em had probably not gotten through that story well enough to send it on to her.

She made a note to ask, later.

A bigger shock was clear down at the far end of the first row, at the opposite end from Rohm.

There was a girl in uniform. Standing at attention with the men. As if nothing was wrong with the world at all.

Such women were common in *Aquitaine*, where they were encouraged to serve. Casey had had to take the Imperial Throne itself in order to be allowed so simple a thing. She made a note to ask there, as well.

That story intrigued her far more than Arald Rohm.

"It's cold and nasty out here, General," Casey brought her eyes back to Arlo, towering over her like a fortress. "Let's get inside so you can brief me on what I need to know. And the men can get warm."

Vo nodded to her and stepped out of line. She felt like she was standing next to an oak tree as he glanced down and back at her, and then walked down the two lines of troops escorting her.

Looking back, Casey saw Em, Torsten, and Moirrey, joined by Rohm and two other men she didn't know on sight. A transport skiff had been parked close by.

Arlo went in immediately and stepped to one side, so Casey followed. The interior had the feel of a staff car rather than something that soldiers rode into battle. The Navy didn't waste much time or money on comfort in jumpseats, so she presumed that the Army would be the same way. Instead, these were leather seats with good padding to ride comfortably. A ceiling high enough that even Arlo was able to stand upright as he had walked to a nearby seat.

Quickly, everyone was in and buckled.

"All set, pilot," Vo said aloud.

The skiff moved to hover, and then transitioned to flight in a smooth curve. How one was supposed to transport an Emperor, she supposed, rather than how the Army did it.

Vo pointed out the others.

"Field Marshal Arald Rohm, on detached duty," Vo said ambiguously. "Alan Katche, Primus Pilus of the 189th. Reese Borel, Command Decurion of the 189th."

Casey smiled at them. Rohm's story she would get soon enough. Katche and Borel were Vo's right and left hands, from the reports she had consumed. It was Vo, that she was gambling on.

"Grand Admiral *zu* Wachturm," Casey stressed the new honorific, granting her uncle the right to truly speak for the throne, rather than the assumption that decisions made in haste and emergency would be acceptable later.

"Torsten Wald, Chief of Deputies," Casey continued. Civilian head of Karl VIII's government. Her only voice, until the House of Dukes could be reconstituted, and the House of the People re-elected.

"Moirrey *zu* Kermode of *Ramsey*," the Emperor concluded.

Jessica's Evil Engineering Gnome needed no more introduction to these men, but they needed to remember that she could also speak for the throne.

Like Vo could. The galaxy had turned into the strangest place Casey could have imagined, once upon a time.

Now she just had to take ownership of that future, and shape it into the place she needed it to be.

PART 4

EXPEDITION

CHAPTER XXXIII

The bridge of the Galactic Survey Cruiser (GSC) *Ballard* was quiet, this evening. Watching from the darkness, as they did.

Hide with pride.

Normally, Kanda would have happily sent one of the smaller escorts, like *CP-406* or even *CS-405* into the breach here. GSC *Ballard* was not a warship, even if she had guns. She was too valuable to risk in front-line confrontations with hostile navies, except in the worst emergencies.

Like holding an entire flank for Jessica at *Thuringwell*.

However, GSC *Ballard* had something neither Glenn nor Kosnett had: the best Science Officer in the fleet, bar none. Senior Centurion Elzbet Aukley.

This was not a mission to locate stations and defenses around a hostile planet, prior to a simple raid. Almost any of the corvettes could have handled that task just as easily.

No, this required an *artisté*.

They weren't here to merely locate every ship that might shoot back. Jessica wanted to kill things. To unleash the merciless wrath of Tom Kigali and Alber' d'Maine. To have the metaphorical gutters running red with freshly-spilled blood in *Stanovoy's* orbit.

To do that, Jessica needed to know where every single vessel in orbit was located, where it was headed, and how quickly it could escape the devastation *First Expeditionary* was about to wreak on them, including a simple survey cruiser. Kanda and her crew owed *Buran* a debt of pain as well. Being explorers and not berserkers didn't lessen the fury they felt at what those people had done to *St. Legier*.

It just made it that much more important that the rage be tempered for now. Held at bay while scanners listened and Elzbet marked vectors. A fox, waiting at the edge of the barnyard as the chickens settled into their coops.

Ballard was about four light hours out from *Stanovoy*. They would miss some targets, just because the signals intelligence they gathered was that far out of date. However, there was nothing down in closer that suggested any sort of military awareness.

This was a civilian system in all the ways that mattered. There was a rich asteroid belt, thicker than the one once reputed to share the home system. A couple of planets down in the habitable zone. A few lesser gas giants farther out in the cold.

Seventeen stations in orbit, most of them commercial ones of one sort or another. Truck stops. Foundries. Chandleries for small ships that mined the rocks left here during planetary formation.

One hundred and ninety-three signals indicating a ship big enough to make it to orbit, or to move around in deep space. Those tended to be clustered around the stations. Picking up. Dropping off. Hanging around waiting their turn for docking.

Chickens settling to roost.

"Time?" Kanda called.

Elzbet checked her boards and looked up. Every sensor was quietly drinking as fast as it could, feeding everything to the woman seated at the sciences station, a warrior no less fierce than one of d'Maine's Goddesses.

"Two minutes," Elzbet replied.

"All hands, stand by for maneuver orders," Kanda called over the comm.

They were already at battle stations. Had been since they dropped out of JumpSpace three hours ago. Waiting.

In two minutes, the rest of the battle squadron would join them, led by *Vanguard*. At this point, every minute of delay meant that someone farther out might have noticed *Ballard*, hiding in the darkness, figured out what she was doing, and run down to the authorities at *Stanovoy* to warn people there was a wolf in the hills.

Jessica wasn't even waiting to review the targeting plan as laid out by

Elzbet. That was how much the Fleet Centurion trusted them. Trusted her.

And First Expeditionary wasn't going in as a formation. Elzbet was routing every warship onto a different vector and orbit, one that maximized the amount of targets they could hit, with the minimum amount of maneuver. As long as no new *Buran* warships suddenly cropped up, and none had been seen, this would be a mob action.

A chime drew Kanda's attention.

"*Vanguard* and *VI Victrix*," Elzbet announced. "Transmitting now."

In seconds, the rest arrived. *VI Ferrata. CA-264. CE-401. CE-402. CE-403. CM-404. CS-405. CP-406. II Augusta.* Each got a file, acknowledged it, and blinked out of existence.

"We're last," Elzbet said quietly.

"You have Tactical," Kanda said.

She watched Elzbet turn to Centurion Lazlo Moushian across the gap.

"Pilot, your course has been laid in," Elzbet growled. "Take us into Jump."

CHAPTER XXXIV

Jessica almost felt bereft, sitting on the flag bridge of the Heavy Dreadnaught *Vanguard*. This wouldn't be a fleet action. She wasn't sending well-constructed maneuver plans and firing solutions to the ships around her, guiding them in. *Ballard* had handled that. And done it well, from what she had reviewed.

No, today she was seated in her flag bridge with Enej still off to her right, rather than directly across the table from her, as if Casey would join them at any moment and take her space with a warm smile. Around the two of them sat the rest of Enej's flag team, men and women watching their boards but mostly silent.

Vanguard was going in alone. First. *Warlord of Battle.*

She knew Denis and Nina had been looking forward to today with something approaching glee. Aukley had spotted two Hammerheads in orbit, escorts roughly the size of the old destroyer class Jessica had commanded a lifetime ago. *Rubicon* or *Vigilant*. Smaller than *Brightoak*, but not by much. Still, more than enough to take on one of the corvettes.

Completely out of their league against an Expeditionary Cruiser, to say nothing of a Heavy Dreadnaught coming out of JumpSpace.

The countdown clock ticked to zero. Nina's targeting channel was routed down to the flag bridge, not because Jessica would get involved but so she could listen. Nina was in charge until something happened that required a bigger decision.

"Gunnery, we'll be bringing him down our centerline," Nina called. "I want him hammered with the Bubble Gun as soon as you have a lock. Follow that with the Type-3's into his bow and then the second targeting location designated. You have your other targets for the Type-4's in firing sequence, with *Anna* and *Laura* turrets targeting the station itself. I want the platform knocked down hard before he can get off any missiles. *Rachel* and *Zebra* to go after that pair of what look like big bulk freighters waiting in close orbit to dock."

"Roger that," Centurion Afolayan replied.

He had been with them since the early days and knew how to lay the guns the way Nina demanded.

Jessica gritted her teeth rather than override. She knew what Denis and Nina were up to. Had even approved it in the general planning sessions. But it made her nervous to actually try.

However, if they could succeed…

"Emergency Bridge, you have control of the waist and aft Type-3's until I override," Nina continued. "Same rules. I have laid in the targeting sequence I want pursued, but the Gunner is going to be facing forward and doing brain surgery. I want you splattering things. You're good at that."

"Acknowledged, Tactical."

Jessica could hear the blush in Tobias Brewster's voice as he replied. She flashed back nearly a decade to the time she had chewed that kid's ass after that first, disastrous training run at *Simeon*. The young man had redeemed himself at *Qui-Ping*. Turned into a pretty damned good officer along the way.

As well as being an artist with big guns who still held the training sim record for accuracy while tumbling in a cruiser-sized vessel, even if he had done it for real.

He had chosen to stay here, with them, when offered the chance to be promoted to a true First Officer slot somewhere else.

Somewhere likely to be far more boring.

"Stand by," a new voice came over the channel. "Ten seconds."

Nada Zupan. Pilot Extraordinaire. Jessica could imagine her pony-tail bobbing to some internal beat as her hands flashed back and forth across her control board.

A pianist intent on defeating Rachmaninoff.

Jessica drew one last breath. It was all out of her hands now.

She had trained this team. Forged them. Pushed them. Washed out very few. Said goodbye to a few more who had wanted to retire rather than have another adventure. Amazingly few.

She knew d'Maine had gone through more people. The most to date, as a percentage of his overall crew. But Alber' was also a brutal perfectionist looking for the hardest warriors, the meanest, toughest people he could recruit. And his Goddesses of War.

The other Hammerhead escort in orbit, quietly hanging in the skies half a world away, would be facing *VI Victrix* shortly, surprised and alone.

Jessica had made a private bet with herself that *VI Victrix* wouldn't even leave rubble big enough for pieces to survive re-entry.

This wasn't a raid. Economic warfare wasn't her goal. They weren't even here to put the fear of the night into the people of this sector.

This was purely vengeance for *St. Legier*.

About destroying as much material and personnel as they could reach in one afternoon. Because only two of those ships out there were likely to be controlled by *Sentient* systems.

The rest would have to program their JumpDrives by hand in order to escape her wolfpack.

Best of luck.

Emergence.

In the big projection, Jessica watched a target appear. A Hammerhead-style escort. That long, slender hull-type common with *Buran*, triangular when seen face-on, with a flat dorsal surface and sides angled down to a keel. Instead of the black maw from which the Mag-Shear beam emerged, this class had three small, perpendicular cylinders at the bow, holding sensor arrays and extra beam emitters, elevated from the hull so they could rake fire in all directions as well as scan.

The mark of a good escort.

Wouldn't help him now.

Vanguard was set to pass close below the craft, like an orca swimming underneath still waters.

"Boarding teams, launch now," Nina called over the comm.

The projection showed all four shuttles and both couriers pouring out of their aft bay. As many marines as could be stuffed into them, with more men and women in EVA armor strapped on outside.

Everyone who could be thrown into the mix.

The *Reversed Field, Pinch, Plasma Implosion Generator* fired. The thing Moirrey had jokingly referred to as a *Bubble Gun*, unaware at the time that Yan Bedrov would put it into his notes that way, and then forget to clean up all the references before the design was published. Before it became famous.

Beams moved at light speed. Missiles accelerated from a dead stop relative. The Bubble Gun fired a lozenge-shaped bolt of magnetically-contained plasma that moved at roughly fifteen percent the speed of light. Slow enough to be picked up by the human eye. Too fast to stop, even for a *Sentient* warship.

And they caught him asleep, or something. Whatever a *Sentience* did when it wasn't paying enough attention to his surroundings.

The bolt raced out to the perfect range and detonated, flipping the magnetic fields such that the thing turned into a bubble of energy, wrapped around the target vessel.

Then it imploded into him, fire striking every power absorption panel equally and simultaneously. Nowhere for all the excess to be bled off to, and too fast for the batteries to channel it safely in. For the briefest moment, St. Elmo's Fire engulfed the tiny ship.

It faded a moment later as every panel collapsed under the load and the extra energy began thrashing the bare hull.

And then the Type-3 beams cut loose.

Nina had tuned most of the forward beams for short-range damage, planning this sort of scenario out ahead of time on the expectation that they would get to do this.

Some of those pounded on a spot about a third of the way back from the Hammerhead's snout like an angry woodpecker. According to the best estimates, that was where the control systems and the Capriole drive should be located.

The rest centered into another spot, well aft, aimed to shatter the JumpDrive arrays on the *Energiya* module so the ship couldn't escape. *Vanguard* rattled a different chord from Brewster's aft beams striking out at various civilian ships.

On the screen, the Hammerhead was suddenly shown with a red tint. Best estimate that they had done enough damage to cripple the vessel. Hold him in place. Perhaps set him to tumbling as internal systems failed and damage control parties raced to fix things, against an unforgiving clock.

The Gunner put another salvo into the ship as *Vanguard* passed beneath. Jessica could see large pieces shattered off the hull, along with smaller chunks that her imagination showed as crew members suddenly blasted out into space to die the worst death any spacer could imagine.

"Gunner," Nina ordered. "Stage Two complete. Move on to Stage Three targeting. Archer Force, you have the field."

Stage Three. Anything that moved. Around them, a number of freighters still hadn't awoken to the wolf in their midst.

The station was well aware. It had been shaped like a snowflake, flat and with six arms coming out from the core for ships to dock. The third shot from a port Type-4 had managed to torque a section hard enough that one arm and part of the core itself had separated, bounced off another arm, and was floating away from the station at a fast gallop.

Afolayan put a fourth shot into the station anyway. It went all the way through the core engineering hub and emerged as a flash of heat and a pulse of explosive decompression on the far side. The station started to break up under the pounding.

Jessica wasn't happy to be doing it this way. But this was the only military platform in orbit and she needed to teach *Buran* a lesson.

If she had to kill all his minions to do it, that was a price she was going to have to pay.

CHAPTER XXXV

Every second counted.

Senior Centurion Harun Chong had a count going, both in his head and in the Heads Up Display (HUD) screen inside the Heavy EVA armor that cocooned him. How many seconds since the shuttle had cleared the lockshield. How many seconds since *Vanguard* had tried to cripple his target with accuracy and beamfire. How quickly the various craft could decelerate, crossing the gap. How soon he could get his men and women aboard the alien craft.

Today, he really missed *Auberon*. He could even imagine missing *Gaucho*, although he would never admit that in public. They were doing this in transport shuttles rather than a pair of DropShips. Rugged, but not the sort of desperately-overpowered chariots that could bring his old team, *Auberon's* entire First Battalion, on a single raid, like *Cayenne*.

He had settled for strapping every suit of EVA armor possible to the outside of one of the shuttles, until he had run out of space. Then every marine in the lighter armor that he could cram inside as well, stripping out everything that wasn't welded to a bulkhead in the process.

"Archer Transports, this is Archer One," Chong said over the comm. "Cut thrust now. Archer Force, begin your assault."

The target, a *Buran* escort/destroyer, had been sitting still in orbit, hardly moving relative to *Vanguard*, the dreadnaught crossing the lesser ship's beam at a slow pace. Still, there had been a lot of delta-V to kill.

Clearing the locks, every ship had gone out a different direction, flipped end-for-end, and gone hard on the engines.

It had worked. At least well enough. They were still closing on the hulk, but at a pace soft enough that the thrusters on his armor could bring him to rest. All shuttle engines shut down. It was up to him and his team now.

And time was more important than pretty, as Navin the Black always liked to say. The shuttles shed warriors like lice escaping a sheep about to be dipped. Chong lit his thrusters with the team and moved to where he had a better view.

About a dozen figures in light armor held boarding axes, two-meter-long boarding poles with blades at one end. Perfect for prying things open when the power goes out. Or hitting people who didn't want to surrender.

Chong watched that force take the lead. There were a couple of engineering experts over there to help, in case they had to breach the bulkheads inside, and one Command Security Centurion who had no business being out here, except that he still qualified high enough on this sort of thing that he could displace a younger marine. Expertise mattered, with these risks.

And Navin was generally willing to take orders here. Hell, even the Fleet Centurion had come around, once Denis Jež weighed in on the need.

Fast over pretty.

The heavy assault team came to rest relative to the ship. The escort was tumbling slowly on the roll axis, but not so much that they would have problems. Enough that time was still of the essence.

If anybody moved, they could engage it with beams.

Nobody had ever attempted anything like this before, against a *Buran* warship. *Fribourg*, *Aquitaine*, or a pirate would have considered themselves too deep into the gravity well to risk cooking their JumpSail matrix escaping. *Buran* could flee just fine with JumpDrives.

Harun Chong and his team had to convince the bastard otherwise. They would do that by getting aboard and killing all the power systems.

Prisoners would be nice, but not necessary. Fleet Centurion wanted the technology. She already had a tame-enough prisoner who had briefed them on the expected layout of the corridors and systems that needed to be disabled.

Harun would have liked to bring Seeker along on this mission, just to make sure this wasn't a pig in a poke, but the leaders trusted the man. Good enough.

More bodies began pouring out of the shuttles themselves now. They didn't have the sort of heavy EVA armor to engage defensive systems, but Harun wanted everybody deboarded, in case the bastard still had a gun handy to kill the transports.

The airlocks were a close enough fit to standard, but Harun wasn't planning on using them.

"Archer Force, this is Archer One," Harun ordered. "All teams breach soonest."

"Archer One, this is Viking One," Harun heard Navin's voice call back. "Stand by for breach."

Harun counted to three, and a flash of light appeared.

In a vacuum, you only had to get out of the way of blowback when using a shaped charge on a metal hull. Avoid anything that would hole your suit in death pressure. Navin and his men were through the gap that had been an airlock door previously, and inside the ship.

Now, the risks began to accelerate.

How soon until the ship could leap to safety with an infection aboard? How many marines could board and stop the crew from scuttling the vessel? Who might be lost forever or taken prisoner?

Other flashes of light indicated three more places where teams were blowing airlocks to get inside, as close as possible to their targets. Navin was in basic armor. Good enough, and light enough, for the inside, even if the ship had lost gravplates.

Harun regretted having to stay outside, but he would have Navin inside, and the EVA armor he was wearing was exactly wrong for a close battle where speed counted. It was slow, and heavy.

And extremely well-armed.

"Gunner Force, this is Archer One," Harun called to his heavy team, grinning as his fun started. "Begin icepicking the hull."

Harun picked out a spot where his sensors showed a closed porthole. A weak spot in the metal of the hull. His armor had a shoulder-mounted beam weapon. Heavier than a pulse rifle. More awkward, too. That wasn't a problem when you were sitting in space.

He lined up his shot and fired. The first bolt didn't do the trick, but it did flash the hull dull red for a second. The second shot ruptured something. The hull didn't fail, but he could see air escaping and turning to an icy mist. Other shooters would be going after sealed airlocks, beam arrays, or whatever looked like it might be dangerous.

Anyone inside would be suddenly facing death pressure, which ought to do a lovely job of distracting them from the marines pouring through internal corridors behind them.

Harun puffed his jets enough to move towards the bow of the doomed ship, looking for his next target. Gunner Force was all about sowing chaos at this point. There was no way to capture this ship and take it home, so they didn't need it in any shape to fly. If it did somehow escape them, his men and women might end up anywhere in the solar system,

So he needed to make sure the damned thing couldn't go anywhere.

Harun picked out another interesting spot on the hull and fired.

CHAPTER XXXVI

Carnage. Wrought in shattered steel and lost lives. The images in *Vanguard's* holoprojector were graphic, if distant.

Jessica had ordered the attack in cold blood, though she doubted that *Aquitaine* historians would see that. Certainly both *Fribourg* and *Buran* would most likely record today's events as blood-thirsty, well-deserved, raging vengeance.

She couldn't even call today a true battle. Exactly one station had managed to fire two beams and one missile before Hardie Glenraven and *VI Ferrata* had spiked it with beam fire. The remains looked like a bug that had hit a windshield on the highway, slowly de-orbiting in large pieces.

No, this had been a slaughter.

All *Aquitaine* vessels had finally moved out of close orbit, leaving devastation in their wakes. With just beams, it was extremely difficult, if not impossible to actually kill something as rugged as a freighter, to say nothing of a dedicated warship. You had to stab them to death with icepicks.

There had still been a lot of death to go around. Every single station hammered far harder than it probably warranted if they didn't immediately surrender and begin evacuation, but those were the only points of possible armed resistance, once *Vanguard* disabled the first Hammerhead and *VI Victrix* annihilated the second.

You actually could kill a destroyer, if you put four Type-4 and eight Type-3 beams into it point blank, immediately on the trail of the Bubble Gun knocking all the panels down. Jessica noted that Komal MacInerney, one of Alber's Goddesses of War, had settled short of breaking the craft into shuttle-sized pieces. It still looked like someone had taken a badly-tuned laser saw to the hull, with three major pieces flying in close formation amidst a cloud of lesser debris.

Over one hundred and twenty freighters had been hit at least once in the fracas. Few bad enough to be permanently decommissioned, but Jessica's gunnery officers had been going after the biggest targets first. The most expensive to build. The hardest to actually hurt. The slowest to repair.

The most psychological damage she could wreak on this system.

A ping brought Jessica's eyes down from the projection to a screen in the table in front of her.

"Dead, fled, or surrendered, Fleet Centurion," Nina Vanek announced in a voice that mixed professional pride with dread and morbid understanding of what she had done here. Chickens facing a farmer had a better chance. Or sheep about to be culled.

"Thank you, Nina," Jessica replied. "I'll take it from here."

She turned to Enej, noted the emotional distance her Flag Centurion had put between himself and the readouts in front of him from the hollowness of his eyes.

"Put me on a clear channel, Enej," Jessica said. "I'm talking to everyone."

He nodded with a gulp and pressed a switch. After this many years together, he probably could read her mind about the next steps.

"*Stanovoy* system, this is Red Admiral Keller of the *Fribourg* Imperial Fleet," she said in a dark, angry voice. "I have made my point, I presume. This is now declared a salvage and rescue operation. Anyone who has managed to get away undamaged should consider themselves lucky. Starting now, my fleet will coalesce around their prisoner. All other vessels that keep their distance will be unmolested. If any vessel fires on one of my ships, I will annihilate every vessel in this system and then begin bombing targets on the planetary surface. There will be no second warning. You are otherwise free to conduct any rescue operations that do not get too close to my fleet. I will depart soon and then you will regain control of this system at that time."

Jessica nodded to Enej and waited for him to speak.

"Transmitted," he said.

"Put it on a slow loop in the clear," she ordered. "Pull the corvettes into a defensive laager around the cruisers and have them keep polite company. Some of the ships out there are likely to drift under our guns because they can't stop themselves. Command Centurions should behave themselves for now."

"Got it," he nodded grimly, turning to relay her wishes as well as her words to the team.

Not that most of them needed it. Alber's folks were likely to be the least trigger-happy now, having made their point the most graphically. Some of the corvettes were still getting used to exercising mercy so soon after battle.

She focused her mind now on the vessel she had referred to as the prisoner. It was an odd way to look at it, but the ship itself was a *Sentient* being, even if the crew had turned the cognition way down while resting in orbit. The Hammerhead's systems had been about as smart as a sheep, at the moment when *Vanguard* came calling. She didn't think they had gotten it back up to anything useful before everything went sideways.

The little shark was quiet now. Surrounded in a tetragon by two cruisers, one carrier, and a heavy dreadnaught, all of whom were locked onto it with some level of destructive firepower, with the rest aimed outwards, just in case some other warship came calling.

Jessica didn't think *Buran's Sentient* starships would be suicidal, but you never knew. Making a strafing run into this force right now would probably end up with a Mako out of control and going face first into the atmosphere like a javelin.

"Yeoman Robles, on a secured channel for the Fleet Centurion," one of the women, Enej's comm-techs around the outer wall said, looking up from a screen.

Jessica unbuckled and rose from her chair.

"I'll take it from my office," she said. "Enej, join me. Denis, you have the flag."

Enej's eyebrows tried to climb all the way up to his hairline, but he rose as well. Well, halfway, then unbuckled and tried again. He eventually followed her out the hatch of the flag bridge and into the office that was attached to her suite, the space exactly between their cabins.

Jessica sat behind the desk and gestured Enej to sit as the hatch closed.

"Enej, enough time has passed for now that I am willing to tell you a secret that must never be repeated, for reasons that will be obvious shortly," she said gravely. "I had this same conversation with Robles before she left, but she's Moirrey's right hand, so we both trust her."

Enej gulped and nodded. There wasn't much he hadn't seen as her Flag Centurion over the last decade, so she had him off-balance. It had been easier with Saana Robles, since she hadn't been there at the time.

"In order for Yeoman Robles to know what systems to disable over there, I had to describe them in extremely precise detail," Jessica said.

Enej was perhaps the smartest person Jessica knew, in his ability to process a tremendous amount of raw data and boil it down into information quickly. That he was psychologically a chess player rather than a warrior just meant that his career had bloomed as her right hand, when it would have faltered long before he would have ever been put in command of a ship.

She watched his eyes grow big. He blinked three times in rapid succession. Blew out a breath. Shuddered with his whole body, like a dog that came in from the rain.

"But you were never aboard *Alexandria Station*," he said accusingly.

"No," Jessica agreed. "But Moirrey wasn't alone when she went into that escape pod, just before the *Blackbird* managed to kill the station."

"Alone," Enej repeated slowly. "Arlo and the scientist had already evacuated. The assassin was dead. Who was left?"

"Suvi had spent a long time planning how she could escape from the station if she ever had to face exactly that situation," Jessica replied. "She had built for herself a human-shaped body, what she called an *android*, that could pass for human to anything short of a medical exam. She couldn't physically inhabit it without assistance. The bits that made up her mind, her consciousness, were on a set of boards about this size."

Jessica indicated those chips with both hands, as Suvi had shown her inside the android woman's torso in a rest room.

"Moirrey had to pull them from the computer systems where they had resided for over a millennium, and then plug them into the new body herself, so that Suvi could escape destruction."

"But they rebuilt the *Sentience* that is going into the new Temple of Knowledge."

Enej was grasping at straws now, probably feeling all his logic erode. Jessica had felt the same way.

"They did," Jessica agreed. "And the new Librarian is a copy of the old one, done from a backup. But she is not the original woman. I met Suvi on the surface. Moirrey, Marcelle, and I had dinner with her in a burger dive. Her announced plan was to disappear from recorded history so that she could finally discover what it meant to be human. As far as I know, she has succeeded."

"And the Hammerhead?" Enej challenged faintly.

"Robles needed to know how to kill the beast," Jessica said. "Moirrey wasn't here, so I had to explain it. The two of you are now initiated into the most dangerous secret in the galaxy. One that could result in Moirrey, Marcelle, and I being executed as traitors to the species."

Enej's eyes lost focus and he muttered the sort of profanity that would have gotten either of their mouth's washed out with soap by their respective mothers.

"Yup," he finally looked at her. "You've topped anything I imagined, Jessica."

"Good," she said. "Now you understand the stakes."

She reached down and pressed a button to open the comm line, and then typed in the ten-digit string she and Saana had agreed to before the engineer went about the hulk.

"Keller here," Jessica said. "Enej is present and understands."

"Acknowledged," Saana said after a moment. "As you indicated, everything fits into a knitting bag. Oz is sure that all drive and weapons systems have been disabled. Both Capriole and JumpDrives were badly damaged in the initial round, and damage control parties were just pulling panels off to effect repairs when Archer Force got to them. Navin took a lot of prisoners and has them corralled forward for now. Life support is spotty, but good enough to hold until we depart. Miss the gray lady. Would have made my job so much easier."

"Understood, Saana," Jessica said, also missing her Star Controller. "I want the ship's *Sentient* control systems and the data core for intelligence purposes. Any damage control team computer slabs will probably have enough of what we need if you decide that the Capriole is too damaged to cut out. I would still like a functional Power Absorber panel and battery system intact, as your first priority. We know how their beams work."

"Working on that now, sir," Saana said. "Gunner chopped us a nice line along one of the frames, so we might be able to separate the ship into sections where we can just steal one. Might be too big for the shuttle bay, though."

"Talk with Tamara Strnad," Jessica said. "She can shift some of her strike bombers onto *Vanguard* and the cruisers to free up space. We're going directly from here to Forward Base Omicron."

"Very good, sir," Saana replied. "Probably twelve hours and we should be ready to run. Will check in."

And she was gone.

Jessica keyed the comm closed, but didn't move.

Enej had a sheepish look on his face.

"So now I'm guilty of a conspiracy against the human race?" he began. "That about cover it?"

"Yes," she replied simply. "What do you need to know at this point?"

"Why we're stealing parts off a Hammerhead," he said. "I thought we understood all the basics of their engineering. I mean, physics is physics."

"It is, but we've just done something nobody else has ever managed, Enej," she said. "Every other time someone has managed to capture a ship like this, it has self-destructed before anybody could do anything. Because the boarding teams didn't know how to disconnect the *Sentience* before it did something catastrophic."

"Because they didn't know what we know," he observed neutrally. "How do we explain it, when the Grand Admiral's people ask? What lies do I need to prepare?"

Jessica grinned. She had been pretty sure Enej would be on her side, but there was always a risk.

"I'm Jessica Keller," she said with a laugh. "The infamous Fleet Centurion. The Red Admiral. The Queen of the Pirates. This is where we fall back on the magic of that legend and do a lot of hand-waving. I learned all sorts of dark secrets at *Ballard*. And that's the truth. We just need to keep the timelines fuzzy, is all."

"Wish I'd gotten a chance to talk to Suvi more," Enej said wistfully. "She must have been one hell of a woman."

"She was, Enej," Jessica replied. "She absolutely was."

CHAPTER XXXVII

After the first week home, Casey had considered how she might steal the Arcidiacono family and turn Melina and her husband into her personal chefs. After the second week, it was obvious that the 189th just might mutiny if she tried. It was hard, though, seeing the love flow back and forth between the family that had lost nearly everything and the soldiers that they had adopted in place of the town and clan that had largely vanished. But it also gave Casey hope.

Vo had called on the entire planet, the entire Empire, to open their homes to complete strangers and shower love on them. And they had responded. Melina and Thurman, plus Christina, Nicola, and little Celine had adopted the legionnaires instead. Kept them warm and fed. Energized them to go back out into the continuing winter and find more survivors. And to bury the dead.

But living in Mejico, setting up her Imperial Household here, had absolutely been the right choice. And not just because Arald Rohm was assigned to Strasbourg for now. The Field Marshal was doing good work, leading a mixed force of construction engineers and marines, but the way he had always looked at her in person left her no doubts as to his designs for the future. For her.

Casey kept her personal revulsion to herself. She needed the man's loyalty intact. Vo had already broken Rohm to the bit. She had watched the recordings. Better to gamble with Death, than to draw Vo *zu* Arlo as an enemy. Rohm had learned.

Casey had arrived at the restaurant, reading the name *Tenochtitlan* in bold, flowing script on the front door, with both Torsten and Moirrey in tow. She had learned to come in mid-morning, rather than first thing, because the men were up and going before the dawn. By now, the space was mostly empty.

Three weeks and they had settled into a rhythm.

Vo and Alan Katche were seated when she arrived. She joined them at the table, relieved that they had gotten to the point where she didn't have to order them to sit down at her arrival.

Moirrey liked her coffee with all sorts of additives. Torsten, like Casey, wanted it black. Nicola delivered three prepared mugs with a smile and departed. Casey took a sip and relaxed.

Before she could speak, a sound intruded on her. A low rumbling in the distance, like one of Vo's tanks approaching. Casey felt the first bite of panic nipping at her heels, but both Vo and Alan simply looked up, judged something unseen, and shrugged, almost in unison.

"How can you simply ignore a ground quake?" Casey hissed, grasping at her coffee and lifting the mug before it spilled.

It wasn't the first since she had returned. Nor the strongest. It was still the entire room swaying slowly back and forth.

"We have them almost constantly underneath us, Your Majesty," Alan replied as the sound peaked and began to recede. "I would guess that one to be barely a five, reasonably deep, and almost straight down. Enough to rattle snow off rooftops, but probably not even knock over glasses."

"How long will this go on?" Casey asked the table.

St. Legier was tectonically active, but there had never been anything interesting in the close vicinity of Werder.

"The planet's ringing like a bell," Vo interjected. "Pulses of energy headed out in every direction, like dropping a rock in a pond. They bounce back, reflect off each other, and then pass. The bad ones were in the first week, as the compression relaxed."

"And now?" Torsten leaned into the conversation.

"Fading slowly," Vo shrugged. "One of the geologists on staff suggests another rash come spring, when the snow melts and lubricates things, and then it should settle into whatever pattern will become normal, in a year."

Casey sipped her coffee and glanced warily around the room.

"Are we better off building a new palace half a world away?" she asked, meeting the eyes of all four of her cohorts. "I had been of a mind to do it here, perhaps on the shore of what will become Lake Werder in a generation. Or perhaps Strasbourg. Would Yuular be a better choice? Or perhaps Santiago?"

"Not my call, Your Majesty," Vo replied, pointing at Torsten. "That should be a civilian question, at the end of the day. Personally, I'd build somewhere else, because it lets you get in motion immediately, whereas we're going to be a year just getting enough infrastructure in place to start."

"Torsten?" Casey turned to the quiet man.

She liked to think of him as spending most of each day with a mighty axe of legend, chopping down electronic forests that contained all the information flowing inwards towards her. Certainly, he didn't look the part of a lumberjack, though. In a sedate, navy blue, business suit, he looked more like a well-dressed professor, and spoke like one, as well.

"I lean towards Strasbourg, or Lake Werder," he agreed with her. "Perhaps along a canal we should cause to be dug between the two to regulate water flows in the immediate area of the two lakes. That will facilitate transporting heavy materials, and provide a recreational element to the new construction that will be of benefit to the entire region and its coming tourism component."

"And that is why I am a soldier, and not an economist," Alan laughed heartily. "My brain wants to set back everything on the other side of a huge moat, with forty meter tall walls holding secondary shield generators and a couple of beam emplacements."

"Oh, those will be there, too, Alan," Torsten reassured the man. "I'm still a sailor at heart. Even if I seem to be most of the government right now."

"Which brings me to my second question," Casey said glancing cautiously around the entire room.

When this group was having official meetings here, everyone else had made it a point to move to the far corners on her arrival. And even Celine, the youngest daughter, would happily read her books until her mother roused her to refill coffee.

The people at the table waited for her to speak.

"The House of Dukes has been destroyed," Casey said. "Seating a new generation to replace them will take years unless we create an even larger emergency than we already have."

Everyone nodded. A few sipped their coffee.

"The House of the People was not in session," the Emperor continued carefully. "It could be called to sit quickly, as all the members are already credentialed. In normal circumstances, it is nothing more than a salon for intellectuals. Monarchists arguing with Chartists. Regional blocks arguing over sports teams. And it has little power, in itself, because the House of Dukes exercises an additional veto, separate from that of the Crown."

She left the rest of paragraph dangling. Not bait, exactly, but in the same neighborhood.

"Are you proposing to enact the Charter of Man?" Alan Katche, of all people, asked, almost expectantly.

Casey would have thought a career soldier like him would be the last person to be interested in the Charter, especially as his family came from the lowest ranks of the nobility, rather than the general population. His father was a *Freiherr*, a free holder with hereditary privilege.

"I am not," Casey said as Torsten began to bristle. "That sort of thing would undo everything that my father was trying to do and that I plan to accomplish. The Charter would be the thing that would cause the nobles to rise up. It would split the Empire at the very moment where all the seams and fractures are visible."

She smiled the smallest possible smile she could as she watched Torsten relax. Honestly, she had been expecting Torsten and Alan to give her exactly the opposite reactions. Maybe that was an even better indication. She noted how quiet both Moirrey and Vo had remained, even today feeling like outsiders in someone else's city.

"However," Casey continued before everyone relaxed too far. "If we do not harry the Dukes to sit, and then follow that with the worst bureaucratic paperwork messes possible to credential each and every one of them, the House of the People will have no choice but to step up and handle the hard work of governing. They would have to go beyond matters of planetary trade and criminal law, and inject themselves into Empire itself."

"Wh'limitations does ya 'nvisions, Casey," Moirrey drawled sideways.

Nobody else was willing to address her with anything but formality, these days, but Moirrey had understood the need to have someone to talk to. And that it wasn't going to be any of the boys. At least, not yet.

"Something like a reverse of the ancient Magna Carta," Emperor Karl VIII replied succinctly. "Limitations on the House of Dukes as a result of ceding certain powers to the House of the People. Not going so far as a constitution, with all those limitations, but the Crown cannot do everything."

"So a quieter revolution?" Torsten asked. "But not necessarily a slower one."

"I envision a set of emergency decrees drafted by you," Casey focused her attention on the man. "Modified over time, but necessary to deal with the immediate situation. Nobody will be able to persuasively argue with that. Over time, they may become permanent, depending on how that House behaves itself. I will still retain the ultimate veto. And I can dissolve that House if it decides to transform itself into a parliament. Anything like this must be done over decades, not weeks. The Empire is too fragile right now to handle another major ground quake."

The lack of argument did not suggest that this group of people necessarily supported her mission. She understood that. It meant that they would give it time to process, and then probably argue with her in private. But it would take the form of questions rather than outright hostility.

Emmerich would be the hardest one to bring over. He saw himself as one man holding back the entire sea. Men like Tom Provst and Vo Arlo were fingers stuck into the dyke as leaks appeared. She would enrage him if she were to take a hammer to the wall. But Casey would also drown with him, and she understood that, both intellectually and emotionally.

She could, however, paint new murals on the stone, and it would be years before she could expect anything to significantly change *Fribourg*. Father and Ekke had calculated it would take them fifty years to accomplish it. But she would only be seventy-three at that point. And both Wiegand and Alkaev were long-lived families when they didn't die in accidents and wars.

Perhaps she would need to learn more about the three, ancient, English monarchs known as *Elizabeth*, among Moirrey's historical favorites, to see how a crown could survive its culture attempting to come unraveled around it.

"So now I must ask a very personal thing, Vo," she said, letting the warm heat of the man's presence protect her. "Is it wise to allow Victoria Ames to continue her charade?"

It was painful, almost physically so, for Casey to ask that. To challenge another woman's dreams and perhaps squelch them in the name of Imperial survival. She expected Vo's gaze to grown thunderous, terrible in the ways of the ancient gods of the Homeworld's religions.

His wry grin wasn't anything like she expected. Nor was Alan Katche's. Clearly, she did not understand soldiers in the ways she had learned about sailors.

"Not your call, Your Highness," he said simply, eyes bright and smiling.

"I beg your pardon?" Casey fired back, feeling her back come up as some *Man* had the audacity to tell her *No*. Worse, some man other than her father or her uncle. Even if it was Vo.

"You placed me in command on this planet," he rumbled. "That means I make those decisions."

"I'm still the Emperor," Casey growled.

How dare he?

"You have exactly three options, Your Majesty," Vo growled back. "You can relieve me of command. You can court martial me and remove the *zu*. Or you can ignore the entire situation. I will not accept an order to do anything else with Trooper Ames. No, that's not true. In a couple of years, she'll be ready for either Officer Candidate school, or whatever we do to rebuild the Ground Forces Institute. At that point, it will be time for higher education and I will order her to report, if it is still in my power to do so."

"As a soldier?" Casey was aghast.

Inside, she was as angry with herself as she was with Vo. This was that suffocating corset known as *Imperial Responsibility*. Things she would like to do, balanced finely against things she must prevent in the name of stability.

"As a soldier," Vo agreed. "She's already as good in the field as my Cutlass team. Danville is a better scout, but Ames is a better forager. And she shoots as well as ten-year veterans. I'm keeping her in place until she changes her mind. Any orders to the contrary be damned."

Casey saw the mountain of doom known as Arlo at that moment. The terrible ogre that Moirrey had described as they stalked a would-be Emperor and thwarted a coup attempt. The quiet, deadly killer inside him used to be much farther from the surface than he was today.

This was the being that had caused Arald Rohm to bend the neck.

"Can Army discipline handle a woman in ranks?" Casey tried another track.

Aquitaine handled it just fine, but that was a culture built on such a bedrock. *Fribourg* was still reeling that a woman held the crown.

"She's not a woman, as far as my men are concerned," Vo said. "She's a rookie trooper who has to get up every morning and prove herself worthy to wear the uniform, same as them. More so, when that uniform has the 189th Legion patch on the shoulder. *We stood.* They consider themselves the best, toughest unit in your entire Army, so nobody is allowed to slack the rope. Personally, I'm more concerned for the first poor bastard who comes along and catches her eye as a prospective boyfriend. He'll have to deal with *Cutlass Ten*, Reese Borel and Iakov Street as protective uncles."

"She's sixteen years old," Casey observed. Perhaps pled. She wasn't sure how to move this man. "Do you think she can handle all this?"

The way both Vo and Katche laughed, a harsh bark in unison was even more unnerving.

"Let me tell you a story, Your Majesty," Vo began slowly, leaning forward to place those enormous hands on either side of his nearly-empty coffee mug. "I've only gotten part of it, and do not intend to pursue the topic any deeper. But it should assuage your concerns about Victoria Ames."

He stared at her, waiting for her to nod. Casey felt like the entire room had fallen so quiet she could hear the planet itself breathe. Her nod was just enough to convince this hard, hard man to speak.

One did not compel Vo *zu* Arlo to do anything he didn't want to.

"Ames had been living in that hole in the ground for fourteen months when we found her three weeks ago," he began in a quiet, intense voice that caused her to lean towards him. "At some point in that stretch, a man decided she would be easy prey. A teenage girl, living rough in the middle of a forest. She described him to us as an older man, but at her age that might have been thirty as easily as sixty."

Vo paused now, just long enough to empty his mug. And insert metaphorical pins under Casey's fingernails. On top of everything else, Vo *zu* Arlo was a gifted storyteller. Who knew?

"He stalked her, Your Majesty," Vo continued. "I didn't ask. None of us did. But it wouldn't be too hard to guess why he knocked her down instead of killing her outright."

Casey flushed. At first, she thought it was embarrassment, but then she understood that the feeling was rage. Ames was tall and lanky for a girl, but nothing against a full-grown man. Casey barely suppressed the growl that wanted to escape her lips.

"But that was his mistake, you see, Your Majesty," Vo rumbled, slicing her with his words, like a bird ripping pieces off its prey. "Victoria Ames had a knife hidden in her boot. She killed him with it. Buried his body because the authorities would never believe her story. I've never inquired about her background, but I would suspect that Ames was just a commoner, like I used to be, and the man she killed was probably somebody important. Important enough, anyway."

Vo stared at Casey for a hard moment before he spoke again.

"We interviewed her for induction, same as we do with all new recruits," he said in a cold, stone voice. "In the world before, we would have had to bring in the authorities and investigate deeper. Perhaps uncover something ugly when she took us to the place where she dug his grave, as she offered to do. But that was before. Today, we're short on bodies and she wants to serve. She gets up every morning and has to prove to the soldiers of *Cutlass Force* that she deserves to be here with them. And those are hard, unforgiving men, Your Majesty. She's safer than you are, Kasimira *zu* Wiegand, because you are just their Emperor, and you know how much that means to the 189th Legion. Victoria Ames is their daughter. Their sister. Their niece. One of these days, Good Lord willing, their commander. I will not budge on that."

The eyes looked like one of the angry gods, now. The sort of thing Casey might paint for a summoned demon, the kind about to fly out of a picture and claim your soul. Interestingly, Alan Katche was a close second for power, right now. Yes, Arald Rohm would bend the knee. It had been the only way he was going to survive an encounter with the 189th.

Casey nodded. There were no words to inject into the conversation, at this point. Vo *zu* Arlo was a man known for his strength of will and was willing to go head-to-head with his own Emperor on the topic. He was the right man for the job. It didn't even really matter what the job was. No, there was only one thing she could say.

"Thank you," Casey said in a subdued tone.

Vo would always be there when she needed him.

CHAPTER XXXVIII

Hendrik Baumgärtner had served his Empire and its Fleet for thirty-nine years. He was an Admiral of the White today because Karl VII had needed him to be the face and voice of the Imperial Fleet when the Grand Admiral was away. *Flag Captain* would not do when Hendrik needed to speak with the voice of Emmerich Wachturm or Johannes Wiegand. He was the Chief of Staff because Emmerich had precious few people he could trust, even after thirty years' service himself. Too many worms still hiding in the apple.

Hendrik had first met the current Emperor when he was allowed to hold a three-week-old baby, twenty-three years ago. Hendrik had served three Emperors in his time, and God willing, he would die of old age before he ever saw his fourth.

Regardless of the number of men he had to kill to do that.

Hendrik looked up from the report he was reading and studied the man seated at attention on the other side of his desk. The man who had written it. Commander Gunter Tifft had emerged from the craziness of the last few years with a gold star next to his name, having impressed Tom Provst and the Grand Admiral with his competence and diplomacy.

"How did a logistics officer get so good at intelligence and espionage, Gunter?" Hendrik asked pointedly.

For the umpteenth time, it felt.

"There's really little difference between the two, Admiral," Tifft replied in a tight, angry voice, unbending that tiny amount from the rigidity he had held as he waited. The contents of the report were unsettling reading for any honest and loyal officer. "Other than a logistics officer is more likely to carry a gun, and more likely to use it in his career."

Hendrik nodded and looked back down to reread the executive summary on page one. He felt a terrible fury form. It was something that might have impressed one of Lady Moirrey of *Ramsey's* favorite writers. That Hellenic fellow from the early Iron Age on Earth.

Homer had understood that kind of anger when he asked that Muse for a song about the *Rage of Achilles*.

"You have reported your projections to the correct place, Commander," Hendrik said as he held back his wrath. "This does not need to be communicated to the Grand Admiral, or the Crown, at present. It is purely a naval affair, and we will handle it as such. The gentleman in question was a naval officer at one point and that commission only becomes inactive. It does not lapse. It can only be revoked. That makes him one of ours, regardless of his opinion on the topic."

"Understood, sir," Tifft said quietly, expecting to be dismissed, his job completed.

"I will need you in the field on this one, Gunter," Hendrik continued.

"Sir?"

"You will report to Tom Provst aboard *Firehawk*, Commander Tifft," Hendrik ordered the young man who was fast becoming the Chief of Staff's own sharp blade, just as Hendrik had done for Emmerich over the decades. "He remains in command of the fleet at the Grand Admiral's order. You will provide him a copy of this report, answer his questions, and assist him in dealing with the gentleman in question."

"*Firehawk*, sir?" Tifft clarified. It hadn't been a challenge, but confirmation that Tifft sought.

"This sort of situation needs to be handled with a sledgehammer, Gunter," Hendrik said. "We have gone beyond politeness. It has gotten to the point that we must make an example of someone. He'll do as well as anyone."

CHAPTER XXXIX

Given his choice, Tom Provst would have gladly been the one who died that day aboard *Firehawk* rather than the Crown Prince and Al Kistler. It hadn't helped his state of mind that *Firehawk* hadn't really suffered any significantly permanent damage from the battle. Her own crews had been able to do most of the work in the field, with barely any downtime.

That just meant that he had been able to control the Imperial defenses from his damaged ship rather than having to go aboard the orbital station.

Staying at the scene of the crime, on the *Pequod*, as it were.

As guilt went, Tom Provst knew his was going to drive him mad eventually, but he had only promised Emmerich a year. Tom knew he could hold it together for twelve, angry months, as long as he stayed on this flag bridge deck, forever looking for a white whale he wouldn't find on this side of hell.

Even as he looked.

The chamber was quiet. Tom couldn't get past the rage in his head and sounds of that day to remember if this was quieter than it used to be, back in the world before. It probably was, but he was close enough to the grave these days that those sorts of things didn't bother him as much as they once would have.

A side hatch opened and Commander d'Noir escorted the Grand Admiral's new errand boy into the room. Commander Tifft had been one of Tom's, once upon a time. A damned good quartermaster down on the flight deck, keeping the old battleship stocked and organized far better than the man who had replaced him. But the new fellow was merely exceptional. Gunter Tifft had been so much better than that. The old Tom Provst would have missed the young officer, so the new one tried.

The room fell the rest of the way silent. Only the blowers putting out air and the occasional chirp from somebody's control board intruded. Tom knew that the men wanted to turn around and see their old comrade, but professionalism kept their faces turned away. On one of the newer designs, like the battleship *Valiant* that they were all due to launch from her drydock soon, the men faced in on both the bridge and flag bridge, so that they could see their commanders at work.

Tifft came to attention at exactly two meters and snapped a salute off his forehead.

"Admiral Baumgärtner's best regards, Admiral Provst," Tifft said formally.

Up close, the last few years had done wonders for the young man. He was still a tall, blond recruiting poster, but the last bit of boyishness had been sanded off, leaving only mature and serious. The uniform was as good a fit as the logistics officers always managed, and Tifft carried an imposing-looking leather satchel in one hand.

"You have orders for us, Commander?" Tom asked in voice loud enough for everyone to partake.

It was interesting, watching Tifft hesitate, not at the circumstance, but at the orders themselves. All Hendrik had been willing to say was that he was sending a messenger.

Must be good, then.

"Perhaps a suggested course of action for you to pursue, Admiral Provst," Tifft prevaricated carefully with a vague nod. "I had prepared an intelligence report for the Chief of Staff. He ordered me to put it and myself at your disposal to answer questions and deal with the situation as you felt best."

Tom stared at the man for several seconds, trying to read his soul, but Tifft had grown hard and still in the last year, especially from the young man who used to be so easy to embarrass.

And Tom no longer felt human enough to judge well.

"Join me in my office, then," Tom ordered.

Hendrik hadn't wanted the Grand Admiral involved. And had sent his personal spook with a packet of papers because he wasn't going to say it, even over an encrypted line.

Tom wondered who needed to be killed.

An hour had passed. Tom Provst emerged from his day office and stepped back onto the *Firehawk*'s flag bridge, Gunter Tifft trailing in his wake silently. Tom would have said his rage joined them to fill the room, but that was a constant these days and nothing would quell that. Fade it perhaps. Or focus it.

The noise around him was greater than it had been. Perhaps what it should be, with a proper commander in charge, and not this hopeless soul. He pulled a cleansing breath to the bottom of his being.

"Flag bridge," Tom called in a heavy voice. "Bring the entire squadron to alert status and prepare them for maneuver orders."

Tom walked to his station and nodded as Commander d'Noir moved to stand across the table from him.

"Tifft, you join d'Noir," Tom continued.

He unlocked his keyboard and typed in a series of alpha-numerics.

"Sensors, I have just identified a target for you," Tom said loudly. "Work with System Control and find me that ship. If it hasn't arrived, place a quarantine under my authority and hold it in place as soon as it emerges from jump. If it is here, freeze it where it is."

Charles d'Noir glanced sidelong at Tifft as the man stood close by.

"How bad?" d'Noir asked.

He had been Tom's Flag Officer for several years, another paperwork junky like Tifft, the kind that made the galaxy spin.

"I want boarding teams on a fifteen minute standby, Charlie," Tom said. "Guns and missiles will be unlocked as soon as we have a target."

Rather than answer, the man looked down at his own screen and studied it.

"Tom, this is some Duke's personal transport," Charlie replied. "Maximum crew probably twenty, including his mistress and her maid and cook. What gives?"

Tom considered the implications of that dossier for a moment. How angry it made him. And probably Hendrik. How badly some of these men around them would react.

"Tifft," Tom decided finally. "Show Commander d'Noir the executive summary only. That will be sufficient for our purposes, and not put him in a hole later if something goes sideways and the rest of us are executed by the Emperor."

Charlie blanched, but held his peace.

Tifft nodded and flipped open the satchel. He removed one page from inside, placed it flat against the side of the briefcase, and held it so that only Charlie could read it, and only then by leaning against Tifft's shoulder.

Tom knew when Charlie hit the right sentence by the unconscious recoil and the profanity that burst out of the man's mouth. Charlie started to say something, then thought better of it. Finally, he spoke.

"Should we have a team in heavy EVA armor, just in case you want to order their hull manually breached?" he snarled quietly.

"Charlie, it would be faster to just kill them with beams at that point," Tom retorted.

"I'm aware of that, Tom," Charlie growled.

Tom considered it, and nodded.

"One team only, Charlie," he ordered. "As you said, that's a personal transport of a Duke, not a warship. One EVA marine could probably rip it in half by himself if I ordered it."

"Admiral, I have a target," one of the men called from the outer ring. "Confirmed: *YPL-10006241BRX*. Common name: *Aramis*. Holding at the second boundary for inner system clearance. Zone lock initiated."

Tom smiled. It felt like a smile to him. Others might mistake it for a predator preparing to rip out its victim's throat. Not that there was a lot of difference right now.

YPL. *Yacht, Personnel, Light.*

As Charlie had said, some Duke's private boat. Specifically, Kiril Hahl, Duke of *Blue Essex*, a lovely world Tom had heard compared favorably to both the lost Homeworld and *St. Legier*.

One of his frigates was more than enough to take charge of a YPL, all the more so because it had no guns.

Sending all five frigates perhaps qualified as overkill. Adding three cruisers and a battleship was just icing on an already vicious cake.

"Maneuver orders," Tom said to Charlie and Gunter. "I want the escorts bracketing him when we emerge. Put the cruisers on his flanks. Drop *Firehawk* right on his nose, dead stop relative, close enough that the Primaries can't focus. Then put all of our marines on his hull. After that,

Tifft and I will board his vessel and we will have a conversation with the man."

"On it," Charlie began typing buttons.

Tifft nodded. Tom smiled. He just might get to add another ghost to the ones that haunted him at night. Perhaps he had found his purpose.

Tom made a note to himself, to thank Hendrik for sending him this before he died.

CHAPTER XL

Gunter watched on the shuttle's screen as they closed the last few meters to *Aramis*. He was reminded of a rabbit surrounded by a pack of wildcats. The teams of marines attached to the hull in armorsuits, plus the four men nearby in flying tanks, just added to the measure.

Inside, the shuttle was darker than normal. Perhaps half light. Admiral Provst had set them that way on purpose. Several rows of passenger seats were mostly empty, as well as the cabin aft that could serve as a conference room. Four marines in light, boarding armor and guns, near the hatch and far enough away that the officers could speak without being heard.

If Provst had said anything.

Only he and Admiral Provst knew the whole story, here on the scene. Commander d'Noir had enough information to back them up in case things got weird, but there was an entire battle squadron around them. His old mates. Veterans of the apocalypse itself.

Gunter saw the lines that guilt had carved into his former Admiral's face. Hendrik had warned him that Provst was both on edge and in a bedrock state of mind. Gunter hadn't understood the duality until he met the man today. Solid, but only barely in control of his rage.

A gun, awaiting a target and a finger on the trigger.

Probably exactly the sort of man Hendrik would want here. If the Crown took exception later, Gunter had no doubt that Tom Provst would be the right man to be executed. After the last several hours in his company, Gunter suspected the man would probably look forward to it with a smile.

Gunter couldn't remember the last time he had to play the straight man in such a good cop/bad cop routine. And yet, here he was.

And Hendrik Baumgärtner had been right about guns, as well. Tom Provst had issued him a sidearm and taken one himself. The four bodyguards seated around them felt like guppies trailing a shark and a remora.

On the screen, *Aramis* had grown until she filled the display. As yachts went, she was larger than most, almost a medium hull classification, but Gunter assumed that the man who commissioned her had carefully kept the vessel just below that limit, as well as the taxes that went along with it. She was still over one hundred meters long, and perhaps twenty across the broadest part of the beam. Three decks internal, plus what he would guess to be a stateroom over the engines, from the way the hull humped up there. Probably came with retractable shields so you could sleep among the stars, or the haze of JumpSpace.

Money. Power. And arrogance.

Hendrik and Tom had read the report, but Gunter had prepared it. As Hendrik had said, logistics officers make good spies, collating details and assembling stories. Or, in this case, having feelers out in the right quarters, the invisible places. Letting certain people know that blowing their cover might be more important than just sending a message.

Time had indeed been critical. The vessel had arrived less than twenty hours after the message chain she had triggered. *Aramis* had a better navigator than she should have to make the run that fast.

Gunter looked over at Tom Provst, dressed in his white day uniform. It belied the fact that the Grand Admiral had left the man in overall command of local forces, ranking on Admirals of the Red or Blue who had seniority, but not necessarily the other man's complete trust. The entire Empire had balanced on edge for a few weeks, held safe by Provst and the men aboard *Firehawk*.

Tom Provst was haunted. All the reports agreed, including the one Gunter had filed before they boarded the shuttle. Not suicidal, precisely, but long past the point where he cared about most things, including his career. Gunter had read the transcript of the conversation between Provst and Wachturm. Knew Provst wanted to die, but would not do it without that year elapsing or Wachturm giving his blessing.

It had taken this situation to rouse the man from his apathy. Gunter hoped that it was enough. He missed the old commander he had known.

The shuttle lurched slightly as she docked. Knowing how good most pilots were, Gunter assumed that the man up front had done that on purpose. Rattle *Aramis* with a good, ominous thump, when a kiss might have done. They had already rolled over and bared their belly to the warfleet around them. Anything *Aramis* did at this point would just hasten their demise, as it were.

More clunks. The normal ones, this time, as the two airlocks embraced and began to join. Gunter could never get the juvenile joke out of his head, the one about ships mating, so he scowled instead.

Admiral Provst looked over at him with the faintest ghost of a grin.

"We have mounted them," he said. "Now they will bear our children."

Gunter chuckled in spite of himself. That was the old Admiral. Perhaps some of the man remained alive inside.

The next few hours would tell.

Provst unbuckled and rose. Gunter joined him. The four marines were already up and poised. They smelled danger in the air. Everyone did, with the level of secrecy being maintained.

"Open the airlock," Provst ordered in a gruff voice.

"Should you be this close, Admiral?" one of the marines, faceless inside his helmet, asked. "It could be a trap."

"If it is, then Charlie d'Noir splatters their silly asses all over space," Provst responded in gravel-hued tones.

The marine nodded and triggered the hatch. Three of them crowded the opening as it pivoted inwards, with nobody in the airlock itself.

Gunter could see movement beyond the far lock door, but no one opened fire. And no grenades appeared, rattling off a bulkhead. As a former logistics officer, Gunter had been in charge of tracking all the armaments on his old battleship, so he was aware of how many different ways he could die today.

Still, he had sworn an oath. They all had, including the man on the other side of that wall. He had apparently forgotten that. It was time to remind him.

To remind them all.

Gunter felt the anger billowing off Admiral Provst infect his own soul. He had managed to keep it at bay this long, but it was straining at the leash now. Of course, Gunter didn't figure he would have made it this far in his career if he was unable to adapt to changing circumstances.

That was part of what made a good spy.

"Admiral, perhaps I should lead?" Gunter asked as Provst was about to move. "This is an official situation after all, sir."

"Yes," Provst replied darkly. "I suppose it is. I forget that there are rules again. Good call, Tifft."

Gunter took point. He held the ominous satchel in his left hand, just in case he needed to actually draw the weapon with his right. Logistics officers as cowboys.

Today, he was a spy.

Into the airlock with a firm tread. Careful crossing the threshold, because they had the gravplates running lower over there, maybe ninety percent rather than the one-hundred-two that Provst maintained on *Firehawk*.

Two obvious guards, neither of them with guns on their person, waited in the hall, along with a man Gunter could only describe as a *flunky*.

"What's the meaning of all this?" the flunky demanded.

Gunter stopped and considered the man from close enough to punch him without stepping into it first. The other two appeared more sanguine about the situation, so Gunter mentally upgraded them to the kinds of goons that rich people hired as fixers. Tough, but not dumb enough to start trouble with Imperial marines.

"Are you the captain of this vessel?" Gunter asked solemnly.

"Yes, but…"

Gunter snapped his fingers in the man's face.

One of the real spies he worked with occasionally had taught him that trick to throw people off kilter. It worked. The man blinked and fell silent.

Gunter turned to the closest marine and nodded.

"Put this one aboard the shuttle under guard," he ordered, before turning to the goons. "Which of you is senior?"

The short one nodded without speaking. Again, smart player aware that anything he did might be wrong.

Gunter pointed to the tall goon.

"Him as well," Gunter continued. "Lethal force is authorized, if necessary."

Tall goon understood faster than the captain did. He actually grabbed the sputtering flunky and propelled the smaller man into the airlock and custody, well away from whatever was about to happen over here. They were all just pawns at this point.

Gunter glanced back to confirm that the Admiral was right behind him, and turned to the remaining man.

"Lead us to your principal," Gunter ordered. "Don't do anything stupid and we probably won't need to do anything more than take your statement, afterwards."

Again, the nod. Hard man, used to hard knocks.

Gunter decided he had spent too much time around Hendrik Baumgärtner and that man's spies over the last year. He couldn't remember ever being this…inflexible. This belligerent.

Maybe Tom Provst was rubbing off on him, too.

The hard man moved. One of the marines followed, then Gunter, Provst, and the remaining two gunmen.

The hallways over here were broad and well-appointed. *Pretty*. Gunter had spent too much time on warships to appreciate the lush carpet under his feet or the gold sconces off-set down the corridor. The logistics officer he had been was tracking the quarterly costs to clean and replace the carpet and polish the metal. Effort wasted to make exactly one man happy.

They were headed aft. Gunter assumed that the bridge was the last place this man ever went, so all the crew would be forward. He would have his mistress close to that bubble, so he could open the shields to the stars and pretend to be a god while fornicating. The hallway, the fittings, everything just pointed at that.

Decadence.

A man emerged from a side corridor, spotted them, and froze.

"You," Gunter ordered. "Stay put."

He was dressed like crew, a uniform close to Imperial Fleet in cut, but green instead of blue.

The sight of armed men, Imperial marines, froze him. Gunter grabbed the man's arm as he came even and directed him towards one of the marines aft of the column.

"Bring him along," Gunter ordered.

Part of Gunter's brain found it amusing that Admiral Provst had remained silent through all this. The man hadn't spoken since he set foot on this deck.

Maybe Gunter really was supposed to play good cop here? Who knew? He was the expert on the ground.

Time to expert.

Another long corridor, past a bulkhead hatch. The carpet was even nicer here. It felt handmade, rather than an expensive, machine import, like the other had been.

He considered his prey. The man had only been a number until three days ago. A cypher.

Gunter had not developed a particularly high opinion of the man in the time since.

The goon stopped at another hatch. He turned and grimaced at Gunter.

"Officer country beyond this, sir," he said, indicating a naval background at some point.

That or he had watched a lot of military vids.

"Understood," Gunter replied. "Open it and stand aside."

"Yes, sir."

The man keyed a combination into a pad, waited for the door to chirp, and put his shoulder blades against the side wall as the door moved. Gunter tapped the lead marine on the arm and directed him to take the goon and bring him along as Gunter led the way into a Dionysian paradise decanted in gold and expensive. His inner logistics officer snarled at the effort to keep a place like this up to par during operating conditions.

One man, seated. Youngish, perhaps. Lean and rangy, with golden hair and long arms. A scarecrow knitted out of barbed wire. Possibly forty standard years old. It was hard to tell, through the makeup trying to cover the scars of dissipation.

Duke Kiril Hahl.

Another man, older, obviously a servant of some kind. Perhaps a butler, over-dressed in baggy, black attire that looked wholly uncomfortable. Pudgier, with the roundness of good eating and not enough sun or exercise.

A woman. Gunter was willing to assume she was old enough to be here without a chaperone. He wouldn't have been willing to place any money on that bet. His first guess was a daughter. She was young enough, hopefully over eighteen years standard. But she looked nothing like the Duke. Short and lush to the man's lean sparseness. Dusky skin with black hair. Eyes that appeared empty for a moment, before they locked onto the gun on Gunter's hip. Then he saw a highly-refined intelligence flash into being, before vanishing into the mists of her soul at a dead run.

So, probably a professional. *Hopefully* a licensed one. And *hopefully* of age. Gunter was willing to throw that book at the man, as well, although it really wasn't necessary at this point. Unless he wanted to destroy the Duke's reputation first.

There was always that.

Barely a moment had passed. Gunter had flowed into the center of the room. Tom Provst was right behind him, off to one side in case he needed to draw and fire suddenly. At least one of the marines had entered. The other two had the rear covered. Those men were professionals.

"What is the meaning of this charade?" the Duke demanded in a voice used to abusing servants and underage girls.

Fortunately, he didn't try to move, trapped behind a lovely, oak table by the shag of the golden carpet and how it would hold the feet of his chair with friction if he tried to stand suddenly. The glass of sparkling wine in the man's right hand also rendered him fairly harmless.

The butler stood up from being hunched over to pour from a glass bottle. The look on his face was comparable to a cow chewing cud.

The girl didn't move at all, but that was expertise in her field. He hadn't seen fear, nor anger.

Gunter paused long enough to make sure all the other doors into the vast chamber were closed. Standard practice on a starship, no, check that, on a warship. You had to double-check aboard a flying boudoir like this one.

"His Excellency, Kiril Hahl, Duke of *Blue Essex*?" Gunter called in a very formal cant.

"That's right," the man snarled. "Who are you? What are you doing aboard my yacht? And where's Robert?"

Gunter started to speak, but felt a hand descend on his shoulder. A giant raptor about to grab him and carry him off would have a grip like that.

Perhaps the semi-legendary *Firehawk*.

Tom Provst, Admiral of the White, Supreme Commander, Home Fleet, *St. Legier*, stepped around Gunter and became the center of gravity for the entire room. Maybe the entire star system.

"Kiril Hahl, you are under arrest, charged with treason."

Provst pronounced the words like an oracle who had seen the Face of God. Terrible and destructive. He pointed a finger like a gun at the butler and the girl.

"Remove those two and place them aboard the shuttle with the others," the Admiral continued in that deadly voice. "Remove everyone from this vessel and secure them. Only Commander Tifft will remain with me."

"Yes, sir," a marine barked.

In thirty seconds, the room had come down to the three of them. The Duke might have gone white, but it was hard to tell through the layer of pancake designed to cover up ruptured blood vessels in his nose.

Tom Provst had apparently turned to bronze. The flush under his skin wasn't anger, unless a rage could do that. Considering the circumstances, Gunter wasn't sure it was impossible. Tom Provst had joined him and Hendrik at the peaks of wrath.

Hahl had fallen silent. Occasionally his mouth moved, like a fish, but no words came out. Provst wasn't filling in the space with gabble either. Gunter had an active recording device secreted in his belt, just in case they needed something even more damning to back up their case.

If there was anything more.

Provst took the seat across the table from Hahl. Gunter found a spot with a good view, good audio pickup, and a solid bulkhead behind him.

"Do you know who I am?" Hahl demanded, finally working up the courage, or the bile. It was hard to differentiate.

"Yes I do," Provst replied serenely. "I know your name. But I don't really care. To me, you're just a number on a page. What was his number, Tifft?"

Gunter saw the good cop/bad cop routine take shape now. Provst, seated at the table with the witness. Gunter close by to fill in damning details. The Duke as the only victim.

"Twenty-seven, Admiral," Tifft replied.

"Yes," Provst agreed calmly. "Twenty-seven."

Long pause as Gunter watched both men. They had pulled back into themselves, gladiators about to make the first pass.

"It is an interesting list," Provst continued, almost serenely. "The Imperial Succession Plan, as published by the House Of Dukes. You appear on page three, in space number twenty-seven. As if you mattered."

"She cannot be Emperor," Hahl hissed. "No woman has ever held the throne. She must be put aside. If no one else has the courage, then I will do it."

"But the House of Dukes has been destroyed," Provst continued, as if the Duke had never spoken. "So we cannot even update that list until the new government figures out how to invest a new crop of Dukes, empanel them, and then go about figuring these sorts of things out."

"Admiral, the Dukes will not stand for a woman, you know that," Hahl ranted. "Something must be done, and done right now, or the Empire will fall to pieces and *Aquitaine* will roll over us!"

"So here we have a man who believes that he has the answer to all our ills," Provst said over his shoulder to Gunter, gesturing to Hahl. "The Admiral commanding that sector did not suddenly swear fealty to a newly-proclaimed Emperor. According to what I've read, he even tried to talk you out of this absurdity. He failed to arrest you afterwards though, so we'll probably just court martial him in disgrace, rather than have the man executed. I'll leave that one to a jury of his peers to decide. But I still have to deal with you."

Somewhere in the middle of that speech, Hahl registered Provst's words. Or his underlying anger. The Duke of *Blue Essex* fell silent. And turned even whiter, if that was possible.

"Twenty-seven," Provst continued his slow, lyrical rhapsody. "I know of at least five people above you on that list that survived, Hahl. Hell, I've spoken to two of them this week."

Provst fell silent. He stood enough to push the chair back by lifting over the heavy shag of the carpet, and then moved silently to one side of the table before he turned and lurked over the Duke.

"So under what fucking circumstance do you think you should become our new Emperor?" Provst bellowed, a dragon roused.

Hahl started to rise, until Provst's hand fell onto the sidearm. Gunter found his own pistol, but did not draw it. Hahl fell back into his seat with eyes like a deer on a dark highway. Gunter relaxed. He hoped Provst did, as well.

"Shit-head twenty-seven, that's what you are," Provst roared. "You do not even rate a *who* anymore. Just a *what*. I have read the reports forwarded by Imperial Security, Twenty-seven. They paint a damning-enough portrait without you showing up in the *St. Legier* system to try to rally the fleet. To overturn the law I swore to uphold."

Provst fell silent and began to pace. Except pacing was supposed to be a softer thing, Gunter guessed. It didn't involve stomping back and forth, like Provst was doing. Even the expensive carpet could barely muffle it.

"I presume you thought you'd get here before Karl VIII could return and that would help your cause with the fleet?" Provst probed.

Gunter was reminded of a raven, ripping choice bits out of a fresh corpse.

Or a still-dying man.

Hahl remained frozen, hands like claws on the arms of his expensive chair, white with shock.

"Answer me, Twenty-seven," Provst yelled. "Was that your idea?"

Provst fell silent, a ugly, avenging demon towering over the Duke.

Finally, the Duke broke.

He nodded. Miniscule, but movement. Voluntary, even, and not just a bobbleheaded doll set to bouncing.

Gunter had a hard time hearing the words, but he could read the man's lips from here well enough.

"She cannot reign," Hahl whispered in a voice that somehow managed to be both dead and panicked. "The noble class will never allow a woman. It will be civil war if she tries. Don't you see that?"

"No," Provst countered bluntly. "I don't. I see a woman who took on Sigmund Dittmar and all of Imperial Security by herself. Who became Karl VIII that day rather than allow shit-head number eight to promote himself."

"No woman has ever sat on the throne," Hahl began to find his voice now. Belligerent, even if he never moved. "Karl VII forced the Dukes to insert her by a bare majority, not by acclaim. The nobles, the ruling class of this Empire, they will rise up and sweep her away. Do you know what that harlot has been doing for the last two years? Serving our enemy!"

The sound of Provst's open palm cracking against Hahl's face echoed like a gunshot. He hadn't put any real force behind the blow, or the Duke would have tumbled bodily from his chair. His hand still flew to his face in shock as his jaw dropped open.

Gunter removed his hand from the gun, where it had suddenly dropped.

"I take exception to that word," Admiral Provst growled in a killing-edge-sharp voice. "*Harlot.* That suggests you don't hold a *Ritter of the Imperial Household* in high esteem, Your Excellency."

He turned and Gunter felt the weight of the man's stare, like a physical object.

Wrath made flesh.

"Remind me to inspect the papers of that young woman we found in here when we arrived, Tifft," Tom Provst purred. "She didn't look old enough to be the Duchess, and I believe the Duke's oldest child is barely of school age."

He turned back to the Duke, taking that mad energy with him.

"Mayhap your companion is a *harlot*, Twenty-seven?" Provst asked.

He backhanded the man lightly enough to add considerable weight to the insult itself.

"I would offer seconds, but there's no way in hell the Emperor would ever allow me to have you to myself on a dueling ground."

"So you'll serve a woman?" Hahl sneered. "An incompetent?"

Gunter expected another slap. Hahl tensed. Provst just laughed.

"Do you find Jessica Keller to be an incompetent *harlot*, Twenty-seven?" he asked. "Perhaps she'll offer you satisfaction, when she returns. Blade or pistol, she's an expert with both. Did you know she's now in charge of the entire war effort against *Buran*? A woman. Imagine that. I suspect she'll do better than any of the men who have been there, since the Grand Admiral will be stuck here for years, dealing with shit-heads like you. I'm just sorry you arrived as late as you did."

Gunter nearly chuckled at the look of comic surprise on the Duke's face. Inappropriate, but so very hard to contain.

"Yes," Provst continued after a beat. "Karl VIII rescinded the *Emergency Conditions* that the Grand Admiral declared before he left, speaking in her name. Had you gotten here while *those* were still in effect, I could have just had you shot out of hand given the evidence gathered by Imperial Security. Well, no, that's not true. I would never have subjected my men to that sort of indignity."

Gunter discovered then that Tom Provst had perfect comic timing, something that Gunter had rarely managed. The next words were better than an ice-cold shiv.

"I would have just put you down myself," Provst concluded. "But now I am required to turn you over to the civilian authorities for trial by a Court of your Peers. Perhaps I'll get lucky and she'll let me serve on the firing squad that executes you, assuming she doesn't have you hung instead. I understand that *zu* Arlo is going through wood at a prodigious pace down on the surface, building enough gibbets for all the people he has had to execute."

Dead silence. Even the air systems were too hushed, frozen with utter fear, to speak.

"Nothing to say?" Provst asked, but there was no response. "Pity. Commander Tifft, your prisoner."

Gunter stepped up and took charge of the Duke. Interestingly, as white as the Duke had fallen, Tom Provst's color had returned almost to normal.

Maybe the man just needed fools and rebels as prey. Gunter Tifft suspected that well would never run dry. He had seen enough intelligence summaries to know the truth. There might yet be a civil war at some point.

Gunter was happy he was on Tom Provst's side.

CHAPTER XLI

*P*remier.

By the Creator, it felt good to be back in the saddle.

Senator Tadej Horvat ran his hands lovingly across the flat wood surface of the counter top. The empty Senate chamber was an ancient place, made almost holy by the work of the men and women who had spent more than four centuries upholding *Aquitaine* and making it a shining beacon to the rest of the galaxy. Even when they hadn't.

Still, it had been years since he stood on this side of that dividing bench. As a member of the Loyal Opposition, it was among the highest personal insults a Senator could offer to stand at the Premier's chair and caress the place where papers would rest. Not that he hadn't dreamed of doing exactly that, but Judit Chavarría was an old and dear friend.

Her time in office as Premier had not irreparably damaged the Republic. Had, in fact, done much to strengthen it, but then, she was no wild-eyed radical. She and Tad still went to the opera with their spouses after dinner for regular double-dates.

And he had almost pulled off the upset two years ago that would have returned him to power. Could have hung the minority government sideways on a yardarm had he wanted. But for Jessica Keller.

He had promised Nils that he would protect Jessica from fools at home, and had, but the last eight years she had become Judit's creature as well. Perhaps they would end up sharing her. Certainly, both of them would rate good mentions in the histories of Jessica's life.

Tad found that acceptable.

After all, he had prevailed in the most recent elections. Not by much, but the numbers had come in and enough of the tide had shifted in his favor that he had regained his power and title with enough spare votes to even allow the occasional vote of conscience from fools and Quixotes.

Movement at the top of the bowl across from him caught Tad's eye. He was no longer alone, sneaking in here so late in the evening.

"I had wondered if I was the only Premier who did that," Judit said cheerfully as she began to descend the steps to her new side of the desk.

The wood here was two meters wide. Traditionally, separating legislators holding swords, so that they could not reach someone on the other side without casting dignity to the wind and climbing atop the meter-tall platform.

Tad fixed her with a wry grin as she approached. His hands continued to stroke the polished surface, perhaps almost pornographically.

"I suspect the list of men and women who haven't done so is much shorter, Judit," he replied quietly.

The acoustics of the room were such that a normal speaking voice could carry to the back walls, if the crowd wasn't too restive.

She grinned up at him as she took her place across the way, perfectly manicured nails resting lightly on the side of the Loyal Opposition. She was still a stocky fireplug of a woman, aging gracefully and finally allowing the gray hairs to infiltrate the black on her head. They had been friends for over twenty years.

"All set to undo everything I've spent nearly a decade accomplishing, Tad?" she teased.

"There is remarkably little I disagreed with, you rogue," he offered. "And for the last two years, the War Government meant that everything was negotiated ahead of time to my satisfaction before it ever became law. And you? Still intent on retiring?"

"Had I not been in your shoes, I wouldn't have stood two elections ago, you old fart," Judit laughed. "Now I'm free. You have no idea how liberating that is."

"Indeed, madam," Tad agreed. "I have spent my entire adult life in service, first to the Navy, and then the Senate in many forms. It is all I know."

"You do raise cattle in what little spare time you have," she remembered with a twinkle in her eye.

"And they barely know my name these days, with all my work for you as Chairman of the fleet committee. But I inquire for a different reason. The future we just fought an election over has changed."

Judit sighed and shrugged.

"My analysts tell me that the outcome itself would have barely budged, had that Imperial frigate arrived here with the news a week earlier," she said. "It is frightening that destroying a planet would raise so little fuss."

"Strange things happening to distant foreigners, Judit," he said. "That is always eclipsed by issues of taxes and morality closer to home. But if you truly intend to retire from the Senate, I might ask a favor of you."

"Oh?"

"Tomorrow, this ancient body will conclave again, and begin discussing our response to the disaster at *St. Legier*," Tad said. "As you know, many of us are former fleet officers, and to a man and woman, all have had some fantasy of bombing that planet into submission during their career. Now, instead of celebrating, we mourn, and ask what we can do to help."

"You think I should retract my resignation, Tad?" Judit probed. "Remain here as your foil to keep you honest?"

"Worse," he countered. "I would ask that you accept Palatine authority and travel to *St. Legier*. To serve as my official representative to whomever they enthrone. If it is indeed Princess Kasimira, she will need all the help she can get. If it is anyone else, we may need to rethink our new alliance with *Fribourg*, and perhaps withdraw back to our side of the border."

"In my hands?" she asked tautly. "On my head?"

"Judit, there are very few people on this planet I trust more than you," Tad offered. "Nils Kasum would be one, but he would not be nearly as acceptable to them as a true civilian, even a woman. And you have just had a long run as a successful woman in charge of a government, to provide Lady Casey the ultimate counterpoint to the fools who would suggest she's incapable of out-maneuvering them. Because she will, of that I have no doubts."

"Palatine is a legally-binding thing, Tad," Judit pressed on.

"I'm aware of that," he replied. "Wakely Okafor did a spectacular job on *Thuringwell*. Another successful woman. You would be too far away for me to second-guess your decisions, so you will need space and power to operate. And backing, if you are going to help them create a new future."

She remained silent for several heartbeats, studying him. How many times in the last two governments had their roles, their positions been reversed, with him on that side and her attempting to fathom the dark waters accurately?

"Do you wish to see *Fribourg* succeed?" she finally asked. "Or disintegrate into civil war?"

And that was why she was one of the few people in the galaxy prepared to step into this role. One of the few he would trust. Most would take it at face value: to provide assistance and coordination to the former enemy in their time of need.

Rare were the ones who would consider how easily they could plant worms into that apple. While retaining white hands.

"I have taken Lady Casey's measure," Tad pronounced carefully. "As *Emperor of Fribourg*, she would be at least as capable a foe as her father or uncle ever were, married to a better understanding of us as a people, from having served in our navy. But Jessica Keller has also left a mighty imprint on the young woman. I believe she will guide her people to a different place than the men would have, given the reins."

"So successful, but weakened?" Judit parsed.

"As long as *Buran* is out there, we require *Fribourg* as a buffer, Judit," Tad said. "If we could magically maneuver all the players onto a board where Keller broke *Buran*, from whence we could initiate a subsequent civil war in *Fribourg* that broke them down into a dozen, petty fiefdoms, I would consider that the greatest possible outcome for the future of the *Republic*."

"And then?" Judit's eyes turned black and serious. "Would you accept the fragmented principalities that had once been the Holy Roman Empire, or would you seek to claim them?"

"Gauis Yulius Kaesar bled out his life on the floor of the Roman Senate, Judit," Tad replied. "Done in by Senators. We will pass the anniversary of that date in a little over five weeks, by my reckoning. If you are perhaps too tall to ride in the chariot with me and whisper dire prophecies, that will still be one of your jobs. And my job, for whatever fool replaces me here."

"Remember, thou art human," Judit murmured.

"Just so," Tad acknowledged. "And we are about to initiate the greatest game of Empires ever undertaken."

CHAPTER XLII

Moirrey tooked an extra breath and wiggled, trying ta get the shoulder shields'n torso half-plate ta sets right. Padding just weren't workin'. Maybes time to pull alls that back out and go backs to an inflatable bladder with lots of pockets. Puts it on, hits the inflate button, counts ta three.

Helmet were on tight 'nuff. Had done the inflatin' thing there, on counts'a needs fer hair and pony tails tucked. Wild hair flowing in the wind might look good in pictures, total pain in the arse in the field, even 'fore bugs.

Still, looked totally freakin' awesome, this morning.

Cut down armored field suit like Impi marines wore. *Adjusted* for boobs. Lacquered over with a messy, green-brown pattern fer hiding in the weeds. Pointy head almost tall on tops as Casey. With bright pink feathers off'n the back 'n glittery unicorns painted on both sides.

Cause, ya know, *glittery unicorns. Duh.*

Backpack bits hobnailed tagethers from three zip bikes and leftover stuff from the dude at the motor pool with nine stripes on his arm and a big laugh. Three meters of wings sticking out. With variable lifters, thrusters, and vectors, one on each kidney, one on each wingtip. Metal wings wired to react to windflow and speed and act like three dozen, chromatically-awesome elevens.

Hover like a monster hummingbird, when she finally gots it ta work'n'.

Pulse pistol on the left side in a holster. Telescoping, katana sword two meters long in both hands like bad-ass *nodachi*.

She just needed forty-six more crazies an' a music departments ta completes the stage.

Today's stage were the landing field where 189th vectored ships serving Mejico. Strasbourg had its own, bigger field 'cross Lake Zurich. Place were cleared big'nuff fer hers to show off.

She missed havin' Saana handy, but the six dudes Vo'd rustled up were competent enough. And not one of them were more than twenty, makin' her feels like an old lady, by comparison.

Thirty-six *prolly were* too old ta pulls crap like this. Until the lift motors came on line and suddenly she were flying.

"Jo, what's the forecast?" Moirrey called over the short-range comm. The suit and hat were full of haphazard electronics, but most of it were held togethers with solder at this point. Once it worked, she'd turn the boyz loose on building her a proper set.

Assuming she didn't street pizza today.

"Stable, crazy lady," the one named Jo replied. "Temperature will come up a little over the next three hours. Pressure forecast is flat for that long. Your flight profile today should be good."

Crazy Lady. That's what they all called her. As good a callsign as anything, she supposed. This were crazy.

Jo o'er there were never gonna wanna do this, but he had the best instincts fer flight motors acting up. Frequently, he could do the diagnosis just from hearing her land. Had, a few times.

Other five dudes just wanted suits of their own. Probably go transfer to whatever unit were crazy 'nuff ta use winged demons as scouts, if today worked.

After all, were Jess's approval started this. And Moirrey's patents, trademarks, and copyrights everywhere.

Filthy, stinkin' rich.

"Incoming," Sharad called over the line, pointing to an ugly, gray box cruising across the field towards them.

As she turned to watch, a bunch more popped out from behind, spreading out on both wings like hunting dogs.

Huh. Pretty good driving trick.

But Vo'd only hired the old farts, so they knowed hows ta drive.

Would need crazy kids fer this stunt.

Rather than pounce, the wall of skiffs all grounded'n men poured out.

Cutlass Force. The craziest of the crazies, with the folks she 'membered from the old days.

Boys with guns poured out'n'took up positions. Guns pointed out, up, and a few in at her.

Professionally-crazy folks. She didn't begrudge 'em that.

Big truck in the middle were the last to disgorge its prize. Cutlass Ten. The folks she really wanted here today. Everyone else were just icing.

Since thems had parked fifty meters away, she waited fer what folks were gonna to walk over.

She were insulated in her underarmor leathers from the chill air o'winter. Dudes were bundled up. Everyone walkin' were wearing cold-weather gear.

Still too early in the morning, but soldiers was like that. Up and dawn and off doing stufffff. Parts of why she joined the navy in the first place, thank you very much.

Moirrey wiggled one last time and counted noses.

Vo were easy ta spot. Nothin' on this planet that big moved like that.

Her Imperialness were next, with a half-dozen faceless goons in opaque faceplates that Torsten had rounded up as the beginning of the new Palace Guard. Apparently imported from one of the other palaces that had survived.

Iakov and Hans, plus the rest, with Victoria Ames on a corner.

Two other dudes added in. Musta been a tight fit in the back o'that truck.

Alan Katche she knew. Primus Pilus. Vo's top bad-ass.

Other dude were the one she really wanted ta sees today.

Cohort Centurion Pyotr Martin.

Commander, *Fourth Heavy Scout Ala, Mechanized.* Drivers of crazy scout skiffs, stripped down versions of what the first three Alae drove, light fer speed, same guns.

Finds ya, fixes ya, calls in *CCLXXIII Heavy* ta smush ya.

Aquitaine Legions were three core plus one attached, with a Headquarters unit for five. 189th were three Alae of Armored Rifle, plus Heavy Scouts, *plus* Heavy Armor. Tuff'n'mean.

Reinforced.

If this worked, they'd be reinforcing some more.

Vo come to a stop and stared. Weren't his show'n'he knowed that. Just here for visuals. And to protect Casey.

Casey were here 'cause stuff like this'd need boss-level sign-off.

Katche were here 'cause he were like that.

Martin fixed her with challenging eyes. Man dinna think girls were tuff'nuff. Mean'nuff.

Not killers.

Tall chick beside him could'a taught him betters.

"Jo, we green?" she asked over the line.

Face were staring at the bosses, but no external speakers yet. Needs space fer other stuff.

"Stay away from the Immelmann and you should be okay," the kid replied. "Pretty sure you'll start shedding vital parts if you try a hammerhead today."

"Can do," Moirrey replied.

She turned to the Imperial party, feeling about as alien as she probably looked. Stowed the sword as tall as she were by untelescoping it back to a simple handle and tucking that into a thigh sleeve.

She curtsied to the Emperor, grinned inside her helmet, and spotted the set of posts her dudes had uprighted to her left.

Two quick steps and Moirrey threw herself at the sky, praying to any available deities that all the lifters worked well enough that she missed the planet.

Right hand held the flight control buttons, such as they were. Up. Down. Fast. Slow. Hover.

Ya steered with yer hips'n yer toes, more than anything. Plus fins on calves that would pop up in a wind.

Feathers on the helmet were just for grins.

Moirrey let gravity lose track of her and pulled back, pushin' the motors up a notch. Like Jo had said, every flight required almost as much prep as a fighter craft right now, but once ya locked in a profile for today's weight and atmospherics, you were golden.

All sudden, she were twenty meters up, moving fifty kilometers per hour. Not much compared to a heavy tank er a skiff, but they couldn't do *this*.

Quick dive with a roll and some yaw. Pike turn to reverse course in twenty meters, headed the other way full bore.

Watch the troopers on the ground get twitchy as she were about to come over them at too-low, too-fast.

'Nother turn. Softer, so's they could track her. Pull out the sword pommel, carefuls not ta drop it an'look silly.

Turn it blade-rear before triggering.

She'd made that mistake exactly once, stalling so hard she near broke things meetin's pavement when the suit stopped going forward.

Blade trigger, and now we gots two meters of two-handed, razor-sharp, Japanese craziness, weigh'n 'bouts as much as a pistol.

Line up the first post. Four meters tall, thicker'n a broom, but not much. We're showing off here. Get crazy-stupids later, ya know?

Swoop.

Gods, but this was fun.

Focus. Count the timing.

Leans *into* the blow so's ya don't break yer bloody shoulder goin' by.

Snap.

Like chopping apples, after a few tries ta gets the touch.

Heels down. Head up. Grab sky.

Think about the hammerhead, 'tils ya remember that Jo thinks you'll fall on yer ass doing it.

Smooth turn over, instead of the crazy drop turn.

Orbits once fer effect.

Next pole is shorter and thicker. Timing still good.

Crack of metal through wood.

Pull right, start her pass on the third post.

Uh oh.

Just lost power on the right side. Left side suddenly accelerating.

Ground looks soft. This is gonna hurt.

Toss the sword well clear of the path yer about ta tumble through the grass.

Deep breath. Relax.

Boom.

Pretty sparkles.

Pretty people.

So glad the helmet is tight and filled with air.

And washed easily, to gets all the mud and grass off it.

Moirrey were surrounded when she figured which way were up.

She popped the lock on the helmet, separating the face piece from the back, so she could pull everything apart and see, optics and mud not mixin' well.

"You okay?" Vo asked, squatted down to her level.

"Not the landing I had planned," she observed dryly.

"Bonus points for originality," he grinned, holding out a hand.

She took it and let him pretty much lift her upright. He were good at that.

Moirrey picked out Jo in the crowd.

"What failed?" she asked.

"Telemetry says a connection on the primary transverse coupling," he replied.

She grunted. Damned thing was still too finicky. Maybe Yan could take a look?

Pyotr Martin stepped close and inspected her like a side of beef hanging from a rack. He walked all the way around her before he spoke.

Casey looked appalled, but she weren't in for this sort of fun.

Martin came back into view and stopped.

"How close to ready is all this mess?" he asked in a hard voice.

"Me'n six dudes," she gestured to her ground team. "One garage. Help from *CCLXXIII Heavy*'s motor pool Decurion. Three weeks from first weld. Just over a year since I dreamed it up and presented it to the Fleet Centurion."

"Three weeks?" he gasped in astonishment.

"Yup."

Martin surprised her by turning to Alan and Vo.

"I want a fourth Patrol added to the Ala," he near-demanded of his bosses. "A whole team of the wildest kids we can find, dressed up like that."

He turned back to Moirrey, face *INTENT*.

"Lady Moirrey, your notes suggest that the team should be mechanized on a military version of zip bikes, yes?" he asked, breathless.

"Affirmatives," she said, drawing herself up to full height. Which weren't much. Dude were nearly Vo's height. Maybe half his mass, though. "With Deadman switches built in, and remote flight controls added to the armor."

"We're going to need a new Ala design, Pyotr," Alan tossed into the conversation. "Nothing like this in the Table of Organization and Equipment. Light Strike Scout?"

"Closer to Fourth Saxon. Start with that and adapt. Saves you time," Vo said, drawing a nod from Moirrey and Alan. And two of her mechanics: Andre and Kiran.

Studied cowboys, did ya's?

"What is all this?" Casey asked, a bit befuddled. "What have I just seen that has all of you so excited?"

"What Yan did to warships?" Moirrey said, catching Casey's eye, and her nod. "I just dids to th'army. Boys'll wanna play."

Moirrey locked eyes with Trooper Ames, quietly standing off to one side, being all soldier-like'n'stuff. Got a grin, in spite of serious face over there.

"And girls," Moirrey added.

CHAPTER XLIII

Jessica placed her hands flat on the inclined surface of the lectern and gazed out at her audience. All the senior officers from her squadron were gathered, listening rapt as she had gone over the intelligence her teams had gained. The main conference room was packed.

"Any questions?" she asked as she took a breath.

Stanovoy had been unbelievably successful, shattering the local economy and capturing a Hammerhead destroyer intact enough that they had been able to strip the corpse of all the parts they desired.

Technically, that included a prisoner, in the form of the *Sentience* itself, but Jessica had very pointedly not brought home the actual equipment needed to connect the half-dozen boards into a whole and rouse the beast. He would stay dead, preferably forever.

The rest of the Hammerhead's crew had remained behind. Jessica had no need for more prisoners. All the information she had needed had been in the computer core and the equipment they had stuffed into the flight bay on *II Augusta*.

A hand went up, off to her left.

"Command Centurion Ihejirika?" she said.

The man who had commanded *RAN Mendocino* for the last decade and a half did so because he had found that to be his calling in life. Waldemar Ihejirika wasn't a warrior. He was a shopkeeper. He just happened to bring supplies to forward bases and fleets, instead of keeping a five and dime somewhere in Penmerth.

In person, the man known as *The Mailman* was an average-looking Anglo, skin almost bleached by comparison to Jessica's darker heritage. He had jet black hair that was straight, so she had always assumed some level of Diaspora Chinese in his family history.

"Technically, we're operating under a Flag of Convenience, Fleet Centurion," he replied, carefully ignoring the uniform of an Imperial Red Admiral she was wearing today. Possibly, reminding her of who they were. He had been with her long enough to do that comfortably. "But we're still the *Republic of Aquitaine* Navy. Under what legal justification are we delivering this material to *Fribourg*, instead of hauling it to *Ladaux*?"

From the grunts and muttering around him, Jessica could tell that most of the people here had wanted to ask that question. Only her inner command: Denis, Enej, Robbie, Kigali, Tamara, and Alber'; really understood the whole story. The rest had only heard rumors.

She nodded succinctly to Waldemar, acknowledging his question as she looked for the right words. Casey would have had them on the tip of her tongue, but that woman was born a poet.

She still missed Casey's bright face every morning.

"Because the war is over, *Mendocino*," she finally said to him. "Someone we know and respect is going to sit on that throne, guarded by other people we trust. Centurion *zu* Wiegand will rule. Emmerich Wachturm will protect her. And Vo. If *Buran* defeats *Fribourg*, and they were doing just that before we arrived, then *Ladaux* would have fallen in our lifetimes."

That got the response she was expecting. Angry growls and hoarse negations.

"Because *Fribourg*, for all its militant culture, fought their war predictably, and honorably," she continued. "How many battles have been fought and lost for *Samara*? You can almost set a calendar by them. In their place, we're going junkyard dog on that bastard, to quote Yan Bedrov. Some of you were there for the *Long Raid*, what those damned historians are calling *Keller's Raid*, ignoring the contributions of Denis, Alber', Kigali, and several thousand more of you who were with me. We're not capturing worlds in order to force a peace with *The Eldest*. Karl VII was honorable enough to end the war after *Thuringwell*. This bastard has gone back to bombarding inhabited worlds from space. Emmerich Wachturm estimated twenty million people were killed in the first twenty-four hours, with something like two hundred million at risk over the course of a year."

She paused long enough to grab a water bottle she had hidden in the lectern and suck down a cool mouthful. She could feel her own temperature going up as she spoke.

"That is not the mark of a civilized nation," she stated flatly, curbing the fire before she breathed it out, dragon-like. "*Fribourgers* likes to think they're tough, but before now, they never would have gotten ugly. Today, the problem is that they wouldn't know when to pull back. That's why they need us. We're going to go in surgically, using terror as a weapon and devastation as a tool. We are not the sword. We are the sledgehammer. Their defensive squadrons, in places like *Osynth B'Udan*, live in terror of the next *Buran* raid coming to their world. But *The Eldest* can't risk that while we're rampaging through his hinterlands, destroying his own economy. And eventually, we will defeat him, or cause his own worlds to break away. *Buran* is not a hive. He is a single, God-obsessed machine. His fleets are other machines. Dangerous, but dominated by *The Eldest*. Without his own people, he can't threaten ours. I want them more frightened of us than they are of their own overlord."

Jessica took a deep breath.

"Did that answer the question, *Mendocino*?" she called.

Waldemar grinned.

"And then some," he replied.

Several chuckles emerged.

Maybe Jessica had gotten a little wound up. Even she had never imagined that she would be so deeply entwined with the fate of the *Fribourg Empire*, but Torsten was going to become the husband she had never imagined finding, and Casey had turned into the daughter she never had. Perhaps even more so, now that the woman had lost her mother, the indomitable and irrepressible Empress Kati.

Jessica fixed her attention on the man seated next to Waldemar. The commander of *Mendocino*'s sister ship, *RAN Duncan*.

"Command Centurion Kovack," she tagged him, causing the man to stir and sit up straighter.

Illiam Kovack was as short and squishy as Waldemar was tall and skinny. Kovack had a big, bushy beard, like the winter fairy, although still brown in spots. He did have the mischievous elf's twinkling, blue eyes.

"Fleet Centurion," he called back in a pleasant, tenor voice.

"We have their attention, *Duncan*," she said. "Our next attack will be at *Yenisei*. Because *Mendocino* is leaving to haul loot back to *Fribourg* as soon as he's ready, you'll be on your own to mind the whole squadron."

She gestured to the room around them, and the station itself.

"This station is packed to the gills with supplies right now," she said. "Everyone in the squadron is going to carry as much as they can, and I'll award prizes to the most creative logistics teams for packing, but you'll still be hauling the lion's share. It will be a mid-winter's night, and your bag will have to have presents for every child in the squadron, good or bad."

That twinkle was bright enough she could see it from clear up here. Somedays, she wondered if the man really was part elf.

"Stockings will be full on mid-winter morning, Fleet Centurion," he said in as serious a voice as she had ever heard from the man.

"Any other questions?" she asked.

The room was silent.

"Then your weekend will be over in thirty-six hours and you'll start seeing routing orders for supply shuttles and docking priorities to load."

Jessica Keller looked out over the silent, intent faces staring back at her.

"And then, ladies and gentlemen, we're going hunting."

CHAPTER XLIV

Casey had always walked quietly, even on gravel, so the old hardwood of the converted hotel's upstairs hallway was nothing. The four men around her made even less noise as they moved, but that was partly due to the enclosed helmets they wore, allowing them to talk amongst themselves and the larger team outside.

She had perhaps finally gotten used to being surrounded by armed men every moment of every day.

At least Tobias Inmon had survived the devastation, and volunteered to return to duty. He had been her bodyguard in the Princess days, retiring to his farm when she went off and joined the Navy. He wasn't in the field with her but had accepted a civilian promotion to head the armed side of her personal Household. He would keep her safe.

She paused outside the door to room two-forty-three.

The hallway hadn't changed much since they took it over. The Hotel Arcadia had been a little long in the tooth and in need of refurbishment: new paint, new carpets. Love. The maroon rug beneath her feet was worn and starting to show threads. The art on a nearby wall was a watercolor beachscape done with more enthusiasm than skill.

Still, in her time of need, it had become an Imperial Palace, if only temporarily. The entire ground floor was given over to soldiers, servants, and bureaucrats, imported temporarily from other facilities around the globe. Mostly from Father's favorite hunting lodge near Yuular.

Her government had offices and rooms on the second floor, it being just as easy to live and work here as to live here and evict some lawyers and accountants from empty space across Mejico's main square.

Casey supposed Santiago or Yuular would have been more comfortable. Strasbourg had suffered far less physical damage. But she needed to be here. Closer to the wound in her people's heart.

Her soul needed to be able to talk to all the ghosts and help them find peace.

She laughed to herself at such fancy and knocked lightly.

"Come," a muffled voice answered.

It wasn't worth the argument this morning, so Casey let one of the bodyguards open the door and step in first, taking up his place in a corner with a good view and clear lanes of fire if necessary.

After a while, they will become invisible, if you work at it hard enough.

She remembered Jessica's complaints that the only time she could be alone was in the bathroom with the door locked. Casey had perhaps a little more leeway, but only because the rest of her armed team was never farther away than the next room.

Vigilant.

She entered the hotel room that had been converted to an office and located a chair.

"You are not required to knock, Your Majesty," Torsten said as he looked up from behind his desk.

At least he didn't drop everything and stand, like most people. She was slowly working on beating that behavior out of people in these more informal circumstances. That was correct in public, but she wasn't always on stage. They didn't need to be there, either.

"That is correct, Torsten," she said seriously. "I choose to."

She gestured, and another of the men closed the door. With face shields down, identifying them was difficult. Someone, probably Tobias Inmon, had picked that team to be nearly identical, physically. It made a kind of sense. If you could never tell which trooper was which, suborning one, or knowing his weaknesses, was difficult. But she hadn't learned their walks well enough yet to tell them apart, either.

It didn't help that all six of her normal men were within two centimeters and three kilograms of each other.

"How may I be of service?" Torsten asked as she settled.

He set down his pen and ignored the stacks of papers at hand.

"I'm more concerned about the government," she said. "Should you be here, or is there another location that would be better suited? It has been over four months, and the shock of the emergency is starting to wear off. You don't have to remain at the center to do things."

He grinned at her. Most of a grin, anyway. She could see the lines of exhaustion that hadn't been there six months ago. His hair was starting to come in almost completely gray, making him even more the august professor than he had been, although he was too well-dressed for that.

Another of Vibol's walking art exhibits, though much more professional-looking than what the tailor would put her in, if she gave the man his head.

"I am blessed to have been able to simply order people from Yuular and other places to attend me here," he said with a deprecating shrug. He rarely ordered anything, preferring to sneak up on bureaucrats. "They refer to themselves alternatively as *The Junior Varsity*, or the *Country Cousins*, within the group themselves as an inside joke, and are used to working as a team. For the rest of the planet, I have, as you approved, taken the revolutionary expedient of promoting people to Acting Directors and Deputies from their current positions, with the understanding that Imperial Security and the *Inspectorate Generalé* will be watching carefully. And they will remain in that position for a year, unless they give me cause to remove them."

"Is that wise?" she asked.

At the time, it had been a necessity. But to give some of these men free reign for a year?

"The other planets already generally self-govern, within the Imperial framework, Your Majesty, both through their Duke and their appointed Governor," he said. "While many Dukes were present at Werder, few Governors were, so most places can run themselves for a time. I am exercising direct control of *St. Legier* in your name, until the military emergency subsides."

"But the Imperial staff you have promoted?" she asked. "The civilian one? How many nobles make up the tier you have endorsed?"

"Very few," he said, turning serious. "The civil service is frequently a middle-class career, from which a few outstanding examples are regularly ennobled, or perhaps encouraged to marry into noble families. In Werder, the senior ranks were almost completely made up of the noble class. A few survived by being on vacation or missions. They have been plugged in wherever I needed the most authority."

"And the rest?" Casey pressed.

"You ordered a quiet revolution, Kasimira *zu* Wiegand," he said in a hard, low voice. "But not necessarily a slow one. A place somewhere midway between the Magna Carta and the Charter of Man. The Empire must run. I will bind these people more closely to the throne than anyone imagines by giving them a greater stake in the thing itself. Already, hostile reaction stirs in the shadows, noble men not given over to rule by a woman. We will need the support of those commoners, men and women like myself."

"That is why I am concerned that we move too fast, Wald," she retorted.

Privately, she soared on morning breezes, but that was her soul. Her mind still performed the cold calculus of Imperial leadership, balancing factions against one another.

"It does not help your cause that I am betrothed to Jessica Keller," he acknowledged flatly. "Many fear that she will eventually turn on them and rejoin her conquest of Empire, however fanciful that dream might have become. Others see me as an insurance policy that she will not. But there will always be a hard core of dissidents demanding a return to the ways of Karl V."

Casey fought to keep the snarl off her face. Her great-grandfather had been a reactionary of the worst kind. The Charter of Man had been an organic demand to end the sorts of arbitrariness of that man's rule, by embedding rights for commoners into a law he could not ignore on a whim.

"Do we have the people?" she asked pointedly.

He sighed.

"I think so," Torsten said. "Sales of your books and music have exploded recently, and I have taken the liberty of borrowing all of that money into the Imperial Treasury with notes owed to your personal accounts. Emergencies are just that, but we have been able to finance many things out of your residuals that might have had to wait, otherwise. So I think we have enough of the populace. After a year, we'll have more, God willing. The Fleet is as solid as Em and Hendrik can make it, with Tom Provst as their avenging angel. The Army is more questionable, but Arlo has made it clear that his next task after cleaning up *St. Legier* is to strike directly at *Buran*. As he effectively is Army High Command with the help of the Fleet, they are with him, but rebuilding will be a task to undertake soon. It helps that most Divisions and Armies are self-contained."

"But he is another foreigner in our midst?" she asked.

"Oh, God no, Your Majesty," Torsten laughed heartily. "He *is St. Legier*, right now. The complaints I hear whispered are more from the well-bred that a commoner holds their reins. And that he is a man they fear, having watched Rohm taken down."

"Would Rohm be a good commander?" Casey leaned back into the chair and studied the art on the wall behind Torsten. More bad watercolors, but it had a certain flair. "Should he be the next Grand Marshal?"

"We would need to have a long conversation with Wachturm, first, Your Majesty," he replied after a moment of thought.

Casey wondered what art Torsten Wald had hung on the wall behind her, where he would see it every day. She hadn't thought to look when she came in, hotel rooms being, by definition, impersonal spaces.

Who was Torsten Wald, when he was alone?

"We will need to solve *zu* Arlo, at some point," she half blurted.

Wald fixed her with a neutral stare and a raised eyebrow.

"As you have said, he is *St. Legier*," Casey continued in a rush, trying to find the right words. "The people are invested in him to protect them, possibly more than they are me as Emperor. How do we leverage that? How do we leverage Vo?"

"I don't know," Torsten admitted. "Have you asked him what he wants?"

Casey blinked. Shocked still by the question.

No. She had not.

Had anyone asked Vo what he wanted?

Ever?

She had heard rumors and stories. Tidbits and insights from Jessica, Moirrey, and others. Arrested at seventeen and given the option of naval service or jail. Highly intelligent. Loyal to a fault. Exceptional in all tasks he set his mind to, according to the spies responsible for knowing these things when her father had decided to make a grand example of the soldier.

A man committed to always doing what he thought was right, consequences and costs be damned.

But had anyone ever asked Vo what he actually wanted?

She doubted it. They assumed the man, like she had. Assumed his strength, his resilience. Accepted him as a force of nature that could be reasoned with, but not thwarted.

If Casey didn't know who Torsten Wald really was, did anyone know Vo *zu* Arlo?

244

CHAPTER XLV

DATE OF THE REPUBLIC FEB 19, 402 FLEET
HEADQUARTERS, LADAUX

The sign on the wall outside of Petia's office read *First Lord of the Fleet.*

Her office. Her favorite Impressionistic art on the walls. Thick, muted carpet she had picked out on the floor. Petia Veronika Naoumov had worked her ass off for a very long time to make it this far. The only thing she had kept in the suite had been the desk Nils originally installed. It fit her as well as him, they being of a height.

Petia could have retired any time in the last fifteen years and measured it a successful career. In any other century, she would have been ranked among the giants, but it had been her fate to serve in the same fleet as Nils Kasum and Jessica Keller. Those names would be immortal. Of that Petia had no doubt.

The man who had led the fleet to perhaps its greatest strategic victory: a lasting peace with *Fribourg.* The woman who might be the greatest commander *Aquitaine* ever produced.

But Petia was here. Now. And she was going to make damned sure that they didn't lose everything in the aftermath, relaxing at the very moment when things got worse.

Buran. The Eldest. A death machine commanding more stars than *Aquitaine* and *Fribourg* combined.

Who had just declared war on the entire galaxy.

Petia felt her chin come up and a snarl form on her face as she

245

reviewed the notes set down by none other than Emmerich Wachturm and communicated to her personally by one of the frigate captains that man trusted to make a regular, high-speed mail run between capitals.

It would be fascinating reading to a civilian, but Petia had just spent several days reviewing footage of the battle itself and reading reports assembled by her analysts. The tactics. The ships themselves.

There was nothing at all new technologically, other than that new warship/super-bomb that had cracked the shields protecting the Imperial capital with what Imperial scientists thought was a shaped anti-matter charge. Dangerous and unstable, but not all that innovative.

Nothing the beast did was new. It was as if he had frozen his technology and tactics at the moment when his kind had destroyed *Earth* two thousand years ago, and then coasted for better than two millennia since. If some of his tools were better than hers, Petia had no doubt that people like Yan Bedrov and Moirrey Kermode had dedicated themselves to beating that mark.

Petia made a note to send a team back to *Ballard*. The Librarian had been reborn in her golden cage. Perhaps it was time to dive deep into her records and see what other ancient technologies might be within reach of the ancient beast. Or coming and as yet unseen.

A chime let her know that the next appointment had arrived.

"Come," she called, pressing a button to open the hatch.

Senior Centurion Roderick Stone entered first. When Kamil Miloslav had been promoted to Fleet Intelligence, Petia had hired a nephew, her sister's son, someone that she had known since birth. Convinced him to remain in service rather than returning to civilian life and going into politics.

One of these days, the man would probably be a Senator, if he wished. He was that good at his job. It made her life easier.

Rod nodded and stepped to one side.

"Command Engineering Centurion Vlahovic, First Lord," he said.

Iskra Vlahovic entered behind the man and came to attention. She hadn't changed, a medium-sized blond, tiny compared to Petia's great height. A former fighter pilot who had survived a dogfight that should have killed her. Who then used her time recuperating in a hospital bed to retrain herself as a flight deck engineer before eventually taking charge of the deck on the old *Auberon*. And the new one.

She was the quiet, stubborn woman who had commanded a badly-broken Star Controller *Auberon* on her final flight home to the wrecker yard, with a mostly Imperial crew aboard and all but one of the original, surviving pilots.

"First Lord," Iskra said quietly.

Everything she did was quiet. Firm, though. Unbending.

"Please sit," Petia offered. "We're awaiting one other."

Iskra had nothing to prove to anyone. One look at the woman's record and Petia had known that. Had she been of a bent, Petia had no doubt that Vlahovic would have been commanding a dreadnaught these days. She did not fidget, but carefully scanned the entire room exactly once, perhaps seeking clues of her new First Lord.

They had known of each other for many years, but Petia couldn't remember if she had ever actually spoken to the woman before now. Iskra Vlahovic would have made a big-enough impression, so she presumed not.

The chime rang again, and the door opened a moment later.

Stone did not enter, but waited in the outer office.

"The Premier arrives, First Lord," he called softly.

Tadej Horvat entered and took the empty seat, placing himself on Vlahovic's left without a word. The grin that flashed on the man's face for a moment was enough to know his mind. Unlike Iskra, Petia had known Tad for better than forty years. The Fifty Families were a tightly-wound tapestry, if you looked close enough.

Vlahovic responded with a single, sardonic eyebrow as she glanced at the newcomer.

"Iskra, there are going to be a number of responses to the attack on *St. Legier*," Petia began. "Both official and unofficial. Big news and little news."

It was telling, the way the woman responded. Or the near lack of response. A single eye cast at Horvat, and then sternness. Not stubbornness, but a woman expecting to have to eat a badly-cooked meal and smile about it afterwards. Petia flashed back to the early days, before her husband Artur had learned to really cook.

"Part of the official response will be to promote *Digger* Wolanski to Legate and expand his normal Construction Ala to an entire Legion by pulling in other teams for the duration," she continued. "We'll load up two Assault Carriers to transport them to *St. Legier*, so they can help rebuild."

"I see," Vlahovic replied as a placeholder, using so little emotional loading that it might as well have been invisible.

"That's the official bit," Petia admitted with a grin. "Unofficially, we're sending a few other ships along, who will continue on past *St. Legier* and join up with Jessica and *First Expeditionary*, out on the frontier."

"Who?" Iskra asked bluntly.

"*RAN Arad* has passed her Induction Trials and come out of dry-dock ready to fly," Petia said. "Plus a brace of corvettes."

"*Arad* is a converted bulk freighter," Vlahovic observed dryly.

"That happens to now carry fourteen, modified *Kartikeya*-class GunShips, Iskra," Petia replied. "Designed to engage on the *Buran* frontier. It was actually Jessica's idea originally, since that design has a short range JumpSail that could be used tactically, once the ship itself was carried to battle."

"Yes," Iskra said minimally. "We used the trick with *Necromancer*, back in the old days."

"So, three carriers, and three escorts," Petia said. "I know you are close to retirement, but I wanted to ask for one more big mission from you, Iskra."

Again, the eyebrow, and nothing more. Fortunately, Jessica's notes on the woman were extensive and accurate. Petia wondered if she should have conducted this entire interview via scrolling marque text on a screen, just to make Iskra more comfortable.

Petia nodded to Tad to finally join the conversation.

"That force needs a chief, Command Centurion Vlahovic," Tad said warmly. "One familiar with Wolanski and his *peculiarities*. Plus one also familiar with exotic flight deck operations, and with Jessica Keller. It would mean delaying your retirement some, but the government is prepared to promote you to Fleet Centurion and place you in command of said Task Force."

Telling, how Vlahovic's entire head turned to stare at the man. Petia suppressed a grin. Jessica's notes were extremely useful for predicting Iskra Vlahovic's behavior. Which sticks, which carrots to use.

"Fleet Centurion," she observed carefully. "Not Fleet Engineering Centurion?"

"That is correct," Tad replied. "Fleet Centurion. The line commander over the Task Force."

"You already have two Fleet Centurions in place," Iskra said.

"You will be carrying orders with you," he grinned even broader as he offered the bait. "Promoting Jessica Keller to First Centurion. Emmerich Wachturm has, by now, already given her field command of the war with

Buran. The least we can do is match the man. That's the unofficial bit, lest *Buran* come to understand just how much my government is committing to the war effort. At least until she reminds the creature."

A moment of stillness passed, like a pond at dawn before the birds awoke.

"*RAN Arad,*" Iskra finally said. "Who else?"

"The Assault Carriers *RAN Akatsuki* and *RAN Archangel,*" Petia replied. "The corvettes are *CA-410, CE-411,* and *CE-417.* The Fleet Replenishment Freighters *Leggett* and *Redding. California*-class, like your old friend *Mendocino.*"

"*CA?*" Iskra asked.

It was Petia's turn to grin. She had the woman now. That much was obvious from the change in body language: leaning forward, eyes squinting as she made plans, fingers twitching like playing a piano, or typing on a keyboard.

"*CA,*" Petia confirmed. "Tomas Kigali has proven the worth of such a design, in the hands of someone crazy enough to fly it like a battlecruiser. I know a few men and women who fit the bill."

"Very well," Iskra said with a sharp nod. "I accept the commission."

From the gleam in her eyes, Vlahovic was more than accepting. Excited. Petia could see the woman awakening to one last mission, like Roland hearing the horn. And her force would also help Arott Whughy, letting them extend the war ever-deeper into enemy space as construction yards delivered enough of the new designs that Petia could spare ships for the front line, and not just defending against the first *Buran* attack here.

Nils Kasum had spent most of his career as First Lord on defense, saving *Aquitaine.*

Petia Naoumov was going to see how much of hers could be spent on offense, on the other side of mid-field.

CHAPTER XLVI

IMPERIAL FOUNDING: 180/03/01. MEJICO, ST. LEGIER

Vo stared out the window of his office and contemplated the morning's weather.

St. Legier had been originally colonized for the near-identical conditions to the fabled *Earth* of distant history. The Homeworld from which humanity had originally sprung, some ten thousand years ago. The same orbital length, the same inclination, the same over-sized moon. Leap years followed a slightly different cycle, but one that only numerologists noticed.

So it was still the depths of winter at this northern latitude, according to the calendar, but on the back side and beginning to think about spring. Except it wasn't. It hadn't been. The planet couldn't make up its mind.

Instead of a hard, unrelenting cold, the disruption of weather patterns had caused a sudden warm spell to come over them. Outside, the rain was almost pleasant, by comparison to two weeks ago.

Everything was mud, as a consequence.

Still, it helped harden the men, and form a tighter comradery, laughing at the poor space marines who weren't used to dealing with mud and water getting into everything. And bitching about it to Army troopers for whom it was second nature.

The only thing that might make the whole thing better would have been throwing in a Hussar of horse cavalry, so the men had to muck stables and curry whiny princesses every morning.

Vo felt a smile, in spite of himself. Still, he kept it to himself. He kept all of them to himself, since they were as rare as hen's teeth, these days.

A knock at the door, followed a second later by Reese Borel entering.

"Alan's here for your seven o'clock," he said, standing to one side so the Primus Pilus could enter.

Vo went back to his desk and sat. The piles of paper were low today, but that was him staying up later than normal last night, getting things done.

Alan Katche sat at the desk with almost a grin on his face and sipped coffee from a mug he had obviously stolen from somewhere. Or walked out of Tenochtitlan with, where they had found it somewhere along the line. It was from a television show popular in *Aquitaine*: *Beyond the Dragon Gates*.

How the hell had something like that made it to *St. Legier*?

Vo stared at the man who was his right hand. They had been together a year now. Alan waited patiently for him to speak.

"We've done all the rescuing we're going to, at this point," Vo announced. "Things have settled into garrison and security, with some construction work."

"Affirmative, Vo," Alan said. "Having the Emperor here with us has drawn in more volunteers and experts to rebuilding, but the area of devastation is simply impossible. We'll be working across a zone nearly one hundred kilometers across, subject to ground quakes and bad weather for at least two years. Maybe longer."

"I'm about ready to walk away and get back to soldiering, Alan," Vo said.

The Primus Pilus responded with a bit of a start.

"So soon?" he asked.

"Not much left that requires us here," Vo said. "The Emperor will decide where she wants her new capital, but that won't be our job. Strasbourg is turning into the northern financial capital, at least for now. The civilians can handle it from here."

"Have you told her?" Alan probed.

"No," Vo countered. "And I haven't told Torsten Wald or the Grand Admiral, either. I wanted your thoughts. Are the men starting to get blunt?"

"Not these men," Alan laughed. "The biggest problems I've had with discipline have been a few men who got overwhelmed by things and had to be talked off ledges. Survivor guilt, but more, because they see themselves as failures, for not having stopped it. There's nothing fat and lazy with these men. Probably won't be, for another year."

"Understood," Vo nodded. "I sleep with those demons every night. And I think it's going to get worse, as time goes. That's why I want to focus them on a new task."

"Which would be?" Alan asked.

"Vengeance," Vo snarled quietly. "We can't hold an enemy planet, not with anything less than about fifteen divisions of troops and complete orbital control. But we can land, and cut a swath of devastation across a few before we withdraw. I would like the folks over there to understand what it means to have their world shattered by monsters from deep space."

"What will she say?"

There was only one woman Alan would refer to that way. Emperor Karl VIII, the former Lady Casey *zu* Wiegand.

"Alan, I'm not going to ask her for permission," Vo retorted. "*Maybe* her blessing, but that's it. I promised the people of this planet that I would carry the sword to *Buran*. Not even an Emperor is going to stop me from doing that."

Alan was silent for a few seconds, considering.

"What if she forbids it, Vo?" he finally asked. "Or worse, promotes you to something like Grand Marshal and chains you here?"

Vo considered the man, in turn. Alan Katche wasn't someone he drank with off-hours, except when the cohort centurions were having dinner. Wasn't really a friend, in that sense, but Vo was hard pressed to identify his true friends.

Jackson Tawfeek, once upon a time, but he hadn't seen the man in years. And he was a Chief now. Moirrey, but she was busy as a Lady-in-Waiting *cum* Mad-Scientist these days. Hans and Iakov and a few of the men from the old days, perhaps, as far as that went, but they were enlisted grunts now and he was an officer, and that was a big divide. Dash and some friends from Fourth Saxon.

All people he had served with, and liked. None who knew the inner Vo. He had managed to keep the entire galaxy at arm's length. Even Rebekah Kim had moved on, eventually, unable to accept that distance around him.

What if she did forbid it?

"I would resign, Alan," Vo finally admitted. "All my commissions and ranks. Every award. The works. And then I would go find a banker willing to loan me enough money to start a mercenary company, with returns paid on loot or sense of patriotism for the worlds I would shatter under my fist."

Alan blanched in surprise.

Then again, he might be the first to see the inner fire that drove Vo. At least since a scrawny eighteen-year-old first stood at attention on Navin Crncevic's deck and took the oath.

Navin had known the truth. Vo supposed that they might be peers enough, these days, that they could be friends. Perhaps when they both retired, if old marines like them ever did.

"Walk away?" Alan sputtered.

"Nobody has any hold on me, Alan," Vo stated. "That's part of the reason I can be successful in this job. I was willing to meet Rohm on any dueling ground and kill him like a chipmunk. Before that, there were others who thought their noble birth and careful breeding made them better than me. I would have happily crushed any of them, as well."

He tapped an angry finger on the desk between them for emphasis.

"I promised these people that I would do something, Alan," he ground out the words in the rage he had been hiding. "Nobody will stop me. Not her. Not the Grand Admiral. Not even the Fleet Centurion. The only question I have for you is this: When I light that fuse with them, will I be going out there alone, or will I have the entire 189th behind me?"

"Vo, I haven't kept you up to date on the recruiting tasks I have to handle as Primus Pilus," Alan countered in a hard voice, smiling slightly. "We could spin up an entire second legion just from the men trying to find a spot with us now, because they know where we're going. Perhaps an entire Corps. If I pushed, you might have access to something like Seventh Guards Army backing you when that day comes, so don't you worry about us. You work on those three people. I'll bring the rest of the damned Army along behind you."

Vo nodded. Primus Pilus meant *First Spear*. The man closest to the enemy. He had chosen Alan Katche for exactly that personality, that temperament. He would be first.

But Vo *zu* Arlo would only be one step behind him.

CHAPTER XLVII

"*First St. Legier?*" Torsten sputtered, staring in shock at the document General *zu* Arlo had brought along to their regular meeting. "Don't we already have enough divisions of troops?"

"This isn't a division, Chief Deputy," Vo said carefully.

Torsten was always amazed at how little the man moved. How emotionally compact Arlo had grown in the last two years that Torsten had known him. Vo *zu* Arlo would make an amazing poker player with so few outward indications about him.

Torsten set the paper down again and rubbed the bridge of his nose. He should have known Vo would have something big in mind when he asked for their weekly meeting to stretch to two hours from the sixty minutes he normally allotted.

Vo wasn't one to sit around and chew the fat.

"So let's pretend I'm an old, Imperial Fleet hound, Vo," Torsten offered. "Who's easily confused and a little lost here?"

That got a grin out of the man. Just a ghost of one, but the first he could remember from Arlo since they were both aboard *Auberon* together. In the distant past.

"Division is what *Fribourg's* Imperial Land Forces calls their single, largest, maneuver unit," Vo said, stacking his hands on the desk for emphasis. "Squads form platoons. Companies. Battalions. Regiments.

Divisions. Corps. Armies. Fronts. Depending on the type of division, you'll have somewhere between three and twelve thousand men involved."

"Why such a disparity?" Torsten asked, engaging the econometricist side of his brain rather than the politician.

"Smallest number of men is a tank division," Vo said. "Largest is pure infantry, with just enough attached transport to move the headquarters around in a pinch."

"Got it," Torsten said. "And you want to raise a new unit, but not a division? A legion on the *Aquitaine* model, right? Why?"

"Correct, Torsten," Vo agreed. "Because the 189th has so many men trying to get into it that there are no empty billets, anywhere. And more keep trying, plus all the civilians rushing to sign up for service. This is a way to channel that enthusiasm. Most Army units are designed for garrison and defense."

"But not a legion?" Torsten let the doubt creep into his voice.

"Oh, most legions as well," Vo agreed. "But not the 189th. I specifically designed it for planetary assaults."

"I see, and you can't just add more…what are the various units called?"

"In an Armored Rifle Legion, like mine, the smallest unit is a lance, made up of three transports, with nine crew and twenty-one passengers at full load," Vo explained, patiently even, which Torsten appreciated. Land forces were not something he had ever studied in detail. Certainly not *Aquitaine's*.

"Three lances make up a squadron," Vo continued. "With an extra command vehicle and team thrown in. Three squadrons makes up a patrol, with a Support Lance of three engineering vehicles. Three patrols makes up an Ala. Around eight hundred and fifty men when fully equipped. Plus another hundred or so mechanics and armorers."

Vo paused until Torsten nodded, absorbing the details rapidly.

"Good," Vo said. "So a normal legion has four Alae, plus a headquarters unit that has the artillery, transport, construction, and support teams. Except that one of the four Alae is almost always swapped out to another Legion, to provide training and expand that Legate's options."

"Three Alae of horse cavalry, with armor attached, such as at *Thuringwell*," Torsten noted, feeling his feet finally settle under him.

"Exactly," Vo agreed. "189th is *Reinforced*, so we have three Alae of Armored Rifles, with an Alae of tanks, plus an Alae of Heavy Scouts that are then getting a fourth Patrol added as soon as Pyotr Martin can get Moirrey's winged troops idea equipped and trained. Five Alae, all total. As much as I can handle in the field."

Torsten leaned back and considered the man. He had probably known Vo the longest, of everyone in the Empire, having traveled from *St. Legier* to *Ladaux* with him and Jessica at a time when Lady Casey was trying to become an ambassador to the Republic, and later a Centurion. And Torsten possibly knew him the best of everyone, recognizing the unquenchable drive underneath the man, a glacier happily grinding down whatever mountains might get in his way.

"In the field," Torsten noted. "Generals aren't supposed to be in the field with their troops in battle."

"Nor are Legates, Torsten," Vo completed the thought. "But that's why I can only command five combat formations at once. I'll be on the ground with them."

"And a second Legion?" Torsten probed. "What would we do with it? What would you do with it?"

"I wouldn't do anything, Chief Deputy," Vo countered. "Alan Katche, my Primus Pilus, tells me that he could recruit an entire legion just from people trying to join us when we go after *Buran*. Traditionally, a legion is named after the planet where it was first raised, and numbered accordingly. I'm proposing that you raise *First St. Legier* this year, while you have a number of very angry people who suddenly discovered how much they value the Empire."

"And not divisions?" Torsten asked.

"Divisions are the old way of fighting, Torsten," Vo said. "They'll hold ground, and put down uprisings. It's what they have always been used for. Legions go out and conquer worlds."

"If you were interested in taking supreme command, you could just order it, Vo," Torsten trod lightly.

He was rewarded by the most sour, angry face he could ever remember Vo making. It reminded him of an angry dragon, just waking up to find you in his hoard uninvited.

"No," Vo said. "Next stupid idea?"

Torsten grit his teeth rather than take the bait. He knew Vo wasn't angry with him, just with the entire, galactic situation.

"Who would you suggest, then?" Torsten continued. "Is Rohm good enough to handle it?"

"Arald Rohm is a political general, Torsten," Vo echoed Iakov Street's assessment, reinforced by personal experience. "You'll need political acumen and maneuvering, once you start to pull together elements from regional commands and schools, and tell them they have to re-invent Imperial Lands Forces itself. There are a number of Flag Generals and Field Marshals out there who will need to be soothed and assuaged after the rough treatment I've given them. We'll also need the support of the Crown, the government, and the Grand Admiral during the rebuilding phase."

"But you won't be involved?" Torsten said. It was in the nature of a question, but they both knew the answer.

"I'll be out wreaking my terrible vengeance on *Buran*, Chief Deputy," Vo said. "I had this conversation with Alan Katche, and I informed him that I would rather turn into a pirate if that was what it took. I know a few who would help, so it's not an empty threat."

"And you'll leave me to explain it to her?" Torsten asked.

"I'll handle that," Vo said. "I want you providing calm analysis rather than emotional reactions when it comes up. You and Wachturm will be the first two people she asks."

Torsten considered the hard-headed man in front of him. And the equally stubborn woman ahead of him. And the things that maybe nobody else saw. He wondered if those relationships could survive.

CHAPTER XLVIII

Jessica confirmed her next appointment on the schedule, one final time. She had a standing meeting with Denis going back years. It had been daily, back when she commanded the first *Auberon* and he was just her amazing Executive Officer. When he took command of the second *Auberon*, they had gone to three times per week in his role as flagship commander of her Task Force.

They had retained that rhythm, spending thirty minutes going over anything that needed to bubble up from the ship to her as Fleet Centurion or Admiral, but Denis had a good crew and rarely needed anything from her except to check in.

So him adding a meeting off-schedule had her concerned somewhat. Not much, this was Denis. But still.

She was drinking freshly reconstituted fruit juice this morning, one of the thousands of containers stuffed into every available space on the ship and in the squadron. One freighter had to be the general store for everyone, and she wanted to strike deep, so they would be gone for a while.

Not so long as to constitute a risk to food stocks, but it was always better to have too much food for the crew, rather than too little, when a navy was only as good as its larder.

The hatch signal chimed, followed by its opening and Marcelle poking her head in.

"All good?" she asked.

Jessica nodded. Worse come to worst, she could sneak off to her private stash of more juice in her attached cabin, or run off to pee and leave him here for a few moments.

Denis entered as Marcelle withdrew. He had a serious look, which just threw Jessica further off-center. Denis was usually the calm anchor of the crew. Plus, he was wearing white, the day uniform of an Imperial Admiral, rather than his traditional black-and-green, so she had no idea what was coming.

It was likely more serious than office gossip and romances.

He sat. Studied her for several seconds.

"So I might be out of line," he began, awkwardly. "But I also made a promise to the Grand Admiral, and that kind of eclipses the normal order of things."

"Did you now, Admiral Jež?" she teased.

He was grinning, so she joined him.

"Emmerich instructed me, in no uncertain terms, to watch over you, Jessica," Denis said. "To keep you safe and sane. He reinforced that when he came for Casey."

"I see," Jessica said as a placeholder, unsure of what the two men might have discussed.

"So I'm speaking as a friend, a colleague, and for your guardian angel," Denis continued.

Jessica nodded. It was obvious Denis had worked himself up to this speech.

"We're going to *Yenisei,*" he observed. "Scout, strike, withdraw. The classic maneuver of a strike carrier squadron. But we're doing it so far behind enemy lines that we might set a new record, especially given our linear distance from *Ladaux.*"

Jessica just waited rather than speaking. Best not to betray her inner thoughts, whatever they might be.

"Plus, we're doing it with a sledgehammer that might be big enough to fracture *Samara,*" Denis continued.

"And you're here as the personal representative of the Grand Admiral," she stated flatly.

"I am," Denis agreed. "He wanted me to remind you occasionally that you don't have to win the war in a day. That they've been fighting this front for nearly forty years, off and on."

He fell silent, perhaps unsure of his next words.

"And what brings you here today, Denis?" Jessica pressed.

"What happens after *Yenisei*?" he replied. "We didn't need to pack so heavily for a single hard run in and out. I can see being careful and retaining the tactical edge to do things while we're there, but you're up to something. As the commander of your flagship, I'll do whatever you order, but as a representative of the Grand Admiral, I want to make sure you aren't planning a second hop, deeper, to jump out and hit *Winterhome*."

Jessica grinned. She had considered that option, but didn't have the right formation for an attack on *The Eldest* himself, even just to pull another *2218 Svati Prime* on them.

"Yeah, I thought so," Denis said after a beat, finally relaxing from his rigidity. "Where are we going? And why couldn't you tell anyone?"

"Because I won't know if we can even try it, until I see what *Yenisei* has protecting it," Jessica admitted. "I nearly got us all killed at *Trusski* by making bad assumptions based on how *Fribourg* did things."

"Well, you've got *Vanguard* this time," he said, gesturing to the mighty warhorse around them. "What did you learn at *Stanovoy* that you won't even whisper to yourself in the dark, let alone tell the rest of us?"

He was serious today, and wouldn't be brushed off lightly.

"*Buran* is an egg, Denis," she admitted finally.

"An egg?"

"Tough shell," she continued, holding up her hands as pantomime. "Hollow, gooey center. Yolk. Once we pierce the outside, we can run rampant, as long as we go sideways. The yolk, the oldest stars in *The Holding*, are going to be better defended, all the more so because we'll be operating so far from any *Fribourg* bases."

"But we've got Forward Base Omicron," he countered.

"Yes, we do," Jessica said. "And we know how their navigational system works now, so we can avoid *Holding* vessels for the most part, if we're careful. *Pochtovyi Trakt*, the Postal Road. Those are blood vessels carrying oxygen to the systems. Nerve bundles carrying commands to the muscles. *Stanovoy* was a remote system, far from anyone important. The kind of place I'm known for hitting, after the *Long Raid*. *Yenisei* will hold to that pattern. Closer in, but still not all that important, except that now we're getting closer to the home systems. The yolk."

"So we're likely to go hit a second system after we presumably hammer the shit out of *Yenisei*?" Denis asked. "Who?"

"*Severnaya Zemlya*," Jessica pronounced. "The capital of the *Altai* sector."

"When everyone would expect us to go after *Ninagirsu*," he breathed. "The bulwark defending the *Altai* sector."

"They would," Jessica said.

"Okay, so now I'm here, representing Wachturm," his voice hardened. "Are we taking too big of a risk? As you said to me, early in the *Trusski* campaign, we can't win the war today, but we could lose it."

"We absolutely could, Denis," she said. "But *Yenisei* has absolutely nothing of military or economic value. Us hitting them is a black swan event. Just bad luck that they drew the short straw."

"And on our way home, we are supposed to make a run at *Ninagirsu*," he realized.

"We are," Jessica said. "But we're not. We're going deeper. And I plan to hop sideways and give *Severnaya Zemlya* time to absorb the essence of the calamity so they can send help, both to *Yenisei* and to reinforce *Ninagirsu*. What idiot would dare attack *Severnaya Zemlya*?"

"Indeed," he admitted. "So I'm doing my job for Wachturm. We've pushed *The Eldest* back, like you intended. Pissed him off, if *St. Legier* is any indication. Materially damaged him at *Trusski* and *Stanovoy*. Should we wait for help?"

"Absolutely not," Jessica countered. "He's built that assumption directly into his planning. He is a machine, Denis. Logical, but not creative. He can play chess better than anyone because he thinks thousands of times faster and can try millions of moves. He can make checklists so he doesn't forget anything. But he cannot make an imaginative leap. All he can do is assign probabilities, and then work to mitigate the biggest, because his fleet is tiny for the number of worlds he has to protect, particularly in relationship to *Fribourg*. If we were to build a thousand CA-type corvettes, we might be able to simply overwhelm the bastard, purely on numbers, like a nest of fire ants."

"Have we considered doing that?" Denis asked. "Fire ants and corvettes?"

"No," she stopped cold, surprised at so obvious a possible solution. "No, we have not. Damn. And Yan went back to *St. Legier* with *Mendocino*. Grab Tobias Brewster and have him spend some time working up some scenarios and then fighting them with his crew down in the Emergency Bridge. He's better at that sort of thing that most people, and

I'm sure he's been refighting our battles to learn to be better. He got that from me and you."

"Got it," Denis said. "And waiting?"

"*The Eldest* must rule people, but allows them no independence," Jessica noted. "A human might guess at what we're up to, but the machine will assume the logical outcome. We will defeat him with chaos and by making him look fallible. All we need is enough of his people to doubt him, and they'll stop listening."

"And then what?" Denis asked seriously. "Peace?"

"No, Denis," Jessica said. "And then they won't stop us when we come to kill him."

CHAPTER XLIX

Casey remembered her previous interactions with Arald Rohm: Field Marshal, Commander of the Seventh Guards Army.

They were not pleasant memories.

He was not a pleasant man, on the whole, being solely dedicated to apparently two tasks: achieving supreme command and marrying into the Imperial family.

Lady Heike might have been acceptable to the man, but Emmerich Wachturm had never expressed anything remotely like interest in such an alliance for his favorite daughter.

Casey supposed that, in another world, Father might have considered a man like Arald Rohm as a prospective son-in-law, married to Steffi. Casey's sister had only ever aspired to a happy home and a large brood of children running around. Steffi had always been the most practical of the Imperial children. So Casey had watched the man maneuvering with a careful eye.

Marriages at this social level were rarely love matches. Most families approached them like long-term business deals, where everyone was *satisfied enough*, even if very few turned into the kinds of romances for the ages like Mother and Father, or Uncle Em and Aunt Freya had.

When Steffi had been murdered, Rohm's cold eyes had turned to Casey next. That he was approaching fifty now, and had more than twenty-five years on her just meant that she could have expected to outlive the man by forty or fifty years had Father determined that to be the best match for his remaining daughter.

With Father and Ekke dead, Casey *was* the Imperial Household today, as far as that went. Arald Rohm might have turned his covetous eyes on her, but she was no longer a child, and no longer a mere woman. She was an Emperor, now. His avaricious dreams would have to wither and die on the vine unless he was willing to settle for one of her more distant, distaff cousins, the kind who hadn't been important enough to reside anywhere near the Death Zone on that day.

Casey banished the evil grin from her face as she made a list of prospective names, inversely ranked according to her personal opinions of them. Lady Moirrey was staring at her with a weird grin, like she could guess at Casey's thoughts.

"What?" Moirrey asked.

"Nothing good," Casey admitted. "Planning who we could marry Rohm off to, to get him out of my hair."

"Ya considereds findin' him a foreign brides, m'Lady?" Moirrey giggled. "We know lots back home. Maybe he likes hisself a pirate? Oh, I knows. *Wiley*'s be awesome good fer 'im."

Casey nearly spit, laughing at the thought of Arald Rohm wed to Shiori Ness. *Wiley*'d probably kill them for suggesting it. But she might also like the idea. Take it as a challenge.

Casey wondered if she could steal Jessica's Flag Commander and make the woman the second admiral in the history of the *Fribourg Fleet*. That would be fun, just watching Em and Rohm fume.

"Hush, you," Casey finally whispered amidst the giggles.

They were seated in firm chairs in a solarium kind of porch, at the hotel that was the temporary Imperial Palace until she decided where she wanted to build her new one. Plants filled the space with greenery and hints of flowers. It was warm with today's partial sun, but not terribly hot, nor bad with the kind of humidity that she was unaccustomed to from serving on a starship.

She and Moirrey had the space to themselves, not counting two bodyguards in the corners and a couple of quiet girls coming and going, running errands. Locals. Survivors who had volunteered to serve, and been vetted by Melina Arcidiacono personally, her own three being too young for the job right now. Maybe in a few years.

One girl entered now with a tea service for four on a nice tray. The Imperial silver of Casey's great-great-grandmother was gone forever, presumably. This had been functionally looted from one of the surviving stores in Mejico, like so much. They would be a generation sorting out things like that.

Moirrey had fallen silent, but the giggles were still there in her eyes. Casey assumed she was just waiting until this afternoon, when she could go flying again and play aerial games with Vo's new scouts.

"Thank you, Anna-Katherine," Casey said as the girl placed the tea and sandwiches on a close table. "We'll serve ourselves. Send the gentlemen in."

"Yes, Your Majesty," the girl quietly said as she withdrew with a quick curtsy.

Girl. Casey considered Anna-Katherine. Perhaps three years younger than she was, at most. The product of a family at the lowest rank of nobility, with Anna-Katherine's father being local Freiherr. The girl had barely any formal education in scholarly or artistic pursuits, having been raised to marry well, perpetuate the family line, and keep a proper household. Nothing more.

Nothing else was needed, for far too many of them.

Casey grit her teeth rather than say something rude. It wasn't Anna-Katherine's fault, or even her father's. He was who society had made him, just as the girl was. The solid, stolid backbone of the Empire, just like the Fifty Families that had founded *Aquitaine*.

Casey would be at this for her entire life, and had only just started her revolution.

Shadows at the door. Two men, stopped and inspected by Casey's troopers, regardless of who else might have passed them previously. Men who had failed an Emperor would die before failing a second, regardless of having been half a world away and powerless against stars falling from the heavens.

After a moment, Torsten Wald and Arald Rohm were allowed to join she and Moirrey on the porch.

"Your Majesty," Torsten nodded serenely as he entered. "Lady Moirrey."

Rohm did the same, and then all four of them were seated, with Moirrey on her right and Torsten on her left.

It was an interesting contrast, Torsten dressed in a navy blue jacket and slacks, and she and Moirrey wearing their Ritter sundresses, as the fashion magazines were calling them now. Rohm had gone for what looked like his best day uniform, sage rather than the flashier full dress version. The kind that Vo wore when he had to be dressed up, normally preferring the field utilities instead.

After so much time around Vibol Harmaajärvi, Casey had developed a keen nose for the intricacies of fashion, a thing that the tailor took as seriously as Em took fleet maneuvers. Rohm was in a precisely-tailored uniform, wearing just enough ribbons and tags to be impressive, without looking like a spring peacock. Casey couldn't say if it represented a new leaf in Rohm's life, or if he was just trying to look more like a soldier and less like a suitor.

As if.

Casey still had no interest in being close enough to Arald Rohm to even consider physical contact, let alone wooing. The way he had always looked at her before reminded her of a valuable horse. A prize, a thing, rather than a person. That his eyes had always kept wandering down to her chest and hips, as if measuring her breeding capabilities, had done nothing to improve her humor about the man.

Still, she needed him.

Moirrey took charge, serving the tea, with honey and cream as needed. Casey's favorite dork could act like the most well-bred Imperial Lady when circumstances, or her friend, demanded it. Like today.

Moirrey was still a dork, though, most of the time. That helped keep Casey sane, too, even if she was *never* going flying in a personal scout suit. Those folks were nuts.

Small talk ensued over tea and snacks. Weather. Construction schedules. News about friends and relatives that had happily been off-planet, when everyone had assumed them dead.

Nothing of particular consequence.

Casey decided they had been social long enough. At this point in her life, every moment not spent in meetings and paperwork was time she wasn't sleeping, and there was already too little of that. She placed her mug on the saucer and fixed Torsten Wald with a sharp, penetrating look. Almost hostile, but he had already prepared everything in advance.

Much of this was for show.

Wald, in turn, nodded sagely. He placed his mug down as well and turned to Rohm, who had turned the first bit apprehensive. Perhaps smelling the trap beginning to close.

"The Crown is concerned about circumstances related to events on December Nineteenth, Field Marshal Rohm," Wald began, invoking his authority as Chief of Deputies, one of the few who reported directly to and spoke for the Emperor herself. The Head of her Government, itself. "There are ugly rumors circulating. And a video conference we watched involving yourself and *zu* Arlo."

She had considered having Vo here for this conversation, but had decided that it would push the conversation in the wrong direction, making it too adversarial. Rohm, or someone like him, was necessary, especially as Vo had made it clear he would never agree to take Jenker's place.

Casey watched Rohm turn a little paler. Not much. Probably more tension than fear. As Vo had made clear from his reports, Rohm had started badly enough to possibly warrant his execution, and then had worked like a draft horse to redeem himself in the time since.

Rohm pursed his lips after a beat but remained silent. Casey watched his body language like a hawk, and was surprised when his eyes went down, instead of up. Raising them would suggest lies impending. Grand stories and deflections. About what she expected of the man, all things considered.

Down suggested contrition or internal anger, but she was unconvinced. Arald Rohm, or someone like him, was a necessary evil, yes. And he would have to convince her that he should be the man in command. She would let Wald and Uncle Em, *zu* Wachturm, deal with the situation after that, until she had to get personally involved.

Carrying through on Arlo's threat to have the man executed rose to that level, even if Vo had written subsequent reports specifically detailing the exceptional work Rohm had done at Strasbourg, perhaps to reward the man for earnest effort.

"I made a serious mistake, Chief Deputy, Lady Moirrey, Your Majesty," Rohm admitted in a small, serious voice, finally looking up to meet each of them eye to eye, his lips still compressed. "General *zu* Arlo saved me from compounding it, at great cost to himself, but I still do penance each day, having forgotten myself. In my arrogance, I thought to brush the man aside and show him how to handle such an operation, on the assumption that a foreigner, and a navy man to boot, would have no choice but to fail, while I would gain everlasting glory for myself."

"Indeed?" Wald pressed. "Considering how the two of you met, how was *zu* Arlo able to bring you around?"

"He had made it clear that he would happily annihilate me and my men with no more thought than culling sheep, in order to get me to understand the stakes he was willing to play," Rohm uttered. "After I arrived, he put me to work, Chief Deputy. Made me get my hands dirty, as he intended."

"Work, Field Marshal?" Moirrey asked.

Casey listened to tones as Moirrey leaned in and centered the man in her gunsights. Bad cop, perhaps?

"I was given to understand that he assigned you to take command of Strasbourg's infrastructure tasks and had Admiral Provst eventually drop nearly a regiment of marines for the task."

"That was later, Lady Moirrey," Rohm replied simply, quietly. "On my second day here, serving under his authority, I was out in the field with Cutlass Ten. That was the day we recruited Trooper Ames, and I began to realize how far I had fallen from the man I was supposed to be."

Casey marveled at the choice of words. *Recruited.* She would have expected Rohm to say *rescued,* or something similarly dismissive of a woman living rough. And he called Victoria Ames *Trooper.*

"But that wasn't the day I realized the true depths of my error, Lady Moirrey," Rohm continued. "Roughly a week later, we found…"

Casey watched the hardened soldier stop dead and clamp his mouth shut, eye dilating, as if he was holding back tears.

Arald Rohm?

"What did you find, Field Marshal?" Casey finally broke her silence.

This was not the Arald Rohm she had been expecting. Leopards and spots, but something had changed about the man. Something significant enough to alter his very trajectory.

Casey wondered if it had been for the better.

"We found…" he paused again, drawing a heavy breath in and releasing it before he matched her gaze.

"We found an elementary school, Your Majesty," Rohm finally said. "The bomb had knocked the entire building over. Most of the children and teachers had been killed by walls falling in and other debris, but a few had survived, at least long enough to die of exposure a few days later. Burying those children was the single hardest task I have ever faced. And I did it myself, ordering the others away. I finally understood then the magnitude of what *zu* Arlo goes through every day. Went through, creating the order we have from the shattered chaos left behind."

"I see," Casey said, watching the anguish carve new lines in Arald Rohm's face as he relived that day.

"Afterwards, Daffidd de Bruyne and Thaddeus Gunderson, two of the men of *Cutlass Ten*, took me back to base and stayed up with me, getting me very drunk, and then making sure someone was with me all night, and in the morning," Rohm said. "That was point when Vo sent me off to Strasbourg. He knew the truth."

Casey leaned back and sucked a quiet breath. The man seated across from her suddenly sounded more like Em or Tom Provst than the peacock he had always been before. That had been a reason he had been assigned to Santiago, rather than High Command in Werder. Grand Marshal Jenker hadn't liked the man at all, but found him to be a competent general, an assessment Em had echoed.

Vo had spoken of Rohm in better terms, but had also been there that next morning, obviously.

He knew the truth.

Torsten glanced over at Casey. She nodded.

"What is the status of your command at Strasbourg, Field Marshal Rohm?" Torsten asked as the emotional energy bled out of the man.

Rohm stared at the Navy man for a long second.

"Commander Withers is prepared to take over for me immediately," he replied, deadly serious. Resigned, if not relaxed. "In case I needed to be removed from command today."

So, an intelligent man, after all.

Casey had wondered at the thought processes that might accompany an order to attend the Emperor privately, and alone. Especially when she might have an axe to grind with the man. He could have been tried for mutiny. Possibly still could technically, if someone had determined that Rohm should become an example for the rest.

Certainly, Karl V would have carried through Vo's threat to have Rohm's head on a stake. But her great-grandfather had been an ass, to read even the official, laudatory histories.

"Do you think you should be relieved, Field Marshal?" Torsten continued.

Casey had never appreciated just how implacable a voice that Torsten Wald had when he wanted to use it. But she supposed she had never been in a position where he needed to use it on her. Only *for* her.

"I serve at the will of the government and Her Majesty," he said, carefully enunciating the legalism involved in a voice bereft of any emotions whatsoever.

"And if we determine that you should be transferred to another command?" Torsten ground on.

"I serve," Rohm repeated. "Life with the 189th has taught me something about the uniform I wear. Reminded me. For them, the simple words *We stood* are enough. Because they did. They stood firm and unbending, and continue to do so. I serve an oath. It was only in field with them that I came to recall, to appreciate what that oath meant. The costs to the men, and women, that I serve with. If you have a place other than Strasbourg where I should do my job, you have but to order. What is your will?"

Mentally, Casey revamped her list of prospective bridal options. *Wiley* stayed on it, but Casey could see moving this man closer to the heart of power with a good alliance. Not that she would ever consider him, but he had done something to redeem himself for the last ten years. Perhaps it would be enough.

Torsten turned to look at her. Casey nodded again. She had been apprehensive before, knowing how much that she needed this man. His rank, his birth, and his place in the Army made him a potentially powerful ally, or a terrible enemy, should she have to excise him.

But he had apparently gone into the fires and come out purified. Vo had seen it. Recommended him. Others had agreed.

He knew the truth.

Casey had still needed this. To know the man's soul.

"Our will?" Torsten announced. "It is to have you take Anthohn Jenker's place as Grand Marshal of Imperial Land Forces, for the purposes of rebuilding the Army."

Casey felt bad, but only internally, watching the man recoil in surprise, even just a little bit.

"But I thought Arlo…" he trailed off before completing the thought.

"We will have other tasks for *zu* Arlo," Casey proclaimed. "As Grand Marshal, you will be required to assist him."

Rohm nodded, sharp and short.

"Yes, Your Majesty," he replied quickly as his voice turned wistful. "I had just hoped to be there with Cutlass Ten, when they first hit alien dirt."

That caught her off-guard. Casey had been thinking about Vo in the present tense, not that future where he had gone off to wreak his terrible vengeance for the deaths of Annette Fuchs and Annette's father, Walter. When he left, and she remained behind to hold together an empire with men like Torsten Wald, Emmerich *zu* Wachturm, and Tom Provst.

And Arald Rohm.

Could they succeed?

Would it be enough?

CHAPTER L

Jessica was reminded of the planet *Bunala*, far away home in *Corynthe*, looking at the devastation around them on the screens of the flag bridge. The planet known on the rims as *The Boneyard*, with hundreds of ancient starships, both warships and freighters, abandoned on the surface in one, long rift valley on the southern continent. All of them had been methodically stripped in ancient times of every bit of valuable kit, leaving only the metal skeletons behind, rusting and crumbling slowly in the sand and dust.

Yenisei looked like that today on all screens, every direction. With the added benefit of the pieces tumbling in three dimensions as the gravity and atmosphere of the world below dragged at them with inexorable fingers. And ships dying in real time. Another quiet system, slightly off the beaten path and more of a regional hub for trade than *Stanovoy* had been. At least until yesterday.

There had been a Mako in orbit. Past tense. Deep enough down that he might have had a chance to escape, given the edge of the gravity well above him as a tidewater mark for Expeditionary vessels. Even for Alber' or Kigali.

He should have been safe.

Ballard had taken the lead for the team this time, dropping down on a hard, slingshot orbital path that brought her onto the Mako's rear flank at high speed. A cannon firing from that range might have warned the

Sentience of the Mako that something was amiss, but two sudden searchlights of ECM: hard, electronic static from *Ballard*, had blinded and confused him for just long enough, drawing his eyes down and back in confusion, away from the threats coming from other directions.

Jessica had let Robbie and Alber' have that enemy ship as a joint effort, coming out of JumpSpace and crossing the Mako at high speed, headed in opposite directions at full tilt. Between them, they had shattered their smaller cousin with four Type-4 beams and their full Type-3 arrays, all at once, followed a moment later by the Bubble Guns, fired earlier but arriving as holes had been punched in Absorption Panels and the hull underneath. Kigali, on *CA-264*, had come in a few moments later and finished the bastard off, leaving the three men and their crews free to go after every freighter and country ship in range.

Those folks still hadn't learned the necessity of having an emergency jump programmed, but they also didn't have the money to keep their JumpDrives charged at all times, just in case there was an Imperial raid.

Pity.

Vanguard had taken on the only other warship in orbit, a single, lonely Hammerhead with its snout tucked into the biggest orbital platform. Unlike the berserkers, Denis had come in at low speed from behind, almost at rest *delta-v* to the station. Two salvoes had put paid to both targets, shattering the assembly into pieces with enough drag that they would have to be towed to a higher orbit soon, in order to be kept from falling to earth.

And then the hunting had begun.

At short range, a Type-1 beam or two was sufficient to seriously damage most small freighters, if not disable them, given the tiny number of defensive panels those vessels carried. At longer ranges, a Type-3-Tuned set for distance hit like a Type-2 beam, which could shatter delicate systems and trap a ship in range of a carnivore. Most of the corvettes with Type-3 beams had opted for splitting them short and long, retaining the ability to hit even harder, so they could work their way up to the big, bulk jobs, the kind that hauled thousands of shipping containers, or megatons of grain between worlds.

And they had.

Buran freighters were not armed. No civilian vessel, those piloted by a human, was allowed a beam weapon of any kind, and piracy was unheard of, there being no place to sell looted cargo in a nation where a single, *Sentient* system ruled everything and counted every Lev. Even *Fribourg's* most ambitious raids had never penetrated this deep into the interior of *The Holding*, at least not in records accessible to Jessica.

Nobody knew what might lie on the far side of *Buran*, another thousand or six light years away. Whoever might be over there, if there was anyone still free. After this war, perhaps she could take *Ballard* on a grand tour and find out.

Jessica checked one last time, but there was absolutely no resistance. Instead of a large number of small stations, *Yenisei* had orbited only four large ones. Two had exploded outright under the withering barrage of inbound vengeance. The others had been dismembered with blowtorches.

"Enej, are we ready?" she asked in a companionable voice.

He had gotten mostly over this sort of thing, hardening up after watching the chickens be culled at *Stanovoy*.

"Affirmative, Fleet Centurion Admiral," he said, commenting subtly on her choice of red day uniform instead of white.

It was an *Imperial* effort, but most of them, her and Denis excluded, were still exclusively *Republic*. Only Denis was also wearing white today, forward on his bridge.

"Put me on squadron channel first," she ordered, waiting for his nod. "Task Force, this is Keller, aboard *Vanguard*. I have the flag."

Translation: piracy time was over and you need to start acting like a unit again.

"All vessels move to Point Nineteen," she continued. "Repeat: Point Nineteen for rendezvous and next phase. *Vanguard*, stand by for Phase Eight."

"Roger that," Nina Vanek replied a moment later. "Phase Eight ready, Flag."

"Launch Phase Eight, *Vanguard*," Jessica ordered.

Unlike *Trusski*, she didn't feel the need to make any formal announcements about legalisms and niceties here. *The Eldest* had conducted an orbital bombardment of a civilized world without provocation. She was merely reciprocating, even if she still observed her own code.

Seeker, the man who was once the *Khan of Trusski*, might have been able to enlighten the locals about the finer details, but he had defected wholeheartedly and instead explained everything he knew to anyone in the Empire who would listen.

Ethnographers were having a field day as a result, but Jessica already understood the psychology of fear as a weapon. It translated nicely into all languages without much vocabulary or syntax. *The Long Raid* had been one dramatic example of the maxim that you could drive experimental rats crazier, faster, with a random diet of punishments and rewards, than you could with straight punishment.

The Expedition was just the same, on a larger scale, with the added costs of the number of people she was going to have to kill, to get their attention rooted more on her than their immortal overlord.

Around her, the hull of *Vanguard chucked* once with a hollow thump as Phase Eight went downrange. Moirrey might be gone, for now, but Saana Robles was still down there with what had been *Auberon*'s Art Department, committing glitter and unicorns.

Because glitter. And unicorns…

It was *First 2218 Svati Prime* all over again, except this bomb was going to go lower into the atmosphere before detonating politely and scattering its payload into the prevailing winds, up-range of the capital city and larger population centers.

The ancient term for what the bomb contained was a circular: a small newspaper or pamphlet with a single essay or treatise printed on it, to be handed around in the days before electronic communications. These were a more durable version, a vegetable plastic Arott's team had found that would last for perhaps a year exposed to weather, and they were printed on both sides in four languages, picked for more psychological impact: Bulgarian, English, Mandarin, and Mongolian.

Anyone, *Republic*, *Empire*, or *Holding*, should be able to read them. To know the date and time that *The Eldest* had killed twenty-something million innocent people by dropping an anti-matter bomb on them from orbit. To understand that the ancient beast of terrible legend had returned, and made this a war for the future of humanity. To ask themselves why questioning the overlord was cause for death and not merely re-education.

And to know that the new Red Admiral, Keller Marie Jessica, was coming for them, as long as they continued to wage war on innocents and children.

Jessica wasn't proud of the sentiment she and Enej had worked up, but she suspected that the poet in Casey would have approved of the words. It read like something she would have done, before she became an Emperor.

"Put me on a clear channel, Enej," Jessica said into the silence.

He nodded a moment later.

Jessica studied the debris fields, spread out in all directions of the planet's orbit. The only vessels left whole in the vicinity flew *IFV* flags.

"*Yenisei*, this is Red Admiral Keller of the *Fribourg Fleet*," she announced in a voice that *Kali-ma* might have recognized. "I had a point to make at *Stanovoy*. And a mission. I do not have one today, except to continue to repay *The Holding* for bombing the Imperial Capital world of *St. Legier* with orbital weapons. *The Eldest* must be punished for his crimes. Until you convince him to behave like a civilized being, the destruction of your ships will continue and I will stalk your worlds without mercy. You have been warned."

She cut the signal and nodded to Enej.

"You're back on squadron channel," he said.

"Squadron, this is Keller," she said. "When you arrive at Point Nineteen, we will form up, and then move on to Act Two."

Enej bowed his head, eyes hooded, as he contemplated their next raid. *Second 2218 Svati Prime*, all over again.

Only this time, she wasn't playing a practical joke.

CHAPTER LI

Torsten always thought of the place as the lab of a mad scientist from a bad vidshow, even though he felt guilty at the comparison. It was merely the sanctum sanctorum of First-Rate Spacer Vibol Harmaajärvi, *Master Tailor*, currently on loan to the Imperial Household.

But only on loan.

Jessica would demand him back at some point. As would Amala Bhattacharya and a few others. Lady Moirrey was technically his chaperone, keeping him safe from poaching by Imperial families who thought that with enough money they could possibly entice the man. Nobody would dare cross Jessica though, doubly so as her fiancé was the head of government now.

It made for an interesting dynamic, watching people reduced to only calculating the angles they might pursue, in order to gain temporary entrée to the man. Grand Admiral *zu* Wachturm was possibly more accessible than the man responsible for dressing Casey and her Chief of Deputies. And even Torsten had to pass a full team of men from the 189th Legion to get inside this otherwise-empty warehouse.

The office up front, which had once apparently been the shipping department, had been gutted. Several work stations had been brought in instead, tables of increasing size, each with a different sewing machine installed. The smallest looked like a toy, compact and as precise as a silversmith's tools. Larger one for everyday use. An industrial version that looked as though it could sew field armor. A long-arm device apparently used for quilting. Something called a serger that only made sense when he had watched the Master Tailor use it to do whatever it was called to fix the edge of a bolt of cloth. *Serging*, he supposed. Another machine with a small computer console was used for machine embroidery.

Lab of a mad scientist.

Lady Moirrey didn't have so many different tools and workstations at hand, except when she went down to the garage she shared with her team of hawklings.

A new sewing manikin in a corner caught Torsten's eyes as he entered, surprising Vibol in the middle of committing his esoteric magic at the everyday machine. Torsten recognized the pattern, though he was surprised to find something like that here, of all places.

It was a tunic of the old Slavic style, such as might have come from *Skuodas*, his home world. The front hem came down to just above the knee, split for horseback, with a six centimeter, complicated, Nordic pattern sewn in bronze, white, and black, perhaps four centimeters from the bottom. The same embroidery and pattern was present on sleeves that would only fall to just past the elbow, as one was expected to wear a longer, softer shirt underneath, or studded leather bracers, depending on whether your field of combat was the boardroom or the meadow.

Torsten found his feet drawn closer to the figure as he lost track of the rest of the room. He hadn't seen an outfit like this one in perhaps decades, since he was a boy.

The placard around the neck hole was much wider than at the hem or arms, running almost to the point of the manikin's shoulder and coming down to mid-chest still two handspans wide, with corners and a point at the center, plus a gap down the center that was two fingers wide at the sternum and three at the top. Here, the tailor had repeated the other pattern, around both the outer and inner edges, with a different design Torsten didn't recognize in the larger space between them. A simple, leather belt rested on the hips, held with a plain disk for a buckle.

Torsten felt a ghost at his shoulder. He turned to find Vibol Harmaajärvi lurking. The man was not grinning, but the light was there in his eyes. The tailor was approaching sixty years standard, and taller than Torsten by a few centimeters, but skinny, almost lanky. As always, a number of pins were stuck into his right cuff for quick use, and his hands were covered with tailor's chalk.

"You will be wearing cropped jodhpurs," the man announced in that voice that would brook no argument. "Buttoned on the outside of the calf from knee to ankle, and done in a good bronze seamed with gold, as soon as I find the right fabric. None has been acceptable, as of yet. Black, short boots of a soft leather. White, linen shirt underneath."

"I see," Torsten temporized.

He had come down here to discuss fashions for the Emperor, not himself. If that still remained an option. He might be Chief of Deputies, but Vibol Harmaajärvi was Jessica's secret weapon against the galaxy. Nobody and nothing intimidated the man.

"When was I to be wearing this outfit?" Torsten gestured vaguely at the manikin.

"At your wedding to Jessica," Vibol pronounced. "It will be a traditional event for a favored son of the planet *Skuodas*. I presume Ladies Casey and Moirrey will attend as her *Wardens*. I will need to get accurate measurements for your two as well, so I can complete the wedding party. Admirals *zu* Wachturm, Jež, and Baumgärtner will of course be in dress uniforms, as will First Lord Naoumov and all Command Centurions in attendance."

Torsten turned back to the blue tunic, so simple and almost plain, and yet so laden with potential meaning.

"How did you...?" he began, sputtering quickly to a halt.

Vibol turned suddenly and strode across to a wood bookshelf Torsten had previously ignored. The tailor pulled a worn, green-bound book down and placed it on the work table between them. Torsten had followed. Perhaps *drawn in by the man's serene gravity* was a better term. The desk separated them but offered Torsten scant protection.

Torsten lifted the tome to read the spine. The book itself was old and worn. And this cover had the feel of being a replacement, considering the raw, worn edges of the pages.

Skuodas: Rebirth and Empire.

Torsten could remember reading this book in school thirty-some years ago. The history of his homeworld, one of the few that had survived the fall of mankind and the thousand years of darkness, before wandering merchants and explorers had brought them from the iron age to space in a single generation, like so many other places that had survived.

And then, a century later, the *Kingdom of Fribourg* had arrived, not even yet the *Empire*. As conquests went, it had been quick and relatively painless. And the three centuries since had been good for his home.

Torsten opened the book and noted the little placard on the inner cover page, added after printing.

From the personal library of Emmerich Wachturm, Duke of Eklionstic.

Wow.

Torsten felt his mouth screw sideways as he considered. His day had completely derailed by now.

"I had not given the topic of my Wardens that much thought, as yet, Master Tailor," Torsten finally offered. "I have been in service, both to the Navy and the government, for twenty-five years. Many of the men I would have considered were at Werder with Karl VII."

"Then it will be necessary to locate and nominate their replacements, sir," Vibol said with a firm tone. "I cannot imagine you will lack volunteers, but they must be men of character, whose every association reminds you of how you came to be standing there and why they would deserve such an honor."

"I see," Torsten acknowledged after a moment. "I had actually come to talk with you about Her Majesty."

"Her wedding will not be for several years yet," Vibol pronounced. "So while I have the design, the work itself must be delayed, as I expect her to grow more fully into her figure over that time. The sewing itself will be a matter of a week or so. The embroidery another three days."

"And she already knows what she will wear?" Torsten was surprised.

"She has not given it any thought at all, Chief of Deputies," Vibol countered. "She is an Emperor and will be consumed by more important tasks until then. When the time comes, she will have the perfect attire, as will her *Wardens*: Jessica, Moirrey, and Duchess Freya."

A lifetime's naval training kept Torsten from simply collapsing into a handy chair at the calm certainty of the man's words. He fell into parade rest instead, feeling as if he were back as a new recruit, standing his first watch with that grizzled Chief of Boat handy to keep him from pushing the wrong button.

"No suitors have been identified," Torsten finally offered, weakly.

Vibol just smiled at him. Torsten felt like the man had restrained himself from patting the Chief of Deputies politely on the head, as one would a precocious child.

"What do you know?" Torsten queried nervously.

"One of the most interesting things about being a tailor is that people forget I'm here, even as I have them standing perfectly still atop a pedestal, pinning things in place so I can get the perfect fit," Vibol offered. "Important conversations occur around me, and idle gossip, with the presumption that I am far too busy to listen, and never looking at my principal while I work. Certainly not touching them at the moment when a particular name is spoken, to feel the sudden emotions surge through their body."

Torsten was shocked. And guilty.

How many conversations had he had with Casey in the warehouse through the back door, her standing in that pedestal? Or at the hotel, while Vibol went about his work, crafting a new wardrobe for the Emperor to replace the one she lost here and the clothing of her youth that no longer fit broader shoulders and hips as she turned into a woman?

Torsten realized that he was a fantastic econometricist, but a lousy spy.

"I'm just glad you have as high a security clearance as I do, Master Tailor," Torsten finally acknowledged.

"Just so, Chief of Deputies," Vibol said.

"Please, call me Torsten," he replied.

Torsten had a feeling the man would be a fixture in their lives for years. At least until they both saw Lady Casey married off.

"Torsten," he said, shaking hands. "I am Vibol."

"Indeed," Torsten said. "Thank you."

"It is my duty and my joy, sir," Vibol said. "Now, how may I be of service?"

"I had come to ask if you were including outfits that might turn a man's head, when worn by Emperor Karl VIII," Torsten said. "To perhaps remind him that she was also a woman, and not just an Emperor."

Torsten stopped and bowed deeply to the man.

"I had not given thought to how far ahead of the rest of us you would be on that topic," he continued.

"Just so, Torsten," Vibol said. "It is interesting work, taking a woman who feels self-conscious about herself, or considers herself to be an ugly duckling, and transforming her into a *goddess*. Thus has my career been fulfilling, most recently aiding Lady Moirrey and Ambassador Bhattacharya. Lady Casey will have outfits for all seasons and all occasions. There are formal robes of older rulers in museums and pictures. Those are the easiest to replicate, as I merely need to size them down to a woman of my scale, from her mighty forebears. For others, there will be times when she needs to present as an Imperial matron of breeding and class. Those fashions needed updating, so she will be the plate from which the rest draw, when I am done. In between, I have *carte blanche* into which to cast Kasimira's beauty and resilience, a lure that will draw in any she needs to attract, however it needs to be done."

Torsten remembered to breathe. Eventually.

Everyone spoke of the Master Tailor in hushed, reverent tones. And his genius was an everyday thing, where you could see his work striding the halls of a dowdy hotel that had become an Imperial palace, adorning a young woman.

Everyone had underestimated the man. Except Jessica. Torsten had no doubts that his love had known exactly what she was doing, sending Vibol here, but still making it clear that he belonged to her.

Torsten wondered if Vibol would eventually retire to *Corynthe* with her. With them. He had seen the larval stage of what Jessica was building out there, in his time aboard *Kali-ma*. He could only imagine what a *Master Tailor* might do with such potential. Desianna would be utterly *thrilled*.

Torsten bowed again. Deeper this time.

"Then I will presume that we have both identified the same prospect," he said. "And that you will arm her with the sword and shield she will need, when it comes time for that battle."

"An interesting choice of words, son of *Skuodas*," Vibol replied. "But yes, she will have everything she needs, even if my contributions are merely to frost that cake. I did not bake it."

"You did not, Vibol," Torsten agreed. "But we men are visual creatures, and she will need that to turn his head from the task at hand. Thank you, and I will bid you good day."

Torsten nodded again and departed with a lighter step than when he entered.

He wondered if his Emperor had figured out her own mind.

CHAPTER LII

Vo was just digging into his first burrito when Alan Katche walked into the restaurant and made a beeline towards him. Reese Borel was close behind, so something must be up. Vo took a bite and chewed, cognizant that he might have to wrap it up and eat on the run from the looks on their faces.

No alerts had sounded, so all hell hadn't broken loose, at least not yet. Might, yet, given Alan's grim smile and Reese's total lack of expression. Celine materialized with two more mugs, getting to the table before they did.

Both men came to parade rest. Vo didn't feel like looking up at them this morning.

"No," he ordered, pointing with a fist. "Sitting."

Both men sat across from him. Katche had a slab in his hands, obviously the source of his excitement today.

"There's news," Alan observed in a vague, excited voice.

Vo chewed and ignored the provocation.

"How well do the folks back home like you?" Alan continued.

"Why?" Vo barked around a bite of eggs and chorizo.

"New *RAN* squadron just cleared for orbit," Alan continued. "Hendrik routed them to us. Reese is coordinating the reinforcements, but I might want to get *you* involved personally."

Vo paused, sucked down some coffee, and sat his burrito down. Hopefully, he'd get back to it while it was still hot.

He cocked his head at the men rather than reply.

"*Legate* Digger Wolanski," Alan emphasized the title. "Your old mate from *Thuringwell.* Along with the Twenty-Third Ladaux Construction Legion."

"Construction Legion?" Vo repeated. "A whole legion of those folks? Gentlemen, there's your new Imperial capital city. I suggest you go deep into the operational reports of the time they spent in *Corynthe.* I was here, but I've read some of it. Contact Torsten Wald and get his entire planning department assigned to Digger's HQ. Those boys and girls will be bringing big toys and wanting to play immediately."

Vo sipped his coffee.

"Oh," he added quickly. "And tell Lady Moirrey straightaway. That's her fiancé. Also, if you feel like being a shit, sneak a note to Vibol Harmaajärvi. Moirrey will want some new outfits for her beau. Two days warning and she might greet him like Aphrodite rising out of the sea. She is allowed to borrow a couple of tanks or skiffs, with crews, if she needs a backdrop for her performance."

Both men laughed. Vo snuck another bite. They didn't need his involvement for any of that. Something else must be going on.

"Why are you here?" he asked.

Reese turned his attention to Alan. Vo did the same.

"So," the Primus Pilus drawled. "We've talked, inside the family, of our next steps, but haven't really sprung anything on the Grand Admiral or the Emperor."

"That's right," Vo prompted.

"I'm extremely interested in the ships delivering Twenty-Third Ladaux," Alan said. "I've studied the type, but the fleet doesn't really have anything like it, because they don't do crazy shit like we will."

"Mmm-hmmm," Vo bit into the burrito and let Alan talk while he chewed.

"In about eighteen hours, there are going to be two *RAN* Assault Carriers in orbit, along with several other warships that don't make any sense," Alan said. "Two freighters I can see. They're hauling supplies for the crews and spare parts. Three of the new style corvettes are escorting the force. The flagship has me confused, and I was hoping you had friends we could leverage up there."

"What's the flagship?" Vo asked as he swallowed. Halfway done. If he could keep them talking another three minutes, he wouldn't have a cold breakfast in an hour.

"She identifies as *RAN Arad*," Reese joined the conversation. "A Fleet Strike Carrier."

"Fleet Strike Carrier?" Vo asked. "Fleet carriers are the big jobs. Strike carriers are built on a heavy cruiser hull, or an Expeditionary Cruiser, like *II Augusta*. Old *Auberon* was a Strike Carrier. *Aquitaine* doesn't build combat variants at that scale, because they go right on to Star Controllers. Fleet Strike Carrier?"

"Yes, sir," Reese was emphatic. "Fleet Centurion Vlahovic is in command."

"Iskra?" Vo was shocked. "I would have thought she'd retire by now. Star Controller *Auberon* was her baby, and it was headed for the wrecker after *Trusski*."

"So you got friends?" Alan was hopeful.

"Contacts, at least, Alan," Vo said.

"Good enough that we could borrow a couple of Assault Carriers for six months?" Alan pressed. "Or hitch a ride with them? Firepower like *that* is going to the frontier. That means the Fleet Centurion."

He paused and considered logistics.

"Rohm is taking over as Grand Marshal," Vo said, mostly to himself. "As good a time as any for us to withdraw to barracks, if we can pull this off. You're right that they'll deliver Digger and then have nothing much to do until it comes time to withdraw his force. Two Assault Carriers are enough to put the full 189th on the ground somewhere in two loads, if we pack tight. And we could use the extra space for supplies and replacement vehicles. Normally, that stuff is on one of your replenishment freighters, and has to be broken out of cold storage over days. How quickly could you come up with load plans, Alan?"

"What's our lift capability likely to be?" the Primus Pilus asked.

"If we assume a normal load for an armored division, eight DropShips and two GunShips each," Vo replied. "Since this is a construction legion, those are probably heavy armor carriers, like *Achaemenes* that was with us for *LVIII Heavy* at *Thuringwell*. Even if Digger's in a hurry, you'll have a week before they can get it all arranged, and then probably another week or ten days to deliver everything, since they can take their time."

"We'll have something in a couple of days, Vo," Alan said. "But I won't put the men into motion until you tell me."

"Good," Vo said. "I'd hate to get everyone's hopes up, and then find out that Iskra's orders are to drop everyone and then return home for something, with them not coming back for a year."

"Next steps, General?" Reese asked.

"Get me a call set up with Iskra Vlahovic as soon as she's in orbit, so we can see what our options are," Vo said. "After that, I'll talk to Wachturm and the Emperor and see what support we'll get there."

The two men left quickly enough that Alan still had his coffee mug in one hand, absentmindedly, so Vo could guess where that *Beyond the Dragon Gates* cup had probably originated. Vo finished off his burrito and idled at his coffee, thinking about his options.

Things were coming to an inflection point, a fancy word Vo had learned in business school to describe that arc when a line suddenly turns into a curve and goes a different direction. His life would be going a different direction, shortly. Hopefully, she would let him go do the thing he had promised, with the whole 189th Legion behind him.

If not, he had enough money saved up to go buy a small ship and turn himself into a pirate. And he was pretty sure where he could recruit a crew.

I t was way too bloody early in the morning, or late at night, but *RAN Arad* had been running a little ahead of schedule, so Vo had stayed up way past his normal bedtime to talk to his old shipmate, Iskra. The line was secured, for what that was worth. Mostly, it meant that only Imperial Security and a few others would likely be listening in, rather than anyone with a dish and a halfway competent decryption rig.

Vo had learned more than he ever wanted to know about ground-to-sky operational communications security by invading a hostile planet as a Ground Forces Coordinator. The dude who had to talk to everyone, all the time.

Iskra was aging well, from the last time he had seen her in person. Still a babe. The tips of her hair were mostly blond, and everything coming in underneath was gray and white now. If you looked closely, you could see the fine scars running perpendicular to the wrinkles that she was accumulating.

"Good morning, General *zu* Arlo," Iskra greeted him with a nod and perhaps a hint of a smile. "To what do I owe the honor?"

"I can't call to say hello to an old friend, Vlahovic?" he countered.

Iskra laughed.

"Vo Arlo was never about small talk," she said. "Even as a snot-nosed punk, disciple of Navin. What's up?"

Vo shrugged. She had a point. She had also known him for probably all of his career, even if they had never been all that friendly, nor dated.

"Since last time we talked, my life has gotten a bit complicated," Vo began.

"Ha," she said. "Understatement of the year."

"Yeah, well," he offered. "I was put in command of the 189th and told to turn them into a Legion. So far, so good. Then that bastard blew up Werder and Wachturm put me in charge of the recovery effort until he got back. And left me here when he did. But it's been six months, and while things won't be back to normal in my lifetime, we're at least to a point where someone else can be in charge and I can go do what I set out to do."

"You set out to build a strike Legion, Arlo," Iskra countered. "What's that got to do with me?"

"You brought Digger," Vo said. "And the assault carriers *RAN Archangel* and *RAN Akatsuki*. And you aren't staying long, I'm guessing, considering the rest of your task force."

"What's anybody told you?" she asked sharply.

"Nothing," Vo said. "But a Fleet Strike Carrier isn't something we need here. It's something Jessica might find useful, though."

"And?"

"And so I was wondering what your orders were, concerning those two vessels?" Vo said.

"My orders were to escort them this far," Iskra said. "While I might have additional orders for the rest of the squadron, I'm not at liberty to discuss them over an open line."

Translation: Yes, Jessica's getting reinforced. Maybe picking up a couple of IFV *line vessels as well, if the Grand Admiral feels he can spare something.*

One more vessel wouldn't mean much on the front, especially the way Jessica was apparently slashing at *Buran,* but as part of a larger force, it gave her options. Like Vo wanted to do.

"So who do I talk to about Digger's taxis?" Vo pressed.

Iskra had always had the most evil smile, when she wanted to use it. Like now.

"I brought a *Palsgrave* with me, as well, Vo," she smiled. "You'll have to talk to her."

"A what?" he was surprised. "Who?"

"Former Senator Chavarría," Iskra said. "The former Premier."

"Former?"

"They had an election, just about the time news of *St. Legier* arrived," Iskra said. "Nils Kasum's old buddy Tad Horvat returned to power. She retired, and he sent her out with me."

"Palsgrave, though?" Vo breathed out carefully.

Wakely Okafor had been Palsgrave at *Thuringwell,* exercising legal authority over the newly-conquered planet until such time as a more formal government could be instituted. It went beyond Governor. Way beyond.

"Yuppers," Iskra said.

"How soon until you leave on your next leg?" Vo asked.

"You've got time to work your swindle, Vo," she laughed. "I need to offload two carriers and two Fleet Replenishment Freighters, then reload *Leggett* and *Redding* with fresh supplies. Call it a month, dead minimum, before you run out of possible launch windows."

"This will have to come through official channels, Iskra," Vo said. "But put in a good word for me?"

"You got it," she said. "Anything else you needed?"

"No," Vo said. "Thank you."

And at that, she was gone.

Vo stared at his reflection on the dark screen. The military side of things wouldn't be that difficult. Mostly logistics, to shift all his men and their gear around while handing off to other units and civilians as Digger came on line. That boy was crazy, but an expert.

The political would be interesting. He had never met the Premier when she was in office, but she had personally signed off on the original orders sending him here the first time. Commanded the *Act of the Senate* that made it possible for him to become *zu* Arlo, so she had to know who he was at a pretty good level.

And she was here, with the authority to make legally-binding decisions for the government back home, and the Navy. Plus, she had two Assault Carriers just sitting around, doing nothing.

How bad did *Aquitaine* want to support the war effort?

CHAPTER LIII

Getting Digger Wolanski and his Legion down and engaged had been the easy part, as far as Vo was concerned. Just provide coordinates and time windows to everyone, and let DropShips sometimes flatten ruins with their immense mass, so they could offload the heavy equipment right on scene and go to work.

A Palsgrave was a whole other level of complicated.

Aquitaine had always maintained some level of diplomatic relations with *Fribourg*, even in the worst parts of the war. There were no friendly neutrals who could provide a diplomatic cover, so each side had maintained observer missions. They weren't spies, because everything they did was tightly watched at all times, but it allowed the two governments to talk. To negotiate truces and quiet zones. To arrange prisoner exchanges with a minimum of fuss.

It has only been with *The Peace* that full Ambassadors had been exchanged. Probably professional spies as well, in addition to the sleepers and secret agents both sides had always maintained.

Adding someone with Palatine authority had required a formal *Acceptance* that took several days of celebrations, conferences, and baby-kissing by all the major players. Even Vo had been dragged into it, but had never gotten more than thirty seconds with Governor Chavarría, and not alone. Just enough to ask for a private meeting at her earliest convenience.

Days had passed, but at least he was here.

Less-important folks had been evicted from one of the originally surviving hotels in downtown Mejico, across the square from Tenochtitlan and slightly removed down a side street that paralleled the river. Vo presumed all the rooms on the backside had a good view of the river itself, plus all the construction work happening on the heights across the valley. Mejico had survived because of the depth of the river valley, allowing the firestorm to mostly pass overhead, rather than scouring the earth itself clear, as it had done closer to the epicenter and further out.

Vo was in sage today. He could do the Class Two uniform, since he was coming hat in hand to ask a favor. Alan Katche had joined him, having broken out his own uniform from storage for the day.

There were bodyguards and armed troops everywhere in Mejico, considering the number of important people centered here, but most of them were either 189th troopers, or Inmon's *Household Guards* detachment for Casey and a few others. So it was odd, running into a group of *RAN* marines guarding the outside of the building inside the ring of his own troopers.

Weirder, all the people on the fifth floor wore green and black. It took him back, but it was also something of a shock, since he hadn't worn that uniform in over a year. Still, the men and women on duty were professional and courteous, even if there were no faces he knew among them.

Vo wondered as they climbed stairs if he should have Reese rotate Victoria Ames through this detachment for a week, just so she could see professionally-armed women as a model.

He must have smiled. Alan was smiling back.

"Thinking we should put Ames here," Alan said. "Can you spare half of Cutlass Ten for a week?"

"Absolutely," Vo said. "Was just asking myself that same question."

"You should stop reading my mind, Vo," Alan said. "It'll make at least one of us an accomplice."

Vo was laughing as they emerged onto the top floor and got inspected again. He had left the belt with his pistol back in his office. The sword was in his quarters for special occasions, like parades.

Or duels.

These troopers escorted them into a private meeting with the Palsgrave and a handful of assistants of no particular note. Probably local diplomats and culture experts. Nobody Vo knew or cared about.

He was seated across from her at a dinner table in the suite she was using. It was oak, stained almost black, with a pretty strip of off-white cloth about a meter wide running down the long axis, like a horizontal volleyball net. Judit Chavarría alone on her side, him and Alan on this side.

Probably about an even match, considering all the things Vo had heard about the woman while she was in power.

The small talk was out of the way. He and Alan had coffee. Judit, as she insisted on, was drinking tea. Her famous fingernails were red, gold, and white today, which Vo found interesting, since those were the colors of the Imperial House. He wondered if Judit had brought her own specialist with her across the light years, just to do her nails regularly.

He had seen weirder things in his time.

"So, Vo, Alan," she began finally. "How may I be of service today?"

Vo had hunted enough wild animals in his day to understand a bear trap when he saw one. Even in the form of stocky, middle-aged women. Still, he was here for a reason. Really only one.

"I had a conversation with Fleet Centurion Vlahovic when you first arrived," Vo said. "For obvious reasons, she was not willing to discuss her future movement orders, but it left me with a few unanswered questions. She suggested I talk to you."

"I see," Judit replied. "She and I had a conversation after that, as I will be remaining on *St. Legier* after she departs."

"Yes," Vo agreed. "As will Twenty-Third Ladaux."

"That is correct," Judit said. "The Senate has offered the Empire the full use of Digger's Legion, expenses paid, for a year. After that, we will determine if the contract should be extended or renegotiated, depending on circumstances."

Circumstances. Like who was in charge here, a year from now?

Vo kept the thoughts off of his face. Judit Chavarría was a far more dangerous foe than Arald Rohm ever dreamed of being.

"I am interested in that year of lag, Palsgrave," Vo ventured.

"Oh?"

"Yes," he continued, hoping he wasn't about to stick his foot in that bear trap. "Specifically, the two vessels that delivered Twenty-Third Ladaux, *RAN Archangel* and *RAN Akatsuki.*"

Vo didn't like the spark that seemed to light in her eyes at those names.

"The Assault Carriers," she said.

It wasn't a question, and they both knew it. Vo nodded.

"The Assault Carriers, yes."

"What, specifically, were you interested in, General *zu* Arlo?" she pressed.

It didn't feel like a knife about to enter his kidney. Still, he had asked for this meeting. This joust had been his idea.

"Borrowing them," he said simply. "Perhaps leasing them, but I'm no longer functioning as Margrave of this planet, so the new Grand Marshal would likely get involved at that point, as would the Grand Admiral, since they control the budgets."

"And the Crown?" Judit homed in.

"Her, as well, yes," Vo said. "At least through her Chief of Deputies, Torsten Wald."

"Yes," Judit observed. "The fiancé of Jessica Keller, who is currently out fighting the war for both nations, using forces supplied by both fleets. You had something in mind to further the war effort, *zu* Arlo?"

"I was about nine hundred kilometers south of Werder on that day, Judit," Vo let the emotion creep back into his voice. "I watched a new star being born, falling to earth, and killing a great many men and women I loved. The 189th Legion is going to go out there and repay *Buran* the courtesy. The *Fribourg Fleet* doesn't really have anything like an Assault Carrier, using flotillas of cruiser-sized vessels when they need to land significant forces on a hostile, planetary surface. In the last generation, those have been mostly Imperial worlds in active rebellion, so nothing so concentrated was needed. An Assault Carrier lets me put an entire Legion on the surface in a day and a half, even reinforced, as the 189th is."

"So you would take the war to *Buran*? Personally?" she asked.

"This is Alan Katche, Judit," Vo turned and gestured. "He is my senior commander, but more importantly, his job title is Primus Pilus. *First Spear*. The man closest to the enemy. I don't plan on doing to one of *The Holding*'s worlds what Jessica did to *Thuringwell*. She was intent on capturing one, and knew how to hit the diamond just right. We're going to go blow things up and kill people. Assault Carriers make that much more likely to succeed."

"And my involvement?" she asked, slowly closing those steel jaws on his foot.

"You control them," Vo said. "Regardless of Iskra's orders, you can override them, if you see the need. I studied Palatine authority extremely carefully before we invaded *Thuringwell*, Judit. Technically, the Senate would have to vote to revoke your authority, before they could subsequently vote to overrule you on something. Premier Horvat trusts you more than I imagined possible."

"I've known Tad for nearly thirty years, Vo," she replied. "We double-date to the opera several times each season. I'm the godmother to one of his grandchildren. Yes, he trusts me. Why should I trust you?"

"Annette Fuchs," he said simply.

It was pleasant, getting to watch her grow confused for a second, before enlightenment.

"Walter's daughter," she breathed finally. "Your speech to the soul of the *Empire* itself. This is your revenge?"

"And I have already dug two holes, Judit, as the ancients warned that you should do before setting out for vengeance."

"Tell me," she asked, finally thinking she had caught his leg in the trap. "Would you escalate this to become an *incident*, if I said no?"

"No," Vo smiled like death at her. "You could make it easier for me. Your refusal would not stop us. Just slow us down. Nothing more. The only question now is *when* I will come calling, and *who* will be our first target. That we are coming for them is a given."

"I see," she said.

And she did. This woman had been in supreme command, back home, for nearly a decade. She knew how to deal with hard, dangerous men.

But she smiled.

"Let me have a conversation with your government, then," she offered, still keeping her cards close to the vest. "I would like hear what they have to say on the topic."

Vo took that as a dismissal. He didn't have anything else that needed to be covered here. And she hadn't said yes or no.

He and Alan were up and gone quickly after that. In the stairwell, Alan stopped him.

"Depending on the number of bulk freighters available at the time, it would take me about three to five months to buy, requisition, or build the transports we would need, if they won't go for it."

Vo nodded.

"I don't think she'll refuse us," Vo replied. "But I'll let Casey and Torsten make that pitch to her."

Alan nodded back and they continued down.

Karl VIII had staked her reign on the twin foundations of the 189th and his promise to the people of *St. Legier* and the wider Empire. She would support them. She'd better.

And if *Aquitaine* wouldn't, or *Fribourg*, then it might become a private venture, after all.

CHAPTER LIV

Jessica looked at all the faces projected into the air around the table of her flag bridge.

Auberon had been big enough to pull all her command centurions and tactical officers together for a single meeting in the flesh, where it had helped forge them into a unit. *IFV Vanguard*, while far more dangerous and resilient than a Star Controller, was also significantly smaller, with a tiny flight deck. She would have had to send her few shuttles on a long path to pick everyone up, losing a day in the process.

Time wasn't that critical, but it also wasn't for wasting.

After a year of high risk/high rewards raids, Jessica's team had honed their craft to something of an art. In the old days, you dropped out of JumpSpace a couple of light hours from an Imperial world and sniffed for gaps in their defenses. Maybe you raided, maybe you withdrew.

Against *Buran*, it had been necessary to hide further out, down in the Oort cloud, or in the shadow of one of the frozen worldlets that orbited at that range, because the beings watching the heavens could be *Sentient* systems that might notice you occluding a single star or emitting a rogue radio or laser signal. Plus, at *Trusski* she had been more careful, picking the terrain she wanted to lure *The Eldest*'s warships into.

Henry V at Agincourt, rather than Leonidas at Thermopylae or Horatio at the bridge.

Here, the terrain was already set, so she would have to emulate Drake, raiding ports to stop the Spanish Armada.

Again, there was time for patience. *CP-406* had walked slowly towards the *Severnaya Zemlya* system from a starting distance of nearly one light year, pausing to sniff for any defensive ships hiding there in the dark, while *Ballard* watched from a distance.

They would only get to do this once. Perhaps.

Come in from the galactic south at seventy-three degrees, for no other reason than random deviation. Chaos, in the face of an orderly robot. Stay well away from the Postal Road that ran along the northern part of the primary galactic plane, where the stars were thinner and you were more likely to encounter other ships.

Thief in the night.

CP-406 and *Ballard* had spent nearly a week on their silent stalk and returned safely to her laager, hiding two and a half light years away.

Jessica took a breath and checked that Enej was ready. Without Casey, he was back to doing all the main work, which he occasionally bitched about. She still teased him about it, but not today. Serious business was at hand.

She pressed a button to bring everyone live. Additionally, she began projecting the map that a week of passive scanning from various locations had gathered; washed, filtered, and cataloged by Elzbet Aukley and her team of experts. They were working on a tight network of lasers between ships, but would be long gone before even the reflecting signals might give something away.

"What you are seeing might be classified as ancient Rome, just before the first of the barbarian tribes from the north crossed the Rubicon," Jessica began. "I won't invoke Caesar crossing that river, because we aren't here to conquer Rome or rescue it. We are here to destroy it. To break the empire of *Buran, The Eldest,* the so-called *Lord of Winter.* Our role is Hannibal, hoping they have no one like the Scipios. Up until now, we have been sparring with his legions at the borders, fortifications erected to keep our kind at bay. Today, we begin the campaign for his heartland in earnest."

She paused there, rotating the map a touch and zooming it. She missed having Moirrey, right now. Saana and Elzbet were exceptional technicians, but they wouldn't have been able to find the perfect soundtrack to play with the projections. Music would have been nice.

Jessica made a note to locate a crewmember with talent at musical composition and add them to the informal Art Department down in Engineering. Or recruit one specifically for the purpose. She was the *Red Admiral*, the *Fleet Centurion*, and the *Queen of the Pirates*. She could do those sorts of things and it just enhanced her legend.

"*Severnaya Zemlya*," Jessica said as the planet took shape. "Capital world of the *Altai* Sector. According to *Seeker*, a major manufacturing hub and fleet repair facility for *Buran*. We got to our observation point at the edge of the system faster than any news could have outrun us, since it had to come via human-piloted vessel using JumpDrives, while we could sail full tilt. We were able to spot our messenger when it arrived, blurting out its news to anyone with a radio, about how the terrible dragon Red Admiral had destroyed *Yenisei*."

She advanced the projection that *Ballard* had been able to scan, once they knew the clock had started. In the air above her, a vessel suddenly blinked out of existence in planetary orbit and reappeared next to the freighter bearing bad news.

"We don't fully know what a *Megalodon*-class battleship is yet," Jessica said. "They are new and are replacing the older *Carcharias*-class. There was one at *St. Legier*, so we have some idea about their weapons, but he didn't get close enough to anyone for us to get a hard scan. That ship was a response to the Expeditionary Cruisers Yan Bedrov designed, so it is probably comparable to *Vanguard*. We know they are using a new version of the Pulse Beams that are roughly equal to a Type-3. This one has an extended range, but the same general damage. Think Moirrey's Type-3-Tuned, without losing the focus at that range."

A flag on her screen indicated a question.

"Hardie?" Jessica asked Robbie's Tactical Officer as she paused.

"Carcharias has three Hammerheads as secondaries," the woman said. "Am I right in counting six on this design?"

"You are," Jessica replied. "This hull is almost as big as the Nightmaster we fought at *Trusski*, for length and probable displacement. But it is more a pure battleship, with a team of lighter escorts, rather than the heavier Makos. Now watch what happens."

Jessica resumed the video. The Megalodon rotated to face galactic north and vanished.

Around her, Jessica heard the murmurs, curses, and cheers from the men and women watching.

"As many of you have guessed, we think that ship immediately departed," Jessica continued. "Either to support *Yenisei*, or reinforce

Ninagirsu. It won't matter to us, because they aren't here. What's left are three Mako-class vessels, and three Hammerheads, plus one massive orbital station."

She zoomed now on the station, the thing *Buran* called a *Chéngbǎo*, or Castle. It wasn't a starbase, which was a pure military platform for naval operations. Nor was it an industrial station, but a facility that incorporated elements of both. As such, it was bigger than even Fleet Headquarters orbiting *Ladaux*, but no better armed, if Seeker's notes were accurate. Possibly not even as well.

"Like all good, defensive structures, this one sits down below the line of the gravity well as JumpSails consider it," Jessica said. "*Buran*'s JumpDrives use an older technology, and one not limited so much by gravity, so it doesn't matter to them. This is purely for our detriment."

She paused long enough to locate the sealed mug of coffee Marcelle had delivered earlier, half-forgotten, and sipped a bit, letting the warmth spread through her.

"In the past, such a fortification would have been impregnable," Jessica continued. "Even tuned for range, the Type-3 beam hits no harder than a kitten at the distance of the gravity well edge. Even coming out of jump at full tilt would still give them nearly thirty seconds to notice you and bring their power absorbers to maximum defense. That is an acceptable trade for *The Eldest* to make. And it has stopped *Fribourg* at *Samara*, because any vessels trying it would find themselves surrounded by the defensive fleet maintained there. It would be a wild dog attacking a herd of elk. You might wound one, but the rest would gore and stomp you to death before you could escape."

Through the projection, Jessica watched every face in front of her, each watching with the same rapt concentration. Not fascinated, but busy trying to calculate the best way forward. If Jessica had found a path, there must be one. She nearly laughed, but she had seen this too many other times.

The mark of the warrior.

She let the pause build.

"Comrades, I have studied Emmerich's records on the topic, and found something he never tried," she finally admitted. "But he also didn't have the tools we do. The capabilities. *Il Augusta* will lead the charge."

She spotted Tamara Strnad and her top officers by the way they all recoiled in surprise: Tactical Officer Kichirou Uzun; Flight Deck

Commander Ryanne Mauld; and Augustin Petrović, *Merman*. Interestingly, it was Uzun's flag that turned red first.

"Senior Centurion Uzun?" Jessica prodded.

"Are we hot-launching the wing before we make our run, or in the middle of it?" he asked.

Spoken like a Strike Carrier officer. Some of the craziest people in the fleet, to charge into combat in a weakly-armed carrier, just to force the enemy to either divide fire between you and the flight wing, or ignore one completely and hope that decision didn't kill you.

If *II Augusta* had any advantage there, it lay in being built on the same massively-overpowered frame as the cruisers, without the bigger guns. She could reinforce facing shields and generate ECM on a far greater scale, and still keep the Type-3 beams firing as fast they charged and cooled.

"Neither," Jessica grinned as everyone got confused. Why else lead with a strike carrier? "We'll rendezvous first at distance of around fifteen AU out and form into our assault pattern there. Then drop the entire squadron out at a distance of six light minutes. That gives you four minutes to launch the wing and get them formed up and moving. They'll jump as a separate team and strike the base directly from jump, hopefully catching him cold just as the rest of us come out of jump running as hard as we can, firing into the gaps *Merman's* team has hopefully blasted in their defensive panels. What's your team's best launch, *Merman*?"

"Three minutes, forty," he said. "Average four minutes, ten."

"There you have it," Jessica said. "They'll fire and blink out, just as the defenders wake up to them."

Denis's flag lit next.

"You said lines, Jessica," he said. "As opposed to line, singular?"

"That's correct, Denis," she replied. "*II Augusta* in the center, led by *CA-264* and *CP-406*, trailed in turn by *Vanguard*. *CM-404* and *VI Ferrata* on the starboard wing. *CS-405* leading *VI Victrix* to port. *401*, *402*, and *403* across the back, with *Ballard* remaining well off to one side quietly watching and not participating."

"Preparing for our second run?" Denis asked. "After we loop around the back of the planet and come at him again?"

"Nope," Jessica grinned. "This is where most commanders would get greedy or stupid. I'm confident we can do significant damage to that base on one surprise pass. Maybe enough to make a second run worth considering. We're not going to even bother unless somehow we manage to get the sort of lucky kill shot that triggers secondary and tertiary explosions as reactors start to cascade inside. No, instead of looping, we'll blast hard and straight out the back, form up in a traditional line, and come to 015/022/0 and go for max burn."

For that sort of thing, Denis was always the best astrogator she had ever served with. She watched him mouth the numbers, seeking their significance, before his eyes got big.

"*Winterhome?*" he gasped.

The murmurs exploded across the comm line. Jessica waited for them to die down before she spoke.

"As far as they know, yes, *Winterhome*," she said. "Their capital world. Let me be clear: I have no intention of actually going there on this run. We'll transition to JumpSpace and then loop down and port to our meeting point for the run home to Omicron. However, they won't know that. Their ships have to point in the direction they are jumping, so people will see our bows and draw the same conclusion."

"Second star to the right and straight on until morning," Denis quoted with wonder in his voice.

"Just so," she replied. "What will *The Eldest's* servants on *Severnaya Zemlya* do?"

"Panic," Denis said. "Possibly wet themselves if we've just killed a Starbase in passing."

"Correct," she said. "As I have reminded you in the past, for many of these battles, we can't win the war in an afternoon, but we could lose it with the risks we take. This will be an even bigger risk, but we're not conquerors. This is *Second 2218 Svati Prime*. This is a pack of foxes in the henhouse, and then gone. We won't stay, we won't slug it out, regardless of the temptation. We're going to look like we're going after *Winterhome* next. And make them worry. Any other questions?"

There were none. She had answered the important ones. The rest were maneuver orders and timing, and they would expect those soon. They were prepared.

"In twelve hours, we'll transition to JumpSpace and begin our attack run. *Duncan* will meet us at the next waypoint with supplies, but he's leaving shortly, so stock up if you have needs now."

She cut the line and stretched. While it might be her most audacious surprise ever… No, strike that, *yet*; it wasn't all that great a risk, compared to some of the others. In, out, and gone.

But she really wished she could go after *Winterhome* itself. Gather up all of the *Empire's* Grand Fleet, throw in elements of *Aquitaine's* Home and War Fleets, and throw them at the beast. Then go hunt down every *Sentient* warship they could find and kill it, until there were none left anywhere in the galaxy and Suvi really was the *Last of the Immortals*.

Severnaya Zemlya would have to do for now.

Until the tide came in for the last time.

CHAPTER LV

As galactic speeds went, *Vanguard* was a sluggard right now, even with the engines running wide open at the redline of safety and pushing the warhorse hard. Still, Jessica felt the same sort of adrenaline she got when Marcelle wanted to push the margins while driving, or any landing from orbit with *Gaucho* flying.

Going all in.

And blind, to top it off.

Merman's Flight Wing had managed three minutes, fifty-six to get all twelve Fast Strike Bombers clear of the lockshields and formed up with acceleration. Still ahead of schedule when they blinked out of existence for their rendezvous with destiny, or at least history, as the first time the JumpDrive element of Bedrov's design got used as he intended: leaping into battle, rather than chasing someone trying to get away.

Doing to *Buran* what they always did to everyone else.

Vanguard would be in the middle of the formation, more or less. Every vessel had a different engine signature, and different tolerances, so the level of fine tuning on the sails would determine how far down the edge of the well was finally enough that the matrix failed and they came back to RealSpace.

Everyone would miss the planet on their trajectories, but it was entirely possible that *Vanguard* might come out last, with the newest engines and, as far as Jessica was concerned, the best engineers in the fleet under Oz, even without Moirrey's magic. That might put them closest to the base when they came out.

One could only hope.

She watched the timer click down to the normally-expected edge of the gravity well, according to *Ballard's* charts. This was where things got weird. The trigger on the sail matrix was a zone, not a line. A probability curve, until the engineers couldn't hold it together any more. Robbie, Alber', and Kigali had gotten to be masters at that sort of maneuver, but *Vanguard* was newer, with a design that had been tweaked after Yan had seen what those boys could do.

And Denis might push a little harder, having had to miss so many parties when he commanded a mere Star Controller. She laughed to herself at the comparison, but maintained the outward sternness for her flag bridge crew. Fleet Centurions weren't supposed to laugh out loud during battles.

Sane ones, anyway. Let's not give them questions.

The screen showed the ships cross the high water mark and keep going without transition. Every instant now was distance cut off her attack.

There. *Transition.* RealSpace. Denis and Oz had managed the impossible. *Vanguard* was there in the van, everyone else having come out as much as a half-second earlier, from the scattering of their previous orderly lines.

Again, *Fribourg* would order everyone back into some formation now, just because escorts were supposed to be protecting capital ships and cruisers. But there were hardly any missiles here, and no fighters. Just ships that could land anywhere they wanted at any time, to savage whatever vessel was their target.

And *Buran* would be expecting a few moments of chaos on the *Imperial* side as orders from stupid admirals wasted time on pretty lines. It would give the sharks time to react.

Jessica just had time to see the last of *Merman's* strike team vanish into their second jump. The fast bombers didn't have missile racks, relying solely on beams, but they had a JumpDrive and enough batteries for two jumps before recharging.

In. Hit. Fade. Thinking like a pirate. Bedrov's forte. They would go to ground now, recharging out in the darkness so they could make it to the next checkpoint and their ride home. But they had accomplished their task, that much was obvious. Power Absorber panels that failed at low power couldn't be raised to full defense until they were repaired, which might take minutes.

Minutes that station didn't have, as the blue-painted Picts came over Hadrian's Wall, howling for blood.

The Bubble Guns on *VI Ferrata* and *VI Victrix* took a blink of time to track, implode, and immolate. Slow enough that a human could follow it. The beams always hit first.

Moirrey had envisioned the Bubble Gun as a way to damage all shield facings simultaneously, so that an enemy vessel couldn't turn a damaged shield away from you for a full one. Power absorber panels normally took the incoming energy and captured it so that it could be bled off to batteries to be fired back, but that took time. And the panels held more power than the batteries. If you filled them, there was nowhere for the power to go, for several, precious seconds, perhaps as much as a minute.

If only one panel was full, the commander over there could route power to an empty panel on the far side of the vessel quickly, adding layers of security as he did.

Bubble Guns filled all the panels at the same time. There was nowhere for the energy to go. And they would still hit gaps in the defensive array. *VI Ferrata* was in line with the gap the bombers had blasted, but *VI Victrix* was too far off to one side.

Not that Alber' would care. Nor Komal MacInerney, his tactical Goddess of War.

And everyone was firing as fast as they could cycle. *Vanguard* pinged and bumped as beams fired and the Bubble Gun erupted. Jessica felt the ship groan as Nina cut the engines and actually began to yaw a Heavy Dreadnaught on her flat axis, torqueing on all those extra gyros that the design came with, twice what a normal dreadnaught or battleship carried.

Because crazy people are the most dangerous warriors, and Jessica had a whole fleet full of them. Her people.

More fire from the port-side beams and turret as *Laura* came back to bear suddenly. Eight Type-4 beams outbound from her squadron. Depending on damage to the station and how she lay in relation to the attackers, up to eight inbound. Her team had one target. The *Sentience* on the station had one big target, three cruisers, and a swarm of corvettes to pick from. Hopefully, he was dumb enough to spread out his fire.

Vanguard could resist Type-4's longer than anyone else, unless Tamara slowed her rate of fire to keep everything in shields. Looking at her readout, Jessica could tell *II Augusta* wasn't conservative with her fire, but not putting everything on the line, either. Enough to keep the station honest, and hopefully still make it out to pick up her flight wing. The pilots could be rescued without the carrier, but the ships would be lost without their base.

Flag bridge lights flickered, and then failed, but only for a second, before emergency lighting came on.

"Enej?" Jessica called.

"Working," he said, furiously punching buttons and scrolling. "I think we've pissed them off, boss. He's concentrating fire on us with the big guns, and firing the lighter stuff at corvettes. Seems to be ignoring the cruisers completely."

"Alber' will be insulted," Jessica laughed. "Good thing he's going too fast to stop and demand a duel."

"Something like that," Enej said. "Robbie seems to be taking it personal. Or wants to show Nina that's she's not the only crazy one here."

Vanguard had continued to yaw like a sundial chasing the day. Front shields were taking a pounding, but all four big beams could track, and the Bubble Gun fired a second time as Jessica watched. Coasting on inertia, the excess power from every generator and all the engines was going into the shields. It wasn't enough, but the station had no shields on this facing until the squadron passed to a different side, and even then the Bubble Gun had long, deadly fingers.

And *VI Ferrata* was also twisting like a worm on a hook. *VI Victrix* had turned the other way, stern-on to the station so that both Type-4 beams could fire over the shoulder, Parthian-style.

The result was the squadron splitting into two parts with most of the corvettes firing their rear weapons while continuing to accelerate with Alber', as Denis and Robbie coasted, firing aft with the heavier front weapons suite.

That was bad, there were still Makos out there.

"Denis, Robbie, abort and stay with the rest of the team," Jessica called over the comm. "We haven't escaped yet."

On the side screen, Nina made a face like she wanted to argue, but she turned to one side, nodded, and subsided. Probably Denis snapping the whip on her personally, instead of over the team channel.

Aft, she felt *Vanguard's* engines engage as the ship began to yaw the rest of the way around, so she would rotate on her flat axis once. Jessica would have waited until they were lined up, because this would push *Vanguard* out of line with the rest of the force, but *VI Ferrata* was doing the same. Robbie could fly escort for the Heavy Dreadnaught until they caught up.

Alerts sounded and Jessica felt a crunch in the hull as fire penetrated a shield.

"Who's hitting us?" she yelled.

A moment later, the sensors and projection caught up to reality to show the three Makos well off to one side and firing. She had expected them to make a run with their Maulers, but that would require them to jump right into the middle of a buzzsaw. These were using something else. Something that let them hit from the range of the Type-3's tuned for distance.

Denis was on the screen signaling.

"These are the same Pulse-Ex that the Megalodon was using at *St. Legier*," he said, more or less calmly as the beams carved lines into his ship's flank. "Thing's almost a Type-4 for range and power, near as we can tell."

"Gold star for Nina," Jessica said. "Glad she lit the engines and moved us off line. They can't accelerate enough to catch us, and jumped where they expected us to be, rather than where we are."

Another crunch as a second vessel fired. Again, ignoring the cruiser on her flank to go after the terrible Red Admiral. Jessica had a feeling she was going to need *Valiant* and Tom Provst on her next raid, just to confuse *Buran* commanders as to which chariot their dreaded nemesis was riding.

Robbie and Hardie fired back, but dueling at long range with a ship like that was almost a waste of time. There were three of them, taking turns hitting *Vanguard* on a soft flank as the dreadnaught raced to catch up to the rest of her escorts.

One of them lit up with St. Elmo's fire as Jessica watched. And then all three blinked out of existence.

"What happened, there at the end?" Jessica asked.

"Fool forgot about us," Senior Centurion Komal MacInerney growled over the command line. "Lost track that *VI Victrix* had the range to hit the bastard hard, even headed away. Like we never practice that sort of thing."

On the screen, Jessica noted that the other cruiser had spun on her axis far enough to bring a Bubble Gun shot to bear, firing in a single salvo with all the corvettes around her, rather than everyone firing on their own.

Again, a big splash of damage hitting. And shocking surprise. Enough to make those cruisers blink and flit, even if the damage wouldn't be that great.

She checked her records.

"All ships, designate that new class of Mako as a *Tigershark*, and note that they're snipers, and not knife fighters," Jessica said. "Bedrov was right, again. *Buran*'s learning. All vessels turn 345/350/350 and push your engines hard. I want us off this line before they come back for more, and then I want us gone. *Buran* might count this a victory, but they won't forget what we just did to that station. Ever. Now, prepare for Act Three."

Jessica couldn't see it from here, but her mind was tracking the spot of darkness that would be *Winterhome*'s star if she was close enough for it to become visible at this range.

Second star to the right and straight on 'til morning…

Not today, you bastard, but soon.

She just needed Tom Provst and *Valiant*. First Expeditionary, reinforced. Moirrey and Yan.

And then she would see what *Winterhome* looked like from orbit.

As bombs rained down.

CHAPTER LVI

It was a new and uncomfortable feeling for Casey. All her life, she had been decisive, even when she wasn't entirely sure what she wanted. Father had taught her that lesson. That it was easier to adjust things while in motion than it was to impart momentum on a still object.

Tonight, she was unsure. And worse, she was standing in the middle of her closet considering how she should dress for the coming meeting. Nothing she had worn previously seemed to convey the mixture of her needs right now. Powerful yet feminine. Imperial but approachable. Capable nonetheless uncompetitive.

She had showered, toweling her long, blond hair dry and brushing it back and down. Simple and elegant, without requiring an hour of Moirrey's time, or the attention of someone like Anna-Katherine, to pull it into more-demure braids. The warm robe around her protected against the odd drafts from the old building, coupled with thick, wool socks comfie enough to wear indoors without shoes.

Idly, Casey touched one outfit, and then another. The Ritter sundress was too official, the Imperial robes too severe. Some things here were only for summer, and she would be freezing if she picked one. She wondered if field utilities would make the right statement, but realized it would look too desperate.

Slowly, she worked her way down the length of the walk-in closet, touching and rejecting one after another until she reached the dark end. Down here were the outfits she hadn't tried yet. New things from Vibol that had not spoken to her in the ways necessary to move them closer to the door.

One spoke to her now. Made promises as she *considered.* She wondered what had inspired Vibol. As far as she knew, the man didn't even like women that way, although it was probably best to say that he was wed entirely to his art, and everyone who had ever entered his life merely qualified as either inspiration or customer.

Casey pulled the hanger and held the piece in one hand. It was so new that she hadn't even separated it into component parts, to be mixed and matched as she needed. Long, skinny pants that would hang to her ankles and cling to her thighs and hips, done in a black denim that had been softened from normal dungarees. Two slit pockets at her hips, and a wide, fabric drawstring to hang it from her waist.

She would have never worn the accompanying red-and-white top alone, at least not when she was expecting anyone around, but it came with an outer piece. The first piece was like a halter top, except that the straps didn't tie, but slipped over her head, letting the rest of the outfit cling too much for most public company. Too much skin exposed.

She supposed that the other piece, the forest-green outer top, might be considered a minimalist's bolero jacket, perhaps. Long sleeves that would fit tight, all the way down to her knuckles, in something stretchy, heavy, and warm. At the shoulder, the jacket crossed her shoulder blades and in front ran in from flank to neck so as to barely cover her collar bones, ending in a standing collar that only went from earlobe to earlobe across her neck. Tiny, but it would frame the top, and cover enough skin that she could still be demure, even as it would accentuate her muscles and shoulders to best advantage.

Casey dropped the robe and pulled on just the halter top and pants, tucking the former in and tying the latter. The bodice of the top was a soft white, in a heavier fabric midway between the toughness of the pants and the stretchiness of the bolero. The hand-wide straps were a dark maroon that was almost a merlot, mirroring with a stripe that ran up both of her flanks.

Casey turned and located the cheval mirror in one corner, full length enough to show off even a woman as tall as she was.

The outfit wasn't right. Too girly. This was the sort of thing she might have worn five or eight years ago, a teen princess trapped in a loving palace, but still plotting her escape. She started to remove it, and then caught sight of the bolero, still waiting on the hanger.

She trusted Vibol. Her entire public image was wrapped up in that man's understanding of appearance. She would trust him now.

Casey grabbed the bolero, figured out which way was forward, and pulled it on. There were thumbholes at the wrist, she discovered, that would hold it in place when she moved and still let her grasp a paintbrush. The collar was weird, having been possibly starched just enough to stand up, and just tight enough to cuddle her shoulders.

The feel of the cloth on her skin was something she had never appreciated, even as the spoiled princess with her pick of fashion designers desperate to dress some member of the Imperial family. Almost a warm, second skin.

Casey turned to the mirror and her breath caught in her throat. Who was that person? The precocious teen was gone. In her place was a young woman, sexy and female in ways that Imperial culture didn't really understand, and rarely permitted, at least at her station.

This was something a young, university student-athlete might wear on her way between class and gym on *Ladaux*, flattering her curves and lithe shape. She turned, right and left. Hair would need to be up in a simple ponytail, perhaps with a few bangs loose. The difference between teen, matron, and *woman*.

Quickly, she grabbed a pair of warm, dark socks and house slippers from their shelf and emerged back into her bedroom, plopping down on the bed and considering her next phase.

Makeup needed to be light. A little color, and little base. Just enough to connote strength and independence. Moirrey had already offered several good suggestions, and it took Casey all of five minutes to get it just right.

Jewelry was the hard decision. Casey's ears were pierced twice on each side, but the only earrings she had worn since she became Emperor were a pair of small, gold hoops given to her by Father and Mother on her eighteenth birthday. The rest had stayed in the jewelry box, along with rings she had accumulated and a variety of necklaces.

There was one piece she would wear tonight. It was a platinum pendant, roughly the size of her thumbnail, with the Imperial eagle worked into it and decorated with rubies and sapphires. She found it in the back of the box, strung it on a short, silver chain, and hung it around her neck.

Originally, her grandfather, Karl VI, had given it to his young wife Ailina as a wedding present. Here, it set off the rest of her outfit, resting right at the pit of her neck as a cool spot against her warm skin.

Casey took a deep breath as she rose, facing the door to her bedroom as one might approach the guillotine. She paused with her hand on the knob and forced herself to relax.

In the outer chamber, Moirrey looked up from the slab she had been reading. Her eyes got big.

"Wowsers," she exclaimed, following up with a wolf whistle that made Casey blush.

"You think it will work?" Casey asked.

"Babes, if'n I weren't all sets to let Digger make an honest woman o'me, *I'd* be chasin' ya," Moirrey grinned. "Rawr."

That just made Casey blush worse, but it also helped her focus on her goal. Approach him like a woman, and not an Emperor.

"Thank you," Casey said.

"Don' be nervous, Casey," Moirrey said. "I'll be's yer Marcelle an' all will be good."

Casey nodded.

She let Moirrey carry the conversation for perhaps fifteen minutes while they waited. Gossip. News. Some strange new design she and Yan Bedrov had submitted to Em for consideration. Something called a butterfly.

Calming things.

"He's always dead accurates fer time," Moirrey said, checking a clock. "I'll sets the tea ta steepin' now. You waits here an' I'll brings him in when I'm ready."

Casey drew a breath. Held it meditatively. Willed her limbs to relax from their current stiffness. She studied the hotel room one last time.

Gray sofa and two, unmatched chairs, the brown one firm and the blue one so overstuffed she feared falling into it. Sometimes that was good, but she was in the brown one today, perched as much as anything. Two side tables. A rarely-used desk where she could sit and type out messages, if the couch wasn't working for her peace of mind.

Across the sizable suite, a wet bar where she frequently made her morning smoothies from fruit stocked in the refrigerator, and next to the bar was a sliding, glass door with a view of an interior courtyard and the empty swimming pool.

She hadn't made a decision about having it refilled, come summer, unsure where she would reside. With Digger and a whole legion, she might already have the beginnings of a palace compound somewhere, by the time this hemisphere got warm.

Another decision to approve. Another brick in the foundation of her rule.

Footsteps in the hallway drew her attention. As Moirrey had said, he was always on time. Dependable. Reliable.

The door opened and Moirrey came first, hauling a teapot and service on a silver tray.

And then he was in the doorway, calm, but she thought she detected the faintest hint of apprehension in the man's face. It was gone like dew, leaving no trace that it had ever been there, but it gave her hope.

If he could be unsure, she had an opening.

"Lady Casey," Moirrey announced as she placed the tea off to one side and gestured to the two of them. "Lord Vo."

"Your Majesty," Vo rumbled as he took exactly one step into the room and stopped.

"No," Casey said sternly, unwilling to let him fall into that place in his mind. "Tonight I am merely Casey, and you are Vo, and this is Moirrey. Please close the door and sit. I'd like us to chat about various plans for the future."

Again, a flicker of emotion across his normally impassive face. A magnificent stag scenting the hunter, perhaps.

He closed warily and put just enough of his bottom on the couch to qualify as seated, while leaving most of his weight forward, as if he might need to flee on short notice. While she was dressed for comfort, Vo was wearing the sage uniform he always referred to under his breath as *business*.

"Casey," he said, as if tasting her name for the first time.

Thinking back, she couldn't remember if he had ever addressed her by name. Even on that first flight to *Ladaux*, after the coup, she had always been *Lady* Casey, or more frequently, *Princess*. Later, *Centurion*.

But that had been more than three years ago, and much water had vanished under that bridge.

They fell to an awkward silence as Moirrey served tea and adjusted it to taste. Tonight was a night for decaffeinated leaves. Casey felt she was already so wound up she might not sleep until daylight anyway.

Finally Vo fixed her with his own hunter's gaze. He studied her with such intensity that she felt a blush creeping. Perhaps she had always been a symbol of something to him, and now he was seeing her for the first time as a person. A woman.

Casey glanced once at Moirrey, mostly to confirm how serious the little goofball was being, serving them tonight as a chaperone and matron, in addition to being a Lady-in-Waiting.

Vo sipped the tea and turned to inspect the room itself for several seconds.

"Based on the setting, would I be safe in presuming that it is not official business that brings me here tonight?" he asked in a low, gruff voice.

She had heard that man angry. And emotional. This was him almost emotionless.

Tightly-wrapped.

"It is official business, Vo," she replied quietly. "And personal."

"Personal," he repeated.

"It touches on a broad variety of things," Casey offered.

Rather than speak, he fixed her with those eyes, dark hazel that might be almost a burnished gold in the softer light of her salon. A sip of tea seemed to communicate the questions he would not voice.

But she had known that. Vo reminded her of Torsten Wald that way, and she and Jessica had spoken often about quiet, resilient men.

"I have spoken to a number of people recently," Casey began as Moirrey seemed to fade into the background, as she had promised she would do. "Torsten, Alan Katche, and Judit Chavarría, most importantly. The arrival of Digger Wolanski, however much Moirrey was thrilled, has forced my hand earlier than I had hoped we might have this conversation."

Breathing, blinking, and sipping tea were the only indications that Vo *zu* Arlo hadn't turned into a granite version of himself.

"Anthohn Jenker tasked you with turning the 189th Division into an *Aquitaine*-style legion, yes?" she asked, just to force him to stay at the surface, rather than withdrawing completely from her.

"He did, among other things," Vo rumbled.

"And after the Catastrophe, you promised the people of *St. Legier* vengeance," she continued. "Your sword taken to worlds of *The Holding*. Your Legion falling on them like demons from the pit."

"Yes," he replied.

"But until now, you did not have the final piece you needed to put your mission into action, am I correct?" Casey pressed.

"Alan and I had given it some thought, Your…Casey," he said. "There is nothing like an Assault Carrier in the Imperial Fleet, which would have required us instead to either assemble a mismatched set of smaller vessels, or have Bedrov design us something for *zu* Wachturm to build. That was a task for the coming spring."

"But now Digger is here," Casey noted. "And Fleet Centurion Vlahovic was going to take the rest of the force to Jessica, leaving those two vessels waiting in orbit."

"That is my understanding," Vo said.

"So you have spoken with Palsgrave Chavarría, and asked her to contribute those two vessels to the war effort, that they could transport a Rapid Assault Legion, Reinforced, to the front, and into battle," Casey continued.

"Yes, Casey," he said, challenging her with his stare. "I will fulfill my promise."

"I know that, Vo," she let her voice relax, realizing she had started to become an Emperor again. She pulled back sharply in her mind. "Judit asked me for an official position. I had considered forbidding the entire enterprise, intending to keep you here, close to the throne, but then I spoke with Alan Katche."

Jessica had described Vo to her as a deeply reticent man. How she had been speaking to him once and watched him bar the gate and lower the portcullis in his mind. Jessica had been reminded of the light going out in the refrigerator as the door closed, plunging the rest of the cabin into total darkness.

"Alan told me I would lose you forever if I did that," Casey continued. "That it might be the one thing to actually make you angry in a way none of us had seen. Perhaps ever even imagined."

She could taste the rage emanating from him now, that close to the surface but suppressed, by the way he didn't move, except for his eyes dilating and relaxing in synch with his heartrate.

"That is the last thing I want, Vo," she said, dropping her voice down even more, until it was barely a murmur. "I need you to know that. To acknowledge that."

He nodded. Wary. Scenting the hunter, as yet unseen through the trees, but closing.

"Vo?" she almost pled with him.

"I hear you," he offered.

It wasn't much, at least from most men, but it was a sign that he was listening. *Considering.* Had perhaps withheld judgment, for now.

Father had never been so difficult.

Casey took a sip of tea, desperate to find the words to reach him before he set fire to the bridge across the moat.

"I wanted to work my way up to this conversation slowly, Vo," she offered. "Pick the moment when we could talk as adults. But I have run out of time."

"Only if you plan to thwart me," he rumbled.

"And I will not do that, Vo," she said.

"So you will approve it?" he asked in that hard voice.

"I intend to," she said. "That is the official part of this conversation."

She paused, still seeking the words. Vo surprised her by pulling his head back from where it had jutted forward like an ancient gargoyle atop a castle. As she watched, he settled more of his weight onto the sofa, threatening the old springs and pads with utter destruction under his mass.

"And the personal? Casey?" he asked.

If his voice had been emotionless marble before, it had turned to a winter wind now. Not cutting yet, but still threatening to flay the very muscles from her back if she turned the wrong way.

"It still has official overtones, Vo," she suggested carefully. "And I cannot find a simple way to make my case, so I must be reduced to begging you to merely listen and not comment. And not judge until I'm done. Will you do that for me, Vo?"

Those hazel eyes turned to molten bronze as she watched them. She had never know Vo to be an emotional man, at least not around her, nor anyone else she had asked. Jessica had hinted at things, but always came back to the same resting point.

"It would be better to ask Vo directly," Jessica would say. Or Moirrey. And Torsten, come to think of it.

Only Alan had dared speak *for* the man, and that only going so far as to paint a bright, red line. Cutting a mark in the sand and declaring, "You are no longer safe past here."

"I will listen, Casey," he conceded, leaning the rest of the way back and resting those broad shoulders against the back of the sofa.

Casey despaired, but Vo would not be turned by fancy words. Only the truth. That was the secret to this man. Any lies or deflections would just bounce off of his armor and reflect back on the speaker. All words would, but truths would never hurt, coming back.

Only lies.

"You promised the people of *St. Legier* vengeance, Vo," she began in a low voice. "But it was not revenge. It was justice. I know you. You are all about justice. You did not promise to destroy them all, but to carry the sword to *Buran*. My sword. My people. But first you demanded love from them, from those cold, hard, Imperial citizens, nobles wrapped up in their class and superiority. And they gave it. Unconditionally. I never would have imagined that response. Not from those people."

She paused, watching his face for any cues. There were none, but he had not grown angry or distant. She counted that as her first victory. A small one, but they would all be, with this powerful, terrible man.

"You are more beloved of the people than I am, Vo," she continued carefully. "I have seen it in their faces. They will always rely on Vo *zu* Arlo to protect them, to shelter them from the storm. Even to avenge them. From the day I set foot on this planet again, I knew that my reign would be built with you as one of the cornerstones. As Em said to me on final approach, you are *St. Legier.*"

He nodded. Not in anything more than acknowledgement of the rightness of her words. The accuracy of her sentiments. He had seen it, too.

"And now, I must send you off to war," she said simply. "To do anything less would be to lose you forever. As an emperor, I cannot risk that. Cannot risk the Empire itself losing something vital at the very moment when it is at its weakest."

For a moment, those bronze irises flashed like molten gold. Triumph, she supposed. Perhaps he had come here expecting her to bargain with him over that task. Threaten to withhold her hand and make him carry through his terrible promises.

They were not threats, those words.

Casey knew better than to try his might. Easier to bargain with the hurricane winds than stand between Vo and his intentions.

"We must move past that point, Vo," Casey continued. "Assume that you will go to war, carrying my sword into battle. We must talk about the time after that. When the war is won. And here is where all my arguments, all my logic break down."

Confusion on his face, finally. All Vo's emotions were amazingly close to the surface tonight. He was possibly as open as he had ever been, at least in many years.

She paused, waiting for him to move past his own victory and join her at the next plateau.

"Casey?" he whispered, unsure.

Unsure. Good. Vo *zu* Arlo's surety was the strength that mountains grew jealous of.

"I cannot order. I cannot even request," she confided. "For that would be just as bad as the things I am already guilty of. We all are guilty of."

"Guilty?" he echoed.

"Nobody ever asks you what you want, Vo," she explained. "Everyone assumes you will do the right thing, and do it regardless of the personal sacrifice. Alan and Arald Rohm have both spoken to me about what this task has cost you, saving *St. Legier*. For me to speak my mind right now, to make this a personal issue, would make me just as guilty, for you might decide that it is the right thing to do, putting yourself and your happiness aside for the greater good. I will not have that on my head. Not for this."

"Casey?" he repeated.

She felt like a siren, luring this poor sailor onto the rocks. The only way to free him would be to stop singing, at whatever price she had to pay.

"What does Vo Arlo want?" she wondered aloud. "What is the thing that would bring him joy?"

And he closed in on himself, just like that. But this wasn't an angry rejection. This was a man lost in shock and holding everyone and everything at bay while he furiously strove to master the whirling thoughts in his head.

In that, he had finally joined her, at least partway onto that next plateau.

"Want?" he croaked.

Casey felt her chin come up and her shoulders pull back in defiance at the situation.

"Yes, Vo," she challenged him. "What do you want?"

Silence fell, as she knew it would. Casey focused herself on the tea and ignored the small volcano rumbling ominously on the sofa. Vo was no threat to her at all. To either of them, as she glanced once at the nearly-forgotten Moirrey for reassurance.

They had spoken about this task for days. And agreed that there was no other way. None that would be successful, in any event.

"I don't know," he finally voiced with the slightest hint of wonder. "I do not know. It has been so long since…"

Those eyes bored in on her now.

"Even going to visit Holman was fulfilling an expectation," he confided. "Letting the man know how I had turned out. But it was a thing I did for him, and not me."

"When was the last time you did something for yourself, Vo?" Casey pressed.

Silence drawing out.

"Years," he breathed finally. "Perhaps decades."

"Just so," Casey lamented, with as little bitterness as she could manage in her tones. "And now you will go off to war, because it is a task inherit in being Vo *zu* Arlo. It was what was expected of you, not necessarily what you wanted. A promise you made to others, based on a price they had been unable to pay. The cost of being you."

"Yes," he whispered.

"So we must talk about the day that comes after the war, Vo," she said. "I can ask you things, but I must be careful that they do not become duties you must endure for the greater good. They must be things you choose for yourself. On that day, and all days after."

He had returned to silence, sipping his tea and seeking to master his emotions. She understood that place oh so well.

"When you have avenged *St. Legier*, I have hope that you would come back to me, Vo," she admitted finally. "As Emperor, I have official reasons, but I also have personal ones, as a woman."

"Ma'am?" he answered, a voice still tiny with distance.

"As Emperor, I know that you make me feel safe, just by being here, Vo," she acknowledged, gesturing to the room around them and the planet beyond that. "Your terrible sword between me and all threats. But that is the official business, and we need to talk about the personal. And even that is official, to some extent."

"Casey, I don't understand," he pled.

"You make me feel safe, Vo," she implored, finally losing her own emotionlessness to reach him on that distant island. On the other side of the vast, bottomless chasm between them.

"As Emperor, and head of the Imperial Household, I must look to the future, and do so with a blood-thirsty, cruel eye, Vo," she continued. "I must ensure the strength of my reign. And my line. There must be children to carry on the Empire. That is the official business that intrudes on my personal wants. But this is my personal desire. You make me feel safe. No other man does that. Has ever done that. Others see me as a prize to be sought, or an evil to be overthrown. To you, I am a symbol, I understand that. An esoteric object that must be protected and upheld. But you have never looked on me with covetous eyes. Never looked past me. If you have rarely ever looked at me, it was because the universe was making impossible demands of you, and I was perhaps one more thing to bother you, so you ignored me. But here, now, you make me feel safe. I don't want to lose that. I don't want to lose you."

She leaned back and remembered to breathe. Vo had gone chalky white, a color she could never remember for him.

"I could not wait until later to tell you this, because I must send you away now if I ever wish to have you back, Vo," she conceded. "And I want you back. I want you to make me feel safe. I want to know that I have someone I can turn to with anything and never have to worry about them, because you are the most grounded human I have ever met. I want you to come back to me and stay with me, when you are done."

She fell silent at that point, words simply exhausted.

Vo Arlo could not be coerced by force. Only by a guilt that would gnaw at her perhaps more than him, if he were to accede to her desires and sublimate his own.

How does one navigate the Scylla and Charybdis? The fine line between heart and mind, desire and duty?

She had made her case. Hopefully well enough, because tomorrow she would have to officially approve Em's request to temporarily impress two Assault Carriers into Imperial service for a year so that they could take from her the thing that made her feel safest in the universe.

She would have to lose Vo, and hope that he would come back to her of his own volition, and not due to that immense sense of duty.

Vo blew out a huge breath and blinked too rapidly. He set his mug down on the side table a bit too roughly and nearly overturned both onto the carpet.

Rather than speak, he exploded to his feet and stumbled the slightest bit, towering over her like a redwood tree offering her shade. He stared down at her for one long second and then stumbled to the door with a heavy stride.

"Vo?" she implored.

"I will not say no," he conceded heavily. "I will not say yes either. Not today. Perhaps not ever. But I will not say no."

"When will I know?" Casey asked him.

"As soon as I do," he apologized, opening the door and vanishing.

Casey let her own heavy breath go at that point. He had not repudiated her. Would most likely seek an answer for himself in the depths of the war itself.

But she would hold on to the hope that he would return to her, to stand beside the throne that would become her Imperial prison. Be the rock against which all storms would crash first, before reaching her.

She could hope that he would love her.

EPILOGUE: FORLORN

They had stretched their stay as long as possible, and then some, until they were well past the point of mathematical surety. Jessica watched the dark spot on her squadron screen like a tooth missing. All the others were present.

Everyone was dinged up to some degree. Even flying through a battle where you drew no fire caused systems to break down faster than normal. Wear and tear accelerating things. That was nature of war.

They had come out of jump in a tight cluster, spread out over only about ten minutes. Pretty good for this long of a hop and this many ships.

But one ship was missing. Had never emerged. As far as anyone knew, *CS-405* had made it to JumpSpace with everyone else. *Vanguard* had actually been the last ship to escape, so Jessica had been able to watch the logs and scans as Kosnett and his ship vanished.

Four days later, they still had not arrived.

Jessica called up the full squadron channel and made eye contact with everyone's images.

"As you know, we've lingered here long past our original intention," she began slowly, as if, by magic, she could conjure the last duckling home. "*CS-405* has not joined us in the allotted window, so we must declare her missing and move on."

Muffled groans met her words, and she longed to join them, but this was the element of command. The lonely part.

"Kosnett and Lau know the itinerary and the plot," Jessica continued. "If they can, they will make best speed. If we hadn't just stirred up a hornet's nest back there, I might be willing to send *Ballard* back to locate their trail, but we have nothing upon which to base our search and a vast number of very angry ships looking for us right now. Perhaps all of them."

Jessica paused long enough to sip from the mug of coffee Marcelle had delivered with the last of the fresh cream. It would be frozen stuff from here on out, so she needed to appreciate it. And settle herself and her team.

"We have waited two days longer than normal," she said. "Any repairs at this point will probably require teams from the *Junkyard Chihuahua*, so we must now sneak home."

Another pause, locating the man she wanted amidst the faces.

"Kigali, in the absence of *CS-405* to take the van, you have the flag."

He nodded. Sharp and brief. She could see the way he was grinding his teeth at losing one of his own.

"Squadron, this is Kigali, aboard *CA-264*, I have the flag," he said in a terse, angry voice. "All ahead standard on this heading and prepare for JumpSpace. Conform to *CA-264*, and I will see you all at *Waypoint Babylon*. Good luck, and Godspeed."

Jessica nodded at the words. Kigali had turned into something of a poet and a fire-breathing preacher, as he brought the corvette team along to what he considered an acceptable level of professionalism.

Long gone was the laconic *Navigator* intent on his personal records. Kigali had thrown that all aside when he became the warrior monk commanding her escorts.

She paused as the ships began their slow acceleration into the darkness. As *Vanguard* vanished into JumpSpace, Jessica said a silent prayer for Kosnett and his crew to escape and make it home.

Standing orders required any disabled ship to be utterly destroyed, rather than risk capture. The same for certain officers who could be compelled to speak before a god. That was probably the hardest part of being an officer, but it was necessary.

On the projection above her table, in the space between she and Enej, Jessica projected near-space as it stretched out behind them, zooming and adjusting the image until she found the light she wanted.

There. A quiet, yellow-orange star in the distance. Once upon a time, nothing more than a long alpha-numeric designation identified the place, but Seeker and others had updated the navigational charts with more fanciful names, as humans tended to do, electronic gods notwithstanding.

Winterhome.

The lair of the Last Dragon. The implacable, ancient *Sentience* that had become the enemy of all mankind.

Buran, the *Lord of Winter.*

I'm coming for you.

TO BE CONTINUED IN...

Two Bottles Of Wine With The War God
Queen Anne's Revenge
Packmule
Persephone
First Centurion

ST. LEGIER CAST LIST

Corynthe
Name / Rank / Position

- Jessica Marie Keller (F) / Fleet Centurion, Admiral of the Red / Queen of Corynthe
- Marcelle Augustine Travere / Chief / Jessica's Personal Aide
- Willow Dolen / Yeoman / Jessica's Bodyguard
- Amala Bhattacharya / Ambassador / Personal Representative of the Queen of Corynthe
- Yan Bedrov / Principle Engineer, Bedrov & Keller /
- Ainsley Barret / Test Pilot, Bedrov & Keller /

IFV Vanguard
Name / Rank / Position

- Denis Jež (M) / Command Centurion / Commander, IFV Vanguard, Admiral of the White
- Enej Zivkovic (M) / Centurion / Flag Centurion
- Nina Vanek (F) / Senior Centurion / First Officer

- Tobias Brewster (M) / Senior Centurion / Asst Tactical Centurion/Second Officer
- Aleksander Afolayan(M) / Centurion / Gunner
- Nada Zupan (F) / Senior Centurion / Pilot
- Daniel Giroux (M) / Senior Centurion / Science Officer, Communications
- Vilis Ozolinsh (M), "Oz" / Command Engineering Centurion / Chief Engineer
- Saana Robles / Yeoman / Engineer
- Phillip Navin Crncevic (M), "Viking One" / Command Security Centurion / Dragoon
- Harun Chong, "Archer One" / Senior Security Centurion / Commander, First Battalion
- Nadine Orly / Chief / Flag Marine
- Jackson Tawfeek / Chief / Marine
- Mahmud Astrauskas / Senior Centurion / Surgeon
- Nicolai Aoiki (M) / Master Chef / Master of the Wardroom

RAN Squadron
Name / Rank / Position

- Tomas Kigali (M) / Command Centurion / Commander, CA-264
- Arsen Lam (M) / Senior Centurion / Tactical Officer, CA-264
- Aki Ridwana Ali (F) / Centurion / Pilot, CA-264
- Alber d'Maine (M) / Command Centurion / Commander, VI Victrix
- Komal MacInerney / Senior Centurion / Tactical Officer, VI Victrix, Goddess of War
- Robertson Aelieas (M) / Command Centurion / Commander, VI Ferrata
- Harden Glenraven (F), "Hardie" / Senior Centurion / First Officer, VI Ferrata
- Tamara Strnad / Command Centurion / Commander, II Augusta
- Kichirou Uzun / Senior Centurion / Tactical Officer, II Augusta

- Ryanne Mauld / Senior Centurion / Flight Deck Commander, II Augusta
- Augustin Petrović, Merman (M) / Senior Flight Centurion / Wing Lead, II Augusta
- Kanda Lungu (F) / Command Centurion / Commander, Ballard
- Elzbet Aukley (F) / Senior Centurion / First Officer/Science Officer, Ballard
- Orn Nwokolo (M) / Centurion / Asst Science Officer, Ballard
- Lazlo Moushian / Centurion / Pilot, Ballard
- Mererid Stella Dimitriou (F) / Centurion, PhD / Security Marine. Geologist, Ballard
- Larsen Romanov (M) / Command Centurion / Commander, Bulldog
- Nero Yamakagi (M) / Command Centurion / Commander, CT-9492
- Waldemar Ihejirika (M) / Command Centurion / Commander, Mendocino
- Illiam Kovack (M) / Command Centurion / Commander, Duncan
- Enfys El-Amin (F) / Command Centurion / Commander, Wombat
- Manaia Nieminen (F) / Command Centurion / Commander, CE-401
- Ariadna Mateu (F) / Command Centurion / Commander, CE-402
- Valerie Maikop (M) / Command Centurion / Commander, CE-403
- Tómasson Ásmundur (M) / Command Centurion / Commander, CM-404
- Phil Kosnett (M) / Command Centurion / Commander, CS-405
- Heather Lau (F) / Senior Centurion / First Officer, CS-405
- Siobhan Skokomish (F) / Centurion / Navigator/Second Officer, CS-405
- Jennifer Glenn (F) / Command Centurion / Commander CP-406
- Takouhi Elouan (F) / Senior Centurion / Tactical Officer, CP-406

- Janel Rouge (M) / Centurion / Flight Deck Officer, CP-406
- Reese Steiner (F) / Centurion / Science Officer, CP-406
- Adnan Kristensen (M) / Yeoman / Gunner, CP-406
- Murdag Rasim (F) / Centurion / Pilot, CP-406
- Anmol Schwartzenwald (M) / Flight Centurion / Black Prince
- Erik Mosiondz (M) / Senior Flight Centurion / Boomerang
- Michelle Nystul (F) / Flight Centurion / Grendel
- Arott Whughy / First Centurion / Commander, Forward Base Omicron
- Iskra Vlahovic / First Centurion / Commander, Task Force Vlahovic
- Digger Wolanski / Legate / Twenty-third Ladaux

The Republic
Name / Position

- Indira (Chastain) Keller / Jessica's mother
- Miguel Keller / Jessica's father
- Petia Naoumov / First Lord of the Fleet
- Roderick Stone / Aide to the First Lord
- Nils Kasum / First Lord of the Fleet, retired
- Kamil Miloslav / Republic Intelligence
- Tadej Marko Horvat / Premier, Republic Senate
- Judit Margrét Chavarría / Senator, Republic Senate
- Calina Szabolcsi / President of the Republic of Aquitaine
- Seth / Bartender, the Marquette Room
- Sigrún / Steward, the Marquette Room
- Svetlana Ognianov / Sergeant at Arms, Republic Senate
- Vresh Nalani / Senator, Republic Senate
- Declan Burdge / Legate, Fourth Saxon, retired
- Dashyl Mitja / Patrol Centurion, Fourth Saxon
- Zorana Arlo / sister to Vo zu Arlo
- Sonja Arlo / sister to Vo zu Arlo

The Fribourg Empire
Name / Rank / Position

- Johannes Arend Wiegand / Emperor / Karl VII
- Kasimira Ekaterina ('Kati') / Empress / Imperial Household
- Casey zu Wiegand / Centurion / Ritter / Karl VIII
- Lady Moirrey zu Kermode / Centurion / Ritter / Lady in Waiting
- Vibol Harmaajärvi / First-Rate-Spacer / Scholar of Fashion, Imperial Household
- Emmerich zu Wachturm / Grand Admiral / Ritter / Commander of the Fleet
- Freya Wachturm / Duchess / Wife of Emmerich Wachturm
- Tiede Wachturm / Cmdr / Son of Emmerich Wachturm
- Jeltje Voight / Burggraf / Daughter of Emmerich Wachturm
- Carsten Voigt / Cmdr / Husband of Jeltje Voight
- Henriette Anne Wachturm / "Lady Heike" / Daughter of Emmerich Wachturm
- Bernard Hourani / Commander / Husband of Heike Wachturm
- Torsten Wald / Admiral of the White, retired / Chief of Deputies
- Hendrik Baumgärtner / Admiral of the White / Chief of Staff, Grand Admiral
- Gunter Tifft / Lt. Cmdr / Grand Admiral's Staff
- Ralf Frankenheimer / Admiral of the Blue / Commander, Fleet Headquarters, St. Legier
- Tomas Provst / Admiral of the White / IFV Firehawk
- Albert Benedikt Kistler / Captain / IFV Firehawk
- Charles d'Noir / Commander / Aide to Admiral Provst
- Karl Ekkehard Szczęsny Wiegand / Lieutenant/Crown Prince / IFV Firehawk
- Arn Colson / Captain / Watch Commander, HQ
- Gerald Siembieda / Captain / Watch Commander, HQ
- Anna-Katherine Kallenberger / Lady-in-Waiting / Imperial Household
- "Seeker" (M) / Scholar / Formerly Ul Banop Cheani Yuur
- Tobias Inmon / Director / Household Guards

- Reif Kingston / Captain / IFV Indianapolis
- Faisul Bumann / Journeyman / Bedrov & Keller
- Mori Zoucha / Journeyman / Bedrov & Keller
- Kiril Hahl / "Twenty-seven" / Duke of Blue Essex
- Jo / / Moirrey's mechanic
- Andre / / Moirrey's team
- Kiran / / Moirrey's team
- Sharad / / Moirrey's team

189th Legion
Name / Rank / Position

- Vo zu Arlo / General / Ritter / Commanding General, 189th Legion
- Edgar Horst / Color Decurion / Color Sgt, Thuringwell
- Reese Borel / Command Decurion / Command Non-comm, Admin
- Erin Stolz / Curator / Command staff
- Michelle Ali al-Inverness / Armourer / Fourth Saxon Legion
- Sunil Ma / Patrol Centurion / Cmdr, Cutlass
- Iakov Street / Decanus / Cutlass Ten
- Hans Danville / Curator / Cutlass Ten
- Colton Formain / Decanus / Draconarius, Cutlass Ten
- Vladimir Amburgy / Curator / Cornicen, Cutlass Ten
- Kamlesh Ozawa / Curator / Cutlass Ten
- Jisaburo Burana / Curator / Cutlass Ten
- Daffidd de Bruyne / Decanus / Cutlass Ten
- Thaddeus Gunderson / Decanus / Cutlass Ten
- Terence Aday / Lancer / Sniper, Cutlass Ten
- Johan Koga / Curator / Spotter/FO, Cutlass Ten
- Victoria Ames / Trooper / Cutlass Ten
- Alan Katche / Cohort Centurion / Primus Pilus. Cmdr, 1st Ala
- Rikard Laferriere / Patrol Centurion / Third Patrol, 1st Ala
- Chakravarthy Sol / Decurion / First Patrol, 1st Ala
- Omar LeCoat / Cohort Centurion / Cmdr, 2nd Ala
- Dylan Moroder / Cohort Centurion / Cmdr, 3rd Ala

- Pyotr Martin / Cohort Centurion / Cmdr, 4th Ala, Heavy Scouts
- Oleg Chilikov / Patrol Centurion / 4th Patrol, 4th Ala, Einherjar
- Erik Windstrom / Decurion / Draconarius, Einherjar
- Alistair Bleushan / Cohort Centurion / Cmdr, 5th Ala (CCLXXIII Heavy)
- Johan Hellyer / Patrol Centurion / Cmdr, 1st Patrol
- Centurion Kevin Hassen / Centurion / 5th Squadron (Assault Gun Team) "Sledgehammer"
- Hermann Gerstenburger / Cohort Centurion / Cmdr, 6th Ala (Headquarters)
- Arald Rohm / Field Marshal / Commander, Seventh Guards Army
- Ernest Withers / Commander / Fleet Marine detachment, 2IC, Strasbourg Command
- Melina Arcidiacono / Owner / Restaurant Tenochtitlan
- Thurman Arcidiacono / Cook / Restaurant Tenochtitlan
- Christina Arcidiacono / Daughter of Melina / Restaurant Tenochtitlan
- Nicola Arcidiacono / Daughter of Melina / Restaurant Tenochtitlan
- Celine Arcidiacono / Daughter of Melina / Restaurant Tenochtitlan

Imperial Land Forces
Name / Rank / Position

- Anthohn Jenker / Grand Marshal / Supreme Commander, ILF
- Anders Tsibin / Flag General / Commander, Field School
- Olaf van Gorzen / Commander / Imp Land Forces

Buran
Name / Rank / Position

- Buran/ The Lord of Winter / God/Emperor / Ruler of Buran
- Xi Ulan Atah Ahn (M) / Director / Ural Starbase, Samara
- Ul Turin Dyana Vor (M) / Director / Glory in Duty
- Ko Yorin Myar Sam (M) / War Advocate / Glory in Duty
- Au Ulav Fara Hen (M) / Director / Defend The Homeland

ABOUT THE AUTHOR

Blaze Ward writes science fiction in the Alexandria Station universe: The Jessica Keller Chronicles, The Science Officer series, The Doyle Iwakuma Stories, and others. He also writes about The Collective as well as The Fairchild Stories and Modern Gods superhero myths. You can find out more at his website www.blazeward.com, as well as Facebook, Goodreads, and other places.

Blaze's works are available as ebooks, paper, and audio, and can be found at a variety of online vendors (Kobo, Amazon, iBooks, and others). His newsletter comes out quarterly, and you can also follow his blog on his website. He really enjoys interacting with fans, and looks forward to any and all questions-even ones about his books!

Never miss a release!

If you'd like to be notified of new releases, sign up for my newsletter.

I only send out newsletters once a quarter, will never spam you, or use your email for nefarious purposes. You can also unsubscribe at any time. http://www.blazeward.com/newsletter/

ABOUT KNOTTED ROAD PRESS

Knotted Road Press fiction specializes in dynamic writing set in mysterious, exotic locations.

Knotted Road Press non–fiction publishes autobiographies, business books, cookbooks, and how–to books with unique voices.

Knotted Road Press creates DRM–free ebooks as well as high–quality print books for readers around the world.

With authors in a variety of genres including literary, poetry, mystery, fantasy, and science fiction, Knotted Road Press has something for everyone.

Knotted Road Press
www.KnottedRoadPress.com